Immaculate Deception

Ken Baumbach

Cover art created by Kathryn Baumbach

Immaculate Deception
Ken Baumbach

Copyright 2014, Ken Baumbach

Leviathan Press

http://www.kenbaumbach.com

* * * * *

All rights reserved. Without limiting the rights under copyright reserved above, no part of this publication may be reproduced, stored in or introduced into a retrieval system, or transmitted, in any form, or by any means (electronic, mechanical, photocopying, recording, or otherwise) without the prior written permission of both the copyright owner and the above publisher of this book.

Disclaimer

This is a work of fiction (and a satirical parody at that). Its content should in no way be interpreted as an actual record of events, unless a story specifically states its contents are an actual recording of events. These stories are not intended to be, nor should they be construed as, attempts to predict the future course of any individual or entity, and should be viewed only as parody. Any resemblance to any person, politician (who are not people, of course), location, flora, fauna, bacteria or any other thing living or dead is purely coincidental. Any quotes from public figures are pure fiction unless the quote is properly credited.

There are certain religious and political themes running (for cover) throughout this novel. Please remember, before you write me nasty notes or threaten me in some way, this is a farce. I am not making fun of your religion or politics, I am making fun of everyone's religion and politics (including my own), and so at the moment you get offended in the novel, that's when I'm helping you to belong to the great group of everyone.

If you are squeamish about the amount of sex in this novel, you can blame my wife. I originally wrote fairly terse sex scenes and she kept telling me to rewrite and expand the scenes. Yes, I realize I am very, very lucky.

Also, remember, this novel is all a figment of my warped imagination. In fact, you are a figment of my warped imagination, which is why you bought this book, of course. Thanks!

Acknowledgements

Excerpt from Messiah's Handbook: Reminders for the Advanced Soul by Richard Bach. Copyright 2004 Richard Bach.

Many thanks to the Williamson County Writers Group (Ken Meinen, Lora Negrito, Lydia Cole and Dave Ogle), Kristi Baumbach and Hal Baumbach for their feedback and editing expertise.

Special thanks to Ken Meinen and Lora Negrito for rewriting several "articles" to provide a unique voice.

Dedication

To my wonderful daughters, Kathryn, Emily and Megan, who warm my heart everyday…

This almost happened…

…then again, it still might…

PART I

EMPIRE PART 1: 2000-2011

"I have the same goal I've had ever since I was a girl. I want to rule the world."
   --Madonna

Immaculate Deception

Chapter 1

2000

Bobby Roderick sat alone behind the Resolute Desk in the Oval Office. Dismayed, he reviewed yet another stack of meaningless House bills, pondering his legacy. His presidency was going to be over in about seven months.

How was he going to be remembered? As a great president? Shit, he was going to be remembered for bedding trollops like Ginny LeFleur and Mandy Lewis. That and being terrified of Dolly.

He remembered back, long ago, to a time - a brief time admittedly - when he actually loved his wife. He loved her through their college days and most of the honeymoon year, until he realized that she was a frigid bitch not even remotely interested in sex. He never fooled himself into believing Dolly had the same raw animal attraction for him most women did. With most women, all it took was five minutes. He could simply flash a big smile, flirt a bit and bang, his quarry would be locked in a bathroom with him, stroking what was now the First Penis.

Dolly was different. He had to admit that was why he was attracted to her at first. She wasn't an easy lay---and she was so ambitious. Dolly was the only woman, maybe the only person, in the world more ambitious than he was. That ambition carried his love through the wedding and most of their honeymoon year. Unfortunately, it was soon evident that the only reason she married him was her ambition. She wasn't a gold digger like most women he had run into over the years, wanting to be pampered, spoiled and showered with gifts.

No, Dolly was far worse. She was a power monger. She simply wanted to ride the Roderick train to the White House. Bobby had to admit, her plan worked perfectly, and although Dolly may have been impressed, perhaps even proud of his political prowess and power, she wasn't even vaguely interested in having sex with him. In fact, she treated him more like a son or a player on a team she was coaching.

He should have known what his life portended. After their honeymoon coupling, sex was allowed every six months and then drifted out to every three or four years. Knowing that, how could he be blamed for Ginny LeFleur? Dolly never forgave him for Ginny, but a man has his needs. Dolly should have known that a man as ambitious as he would have stronger sexual urges than an average man, he justified to himself for the umpteenth time. She brought all this on herself. After all, it's not as if he totally ignored her. Bobby convinced himself he tried to be close to her, but she was the one who wasn't interested. She got what she wanted from him, first becoming the most powerful woman in Alabama, then the most powerful woman in the free world. Bobby grew weary of thinking about Dolly.

Only God knew what would happen when he was no longer in office. Would he still be necessary in her future plans? Probably. What was he going to do when the term ended? Was there any real future for them? He knew he'd never be free from her or Washington. Dolly always had a plan. She was already running for the Senate. If she won, it was only a small step for her to run for president.

Dolly needed Bobby for her grand scheme. She couldn't win without him, he knew. Hell, what will they call him? The First Gentleman? The First Person? Bobby and Dolly made a pact four decades ago. She'd get him to the White House, then he'd return the favor. Shit, that meant he wouldn't be free until at least 2009. He shrugged.

That was assuming that straight-laced, worthless piece of crap of a Vice President, Bert Francis, lost the presidential

Immaculate Deception

election to Keith's boy, that dumbass from Texas, this fall as he and Dolly planned. If Bert somehow managed to win, he'd have to suffer an extra four years in a loveless marriage before he was free.

Thirteen more years? Bobby shook his head, sickened. He wasn't sure if he could take thirteen more years of Dolly, but he owed it to her to stick by her.

He grabbed his iced tea. Taking a swig, he cleared his mind and focused back onto the business at hand, the stack of bills in front of him.

A few minutes later, as he continued to quickly scan the bills, he thought he heard something. He looked up and listened.

What was that? Sanding? A wild dingo in heat? Sobbing? The noise came from the sitting room just off the Oval Office. Bobby walked over to the sitting room door, opened it an inch and peered through the crack. He was shocked to see Dolly's favorite little ice-cold bitch intern, Mary Ellen Martin, sitting on the couch.

Martin was one of the heirs to the M-Mart fortune. Someday, she would probably be worth billions. Her grandfather, Sam Martin, M-Mart's founder, had been one of the richest men in the world and a long-time contributor to Bobby's campaign. That's how she became his wife's intern in the first place. Funny though, she was completely immune to his charms but followed Dolly around like a lovesick puppy. Normally, it was the other way around with interns. Most flirted incessantly with him like groupies while they avoided Dolly and her volcanic temper in fear of spontaneous combustion at one of her outbursts.

Gently sniffling, Mary Ellen looked so sweet to Bobby. She wore a cute yellow print summer dress that didn't quite cover her knees and accentuated her ample cleavage and trim figure. Her long dark brown hair was draped over her shoulders. She was crying her pretty little eyes out.

This could be interesting. Mary Ellen had always treated

him about the same as Dolly did, responding to his flirtations with a mix of disgust and irritation. She had been Dolly's favorite intern for six or seven years, an extremely long time for an internship, but the girl was finishing up a law degree at Yale, Bobby and Dolly's alma mater, at Dolly's urging. Bobby sensed something amiss between them lately. He thought Dolly was pushing the heiress away but maybe it was just the stress of campaigning.

Maybe this was Bobby's chance to finally get into her panties. He reached in his pocket, pulled out a bottle of little blue pills, and popped one in his mouth. He stuffed the bottle back into his pocket and eased into the room.

"What's wrong, Mary Ellen?" Bobby asked softly as he smoothly sat down next to Mary Ellen and put an arm around her, giving her a reassuring squeeze.

Mary Ellen looked up as if she only half realized where she was and whom she was with. "Oh, Mr. President, I'm sorry, I didn't know you were in here."

She tried to stand up but Bobby gently held her in her sitting position. "Don't be silly, honey. Tell me why you're so upset."

She tensed underneath Bobby's arm. "Aren't you busy, Mr. President?"

Bobby gave her another reassuring squeeze. "I'm never too busy for an intern in need. Besides, I don't have an appointment for an hour and a half. I was just reviewing a stack of bills. Very boring..."

Mary Ellen looked up at Bobby and gave him a weak smile. She wiped the tears from her eyes and relaxed slightly in his embrace. "Oh, okay."

"So, what's the matter?"

She struggled to hold back the tears as she said, "Dolly, uh, Ms. Roderick, has been so mean and cold to me this year. Ever since I came back to the White House a month ago, she just keeps getting meaner and meaner."

"I know, I know. I've been there with Dolly many times

myself. What happened?"

"She...she...she is going on a campaign trip to New York for the next six weeks and she wants me to stay here and 'man the fort'."

"Really? You've gone on every summer trip she has been on since you became her intern..."

"I know, I know," Mary Ellen said, sobbing. "When I told her that, she started yelling at me. I don't know what I did wrong."

A little trouble in paradise. "I'm sorry, sweetie. Sometimes Dolly can be so cold. Is this the first time she's been like this to you?"

"Ever since I got back in D.C. this year, I can't seem to do anything right," she said, nestling herself in Bobby's arms for comfort. "She's always snapping at me; her coffee's not hot enough; I get her the wrong file; the appointment is set at the wrong time. It's like she hates me but I didn't do anything..."

"She doesn't hate you. She loves you." Bobby gently cupped her chin in his hand and lifted it so she would look at him. "We both love you."

She reluctantly returned his gaze. "You do?"

He gave a deep, mesmerizing look and a charming smile. "Of course, honey. What's not to love? You're a beautiful, smart, sweet woman. There are many times I've wished Dolly was more like you."

"You do?" she asked, her eyes locked with his.

"Yes, she can be so harsh, so mean-spirited, so cold, so distant. I still have some small scars on my back from when she threw a vase across the room during a fight on the night I lost my re-election bid as the Alabama governor. The damn thing shattered. It took the doctors an hour and a half to dig out all of the glass. I had 27 stitches from seven different cuts."

"Oh my God! I never knew she could be so mean."

"Yes, yes." Bobby rubbed Mary Ellen's back softly. "You might find this hard to believe, me being the president, but I get lonely."

"You do?" Mary Ellen asked again with a sniffle. She tenderly rubbed the back of his hand that rested on her leg.

"Yes, I wish I had a good woman to care about me the way you obviously care about Dolly. Could you care about me like that?" Not waiting for an answer, he brought his hand up to her cheek and kissed her.

Bobby felt her resist for a few seconds, and then she relaxed, succumbing to Bobby's charms, returning his kiss awkwardly.

After a few moments of kissing, Bobby had the top buttons of Mary Ellen's sundress undone and the front clasp of her white bra unclasped to reveal her large, firm, pale breasts. Mary Ellen's breathing grew more intense as he eagerly moved his lips to her neck, nibbling her ear and kissing her neck as he cupped a breast in his left hand and then rolled the hard nipple between his thumb and index finger.

Bobby worked his lips down her neck to her breasts, kissing and sucking her nipples hungrily. His mouth moved back and forth between her nipples, neck and mouth as he reached up her dress, slid her panties to one side and fervently rubbed her clitoris as she moaned with delight.

With a last suckle of her breasts, Bobby gently positioned Mary Ellen on the floor in front of him, unzipped his pants, and pulled his penis out for her. When she hesitated, he said, "We don't have much time." Then he grabbed her hand and put it on his penis.

She appeared shocked. Had she never been with a man before? A virgin? How delicious… This was going to better than a fine Cuban cigar.

His heart racing at thought of deflowering her, he groaned, "Come on, sweetie, kiss the First Penis."

She reluctantly, uneasily stroked, kissed and licked his member.

Bobby sat there, groaning, "That's it, that's it."

The door opened and Dolly walked in, saying, "Bobby, have you…" She stopped. "Jesus, Bobby! Can't you keep your dick in your pants for one fucking day? We still haven't recovered from the whole Mandy debacle."

Aghast, Mary Ellen stopped licking Bobby and looked up at Dolly, trying in vain to button up her dress. Her face turned crimson with embarrassment and guilt, as her fingers fumbled with the buttons.

As Dolly realized who Bobby's latest conquest was, her face contorted in rage, turning fireball red. She screamed, "Mary Ellen?! Bobby, you fucking fuckwit! I should cut your fucking dick off, you fucking dumbass! I can't believe your fucking my intern."

"Ah, Dolly, I'm sorry…" Bobby began, zipping up his pants.

"Shut up, you dumb fuck," Dolly snapped, then she looked at the frazzled intern who was still on her knees in front of her husband, her face a mix of horror, rage and hurt. "Mary Ellen, we're through. You got that? We're through. Pack up and get the hell out of here. I never want to see you again. And this better not make the papers, do you understand?"

Sobbing, Mary Ellen nodded. Dolly stomped off and slammed the door behind her so hard that Bobby thought the door might fall off its hinges.

"Sorry about that," Bobby said with a weak smile. "I told you we didn't have a lot of time. Maybe I can look you up when I'm in Alabama…?"

When Mary Ellen ignored him, burying her head in the sofa cushion as she sat on the floor, weeping, Bobby stood up and walked out the room. Oh well, Bobby was sure a couple of the other interns here were still virgins.

Chapter 2

2002

John Martin sat on the uncomfortable stool in the Cloning Around exam room. His younger sister, Mary Ellen, wearing a paper smock, sat on the exam table. The nurse had left moments earlier after getting Mary Ellen's vitals.

John flipped through a copy of the local newspaper, the Toledo Blade, which was jammed in a magazine rack. "I hope you're right about this place," he said. "Toledo seems awfully boring for this sort of thing."

"And Martinville is a hotbed of excitement?" Mary Ellen asked.

"True enough, but you're not trusting some quack in Martinville with my future niece or nephew, now are you?" John said. "Toledo's paper is named after a weapon, for God's sake. They should update the name though. How about the Toledo Uzi or the Toledo .44 Magnum?"

"Very funny, dear brother. Don't worry. I had Sylvia check the place out thoroughly."

Sylvia was Mary Ellen's executive assistant at M-Mart. She had been her assistant for almost two years now. When Mary Ellen "left" the White House, her uncle Rob offered her a job in M-Mart's Mergers and Acquisitions division as a junior vice president "to learn the biz" as he put it.

Mary Ellen and Sylvia had been close childhood friends who had lost touch when they went to college in different states. Sylvia recently graduated from Columbia with an MBA. When Mary Ellen found out Sylvia was back in Martinville, she looked her up and offered her a job. Sylvia quickly became her most trusted confidant in both business and personal matters. Mary Ellen's business in Toledo was personal and she trusted Sylvia completely to do the research.

Mary Ellen always wanted a child, but after her humiliation with Bobby and Dolly, she decided she didn't want a man involved. Biologically, a man was still necessary, but at least she didn't have to have one involved physically or, worse, emotionally. Never again.

All men, her relatives aside, she quickly learned from law school and the corporate world, were corrupt, thieving, womanizing scumbags with only two things on their minds: power and sex, and the main reason for power was to get more sex. It seemed as if every man she had any dealings with in the last decade was either trying to get into her pants, trying to get to the family fortune, or trying to use her to advance some hidden agenda.

Mary Ellen found out at an early age being part of the world's richest family had its disadvantages. Friendship, especially with the opposite sex, always seemed to involve an ulterior motive. That's why she asked John to join her in Toledo. He was the only man, other than their father, she trusted completely. He wasn't even an M-Mart employee, so there wasn't any corporate sibling rivalry between them, unlike some of her cousins.

John had used his piece of the family fortune to start a venture capital company and a land development company. He was doing very well for himself chiefly because his main client was M-Mart. He scouted out good locations to put new retail stores, handled the permits and palm greasing of local politicians and M-Mart was happy to give him a tidy profit. When M-Mart decided against one of his locations, he promptly sold it to a competitor.

After careful deliberation, when Mary Ellen decided to have a baby by artificial insemination, John was the first person she thought of to bring with her for moral support. When Mary Ellen first started looking into a sperm donor, she knew she didn't just want to get some John Doe's sperm, some movie star, or some socially-challenged astrophysicist savant. No, she wanted to find the perfect person to be the father. Sylvia performed a meticulous, surreptitious investigation and found the ideal place for her.

Cloning Around was a super-secret, ultra-advanced research facility started by a handful of University of Toledo Medical Center professors in the late 1980s. Over the past fifteen years, the group made many incredible advances in the fields of cloning and artificial insemination. Some of their finds were public and others were top secret. In addition to helping several couples successfully give birth to quadruplets, quintuplets and even a set of septuplets, the group successfully cloned several extinct species, including a gaur and a Tonga ground skink. While Cloning Around was very public about the successes for their artificial insemination work, they were secretive about their cloning work. The Bible thumpers would be outraged if they ever found out that the group had successfully cloned a human. The simple act of harvesting stem cells was causing a nationwide campaign to stamp out cloning altogether by the pro-lifers. Then there were the archeological digs, collecting ancient DNA samples and mapping the human genome.

It took considerable research, string pulling and secret, expensive bribes by Sylvia and Mary Ellen to get an appointment with a fertility expert at Cloning Around willing to meet her special requirements for donor DNA.

There was a soft tap on the door.

"Come in," Mary Ellen said.

A lab coat-attired man in his early forties with wire-rimmed glasses and a salt and pepper hair and beard entered. He scanned her chart. "Good morning, Mr. and Mrs. Martin."

Mary Ellen laughed. "Let me clarify, Doctor. I'm Mary Ellen Martin and this is my brother John. He is here for moral support."

"I see," the doctor said, closing the chart. "I'm Dr. Latio, but please call me Phil."

Mary Ellen appreciated that Phil was so confident he didn't need to use his title for credibility.

John looked up from his newspaper. "So, Phil, how long have you been doing this?"

Dr. Latio's face was a mix of concern and irritation. "You did receive and read the literature we sent, didn't you?"

Mary Ellen silenced John with a scowl. "No, John didn't, but I did. John, Phil's been doing this for over a decade. Please enjoy your paper. If I need your help, I'll ask, okay?"

"Uh, sure, Sis." John found the Sports section.

Phil looked at Mary Ellen. "So, do you have any questions?"

"No, it seems pretty straightforward. I'm ready to go."

"Excellent." The doctor scanned through Mary Ellen's chart again. "It looks like everything is in order. All of the forms are signed and your vitals look good. The mitochondrial DNA your lab sent us has been tested and is viable. As you read in our literature, we'll be doing a somatic cell nuclear transfer. Today, we will be performing a transvaginal oocyte retrieval, harvesting about dozen of your ova, more commonly referred to as eggs. We take the eggs to our lab, work our magic and, assuming all goes well, and it should, in three weeks we'll implant the viable embryo into your uterus. From that point, you should have a normal pregnancy. Our success rate for the procedure is 68%. Very good odds, I think you'll agree."

Mary Ellen nodded.

"It is an outpatient procedure. We'll be done in time for your brother to take you out to lunch. Ready?"

"Yes."

"Great. I'll send the nurse in a moment to get you ready and move you to the operating room. I'll see you in about an hour."

* * * * *

An hour and fifteen minutes later, Mary Ellen lay on the operating table, clad only in a hospital gown, her legs propped up in stirrups. The nurse had given her a painful shot on each side of her vagina, making her vagina and rectum feel strange. The sensation was mainly numb, but with a tingling that she feared might turn into arousal. She hoped she didn't embarrass herself by farting, wetting herself, or, much worse, having an orgasm.

As Dr. Latio harvested Mary Ellen's eggs, he asked through his surgeon's mask, "Miss Martin, do you mind if I ask you a question?"

Trying to not lose focus on her bowels, she replied with labored breath, "Sure, Phil, what?"

"The DNA your lab sent is obviously a human male in excellent health but the lab results were slightly abnormal."

"Abnormal?" Mary Ellen asked in a half-grunt.

"Well…the DNA is very old…," the doctor said. "Do you know the donor?"

"Doctor, you know I'm a Martin, right?"

"Yes, you're Mary Ellen Martin," Phil replied. It was a common enough name.

"Of the M-Mart Martins."

"Oh…" Dr. Latio's eyes widened. "So you used your resources to get the DNA from someone like Hemingway or Lincoln…?"

"Something like that," she replied stiffly, her forehead sweating from the concentration.

The doctor pondered the implications for a moment. "Hmmm, so that's why you needed our services. Now the whole line of questioning by your colleague, Miss Byrne, makes sense. Don't worry, your secret is safe with us."

"Right. Can we hurry this up please? I really need to pee."

"Oh. Right. Certainly." Dr. Phil turned his focus back to the procedure. After he finished, he asked, "Would it be too much to ask whose DNA you chose?"

Mary Ellen gave him a wry grin. "Yes, actually it would."

Chapter 3

"Push, Mary Ellen," Dr. Latio said, trying to sound firm and insistent, yet soothing at the same time. It was a strange combination that didn't quite work for the doctor.

Sweating, grunting, and embarrassed by the lack of composure she maintained through the whole experience, Mary Ellen Martin was outraged by the injustice of it all. She was in the most pain in her entire life and had no one to blame but herself. She felt as if she was trying to pass a kidney stone the size of a walnut or maybe had a bout of constipation that a gallon of stool softener wouldn't cure.

In the movies, the wife could yell and scream at the husband, threaten to kill him and throw cups of ice chips at him, but Mary Ellen had no husband to scream at, so she did the only sensible thing she could think of and yelled at her brother. "Damn you! It's all your fault!"

John was in the delivery room, alternating between holding Mary Ellen's hand and giving encouragement, holding the video camera, patting the sweat from her forehead with a towel, and, of course, deflecting her wrath. "My fault?" he asked, amused, as he wiped her brow. "How so, Sis?"

"You…" she grunted. "You should've talked me out of this. I didn't know it would hurt so much…aaargh!"

John noticed Mary Ellen's face was turning a color strikingly similar to his first car, a 1978 candy apple red Camaro Z28. John really loved that car… "Talk you out of what might be my only shot at being an uncle? I don't think so. Besides, how the heck am I supposed to know how much labor hurts? I've never been pregnant. Blame Mama for not telling you about the pain."

"Nurse, give me something to throw at that bastard," she yelled as sweat exploded off her face.

Thankfully, the nurse gave John a knowing look and ignored Mary Ellen. His sister was acting ten times more deranged than he ever remembered. John leaned over to the nurse and whispered, "Do all mothers act like this?"

"Not all, but enough to keep my job interesting," the nurse replied. She gave John a weak smile.

John whispered back, "If I ever get married and have kids, I'm staying in the waiting room."

The nurse giggled. "Good luck with that. Tell me how that works out for you."

An alarm went off on one of the machines next to the delivery table. The doctor went over to the machine and analyzed the readings on the monitor.

"Phil, what's wrong?" Mary Ellen grunted, her grip on the delivery table rails so strong John wondered if she was going to bend them.

"We have a minor complication. The labor is taking too long and the baby is in fetal distress. We need to do a C-section and get the baby out. Don't worry, Mary Ellen, everything is going to be fine. John, you're going to have to leave."

A panicked look overcame Mary Ellen's sweat-ridden face. "But I need John here!"

Dr. Latio said reassuringly, "It's going to be okay but we are going to use general anesthesia on you and you'll wake up in a couple of hours. We need to get started right now, though. Goodbye, John."

John leaned over and kissed his sister on the forehead. "It's okay, Sis. The doctor knows what he's doing. I'll be waiting for you when you wake up." He walked out of the room, a mixture of relief from being freed from his sister's hormone-induced psychotic break from reality and concern for her and the baby's well-being. He whispered a quick prayer as he went to Mary Ellen's hospital room to wait.

* * * * *

The next morning John awoke to the clank of the metal door handle opening and Mary Ellen again being wheeled back into her hospital room, the baby in her arms.

"Hey, sis, what's up?" John asked with a yawn. He stretched on the futon chair that was folded out into an extremely uncomfortable bed only about three feet wide. He hadn't slept worth a crap last night and the pseudo-bed was only a small part of the problem. The main problem was "Little Sam" as Mary Ellen had nicknamed the baby. Because of the C-section, Mary Ellen could barely move without a lot of pain and certainly couldn't get up and change diapers, so John was stuck with diaper duty, some ten times last night.

John had never changed a diaper in his life and tried to play on the sympathies of the nurse about being the uncle and not the father, but she was a middle-aged battleaxe who was more concerned about her own inconvenience than John's discomfort and inexperience at diaper changing. The nurse showed him how to change Little Sam's diaper once, just once, and handed him a stack of diapers. About every forty-five minutes for the rest of the night, John changed Little Sam's diaper. The biggest shock was the diaper wasn't being filled with poop, but with a nasty tar-like substance that the battleaxe informed him was called meconium, which newborns crap out for the first day or two. He almost lost his lunch the first time he saw it and smelled it, but by morning, he was a seasoned veteran.

Mary Ellen handed Little Sam over to John and had the nurse help her back into bed. "Little Sam and I went for a stroll and I filled out some paperwork, the birth certificate and such."

"So, it's official then? 'Little Samuel Martin'?" John asked with straight face, picking up the baby.

"Right, smartass," Mary Ellen said reprovingly. "I'm sure he'll go by Sam eventually."

"The namesake of the richest man in the world." John handed the sleeping baby back to his sister after she settled back into her bed. "Big shoes to fill indeed, but I bet you can do it, champ."

Big shoes? How little did he know? The thing she hadn't told her brother or parents or anyone else was that Samuel was the baby's middle name.

Chapter 4

News Items from 2008
Excerpt from Penthouse magazine, March 2008 issue:

Leading Democratic presidential candidate, current New York senator and former First Lady Dolly Roderick sits down with Penthouse magazine for the most scandalous interview since notorious "call girl" Ginny LaFleur "blew the whistle" on good ol' Nobby Bobby in the pages of this magazine in 1992.

Penthouse Magazine: Considering the numerous and well-documented affairs your husband has enjoyed through the years, you've received a lot of criticism for not divorcing him. Many people are wondering how you think you can control the good old U.S. of A. when you can't even control your good ol' boy husband. Why have you stood by Bobby all of this time?

Dolly Roderick: God, I am so fucking tired of that question. You idiots in the media never have and never will understand that Bobby is just a stepping-stone for me to get to the White House. America hasn't been ready for a liberated female to be in charge – and if you don't believe me, look at what happened to that dipshit Wallace Mundane when he picked a liberated woman, Gwendolyn Ferrari, as his running mate back in the dark ages also known as the '70's. I had to let Bobby get in the White House so the people of this country could get used to…um, get to know me. Then Bert Francis, that dumbass, fuckwit tree hugger, fucked up everything by losing to Kirby, and I had to become a senator instead of

Secretary of State like I was supposed to, which was going to lead to a presidential run... [Previous text deleted from final printed interview.] Because, despite his faults – and who doesn't have a few flaws? – Bobby is a brilliant man, and a good man at sex...um, heart. You don't trade-in a Rolls Royce just because it has a dent or two. Those dents are character. They have a great story behind them.

PM: So you accept, and maybe even appreciate, the "dents" in Bobby's character?
DR (laughs): Now, I'm not saying I might not trade in that Rolls on a good, dependable, Ford Crown Victoria one day.

PM: So a divorce isn't out of the picture?
DR: Now you fuckers are putting words in my mouth. OK, I'm not trading in the Rolls. But I wouldn't mind "renting" a sporty little Mustang convertible one Saturday afternoon.

PM: OK, you won't divorce Bobby – after all, you rode him to get where you are today. But you wouldn't mind having a fling with a young stud.
DR: Dammit, I never should've listened to that bastard Carver about doing this interview. "Have a couple of drinks beforehand to loosen up", he said. I just remembered he told Playboy about those fucking attack rabbits.

PM: All we're suggesting is you deserve a "stud" or two, especially in light of the whole Mandy Lewis "cigar" scandal and other Presidential flings.
DR: Hey, I've smoked the presidential "cigar" a time or two myself, but I never inhaled...

PM: Uh...thank you for your time, Senator.

Marriage Outlawed in Massachusetts

BOSTON, Mass. – April 4, 2008 – Deval Patron, governor of the Commonwealth of Massachusetts, signed into law the "Civil Unions" amendment to the Massachusetts constitution, making Massachusetts the first state to officially ban the word "marriage" from all of the state's legal documents. Marriage has been outlawed in the state altogether, replaced by the much more liberal term "civil union."

According to the amendment, a civil union is "a voluntary union for life (or until divorce) of consenting adult parties of any living entities; parties to a civil union have all the same benefits, protections, and responsibilities under Massachusetts law as spouses had in a marriage before the term was abolished."

Because of the liberal wording of the amendment and the very active participation of the ACLU in the state capital recently, legal analysts nationwide believe it is only a matter of time before other laws (like those regarding bestiality and polygamy) are stricken from the Massachusetts law books as well.

Famous Texas divorce attorney Pug "Quick Draw" McGraw said, "What the hell is going on here?!?! Those damn Yankees from Massachusetts are screwing up America. The way they have that amendment worded I could marry five women, three men, a goat and two dozen roses (and maybe even an old bottle of wine) and it would be perfectly legal. For Christ's sakes, it'd be encouraged! Will all of the states north and east of and including New York please secede from the union immediately and quit screwing up the rest of the U. S. of A.?"

Condiment Heiress Terry Clauth Dies

CARACAS, Venezuela – April 7, 2008 – In a bizarre turn of events, Terry Clauth, multi-millionaire heiress of the Clauth condiment fortune and wife of former Democratic presidential hopeful Jerry Hertz, was killed while touring the Clauth's ketchup plant in Caracas, Venezuela. She evidently fell into a vat of ketchup and drowned while the plant was being assaulted by the Venezuelan army, who were nationalizing the plant under the orders of Hugo Caldera, president of Venezuela.

When asked about Clauth's death, Caldera responded, "Yes, that was an unfortunate accident. Jerry Hertz has been a close friend of mine for many years now and, although I've never met his wife, I'm sure she was a fine woman. It was a regrettable coincidence that we liberated the plant when she happened to be there on a visit. I'm sure Venezuelan people can accept the slight but tragic collateral damage of these overwhelmingly positive events.

"When the people of our great nation start being able to buy one-liter bottles of Caldera Ketchup for 200 bolivars [9 cents USD], they will forgive a few lost lives. Remember, I am not talking about a regular plastic bottle here either. I am talking about the upside-down no-drip easy squeeze bottle. That's something that will really improve the quality of life for the Venezuelan people. Now if they could just get some food to put the ketchup on..."

* * * * *

Presidential Hopeful Roderick Taps Hertz as Future Secretary of State

New York, NY – May 11, 2008 – After much controversy, World Trade Center's Tower Two was officially opened. Presidential hopeful Dolly Roderick cut the ribbon and gave the dedication speech. Roderick created a stir when she tapped Jerry Hertz as her Secretary of State despite not yet receiving the Democratic nomination.

Polls showed a dramatic rise in Roderick's polls after paying homage to Clauth Condiments' heiress, Terry Clauth, Hertz' late wife that perished two months ago in an industrial accident during a tour of a Clauth factory in Venezuela.

Controversy resumed as speculation regarding Roderick's intentions spread. Hertz accepted the appointment, revitalizing her campaign, a positive sign after Roderick lost several caucuses to Illinois Senator Williams recently.

Republicans claim the appointment had more to do with Hertz' $780 million inheritance than with his prowess. Nate Grolsch, former Speaker of the House and former Republican Presidential Candidate, states, "I'm not trying to point fingers here, but you do the math. Hertz inherits 780 million bucks, which was off-limits until his wife died, under some odd circumstances I might add, and Roderick all of a sudden announces he's the next Secretary of State if she wins. Hmmm...I'm sure there's no connection. No, really."

*****

M-Mart Announces Buyout of ExxonMobil

MARTINSVILLE, AL – May 19, 2008 – M-Mart Stores, Inc., (NYSE: MMT) today announced a hostile takeover bid for ExxonMobil CP (NYSE: XOM) in a stock swap deal worth $450 billion. Once the deal is complete, ExxonMobil would become the M-Oil division of M-Mart Stores, Inc. The merged company would have a market cap of $648 billion if the deal closed today.

Mary Ellen Martin, SVP of Mergers and Acquisitions, said, "This is a great day for M-Mart and the consumer. M-mart, currently the largest retailer in the world, will become the largest company in the world and we'll pass the volume buying power savings on to our faithful consumers."

Rex Humphreys, Chairman and CEO of ExxonMobil, will get a record $7.6 billion payday if the takeover bid is successful. On a side note, 37,800 employees will be able to expand their career growth opportunities with other companies as ExxonMobil will have to lay them off to pay for Humphreys' tough but fair severance package. When asked about his severance package, Humphreys stated, "Mary Ellen [Martin] is an extremely tough negotiator, but somehow I feel my wife, Betty, and our four children will be able to get by on the deal. Does anybody know of a company looking for an executive…?"

Both Democrats and Republicans refused to comment on the pending merger.

Chapter 5

2008 continues...

"You have got to be fucking kidding me!" Dolly screamed, throwing another Styrofoam-filled beanbag at the 46-inch flat screen TV mounted on the wall. Bean bags in the full spectrum of colors---red, orange, yellow, green, blue, purple---littered the floor below the TV, two dozen or more.

The beanbags were Pedro Sandoval's idea. Two weeks earlier, Dolly did over $2,300 of damage to a hotel room and made headlines when she threw an alarm clock at the flat screen TV in a hotel room while watching the Kentucky primary. Pedro spent the better part of a week doing damage control on that fiasco.

If rumors were to be believed, Senator Williams, half-black and having Black Panther and Muslim connections, might be the Anti-Christ. It seemed to Sandoval the closer Dolly came to the Democratic National Convention, the more horns protruded through her hairdo, and not Williams'. In the last two weeks, as Williams inched ever closer to sealing the democratic nomination for presidential candidate, Dolly's mood went from irritated to hostile to rage and, finally, to demonic frenzy.

It was June 3, 2008 at about 11:30PM local time at the Hampton Inn Billings. Though it certainly was no Trump Tower, the Hampton was the closest thing Montana had to a luxury hotel. Dolly and about a dozen of her friends were crammed in the "honeymoon suite," as the hotel didn't have a presidential suite, watching the Montana primary election results. These friends were either so close and loyal to Dolly they were willing to withstand her volcanic tirades or friends not smart enough to figure out a way to get out of being with her as she lost the democratic nomination.

Pedro Sandoval was Dolly's closest adviser and male confidant, even closer than her womanizing scumbag of a husband. She also knew that Pedro had never cheated on his wife, which was a feat in the political arena as rare as someone winning the lottery jackpot three times in a week using the same numbers. There were just too many perky, nubile young groupies, sometimes called interns, who got a rush from bumping uglies with powerful, charismatic and rich men and few men were more powerful, charismatic and rich than a politician. Pedro's fidelity earned him the honor of being the only male in Dolly's inner circle of confidants. Pedro returned Dolly's respect by being the one person who would be truly candid with her. Because of this, Pedro Sandoval was going to have to stay by her side no matter how bad it got, and this had all of the makings of becoming a shitstorm of monumental proportions.

In special election coverage on CNN, Lou Gibbs discussed the winner with Peterson Harper, special election correspondent. "Well, Peterson, with 47% of the precincts reporting, we have Williams with a statistically significant lead over Roderick of 63% to 34%. Based on that, Williams will get a minimum of ten of the sixteen available delegates and perhaps as many as twelve. Even ten would bring Williams' total delegates to 2029, which is over the 2024 delegates needed to secure the nomination, so can we safely say that Brock Williams is the democratic nominee for the President of the United States?"

"I think so," Peterson said. "I think America has spoken and I think what they are saying is they are sick of the Kirby's and the Roderick's. There has been a Kirby or Roderick in the White House for the last twenty years and since 1980 if you include Kirby Sr. being in the VP spot under Reagan. It is obvious America is voting for change."

"Okay," Gibbs said. "So what happens to Dolly now?"

"Who cares?" Harper asked with a chuckle.

Dolly screamed again and sent a red beanbag flying that hit the TV screen right between Harper's eyes.

"No, really," Gibbs prodded in a parental tone.

"No really, who cares about the losers of these things? Where are Thorndale and Ferrari now? Heck, nobody cares about Croissanwich and he was running in this election..."

"I think you mean Kovach. I believe the croissanwich is a breakfast sandwich on the Burger King menu..."

"Whatever," Harper retorted mildly. "Listen, Lou, the fact that I can't even remember this bozo's name must tell you something. I'm getting paid to remember his name. The only thing I, and the rest of the country, remember about Dennis is that he married that hot Fergie, Duchess of York lookalike who is half his age..."

"Now, Petey," Lou cut him off. "Dolly's been in the public eye for almost two decades and I think our viewers would like to know what her next steps might be..."

"Okay, okay, Louie," Harper shot back in an irritated tone. "I see a couple of options. The first and most obvious option is that she could return to her post as New York senator. She still has four years left in her term. Then, if McGarrity wins this election, she has a decent shot at winning the democratic nomination in four years, unless someone comes out of nowhere and steals the nomination from her the way Williams just did.

"However, if Williams wins this November, then, quite frankly, Dolly's done. Unless Williams totally chokes as president, she is going to have to wait until 2016 for another chance, and I mean totally chokes. Look at Bobby's scandals and Keith's performance yet they still easily won the nomination of their party to run for a second term. In 2016, Dolly will be sixty-nine, a number more often associated with Bobby..."

Lou Gibbs cleared his throat loudly.

"...Anyway," Harper continued. "At age sixty-nine, what's her platform going to be? 'One Tough Great Grandma'? As John Tonsils would say, 'Give me a break!'"

This earned another beanbag at Harper's head. Surprisingly, Pam Sausalito, Dolly's failing but militantly loyal campaign manager, threw it. Dolly glanced away from the screen for a fraction of a second, flashing Pam an evil grin. Pam responded in kind.

Sandoval had to give Pam credit. If he were Pam, he would be hiding at the Scott Base in Antarctica or some village in Outer Mongolia. Pedro still couldn't understand how Dolly was losing to a half-breed with a middle name that was the same as the last name of an Arab despot. Heck, Williams was completely unknown until that bimbo, albeit stunning bimbo but bimbo nonetheless, Williams Wench, strutted all over the Internet in a halter-top and jogging shorts. In what must have been near freezing temperatures considering the way her nipples were endlessly threatening to puncture holes in her top, she sang about her horniness for Williams and instantly made both of them a household name. In a rare case of restraint, Dolly hadn't blamed Pam for her impending loss to the neo-Muslim.

"So you think Dolly's chance at the presidency is over?" Gibbs asked. "Her moment has passed?"

"Basically, yes," Harper said. "Stick a fork in her, she's done."

"What about the possibility of Dolly being Williams' vice presidential running mate?"

"I don't see it, for several reasons. First, I don't see the vice presidency helping Dolly at all. Kirby Sr. is the only VP who went on to be elected president since World War II. Francis, Pheasant, and Thorndale all have failed presidential runs. VP Penguin didn't even bother running. Second, I think Williams hates Dolly. Yeah, they appear all lovey dovey on the surface, but I think he despises her and her tactics, especially that cheesy ripping off of the White House china. I doubt she could get him to put her on the ticket, even if she wanted it..."

Images of LBJ and a plan entered Dolly's mind. Wanna bet, you needle-dicked silver-haired fuckwit? She smiled.

* * * * *

The Pepsi Center in Denver, Colorado was filled to standing-room-only capacity for the Democratic National Convention as a dignified, perhaps somewhat defiant Dolly Roderick, wearing a navy pant suit with bright yellow blouse and navy low-heel shoes, stepped up to the podium. Her husband, Bobby, and daughter Cherry, stood on either side and slightly behind her.

"My fellow Democrats," Dolly said into the microphone. "It's been a hard-fought battle and the best man won."

Dolly waited a moment for the thunderous applause to die down. She looked over at Brock Williams, who stood off to the left of the podium, and gave him a professional smile though she really wanted to draw and quarter the bastard. "It is my great honor to give my delegates to the next President of the United States of America, Brock Williams!"

Henry Doone walked up to the podium as Dolly stepped to the side. "It is my pleasure, as the Democratic National Committee chairman, to officially announce that Brock Williams is the democratic candidate for President of the United States."

The crowd cheers rose to a deafening crescendo.

"Not only are we going to New Hampshire, we're going to South Carolina and Oklahoma and Arizona and North Dakota and New Mexico, and we're going to California and Texas and New York," Doone screamed, his arms flailing wildly and his face turning vermillion, the veins on his forehead and neck bulging. "And we're going to South Dakota and Oregon and Washington and Michigan, and then we're going to Washington, D.C., to take back the White

House! YeaAHah!!!"

Williams ignored Doone's histrionics and walked over to Dolly, put his arm around her waist, gave her a light kiss on the temple and waved to the cheering crowd with a big smile. Then, still holding Dolly, he gently but firmly scooted Doone away from the podium microphone. "Thank you, Henry. Thank you, Dolly," Williams said, keeping his arm around Dolly's waist. "Thank you, everyone! I am honored to be your nominee for President of the United States…"

Another liberal dose of applause from the conventioneers (or perhaps it was another dose of liberal applause). Williams smiled as he waited for the applause to die down, looking at the panting and sweating Doone, wondering if he or Dolly was going to have to perform CPR on the DNC chairman before the night was over.

"Dear fellow members of the Democratic party, it is my pleasure to announce my choice for vice presidential running mate," Williams said and gave Dolly's waist a little supportive squeeze. "New York senator Dolly Roderick!" He removed his arm from Dolly's waist, grabbed her hand and lifted it up in victory gesture. "We're in it to win it, right Dolly?"

"You bet, Brock!" Dolly said with a smile though secretly she wanted to cut his pecker off, stuff it in his mouth and sew his lips together while he screamed. The nerve of that fucker using one of her campaign slogans.

The crowd responded with an odd mix of exultation and mystification. It was blatantly obvious that half of the crowd thought the match was brilliant and would cause a landslide victory in November while the other half deemed the choice to be political suicide, tantamount to handing the election over to McGarrity and the republicans.

Dolly grinned, satisfied. She bet that dumbass Harper didn't see that one coming.

"Well, I'll be," Peterson Harper said into his headset from the auditorium floor. "That's a bit of a shock, eh, Lou?"

From the CNN studios in Atlanta, Georgia, Lou Gibbs said, "That came out of left field, didn't it? In fact, Peterson, didn't you say just a few weeks ago what a mistake the Williams-Roderick ticket would be?"

"Indeed, Louie, I did," Harper admitted with a scathing 'you're such an ass, Louie' look. "And I still do. Heck, Doone would be a better choice."

"I don't know about that, Petey," Gibbs said with a chuckle. "He's not looking so good. He might be wheeled out on a gurney before the night is over."

"Boy, it's a surprise, that's for certain. That really ruins Dickson's political future, doesn't it? All of the political analysts thought he was getting the VP nod for backing Williams over Roderick even though Bobby Roderick's administration made him Secretary of Energy and made it so he could make a run for president. Dickson was a nobody governor from a nobody state before the Rodericks. Heck, Bobby Roderick even brought some perky interns over to Dickson's New Mexico ranch for a little 'slap and tickle' in the hot tub while they watched the Super Bowl a few months ago, trying to get Dickson to back Dolly and he didn't. Dickson might as well resign and go find a good book deal. His political career is over. Dolly will bury him."

"True enough," Gibbs agreed with a laugh.

"But why? I just don't get it," Harper continued. "I guess I can understand why Williams is overlooking their differences. He should gain more votes than he'll lose by having Dolly on the ticket, but why would she want to be VP? She always made it clear how worthless she thought Bert Francis was, so why?"

"Why indeed," Gibbs pondered. "I have no earthly idea."

Dolly tuned out Williams' blathering from the podium several minutes earlier and watched Gibbs and Harper on a giant flat screen monitor off the left of the stage. About November 5th, you worthless dipshits will know why.

Immaculate Deception

PART II

PRESIDENCIES: 2008-2011

"My friends, we live in the greatest nation in the history of the world. I hope you'll join with me as we try to change it."
   ---Barack Hussein Obama Jr.

Immaculate Deception

Chapter 6

Election Night, 2008

Dolly Roderick hung up her cell phone. She was backstage at the San Diego Convention Center. Several massive video displays hung from the rafters throughout the convention center's main auditorium. She and a large group of the Democratic Party's major players were watching the election results after a long day of trying to get last-minute undecided voters to vote for her and Williams. She had started the morning in San Francisco and ended here, doing whirlwind stops in places like Santa Clara, Los Angeles, Mission Viejo and a dozen other cities along the way.

She was on the phone with her running mate, the once and future President-elect Williams, who watched the election results in Seattle where he was doing his last minute campaigning. Williams had called Dolly with the news that he just got off the phone with their republican opponent Phillip McGarrity, who had given Williams the obligatory concession call. McGarrity had put up a good, solid fight to the end, she noted, looking up at the election results.

It was 11:14 PM pacific standard time and, with 98% of the precincts reporting, she and Williams had a clear victory with 287 electoral votes over McGarrity's 251. For a change, none of the states were undecided. Even the Floridians managed a clear result, even if it was for their opponent.

Dolly smiled. It was finally over and she had won. Sort of, anyway. Vice president certainly wasn't president, but at least she wouldn't have to deal with McGarrity for the next few years because he didn't even hold any office currently. He would probably go back to his lucrative speaking and writing career. Good for him and good riddance to the annoying prick.

With a deep breath, Dolly felt a blissful peace pass over her like a spring breeze. Soon, very soon, this night in fact, she was going to able to complete a plan some thirty-plus years in the making. Tonight, the world was hers.

She stepped back out onto the stage from behind the curtain to the uproarious cheers of the crowd and stepped up to the podium. Bobby and Cherry, their daughter, were standing next to the podium, smiling at her and clapping as she walked up. Dolly looked quite vice presidential in her navy pantsuit, aquamarine blouse and American flag broach.

She stood there smiling as she gazed out into the crowd, catching the eyes of various big financial supporters and waving to them as she waited for the applause to die down. As it did, she began, "Brock and I want to thank you so much for your support during this long and hard-fought campaign." She waited again as the applause picked up. "I just got off the phone with President-elect Williams. My dear friends and supporters, Phillip McGarrity has conceded the race to Brock!"

The applause became wild as she positioned herself between Bobby and Cherry, grabbed their hands and raised them over their heads in a victory gesture. This was a bittersweet moment for her. These cheers should be for her, not that fucking Oreo. She would rectify that injustice soon enough, but first she had someone else to deal with.

She noticed Bobby trying to be sneaky as he flirted with an especially perky brunette campaign volunteer that was probably ten years younger than Cherry. That dumbass couldn't even keep his pecker under control in front of a thousand people during her moment. Well, he was going to get his, and soon. The applause continued for several minutes as she fumed inwardly, smiling and waving all the while. She grew impatient, thoughts of her ultimate plan flashing through her mind. She said into Bobby's ear, "I have a special victory night planned for us. Have the SS bring the motorcade around. I'll be there in a few minutes." She winked at him.

At first, Bobby looked a little perturbed and confused, glancing for a split second at the volunteer that was going to get away. Then he gave a reluctant put polished smile. "Yes, honey." He waved to the crowd and departed behind the backstage curtain, followed by two secret service agents.

Dolly motioned for Helen Moore, her confidant during all of Bobby's philandering, to join her onstage. She whispered in Helen's ear. "It's time. Go get the hotel room ready."

Helen nodded with a grin, gave Dolly a quick congratulatory hug and darted off behind the backstage curtain.

The applause and chatter was still a loud rumble as Dolly made it out into the crowd, offering handshakes, hugs and quick words of thanks for support to key people in the campaign. Four secret service agents followed closely behind. After about twenty minutes, she made her way back to podium.

"My dear friends, thank you again for your great support! It has been a long day and I'm going to excuse myself and get some rest, so I'll be ready to start building my new administra...err, to help Williams build his new administration early tomorrow morning!" The cheers and applause became deafening as they reverberated throughout the auditorium. With a final wave, Dolly and the guards exited behind the backstage curtain and down the long hallway to the exit at the rear of the convention center where the motorcade waited.

A secret service agent guided Dolly to the third black stretch limo in line where the back passenger-side door was already opened for her. She stepped in and sat down next to Bobby who still had that charismatic candy store grin on his face. Obviously, he had forgotten about his volunteer. At times like these she still felt an odd attraction for him in spite of all of his infidelities and betrayals. A moment of remorse about her plan flushed over her, but she quickly recovered. She knew she was doing the right thing.

The limo started moving. They were alone in this part of the limo. She leaned over, kissed him on the cheek and, grinning, whispered in his ear, "Do you have any of those little blue pills?" Even though they hadn't had sex in several years, she knew full well what the answer was going to be. Bobby always had a ready supply of "Triple P" as he referred to them, which stood for "penis power pills." He was always prepared in case he wanted to get his pecker wet inside some awestruck stewardess or college co-ed while on his never-ending book signing and speaking tour around the world's many universities and business organizations. Helen was diligent about reporting Bobby's many trysts to her. Evidently, he was trying to catch Wilt Chamberlain in the prolific sex department.

She wasn't sure what he enjoyed more about the tour, the endless stream of bubbly groupies or the insane amount of money that universities and organizations were willing to pay him to blather on about his past presidency. She was continuously amazed how he could fetch as much as half a million dollars to repeat the insights that could be found in one of his $20 books. The thought made her pause. He was certainly good at making money. She would miss that, but luckily, she had already come up with several sources to replace that income, one by the name of Jerry Hertz, recent widower and the new front-runner for Secretary of State.

Bobby's expression turned to an uncomfortable confusion for a split second as if he were considering whether to lie or not, but his charming grin quickly returned as he said with a chuckle, "Of course, sweetie. I'm always hoping you'll want to do the nasty with me again."

"Good," said Dolly. "Why don't you take two?"

"Two?" Bobby asked, surprised and delighted. Maybe this wasn't going to be such a horrible experience after all.

She used to be a tiger in bed back in their rebellious college days. Maybe that was why he enjoy boffing co-eds so much. It reminded him of those days.

"Yes, two. It's not every day I become the first woman vice president in U.S. history, right? I know I haven't been seeing to your sexual needs lately with all of the campaigning and I was thinking we could catch up tonight." She playfully rubbed his crotch. "Do you think you could handle a couple rounds of fun?"

"Uh, of course, honey. Let's celebrate!" Bobby groped at her breasts, but Dolly pushed his hands away.

"Slow down, Mustang," Dolly chided. "Let's wait until we get to the hotel. I am the Vice President-elect after all and we're not in college anymore. Let's have a little decorum, shall we? Besides, you still need to take your pills."

"Fair enough." Bobby grabbed a small zip top baggie from his pocket and gulped down two little blue pills and chased them with a couple of swallows of champagne from the limo's wet bar. "So now that your VP, what does that make me? The Second Person?"

No, that makes you a fucking Jew boy rat bastard. "Your title?" She laughed. "The Second Gentleman, I suppose. Don't worry about that. Just work on your champagne." Soon enough, it wouldn't matter.

Within minutes, the motorcade arrived at the passenger drop-off for the Little America Westgate hotel, which was cordoned off by the secret service agents. The Rodericks were escorted to the elevators and up to the top floor where the presidential suite was located. They reserved the top three floors for their entourage.

Helen waited for them as they got off the elevator. "Hello and congratulations."

"Thank you," Dolly said as they all strode to the presidential suite.

Dolly, Bobby and Helen passed two agents stationed at the door to their suite as they walked in.

"Bobby," Dolly said with a smile. "Helen and I need to finish up a little business. Why don't you have a nice hot shower and I'll be ready for our rendezvous in a few minutes, okay?"

Bobby eyed Helen coolly. They had never gotten along and he never trusted her. "Sure thing," he said with hesitant smile, disappearing into the bathroom and closing the door.

Dolly waited until she heard the shower turn on before speaking softly. "Did you do what I asked?"

In response, Helen smiled and handed her a Blatz beer encased in a bright orange Hooters koozie. "Just like Bobby likes."

"Excellent. How many?" Dolly asked, referring to the number of Viagra pills Helen had crushed up and put in the beer.

"Six, just as you requested."

"Perfect." Dolly set the beer down on the coffee table. "Did you put a couple of extra in the fridge?" Helen nodded. "Good, have the agents moved away from the door and stand by the elevator, okay? Tell them we want a little privacy so we can celebrate and they should be able to guard our suite just fine from there. Let me know if you have any trouble, then go to your room and start the arrangements for our other plan. I want it implemented tonight."

"Are you sure you want to do that so soon?" Helen asked, one eyebrow raised. "Won't it attract suspicion?"

"No, just the opposite. Who would suspect a mourning widow fresh off the tragic death of her long-time beloved husband of anything? I'll call you when I need you."

"Yes, Madam Vice President," Helen said with a grin.

Dolly looked irritated at first and then chuckled, knowing Helen was trying to congratulate her, not rub in the fact she had lost the primary to Williams. "Not for long." She erased that melancholy thought and focused on tonight's forthcoming happy events. She gave her confidant a hug and a deep kiss on the mouth. "Now, off with you. I should be calling you in an hour or two if I know Bobby at all."

Dolly shut and locked the door behind Helen as she left. Then she grabbed Bobby's beer and walked into the bathroom to find her husband turning off the shower and grabbing a towel. She handed him the beer and asked, "So, how are you feeling?"

Bobby took a big swig of his beer. "Great, sweetie. What about you?"

Dolly moved close and playfully grabbed his cock. "Why, it's the best day of my life and I believe it's about to get even better." He was already starting to harden in her hands. "Let's go to bed."

Bobby took a huge gulp of his beer, swallowing several times. "Yes, dear."

His cock still in her hands, she guided him to the bed, turned off the lights and undressed as he lay in semi-darkness, the only light coming from the crack at the bottom of the front door and from the partially open bathroom door. He finished off his drug-laced beer.

She hesitated for a moment, wondering if she should ask him to wear a condom. She knew he must have a ready supply. She shook off her concerns, knowing the request might ruin Bobby's mood and cause a fight and that wasn't part of her plan. She just had to hope Bobby had been careful with his myriad of trysts and used protection. It would be just like the dumbass to give her a parting gift in the form of a sexually transmitted disease.

Dolly lifted the covers and slid under them next to her husband, who immediately began kissing her neck and fondling her breasts. His mouth roamed from her mouth to her neck to her breasts and back again as she responded in kind, kissing his mouth and neck and rubbing his chest.

After a few minutes, Bobby whispered in her ear, "How about a mustache ride?"

It sounded so lame, she had to stifle a laugh. She bet the college co-eds and interns loved that line. On the other hand, she did remember from the pre-Cherry years that Bobby was spectacular at cunnilingus. "Oh, yes," she purred, only partially acting now.

Bobby moved down on the bed and enthusiastically lapped at her clitoris, interspersed with an occasion nibble or flick. Thoughts of achieving an orgasm actually crossed her mind. She pulled Bobby up to her and guided him onto his back.

"Are you ready for a wild ride, Mustang?" she asked with a mischievous grin as she climbed on top of him and impaled herself. She hadn't called him Mustang in a long time. Back in their college days she had started calling him that during sex because of his fondness of old westerns, especially John Wayne movies. She must really be getting turned on by her plot. She had almost forgotten what it was like to get aroused by Bobby.

She began rhythmic gyrations on top of Bobby and within a few minutes, with a little help from her left hand, felt a wave of orgasmic pleasure rush over her. When it subsided, she looked down and noticed Bobby hadn't even broken a sweat. Her feelings of ecstasy were quickly replaced by annoyance. Crap. This isn't working. "Would you like to get on top?"

"Really?" Bobby replied with a mixture of excitement and confusion. Dolly hadn't let Bobby get in the missionary position since before she had become pregnant with Cherry and only then because she had read somewhere the missionary position improved chances of getting pregnant. They stopped having sex for the most part when she found out about Bobby's affair with Ginny LeFleur. The rare times when they did have sex she insisted on being on top, except when trying to get pregnant. Bobby and some close political advisers had recommended having a child to further their political ambitions because the average American voter was usually married and had 2.3 kids.

Bobby excitedly jumped on top and began thrusting. After several minutes, he worked up a good sweat but seemed nowhere close to ejaculation. "Gee, these Viagra work great, don't they?" he huffed.

Not as well as I would like, Dolly thought. "They sure do."

After another ten minutes, Bobby was dripping with sweat and panting, his face so flushed that Dolly knew he was close to orgasm, or heart failure.

"I'm king of the hill!" He screamed, as his thrusts grew wilder. "I'm king of the hill!"

Dolly cringed at his Capitol Hill reference. More like you don't fit the bill, you fucking idiot. "Ride me, Mustang, ride me!" she cried with as much enthusiasm as she could muster. Her vagina was getting sore.

"This is it, Honey!" Bobby panted, and then he gasped as his face contorted. Grabbing his chest with his left hand, he groaned. A look of shock swept over him and he fell on top of Dolly with a thud.

Crap, now what? She thought about her situation for a few moments as Bobby's limp body, some eighty pounds heavier than hers, lay on her, trapping her. With some effort, she managed to roll Bobby off her. Calmly, she looked her husband over. His face was still flushed and his penis was still rock hard, standing straight up towards the ceiling, looking vaguely like a miniature Washington Monument, but he didn't seem to be breathing. Those Viagra really did work great. She put her fingers just below his nose and felt no air movement. She also noted no rise and fall of his chest and that he hadn't ejaculated after all. Well, that was a first. Dolly came and Bobby didn't. She chuckled.

Calmly, she proceeded with her plan. She covered Bobby up to his chest. Still naked, she went to her purse and got out the latex gloves Helen placed in there for her. After she put them on, she grabbed his beer, took it out of the koozie, and put a fresh beer from the fridge in its place. Then she went to the bathroom and poured about two-thirds of it into the toilet, sat down, peed, then flushed. With the beer still in her hand, she walked over to Bobby, delicately pressed the can to his lips, being mindful not to spill any on him, and then set it down on the nightstand next to him. She grasped the little trash bag Helen supplied her and put the beer and gloves into the trash bag and placed everything into her purse.

She went into the bathroom and ran the bath water and sprinkled the complimentary pouch of bath beads under the faucet. The presidential suite had a separate bathtub and shower stall. She preferred a nice bath to a shower, and she certainly didn't feel like using the same shower her dead husband used less than an hour earlier anyway. She wanted a clean break from Bobby and now was an excellent time to begin.

As she slid into the tub, she was mildly surprised at a total lack of remorse for her deed. After all, they had been married for over thirty years, albeit loveless for the last twenty-five or more. In fact, she found the whole experience quite liberating and calming. No more wondering if she would wake to yet another scandal like Mandy, Ginny, Pauline or half of dozen others. Finally, the embarrassment was over. No more living in Bobby's shadow simply because he was a likeable man.

She spent the better part of an hour enjoying her peaceful bath. Finally, she unstopped the drain and, as the water slowly flowed away, got in character for a long, difficult night. She stood up, grabbed one of the hotel robes, and put it on as she walked back into the bedroom.

Dolly glanced over at Bobby and noticed the tent-like appearance of the sheets around his groin area had shrunk dramatically and his previously reddish face had turned ashen. She looked at the alarm clock on the nightstand. 3:24 AM. Good. The morning newspapers had already been printed. Even though the news on TV and the Internet would be blasting Bobby's picture everywhere, the L.A. Times and New York Times lead stories would still be about her and Williams today and not Bobby.

Going through the lines she and Helen had rehearsed several times, choreographed tears welled in Dolly's eyes as she picked up her cell phone and dialed Helen's phone number. It rang four times.

"Hello," came the weak, sleepy response on the other end of the phone.

"Helen, something has happened to Bobby," Dolly cried.

"What do you mean?" the voice on the phone now more alert and concerned.

"I don't know. I think Bobby has had a heart attack or something," Dolly replied in a panic. "Get over here!"

"On my way," Helen said, followed by a dial tone.

Snapping her cell phone shut, Dolly walked over to the front door, unlatched and quickly opened it and yelled at the secret service agents, "Get in here! Something's wrong with Bobby."

The two agents, a nondescript male and a beautiful blond female, clad in black suits, rushed into the Roderick's suite. The male agent spoke into his earpiece, "We have a medical emergency in the Roderick suite. Get paramedics up here stat."

The female agent ran up to the former president, quickly checked for a pulse, and finding none, began CPR. She covered Bobby's nostrils with her left index finger and thumb and blew air into his mouth. Dolly looked on curiously with a feigned look of horror at her husband's predicament, noting how gorgeous the agent was and the curves of her full breasts under the suit.

If this doesn't arouse Bobby, he really must be dead, she thought, chuckling inwardly. It was certainly arousing her. She had never noticed the agent before. She would have to get her name later. "Is he going to be alright?" Dolly asked in a concerned tone just shy of panic.

The male agent, who was now leaning over Bobby doing chest compressions, replied, "It's not looking good, Senator. How long has he been like this?"

Helen raced in the room, clothed in a hotel robe like Dolly's. "Oh my god!"

Acting flustered, Dolly slowly responded, "I don't know. Bobby and I were…were… 'celebrating'… When he 'finished,' he rolled over and went to sleep, I took a bath, and when I was done, I came in here and I found him like this. I called Helen, then came out and got you."

"From his looks, I'd say he's been dead for at least half an hour," The male agent said, continuing the chest compressions. "Hopefully, they can revive him at the hospital, but I'll be honest, Senator, I have to say the odds are slim."

I certainly hope so. "Oh no."

Helen came over, weeping, and gave her a deep hug. "I'm so sorry."

Dolly buried her face in Helen's neck, tears streaming down her face. She whispered softly into Helen's ear, "The purse."

Helen squeezed her tighter in response. "Dolly, you need to put something on. The paramedics will be here any minute and you want to go to the hospital with them, right? I'll meet you there. I'll go get dressed too."

Dolly gently pulled away from Helen and composed herself. "Yes, you're right. I should get dressed." Still acting as though she was in shock, she slowly grabbed her clothes off the floor and went to the bathroom.

A pair of paramedics rushed in with a gurney. As the agents shuffled out of the paramedic's way, Helen slipped over to Dolly's purse, discreetly slid the trash bag into the folds of her robe, and then walked to the door. "Ava," she said, calling to the female agent. "Stay with the Rodericks. I'll meet you at the hospital."

"Yes, ma'am," the curvaceous blonde replied.

* * * * *

Twenty minutes later, Helen headed to the UCSD Medical

Center in her rental car, but she wasn't taking the most direct route. On the way, she stopped by a doctor's office and dumped Dolly's trash bag into the dumpster behind the building. From her research, she knew the Waste Management truck would be there at around 6:45 AM to pick up their trash…in just about two hours…

Chapter 7

The Day After the Election, 2008

The five men moved through the pre-dawn darkness with military precision. Two in the group were former Navy SEALs, two more were former Marine Force Recon and the last had been an Army Ranger. The team wore night camouflage gear and night vision goggles, and each was armed with a Glock 19 with an internal laser sight and a Panzerfaust PzF 3 IT-600 recoilless anti-tank weapon. In less than four minutes, they cut through the chain-linked fence on the side of King County International Airport opposite the main terminal.

Crouching, the team scrambled to the safety of the cover of the Boeing Field Air Museum and hugged the building's walls as they advanced toward runway 31L. The leader, codenamed "Captain America," signaled for the group to halt as he checked his Blackberry 8800 for last-minute incoming intelligence.

"Okay," the leader said into his headset for the rest of the group to hear. "The bordello says the satellite images show the area as clear. Airport security just finished their rounds. Batman and Superman, stay here and cover us. Aquaman and Zan, you're with me."

Snickering crackled in everyone's headset.

"Dammit, Mel…" Zan began.

"No names! No names!" Captain America shot back.

"Right," Zan said, slightly hurt. It was an odd look for a six-foot-seven commando who looked like he chased down bears and killed them barehanded for sport. "Why did I have to be Zan?"

"The Joker? Penguin?" Superman offered with a chuckle.

"Jayna? Gleek?" Batman volunteered to the delight of his cackling teammates.

"Shit, even Robin would be better than Zan. The Wonder Twins? Really? They were the lamest superheores ever," Zan grumbled.

Captain America turned around and got in Zan's face; being a good eight inches shorter than Zan, he looked reminiscent of Sergeant Carter chewing out Gomer Pyle. "Listen, Zan, next time don't come in last place in the obstacle course three times in a row. Be glad your handle isn't Wonder Woman or Metrosexual for that pathetic performance. Be glad you're on this mission at all instead of standing guard at ZX-16." ZX-16 was a guard hut on an Aleutian island slightly larger than a postage stamp. As a bonus, the island was really the tip of an active volcano. Three men stationed there had died over the last seven years.

"The only reason you're here is that you're the best marksman we have with these," Captain America said, stroking his Panzerfaust. Then the leader gazed around the rest of the group scornfully. "Now, zip it, girls."

"Aquaman and Zan, with me to position B in three, two, one, mark!"

The three commandos ran crouching to a black four-foot by six-foot metal box in the middle of the grass on the other side of runway 31L. The men hid on the side of the box that faced the short end of the runway.

Captain America whipped out his cell phone and awaited further intelligence dispatches. Three minutes later, he said, "Girls, the Oreo is in the milk…I repeat: the Oreo is in the milk. T minus 840."

Zan did a quick calculation in his head. 840 divided by 60. Fourteen minutes. Why the hell couldn't Mel just say that instead…? They weren't in the military. Why did they have to pretend to be? He hated the fucking military. If he liked being in the military, he'd still be there. Actually, he wouldn't. The pay really sucked compared to this gig, but all of this military shit was irritating.

By the terminal, the men could hear engines from a couple of the Lear jets roar to life.

"T minus 300. Prepare to engage."

Two Lear jets were taxiing to the far end of Runway 31L, almost two miles away.

"Confirmed. The Oreo is in the second glass of milk. Repeat: the Oreo is in the second glass of milk. Girls, everyone but Batman go for the second glass of milk. Batman, wait until second glass of milk has been spilled before engaging the first glass of milk, just in case intel is wrong."

"Roger that, Captain," Batman said.

The first Lear jet's engines roared much louder and the jet sped down the runway. Five seconds later, the second Lear jet did the same.

"T minus thirty. Prepare to fire."

"...Twenty..."

The jets' front wheels pulled off the runway.

"...Ten..."

The jets' back wheels lifted off the runaway.

"T minus five...fire at will," Captain America said, pulsing with excitement.

Instantly, four Panzerfaust rounds were screaming toward the second Lear jet. The men ducked for cover to avoid the fireball and shrapnel as the second jet exploded.

Batman recovered and aimed his Panzerfaust at the first jet when it flipped upside down because of the concussive wave of the other jet's explosion and crashed into grass 500 feet past the men.

"Damn," Batman said. "You bastards took them both out."

"Two for one sale, baby!"

"Shut up, Zan," Batman grumbled. "Or was that Jayna?"

Zan started, "I'm going to fucking kill..."

Immaculate Deception

"Zip it, girls," Captain America spurted. "Mission accomplished. Let's get out of here."

Emergency crews in fire trucks were already exiting the building next to the terminal as the team sprinted back to the opening in the fence.

* * * * *

Later in the morning of the day of President-elect Williams' assassination, Peterson Harper, dressed in a silver wool power suit, red silk tie and black shoes, waited on the sidewalk in front of one of the many brokerages on Wall Street in New York where he was working on his latest story for his TV show, Peterson Harper 180. He tapped his foot, partially from nervousness, partially from excitement of the potential lead. Lou Gibbs, the backstabbing scuzzball that he was, had buttered up senior management at CNN and suddenly Harper was outside looking in on the Williams story, having been told that the story was "being handled" by Gibbs and his crew and Harper should focus on the Wall Street story. What a bunch of crap. An hour earlier Peterson had received a mysterious call from one of Roderick's aides saying somebody important in Roderick's camp wanted to talk to him right away. So here he waited.

At 11 AM sharp, a black limo stopped in the street in front of Harper. A man in a black suit, dark sunglasses and a matching earpiece, opened the middle of the three passenger's side doors, stepped out, gave Harper a quick frisk and waved a metal detection wand over the calm reporter. Peterson had been through this posturing crap before. Most of it was just some moron politician who thought he was hot shit, trying to put Harper in his place. He laughed inwardly as he was patted down. Most of these self-important politicians ended up taking a big fall eventually in some scandal, usually involving their second heads, and Peterson was still plugging away in the business, twenty-two year later. Screw them all.

Whatever it takes to get the story.

The agent motioned for Harper to get in the limo. Peterson stepped in, did a quick look around the limo and saw nothing, both the front and back compartments sealed off by nontransparent windows. He sat down and the lone agent followed him in. The limo immediately went into motion.

The agent, a Buster Crabbe look-alike in both size and appearance, was a good half-foot taller and sixty pounds heavier than Harper, all of it muscle from his looks. He handed Harper a paper grocery sack and said, "Mr. Harper, please strip completely and put on the clothes in the bag."

"What the..." Peterson started at this new wrinkle in posturing.

"Mr. Harper," the agent cut him off. "Did you want to meet with the president or not?"

"Uh," Harper stammered. "Really? But..."

"Mr. Harper," the agent said reassuringly. "It's just a security precaution. If I was a homosexual, which I'm not, and I wanted to rape you, which I don't, you would already be tied up like a pretzel and crying for your mommy."

Not sure why, Harper did feel reassured. With as much dignity as he could muster, he stripped and put on the clothes supplied, which was a pink jumpsuit and fuzzy bunny slippers. He protested.

"Sorry," the agent said. "The president has an interesting sense of humor sometimes. Don't worry, you'll get your clothes back. The president just wants to make sure you aren't going to try to tape the conversation, that's all."

When Harper reluctantly finished changing clothes, the agent tapped the window to the front compartment and the limo slowed and then stopped. The agent got out and placed the sack with Harper's clothes in the limo's trunk. Then he gestured for Harper to get out and get into the rear compartment.

Peterson Harper wasn't prepared for what he saw. Dolly Roderick sat, looking at him with a satisfied smirk on her face and a mimosa in her left hand. "Mr. Harper, don't you look fetching?" Dolly said with a laugh. "Please, have a seat."

Harper hesitated. The agent had said he was meeting with the president... Oh shit!

Dolly laughed again as recognition came to Harper's countenance. "Mr. Harper, please be seated."

The agent pushed Harper into the limo and closed the door behind him. Peterson eased uncomfortably into the car as far from Roderick as he could. Oh shit! That bitch had Williams killed! Oh my God! Oh shit! Suddenly, Harper was awash with a feeling of nausea and dread. So this is what it feels like to be seconds away from death...

"Now, Now, Petey, I won't bite," Dolly said. "I thought we should have a talk." She tapped on the glass and the limo started moving again.

"I just wanted to let you know what a fan I am of your work," Dolly began. "And to thank you for the wonderful idea."

"Idea?" Harper asked, his mind racing. He hadn't interviewed her in months. What was she talking about?

"Yes. Remember when you said my political career was over. 'One tough grandma' or something like that. You said that I would be an idiot to be vice president and that Williams wouldn't take me as a running mate because he hated me. Remember? Maybe not. Who would care, right, Mr. Harper? Isn't that what you said?"

Oh shit! I got Williams killed! Oh shit! Oh shit!

"I bet you care now, don't you?" Dolly asked playfully.

Harper's life flashed before his eyes.

"I know what you are thinking, Mr. Harper, but don't be too hard on yourself," Dolly said lightly. "I promise you that our dear-departed president-elect would have been assassinated either way. Do you really think that the white supremacists were going to let an interracial man take office? I mean, really, your stations were showing videos of Williams' grandmother in Congo, dark as night, looking like a nineteenth century Aunt Jemima in a dew rag and a muumuu, holding a live fucking chicken, for Christ sake. Do you really think the crackers are going to let that happen? In fact, here is that juicy story you were promised." She handed him a piece of paper. It was then when Harper first realized Roderick wore long black gloves. She was dressed all in black---black hat, black dress, black shoes.

Oh shit! She's in mourning. Oh shit! She killed her husband too!

Peterson gazed down at the piece of paper, trying to focus on the words as his mind swam from the implications of everything. It read:

> Dear fellow true Americans,
>
> It is with both profound satisfaction and placid lament that the Legion of the South Triumphant (LOST) acknowledges responsibility for the assassination of the false chief, Brock Williams.
>
> While we are proud of eliminating the impure modern Anti-Christ who propagated an unholy coup on the presidency of our great nation in a similar fashion to the nineteenth century Anti-Christ, Abraham Lincoln, we are intensely disenchanted by the fact so many Americans were so acutely obtuse and so easily swayed by his polished rhetoric.
>
> How could a person of mixed race who was only considered a United States citizen by a happenstance be a proper selection for President? His mother and father weren't even legally married as his father was still married to a woman in Congo.
>
> Williams' childhood was despicable. The man didn't even spend his childhood in America. He should be in Congo with his father right now, assuming we hadn't just killed him and his father

hadn't died in 1982, of course. His father converted from the evil pagan religion Islam to atheism. As we all know, the only thing worse than Goddamn pagan is a God-ignorant atheist.

Williams' education was even more of an abomination. He went to Columbia University and Harvard Law School and became a civil rights lawyer, a term we believe is an oxymoron. Civil rights for who? Not for the Aryans who were the founding fathers of our great nation, certainly.

His wife is black and was raised in the south side of Chicago, the baddest part of town. She has a law degree and a Black Studies degree, but we're positive her views aren't the slightest bit inclined toward jigaboos and anti-Caucasians, just as we're certain she would never whisper evil anti-Aryan lies while she and her husband were engaging in "biblical knowledge."

Williams was patently a career politician with a worldview severely skewed towards porch monkeys and against the God-fearing white founding fathers of this country. Just because Satan has a message we want to hear, doesn't make him the correct choice. Just ask our Lord and Savior about a little meeting in the desert.

Now that we've eliminated the Anti-Christ, can you please, our fellow Americans, start making smarter choices so we don't have to take steps to correct the situation again?

>Warmest regards,
>The Legion of the South Triumphant

As Peterson finished the note and looked out of the window, Dolly said, "That should get you back on the inside track with the higher ups at CNN, don't you think, Mr.

Harper?"

"Yeah," Harper muttered, dejected and still somewhat confused. "I suppose. It's a shame I'll never get a chance to show the note to anyone."

Dolly laughed. "Now, Mr. Harper, what would make you say that?"

Harper looked up at Dolly, a mix of terror and hope in his eyes. "Aren't you going to kill me?"

"Of course not, Mr. Harper," Dolly said, uncrossing her legs to reveal her naked vagina, void of panties, for an instant before the dress covered her again.

Peterson Harper was overwhelmed by a wave of nausea, sickened and turned on at the same time, and appalled that he was aroused by Dolly at all, especially since she had arranged the deaths of her husband and her running mate just hours earlier.

"Hasn't there been enough death in the last twelve hours?" Dolly tapped on the glass and the limo came to a stop again. The agent opened the door and popped his head in.

"Karl," Dolly said. "Get Mr. Harper his clothes. Our interview is over. Mr. Harper, I fully expect our conversation to be strictly confidential. I'd hate to have you locked up in Gitmo for the next decade, for national security reasons, of course, or perhaps for something worse and more permanent to happen to you. Besides, no one would believe you anyway...bunny slippers...ha! Anyway, that note was dropped off anonymously to the CNN offices, understand?"

Harper nodded sullenly.

"Good. I trust you'll care enough to make certain any future reporting of me will be in a more favorable light?"

Again, Harper nodded sullenly.

"Excellent," Dolly said, satisfied. "Now get the fuck out before I change my mind and have Karl take you on a one-way deep sea fishing trip."

* * * * *

As the limo dropped Harper, now in the middle compartment and dressed again in his silver suit, back out at Wall Street, Dolly smiled with deep satisfaction. Tonight, the United States of America was hers.

*****

The next morning the Director of Programming called Harper into his office. The Director told him Peterson Cooper 180 was being canceled immediately to allow for his new assignment, a plumb anchor job on the nightly news on KIWI, New Zealand's third biggest TV station, also effective immediately.

Harper was never seen on North American soil again though he tried several times to visit his relatives. Each time he was denied entrance as he was on the Terrorist Watch list.

Chapter 8

Headlines from 2008-2009

Posted on MSNBC.com:
The Nation Mourns Robert (Bobby) Hamilton Roderick

November 5, 2008, 06:04:19PM: The nation mourns the passing of Robert (Bobby) Hamilton Roderick, the forty-second president of the United States, who died of a heart attack early this morning. The former President will be remembered for the scandals – Mandy Lewis, the "Roderick body count list," Agua Blanca, and the pillaging of the White House heirlooms – which were a large part of his legacy.

Roderick apparently overdosed on Viagra as he and his wife, then-Vice President-elect Dolly Roderick were celebrating her election victory. An anonymous source within the Secret Service revealed a zip top bag with thirteen Viagra pills was found in his pants pocket during the investigation of his death. Another Secret Service agent, also speaking on condition of anonymity, said investigators also found an unfinished manuscript for his latest book, I Still have the First Penis, on a CD in his laptop in the hotel room. Financial analysts believe that Bobby Roderick's estate is worth approximately $56 million.

Senator/President-elect Dolly Roderick (D-New York) issued a comment through her spokesperson, Helen Moore. "I am in a deep state of mourning at the loss of my husband and my running mate in the same day and I appreciate the media respecting my privacy – for a change – during this difficult time. I also would like to thank the good people of the United States for their support in the recent election."

Bobby Roderick's personal aide, Bambi Bazookas, also spoke to the press. Her eyes welling with tears, she said, "This is such a great loss. I can't believe it. He was such a compassionate, caring, loving man...an affectionate, vital, virile man. He will be deeply missed...so, so sorely missed...yes, deeply and sorely missed..." She broke down sobbing without further comment.

Former Speaker of the House Nate Grolsch (R-Georgia) issued the following comments through his press agent: "Bobby was a good guy, if you could get past his womanizing and the fact that he accomplished little of use in office. It's hard to tell what America is mourning more; the fact that Bobby and Brock are dead or that Dolly is now President. It's a tough call. We'll certainly recover quicker from Bobby and Brock's death than Dolly's presidency, that's for damn sure."

* * * * *

Posted on CNN.com:
M-Mart Buys Alternate Fuel Company

December 22, 2008, 07:46:02AM: M-Mart Stores, Inc. announced today an agreement to buy Hydrogen Technology Applications, Inc. (HTA) for $413 million in stock. Denny Klein, founder and CEO of HTA, made quite a stir in 2005 by announcing he had modified the engine of a 1994 Ford Escort Wagon so that it could go 100 miles using just 4 ounces of water as the fuel instead of gasoline. After recovering from the shock that it was actually possible to go 100 miles in an Escort without breaking down, the media was even more impressed with the environmentally- and pocketbook-friendly potential of Klein's invention. Klein had filed for several patents and incorporated HTA back in 1997 but wasn't ready to show the world his invention until 2005.

The company's main patent is for the new hydrogen-based fuel Aquygen, pronounced "aqua gin," but not to be confused with the drink-making practice utilized by some unscrupulous bartenders. Aquygen has been touted to be the next step in evolution of the energy industry. Aquygen (HHO, as opposed to water's H2O) can replace most liquid fuels like gasoline, kerosene and propane and will allow the average car to get about 600 miles per gallon with a cost of approximately 40 cents per gallon (or less than 1% of the current price of gasoline). As if that weren't impressive enough, air pollution is essentially non-existent as the only by-product from using Aquygen is water (H20).

Mary Ellen Martin, M-Mart Stores, Inc. Senior Vice President of Mergers and Acquisitions, said, "M-Mart is thrilled to add this cutting-edge company to our growing portfolio of energy companies. Along with our recent acquisition of ExxonMobil, M-Mart will be strategically positioned to offer a great energy value to our customers now and well into the future."

Denny Klein, who will be kept on as the president of HTA, which will be renamed as the M-Gen division of M-Mart Stores, Inc., said "It is phenomenal to think of the future potential of Aquygen with the immense financial resources available to the largest company in the world that can be leveraged for research and development. This is a great day for people everywhere and for the environment."

*****

Corporate e-mail leaked to the press:

Concerning M-gen
Mary Ellen Martin
[the_dominatrix@m-martstoresincusa.com]
Sent: Wed 12/24/2008 10:28 AM
To: Everyone at M-Mart Stores, Inc.
Cc:Denny Klein [DKlein@m-gen.com]

All,

The Mergers & Acquisition management team met this morning and, with much thought and regret, it has been determined that the M-Gen division is not a financially viable venture and will be immediately shut down. M-Mart Stores, Inc. will retain rights to all patents and intellectual property, of course.

All M-Gen employees who were formerly M-Mart employees will be reassigned. All former Hydrogen Technology Applications, Inc. employees are terminated effective immediately. Security will escort you from the HTA building.

Happy Holidays,
MEM

Mary Ellen Martin
Senior Vice President of Mergers and Acquisitions
M-Mart Stores, Inc.

Share price for M-Mart Stores, Inc. stock shot up 12.4% upon hearing the news, bolstered by the acquisition of ExxonMobil and its new M-Oil division.

*****

Roderick Sworn In, Announces Cabinet

WASHINGTON, DC – January 21, 2009 - The former first lady and New York senator Dolly Roderick took the oath of office yesterday as the nation's 44th and first female president.

In her inauguration speech, President Roderick espoused the virtues of diversity, the dangers of religion, the importance of Roe v. Wade, and the benefits of socialized healthcare. "Ask not what you can do for your country. Ask what your country should be giving to you!" She also announced some of her new administration's cabinet members, including Nanny Moretti as Vice President, Jerry Hertz as Secretary of State, Helen Moore as White House Chief of Staff …

Chapter 9

2009 continues...

Jerry Hertz stood on the top step of the dais of the Saint Patrick's church in Washington, DC, looking out around the crowd of about 1500 people sitting in the pews. Stragglers were in the center and outside aisles, trying to find a seat in the packed sanctuary. He glanced over to his right at his best man, Damian Thorne, and the rest of the groomsmen and took a deep breath.

Lucky number 3. Luck had little to do with it. He had a knack for this, evidently.

As he watched bridesmaids and flower girls begin to slowly walk down the center aisle into position on the other side of the dais, John's life flashed before his eyes; not his whole life, just the last year. What did it mean? Second thoughts? Guilt? It couldn't possibly be a good thing, but it was too late for him to back out now.

The events of the past year scrolled through his mind like a badly spliced movie, jumping from scene to scene in random order:

His secret deal with Dolly to become Secretary of State and eventually follow her as President of the United States in eight years. What had he done?

The death of Bobby, campaigning for Dolly and then for Williams, arranging to have Caldera's troops kill his wife in Venezuela, being sworn in as Secretary of State, his wife's bizarre ketchup (or was it catsup?) themed red funeral.

What the hell was he going to do? He felt like he was stuck in an elevator and the power just went out. Trapped, with no way out.

Jerry eyed the secret service agents stationed on the outside aisles every five rows and loosened his collar. He struggled to breathe as he noticed dozens of news cameras set up in the back of the sanctuary. He managed a weak but polished politician's smile. What is happening to him? He tried to remain calm. The prospect of marriage? His crimes closing in on him?

His head pounding, his heartbeat reverberating through his skull, Jerry understood exactly how the protagonist of Poe's Tell Tale Heart felt. Every fiber of his being screamed to run away though he knew he couldn't. If he did, not only would his aspirations of presidency be dead, he knew he would, in all likelihood, literally be dead. He knew of the Roderick hit list and he was convinced Dolly was the mastermind behind it, not the late sap Bobby. Hell, Bobby was probably the last one added to the list, right after Williams. If Jerry crossed Dolly and humiliated her in front of the nation, her retribution would swift and sure. After all, she had killed her previous husband. Dolly had never admitted it to him or to anyone who might confide in him, but Jerry was certain of it nonetheless.

The wedding march began and Jerry took another deep breath, feeling an eerie peace as his future bride entered the sanctuary, wearing a beige wedding gown, escorted by her brother Hugh and flanked by four secret service agents. While she didn't look stunning or beautiful (nothing could accomplish that) she managed handsome or possibly mildly appealing and that was quite an accomplishment for someone who normally exuded an aura of a drill sergeant or a much-hated nun teacher at a boarding school.

While he was mildly fond of Dolly's power and ambition, he definitely wasn't in love with her and he had never deluded himself into thinking that she had fallen madly in love with him during their affair, if that's what it could be called. During the thirteen months since the first time they flirted and began conjuring grand plans, they had managed to have sex exactly as often as their spouses had died. Twice, a ridiculously small amount, and yet, in a weird way, it made sense. Even though he had made many advances - a man had his physical needs after all - Dolly was always too busy, first campaigning and then with affairs of state. She seemed much more interested in politics than sex, or any kind of affection for that matter.

Being the first male to date a President of the United States, he wasn't sure exactly what the protocol was, but he was pretty sure demanding a blowjob was out of the question. He could see why Bobby cheated on her so much. Jerry would wait a couple of months and set up a discreet lover on the side. He gazed over at the gorgeous, stacked blonde secret service agent, Ava, who discreetly walked two steps behind Dolly. She would be a good choice. She was always near him and Dolly. Maybe...

Jesus, Jerry, he inwardly scolded himself. I'm getting married and already thinking of how to cheat on my new wife as she is walking down the aisle. They'll have to create a new level of Hell just for me...

He was well aware that it was a marriage of convenience and Dolly was getting as much out of the arrangement as he was. He had helped her gain the presidency, after all, but still, thinking of cheating on her during the marriage ceremony made him feel pretty damned slimy. He refocused on the events at hand.

Dolly started up the dais steps, a broad, pleasing smile on her lips. She stopped next to Jerry and took his hand, looked at the priest and then into Jerry's eyes. As they exchanged vows, the temperature in the church felt as if it jumped about twenty degrees. Sweat beading on his forehead and the nape of his neck, Jerry was positive he caught a faint whiff of sulfur. He glanced briefly at Ava and she gave him a positively wicked smile.

* * * * *

"Are you sure you don't want to go, M?" Jerry said as he packed the duffel bag that lay on their bed in the presidential suite of the Buena Vista grand hotel in San Jose, Costa Rica. He had called Dolly 'M' since her inauguration day. It was short for Madam President. It just would not do to use a pet name like Snookums or Love Bunny with the press always around, so they had settled on 'M' as a pet name they both could live with.

"No, J, I'm good. I've got too much work to do and you know the idea of being sixty feet underwater creeps me out," Dolly said absently as she scanned the faxes that Helen had brought her. She looked up at Jerry and smiled. "You go have fun and when you come back, I promise to take the rest of the night off and we can enjoy our honeymoon, okay? We can go out and have dinner at that restaurant your friend recommended. What was it? El Casa Grande de Estreñimiento? Then we can go dancing. You up for the Macarena?"

Jerry grinned, flailed his arms and legs spastically and sang painfully off key, "When I dance they call me Macarena, and the boys they say that I´m Buena…"

Groaning inwardly, but grinning outwardly, Dolly cut in, "I'll take that as a yes. So go have fun and I'll see you in about four or five hours, right?" *God, why did I have to marry another dork?*

"Yep, that works. Try to get as much work done today as you can so maybe, just maybe you can take tomorrow off, okay?"

Dolly eyed Helen and grinned knowingly. "Sure, J, I'll get right on it."

Jerry walked over to Dolly and gave her a peck on the cheek. "See you later." Then he walked out of the hotel room, followed by the secret service agents.

Dolly motioned for Ava to come to her. The voluptuous

agent came over put her ear close to Dolly's mouth and asked, "Yes, Madam President?"

"Are you ready?" Dolly whispered, enjoying a whiff of the agent's perfume. It was a fragrance named after some teen pop star, Britney, Avril, or something like that. Dolly couldn't remember, but it was delicious.

A hint of a grin penetrated the agent's normally stoic countenance. "Yes, Madam President."

"Good luck," Dolly whispered and gave her a quick kiss on the cheek. "Go get him."

A wisp of a blush overcame Ava's face. "Yes, Madam President." Then she trotted off after the Secretary of State.

Helen closed the door behind Ava, bolted and chained it. "Like Jerry said, let's get to work," she giggled.

Clothes flying, Dolly and Helen were half-undressed before they reached the hotel bed. Helen reached Dolly in time to take her bra off for her.

* * * * *

The scuba diving expedition for Secretary of State Hertz consisted of a local dive guide named Don Pablo, who had been thoroughly checked out by the CIA, six scuba certified secret service agents including Ava and two that were also certified in operating boats thirty plus feet in length, and, of course, Jerry.

Dolly had mentioned that it might be more enjoyable to keep the group small to better enjoy the scenery and Jerry agreed so four of the six agents would remain in the boat and watch the weather and keep a lookout for any suspicious boating activity in the area where the Secretary of State was diving. Only Jerry, Don, Ava and an agent named Felix would be going in the water.

As she finished strapping on her titanium dive knife, Ava grabbed her .44 magnum bang stick. "Are you ready, Mr. Secretary?"

"Ava, we've had this talk before. Call me J unless we're in front on the press or dignitaries, okay? Right, Felix?" Jerry scolded gently. How the hell was he going to get to bury his face between the luscious titties if he couldn't even get her past the whole Mr. Secretary thing?

"Yes, J," Felix answered stiffly, seeming vaguely uncomfortable using the nickname.

"Of course, J, are you ready?" Ava asked again, flustered. It seemed odd on so many levels to use his nickname.

"Sure. Don, Felix, you ready?"

They both nodded.

"Can you hear me up on the bridge?" Jerry looked over at Ava, looking distractingly attractive in her skin-tight black wetsuit, wishing he was going down on her and grinned to himself. "Okay, Don, lead the way."

In about a half hour, the four were about a hundred feet underwater, enjoying the pristine coral reefs that were part of the Cahuita National Park. Dozens, perhaps hundreds, of different types of fish, including some dolphins and sharks, swam around in the near distance. Most ignored the divers, save for a few curious small fish.

Don swam in the lead, pointing out geographic features and history of the reef as he went. He was quite well versed on information tourists might find useful or entertaining.

Felix swam behind him, keeping an especially close watch on any shark that loomed too close to Hertz. He held onto his bang stick, sometimes called a shark stick, too tightly. He was obviously deathly afraid of sharks and tense about this particular assignment.

Jerry was about thirty feet behind Felix, either oblivious or simply unafraid of any potential danger the local sea life might present. He happily snapped pictures of the reef and sea life with an insanely expensive underwater digital camera with 87 incredible features, according to the salesperson, of which Jerry knew how to use about five.

Ava followed closely behind Dolly's husband, keeping a

watchful eye on the local fauna and her fellow divers, especially Felix. Felix was her one concern in her "assignment" for Dolly. Ava knew she could handle the other two, but the fellow secret service agent could be a problem. Luckily, his apparent fear of sharks would work in her favor. For now, she would bide her time and wait for the right moment. She still had at least an hour and half left in her window of opportunity before they would have to return to the surface.

Some forty minutes later, a group of a dozen or so bull sharks approached the dive party. They circled the divers randomly, giving the divers a wide berth, with a stray shark occasionally looming closer as if testing the divers.

Felix edgily moved closer to John, saying, "Mr. Secretary, perhaps we should return to the boat."

"Nonsense, we're okay, right, Don?" John asked calmly.

"Probably, Señor J, but it is loco for bull sharks to group. Normally, they are lonely creatures… It's your choice, señor." The guide sounded more puzzled than concerned.

Don would have been less puzzled and a lot more concerned if he knew that Ava had hid a bag of fish blood in her wetsuit. Ten minutes earlier, while the others were distracted with the scenery, she released the blood into the water and let the bag float away.

Now a shark came within a couple feet of Felix and he panicked, hitting the shark in the nose with the bang stick, blowing a chunk of the creature's snout off about the size of a large grapefruit. The shark bolted away from Felix, blood streaming from its wound.

The other sharks thrashed around widely, swimming much faster and circling closer. Don and Jerry now joined in Felix's panic. Ava, on the other hand, remained focused and moved right next to Jerry as the group scrambled towards the surface, sharks circling widely.

Felix screamed as a shark bit into his right leg, blood billowing into the water like smoke from a cigarette. Soon another shark bit into his left arm. Soon the screams stopped.

"What is going on down there?!" came the voice from the bridge.

"Oh my god, sharks just killed Felix!" Ava screamed back.

Sharks loomed close to the rest of the divers. Ava feigned a bang stick strike at a shark approaching Hertz and struck one of his air tanks instead of the shark. Ava was protected from the resulting explosion by Hertz's shattered torso. He immediately went limp and disappeared in a cloud of his own blood.

Ava calmly eased herself away from the dying men, not moving her body at all, just letting herself float away from the scene like a piece of driftwood. The sharks were in a feeding frenzy now, tearing viciously into Felix and Jerry's bloody corpses. Soon, Don, thrashing in desperate attempt to reach the surface and screaming a mix of Spanish expletives and prayers, was their next victim.

"What the hell is going on down there?!" came the voice from the bridge again.

"My god, they're all dead…" Ava's voice trailed off.

"We're coming to get you," the voice said.

"No!" Ava begged. "They'll kill you too. I'm hiding. I can't help them. Oh my god…" Then she turned off her intercom and watched the scene as she drifted away.

Within minutes, the men's bodies were completely gone save for some random bits of cloth and pieces of diving equipment floating aimlessly in the current. The sharks slowly dispersed as they found no further quarry, seeming sated for the moment.

Ava had drifted a few hundred feet away from the scene. She waited a few more minutes to make certain she was safe and then she slowly made her way back to the surface, rehearsing her story as she swam.

Chapter 10

News Items from 2009-2011

Baxter Named Secretary of State in First-ever All-Female Administration

WASHINGTON, DC – May 19, 2009 – President Dolly Roderick announced her late husband Jerry Hertz's replacement as Secretary of State will be Babbs Baxter, U.S. senator from California. The announcement makes the Roderick administration the first in history to be all-female.

When asked for comment, California governor Jurgin Müller, said, "It's about time. They are called secretaries, after all, and everyone knows secretaries should be women. They make better coffee. Besides, now Babbs will quit screwing up California…wait, now she can screw up the whole country…Oh no, this is worse than Gonad the Deflowerer…"

* * * * *

M-Mart Stores, Inc. Sales Top $1 Trillion---Mary Ellen Martin Recognized

MARTINVILLE, AR – February 17, 2010 – M-Mart Stores, Inc. (NYSE: MMT) reported record net sales of $1,034,294,876,213 for the fiscal year 2009 which ended January 31. This marks the first time in history any corporation has topped $1 trillion sales in a year.

The massive growth of M-Mart in recent years is credited to the many key acquisitions the company has made including ExxonMobil, Proctor & Gamble, and Microsoft. The company's buyout strategy was orchestrated by M-Mart insider Mary Ellen Martin, granddaughter of company founder Sam Martin and niece of M-Mart chairman S. Robby Martin.

In an e-mail to all M-Mart employees, Les Scarletti, Jr., President and CEO of M-Mart Stores, Inc stated, "I am very proud of the record results all of our associates have achieved in 2009, but I feel I must single out the efforts of one individual in particular. Senior Vice President Mary Ellen Martin of our Mergers and Acquisition division has made many excellent acquisitions that have tripled M-Mart sales in three short years [net sales were $344 billion in 2006]. In recognition of her great achievements, Mary Ellen is being promoted to Executive Vice President, Finance and Treasurer. In addition, she has been unanimously voted to the vacant seat on the Board of Directors. Please join me in congratulating Ms. Martin."

* * * * *

Marriage Now Illegal in USA

WASHINGTON, DC – October 19, 2010 – President Dolly Roderick signed into law the 28th amendment of the U.S. Constitution. The amendment is officially called the Hertz Amendment in honor of the late Secretary of State and Massachusetts senator, who originally sponsored similar legislation in Massachusetts in 2008 that led to the eventually passage of the nationwide amendment. Unofficially, the amendment has been touted as the No Couple Left Behind amendment.

According to the amendment, which is almost identical to the Massachusetts amendment, abolishes the term marriage in favor of the more liberal term civil union. A civil union is "a voluntary union for life (or until divorce) of consenting adult parties of any living entities; parties to a civil union have all the same benefits, protections, and responsibilities under United States of America law as spouses had in a marriage before the term was abolished."

Upon hearing the news, Carson Kressley of Queer Eye for the Straight Guy fame said, "It's absolutely fabulous!"

Eminem, the white rap artist known for his run-ins with the Gay and Lesbian Alliance Against Defamation (GLAAD) told the press, "This is the kind of shit that makes you want to beat your mother to death with a crowbar. %^&*(^%&^%*$#$#!!!

Debbie Mathers, Eminem's (Marshall Bruce Mathers by birth) mother, could not be reached for comment...

* * * * *

Democrats Lose Control of Both House and Senate

WASHINGTON, DC – November 7, 2010 – In a stunning defeat for the Democratic Party and the Roderick Administration, the Republican Party has gained control of both the House of Representatives and the U.S. Senate for the first time in four years. The Democrats had gained a decisive edge in the House and the Senate in the 2006 elections, during Keith Kirby's second term in the White House, an edge which helped catapult Dolly Roderick into the White

House two years ago.

But the Democratic lead has proven to be short-lived, and the House of Representatives now has 53 Republicans and 47 Democrats and the U.S. Senate has 224 Republicans, 202 Democrats, 7 Independents, and 2 members of the Libertarian Party. The Democrats now face a tough battle to pass their liberal agenda items through Congress. The Democratic Party can claim a recent victory with passage of the 28th amendment, also known as the "civil union" or "Hertz" amendment, which was pushed through the House and Senate before the elections, in spite of heated opposition from the GOP and the general American populace.

President Dolly Roderick said in a hastily called press conference, "This is a disturbing wakeup call for my administration. I pledge that we will redouble our efforts to get the pulse of the American people and to make sure our government is truly representing their wishes."

Shaun McCarthy, popular actor and newly-elected Texas State Senator (Texas Dist. 14-R) was quoted by the Austin American-Statesman following the press conference as saying, "Wow! This is wild! It makes me wants to beat my bongos. I'm livin' la weeda loca!" Austin Police had no comment about a late-night disturbance at McCarthy's Airstream in the Shady Grove Trailer Park.

Chapter 11

2011

"Wow, is that even possible?" Sylvia asked incredulously.

Sitting behind her office desk, Mary Ellen Martin said with a victorious smile, "Of course. Anything is possible with good enough lawyers."

"But it's a union. In fact, it's a union of unions. How can M-Mart possibly buy the AFL-CIO?" Mary Ellen's assistant asked again, still not able to wrap her mind around the whole idea.

"We have the best lawyers in the business and they tell me it's possible. They should know; they've been battling the AFL-CIO for decades."

"My God, Mary Ellen, if you pull this off, it'll be bigger than the Proctor & Gamble buyout, Microsoft buyout, and maybe even the ExxonMobil buyout. You'll probably even get your picture on the cover of Time again."

"That would be nice," Mary Ellen said wistfully. One of her secret goals was to appear on the cover of Time and Newsweek more often than that evil, malicious bitch Dolly Roderick. So far, Mary Ellen had graced the cover of Time twice and Newsweek three times. Dolly had appeared on Time three times and Newsweek six times since the election but Mary Ellen discounted four of Dolly's covers because the lead stories were actually about her dead husbands and she had appeared on the cover with them.

That was a weird business. Who has two dead husbands in less than a year? A gold digger, surely, but Dolly was the President of the United States, after all. It just didn't add up.

After Jerry Hertz's death, Mary Ellen had sent a couple of private investigators to discreetly check out Hertz and Roderick's deaths. She knew they must have been murdered. Nothing was beyond Dolly, but the investigators had come up empty, so Mary Ellen reluctantly dropped the issue after a couple of months.

"So, what are you going to do with it if M-Mart can buy it? What's the game plan?" Sylvia asked.

"Why, that's the beauty of it, love," Mary Ellen said with satisfied grin. "After we buy it, the first thing to do is fire the executive team. How would you like to be the AFL-CIO president, Sylvia?"

"You're not serious, are you?" Sylvia gasped.

Mary Ellen walked up behind Sylvia and began rubbing her shoulders. "Of course, I'm serious. Would I kid you?"

"But I have no know idea how to be the AFL-CIO president," Sylvia stammered.

"Don't worry, love. I'll walk you through it." Mary Ellen gave her a light kiss on the neck.

* * * * *

"Can you hear me, Sylvia?" Mary Ellen said into the microphone. She sat in the back of a van amidst a wide array of sophisticated electronics equipment. On the outside, the blue van appeared unobtrusive, with a white lightning bolt on both sides and lettering that read 'Sam's Electric Since 1994, member IBEW #1324.' The van was parked across the street from the AFL-CIO headquarters in Washington, DC.

"Yes, can you hear me?" came the reply into Mary Ellen's headphones. Sylvia stood in the AFL-CIO boardroom, readying for her first executive council meeting since her presidency was announced two weeks earlier. Sylvia could hear Mary Ellen via a flesh-colored earpiece that looked like a simple hearing aid to anyone other than a spy or conspiracy theorist. Mary Ellen could hear Sylvia and everything else going on the boardroom because she had an elaborate set of inconspicuous listening devices installed throughout the room the same day the AFL-CIO buyout was finalized.

Today was a very important day for Mary Ellen. Buying the AFL-CIO had been extremely expensive, mainly due to legal fees. That prick, John Swenson, the then long-time AFL-CIO president, fought like a ferret trying to escape a Scotsman's pants in a ferret legging contest to save his precious union. He threw the entire union's cash fund into the legal battle in a wasted effort that only managed to delay the inevitable by a couple of months but cost M-Mart Stores, Inc. almost five days of profit. Mary Ellen was so livid she used a legal loophole in the bylaws to fire him for cause for wasting company resources and screw him out of the eight-figure plus CEO severance package so popular with American corporations as of late. Then she used a little known clause in the bylaws to bypass a general election and install Sylvia as union president.

The executive board meeting was going to be a big step toward recouping M-Mart's expenses and eventual profitability. Mary Ellen had, working through surreptitious representatives, worked out payoffs from many corporations who, like M-Mart, had also been trying unsuccessfully to destroy America's main union for many years. Grocery store chains, trucking firms, airlines, hospitals, movie studios, and companies from dozens of other industries were lining up to "donate" to her cause of destroying unions in America once and for all. Now it was time for her to follow through on her promises to those corporations.

It was also a big day for Sylvia. She had never run a board meeting before and she was nervous. She also braced herself for what was bound to be an unpleasant meeting. The attendees would not be happy with the changes she and Mary Ellen were going to make and Sylvia, unlike Mary Ellen, wasn't fond of confrontation.

"I can hear you fine. How are you holding up?" Mary

Ellen asked.

"I'm fine," the AFL-CIO president replied unconvincingly.

"I'll be here with you the whole time. You'll do just fine. I think…"

Sylvia cut her off, "Hello, Mr. Sanchez."

"Hello, Ms. Byrne," Victor Sanchez, president of the Air Line Pilots Association, said gruffly as he entered the boardroom. He, like everyone else who was going to attend this meeting, knew that M-Mart Stores, Inc. buying the AFL-CIO would be a disaster for the unions. He was here to assess the situation and its repercussions and to prevent as much damage to his union and the AFL-CIO as possible.

Over the next fifteen minutes, the two dozen remaining dour executive council members, the heads of various unions under the AFL-CIO umbrella, stiffly filed into the boardroom. They grouped in twos and threes and whispered cautiously to each other, avoiding Sylvia as best they could.

"Good morning, everyone, please be seated," Sylvia said.

The council members quietly sat down and stared at her guardedly. She felt about as welcome as a U.S. Marine strolling around Mecca in his dress blues. The few, the proud, the extremely out-of-place…

Sylvia looked over at Harriet Kelly, her AFL-CIO administrative assistant and the only friendly face in the room, and asked, "Are you ready?"

Showing her pen and notepad at the ready, Harriet replied, "Yes, ma'am."

"Great." Sylvia looked around at the discomfited group seated around the conference table and said, "Let's call the meeting to order." Then she went blank.

After a couple of uneasy seconds, Mary Ellen's voice came through the earpiece. "Start with dues."

Right. "The first item on our agenda is dues. As you all know, the recent acquisition by M-Mart has put a severe strain on the AFL-CIO's finances and almost completely drained our cash reserves."

Several people shifted uncomfortably, snorted or whispered under their breath but no one said anything.

"The legal battle has tapped out our funds," Sylvia continued. "To keep the unions strong, to keep needed monies in our strike and PR funds, we are forced to raise our dues to our entire membership."

"Wait a second," Joe "Pappy" Schroeder of the International Longshoremen's Association cut her off gruffly. Pappy was one of John Swenson's closest friends and was vocal in the boardroom and in the press about his disgust over the former AFL-CIO president's termination. "Are you telling us that you are raising dues to cover the legal costs that the AFL-CIO incurred trying to keep you M-Mart cronies from buying us?"

Sylvia froze again. Mary Ellen whispered a response. Sylvia then said as authoritatively as she could manage, "Regardless of the reason, the AFL-CIO's bank account is dangerously low and something has to be done. Would you prefer we lay off three quarters of our staff and cut member benefits substantially?"

"Sure, let's start with the president," Pappy snapped back. Sylvia wondered if he would hit a woman. She thought he might, even if he did outweigh her by a good hundred pounds. She took half a step back.

"What about M-Mart?" Florence Mockingbird of the United American Nurses added. "Why can't you replace the lost funds? After all, you are the cause of the funds being gone in the first place."

Sylvia didn't have to wait for Mary Ellen's response; she already knew the answer. "A valid question, but as you all also know, M-Mart spent several hundred million dollars in legal costs to acquire the AFL-CIO and the M-Mart board of directors is not willing to invest more funds into it at this point. We must restore the funds on our own. In order to do that, we must raise dues. Otherwise, the AFL-CIO will not be able to send funds to help support strikes, which, of course, will seriously weaken your union's bargaining position. Is that what you want?"

"Of course not," Victor Sanchez said. "How much of an increase are we talking about here?"

Mary Ellen chuckled. Victor's tone gave the impression he actually thought the executive board still had some control over union matters. She whispered into the microphone, "This should be fun."

Right, fun. She steadied herself. "Our finance department has calculated that we can restore our funds to pre-acquisition levels in five years by increasing our dues by 280%."

"Triple?! You want to triple our dues?!" Pappy bellowed. "You can't be serious."

"In fact, I can," Sylvia replied. "The dues increase will be reflected on next month's statements."

Mary Ellen giggled in Sylvia's ear, "Ignore them. Move on to the name change. This should really annoy them."

Sylvia took a deep breath. "Okay, Harriet, onto the next agenda item: the union name. At 1 PM, I will be holding a press conference announcing the new name for the AFL-CIO. Effective immediately, the AFL-CIO will be called M-Union."

Like a bug struggling in vain to the swim out of a flushing toilet, the board members' hopes for the union sank rapidly for the remainder of the hour-long meeting as Sylvia and Mary Ellen continued to dismantle the union's strength.

* * * * *

Corporate e-mail:

Concerning Financials
Sylvia Byrne [prez@m-union.com]
Sent: Wed 08/19/2011 10:14 AM
To: Everyone at M-Union

All,

The finance committee met this morning and I regret to inform you that the financial outlook for our union is rather bleak. We are seriously behind the financial milestones required by the M-Mart board of directors to restore our cash to pre-acquisition levels in the required five-year deadline.

Because of this, the following drastic measures will be implemented immediately:

M-Union workforce will be cut by 40% in all departments. Terminated personnel will be notified on Friday. Please note, as part of the severance package, just in time for back-to-school, laid off employees will receive an 8% off voucher good at any M-Mart.

Moving forward, monies from union dues will no longer be allocated into the strike fund indefinitely. Therefore, strike funds available to member unions will be reduced by 80%.

Disability and retirement benefits to all members are frozen until further notice.

Thank you for your patience and cooperation during these difficult times.

Warmest regards,
SOB

Sylvia Byrne
President, M-Union

* * * * *

Former AFL-CIO declares Bankruptcy

WASHINGTON, DC – November 23, 2011 – M-Union, known as AFL-CIO for over fifty years, has filed for Chapter 11 bankruptcy protection. Since the hostile takeover by M-Mart Stores, Inc. some eight months ago, M-Union has been plagued with many hardships.

Overall membership is down 43% from a year ago. Nine of the 55 member unions (including the International Association of Fire Fighters and International Brotherhood of Electrical Workers) have left the M-Union umbrella.

Three member unions (American Federation of Teachers, Screen Actors Guild, and the Sheet Metal Workers International Association) have already declared bankruptcy after several companies did lockouts and kicked the union out. With no union help, workers only struck for an average of eighteen days before giving up and returning to work with an average pay cut of 26%.

George Cronie, famous actor and spokesperson for the Screen Actors Guild said, "This is a sad, sad thing. The average actor is barely scraping by and can't afford to pay the inflated dues instituted by SAG and M-Union so membership of SAG has dropped by 63% in just six months. Aspiring actresses will have to bypass waitressing altogether and become strippers or hookers just to pay the bills. Who's going to wait on me at Spago now? Not some twenty something hottie with a boob job, I can tell you that. It'll probably be some 300-pound plus forty something former Denny's waitress that needs a Kevlar bra just to keep her boobs from dragging the floor. Crap, I just turned fifty. I don't want to be waited on by someone my own age. I want a co-ed, damn it!

"It's bad enough those bastards at Lucasfilms and Disney are constantly replacing real actors with cartoons and computer animated squirrels. Now this. How the hell am I going to get $30 million a picture now? I'm going to have to charge for going to parties like Paris Hyatt does. Crap, I'm just a glorified gigolo... Hey, that's not a bad idea... No more 14-hour workdays 40 days in a row... hmmm..."

Last month, the M-Mart board of directors demanded a payment of $423,662,962 to cover legal expenses incurred during the hostile takeover of the former AFL-CIO. M-Union had to dip into strike and pensions funds to make the payment. The union also had to raise dues drastically and cut benefits dramatically. The union had to file bankruptcy because it could no longer meet payroll and pay retirees benefits.

When asked about retiree benefits, Sylvia Byrne, M-Union president, commented, "M-Union's resources are almost completely tapped out. Once the bankruptcy is discharged, the court will setup a trust account for the retirees. Our best estimates are that the average current retiree will receive a monthly retirement pension benefit of $47.22. Any M-Union member who isn't already retired will receive nothing. We are deeply sorry for the inconvenience this may cause. Happy Thanksgiving!"

Chapter 12

"Happy Thanksgiving, eh?" Mary Ellen Martin said with a chuckle as she folded the newspaper neatly and set it back down on her desk. "Nice touch."

"Thanks," Sylvia Byrne replied sarcastically, sitting back in one of the guest chairs.

"Well done, love. We accomplished everything we wanted. M-Mart no longer has to worry about the AFL-CIO trying to unionize our stores. Best of all, it didn't cost the company a thing. In fact, we made a profit thanks to the outrageous prices our law firms charged us for the acquisition which, in turn, we charged the union for." Mary Ellen's expression feigned seriousness for a moment. "Unfortunately, you are going to lose your position as M-Union president. I hope that doesn't upset you too much."

Sylvia scoffed, "Hardly. That was the worst job I ever had. I did it for you. Good riddance."

Mary Ellen stood up and moved behind Sylvia, leaned over, massaged her assistant's shoulders and gave her light kiss on the neck. "I know, love. I know it was miserable for you. I'm sorry. I would have loved to do it myself, to watch those union bastards squirm firsthand, but it just wouldn't have worked to have a Martin running the union. I needed to stay in the background."

"I know, I know, but I am glad it's over."

"All of your hard work and misery are about to be rewarded," Mary Ellen whispered into Sylvia's ear and gave it a soft kiss as she continued rubbing her shoulders. "I have a big surprise for you."

Sylvia perked up in her seat. "Really…? What?" A month-long vacation in a peaceful village along the Greece coast?

Maybe a Mediterranean cruise? Just the two of them?

"Now, if I told you, love, it wouldn't be a surprise, now would it? I will tell you this much. You'll be joining me at the board meeting this afternoon."

Sylvia's body tensed up and her mind raced. The board meeting? She had never attended an M-Mart Board of Directors meeting. None of the executive assistants ever attended save for the chairman's assistant, who took the meeting's minutes. What could it mean? She wanted to think it was a good thing but her gut reacted as though she was being sent to the principal's office or being stopped by a cop. "Why...?"

Sensing Sylvia's tension, Mary Ellen laughed lightly and rubbed her assistant's shoulders harder. "Don't worry, love, it's just the board of directors, not a firing squad, no pun intended. Do you think I would bring you to a board meeting just to be lynched?"

"Of course not, not me anyway," Sylvia added with a smirk and then reached up to kiss Mary Ellen on the neck. She frowned. "But what do I do? I've never been to an M-Mart board meeting before."

"It'll be just like the M-Union board meetings..."

Sylvia cut her off, "Great, just great..."

Mary Ellen cut back in, "...but much less confrontational. Just sit back and listen unless a question is directed at you. Follow my lead and everything will be fine. I promise. Okay?"

Sylvia gave a hesitant smile. "Okay."

*****

Mary Ellen and Sylvia walked into the boardroom at ten before the top of the hour. The room was empty except for Mary's Ellen's uncle Robby, the chairman of M-Mart Stores, Inc., and his assistant, TaShawna, who were fiddling with a projector and a laptop computer.

Robby Martin looked up from the laptop and smiled at the women walking toward him. "Good afternoon, ladies."

"Good afternoon, Uncle," Mary Ellen said.

The chairman stepped up to them and gave them each a hug, Mary Ellen's being a much deeper hug reserved for close relatives. "I'm so proud of you both. What a brilliant job you did with the AFL-CIO, just brilliant. Today is a big day for the two of you, eh?" Robby said with a wink.

Sylvia responded with a bewildered look.

Mary Ellen said quickly, "She doesn't know. I wanted it to be a surprise."

"Oh, I see. I won't spoil it then." Rob looked over at the befuddled Sylvia. "Let's just say it will be a big surprise in a good way. Sylvia, have you done any foreign traveling?"

"Uh, not much, sir," Sylvia replied cautiously. Robby Martin hadn't said more than a hundred words in the thirty plus years she had known Mary Ellen and been a Martin family friend. He had always been nice enough but had never really tried to engage her in any conversation beyond a basic hello. She wasn't quite sure how to act. He was the chairman of the greatest company in history, after all. It was like talking to a rock star or the Queen of England.

Robby smiled soothingly. He could tell he intimidated her. He wasn't really intimidating by nature. He was really a mild-mannered, likeable guy but the position often flustered people, especially those much younger than him. "You might want to pack a couple suitcases, you're going to be going on a trip soon…"

Mary Ellen cut in, pleading, "Uncle…"

"Right, I'll stop." Robby gave his niece another hug. "Go ahead and have a seat, ladies, the meeting will be starting in a few minutes."

*****

The board meeting plodded along in normal, boring

fashion for forty minutes. The topics ranged from quarterly forecasts of the various divisions to lists of store openings in such diverse locations like Minnetonka, Minnesota and Kuala Lumpur, Malaysia. Sylvia always wondered why they would put the tallest twin towers in the world in a city named after a cuddly bear.

Finally, Robby Martin glanced over at Sylvia and said wistfully, "Sylvia, I see you're still awake."

Sylvia straightened in her chair nervously. "Yes, sir."

Robby laughed lightly and tilted his head to the far end of the conference table. "That's better than good ole Frank Upton there could manage. Good for you, Sylvia."

Sure enough, Frank's head leaned forward slightly and his eyes were shut. At 84, nothing short of wrestling on TV or Viagra and booth babes at a trade show was going to keep him from nodding off in the afternoon.

"At least he doesn't snore," Robby continued. "But now it's the moment you have been waiting for.

"Dear fellow board members, the team of Mary Ellen Martin and Sylvia Byrne have had an exceptional performance record for M-Mart. Masterminding the buyouts of ExxonMobil, Proctor & Gamble, Microsoft and dozens of other companies, they have managed to outdo themselves with the latest buyout and destruction of the AFL-CIO, one of the biggest thorns in M-Mart's side since the days when my father, Sam, opened all of the stores personally." Robby looked over at the ladies. "We are all very proud of both of you and we feel promotions are in order." He slid a sealed envelope in front of each of them.

Sylvia noticed that their names were typed on the front of the envelopes. She also noticed Mary Ellen ignored her envelope, so she reluctantly did the same.

"As you know, Mary Ellen, we are making you President of M-Mart, China, our fastest growing division..."

Sylvia instantly realized the importance of the promotion. Mary Ellen was going to be the third most powerful person at

M-Mart Stores, Inc., just below the Chairman and the CEO. It was incredible opportunity. It meant that she was next in line to be CEO. Sylvia jumped in her chair as if she had sat on a whoopee cushion, looked over at Mary Ellen, then remembered where she was and stifled a comment.

Robby smiled knowingly. "Did you want to say something, Sylvia?"

"Uh, no, sir. Uh, I mean yes. That's sensational! Sorry for interrupting, sir." She looked as though she would spontaneously combust.

"No problem. Mary Ellen, take a look at your offer please."

Feigning indifference, Mary Ellen opened the envelope and pulled out the letter. It read:

Ref. #081-1521534 (18-0000)

December 12, 2011

PERSONAL AND CONFIDENTIAL

Mary Ellen Martin
8423 Lux Way
Martinville, AL 36420

Dear Mary Ellen:

I am pleased to offer you a promotion to the position of President, M-Mart, China in Shenzhen, China. This appointment, effective immediately carries with it a standard probationary period of six months.

If you decide to accept this offer, you will report to Les Scarletti, Jr., CEO, M-Mart Stores, Inc. and S. Robby Martin, Chairman, M-Mart Stores, Inc. Your salary will be $847,112 per annum, representing pay grade E5 as listed appendix G: Pay Grades of the M-Mart Stores, Inc. employee handbook (rev 08/11).

In addition to your salary, you will be given 10,000 shares of M-Mart Stores, Inc. (MMT) stock with the option to purchase 90,000 additional shares at $58.00 per shares as a bonus for taking this position.

To confirm your acceptance, please sign the second copy of this offer and return it to my office. The original of this letter and the job description are attached for your records.

Congratulations on your promotion. Should you have any questions concerning this job offer, please do not hesitate to contact me at (555) 832-3427.

Sincerely,

Tanika Garret
Staffing Associate

She did a quick calculation in her head. M-Mart stock traded at $75 dollars and change so salary and stock were worth about two and a half million dollars. Nice! That was quite a bump in pay from her 2010 salary of $440,000.

Mary Ellen coughed against her will. Damn it! So much for playing it cool. Clearing her throat, she said calmly, "This is a quite generous offer. I gladly accept the position and I thank the board for its trust in me."

Robby turned his gaze to Sylvia. "It appears to be your turn. Before you open the envelope, I'd like you to know exactly what your boss did for you. Mary Ellen insisted that you and she were a true team and everything she has accomplished in the last decade is owed as much to you as to her. I have never heard an executive give so much credit to an assistant as she has to you. She insisted on this promotion for you and said she would refuse her promotion if you didn't get yours."

After an uneasy pause, Robby said, "Sylvia, open your envelope please."

Tentatively, Sylvia did as instructed. As she read it, she felt the blood rush to her face and she felt like her face was instantly sunburned. From what her mother had described, this is what hot flashes must feel like. She wasn't sure if she was going to burst into song or pass out. The letter read:

Ref. #081-1521535 (18-0002)

December 12, 2011

PERSONAL AND CONFIDENTIAL

Sylvia Byrne
1472 Carrion Path
Martinville, AL 36420

Dear Sylvia:

I am pleased to offer you a promotion to the position of Executive Vice President, M-Mart, China in Shenzhen, China. This appointment, effective immediately carries with it a standard probationary period of six months.

If you decide to accept this offer, you will report to Mary Ellen Martin, President, M-Mart, China. Your salary will be $442,634 per annum, representing pay grade E3 as listed appendix G: Pay Grades of the M-Mart Stores, Inc. employee handbook (rev 08/11).

In addition to your salary, you will be given 1,000

shares of M-Mart Stores, Inc. (MMT) stock with the option to purchase 9,000 additional shares at $58.00 per shares as a bonus for taking this position.

To confirm your acceptance, please sign the second copy of this offer and return it to my office. The original of this letter and the job description are attached for your records.

Please note: this offer is contingent on Mary Ellen Martin's acceptance of her promotion job offer dated December 12, 2011. If she declines that offer, your offer is withdrawn.

Congratulations on your promotion. Should you have any questions concerning this job offer, please do not hesitate to contact me at (555) 832-3427.

Sincerely,

Tanika Garret
Staffing Associate

"Oh my God! Oh my God!" Sylvia screamed and gave Mary Ellen a stifling hug. Mary Ellen returned the hug, laughing.

"I take it you approve, Miss Byrne?" the chairman asked, amused. It had been a long, long time since anything he had done had made him as excited as Sylvia was and it did his heart good to see it.

Trying to regain composure, Sylvia replied with gasping breaths, "Yes, sir. This is fabulous. Most generous. Thank you, thank you."

"It gets better," Robby added. "In this position, you will be Mary Ellen's true second-in-command in China. If she is ill, you will act as president in her place. You will now have your own executive assistant. Do you understand?"

"Uh, yes, sir. I think so, sir."

"The only downside is the travel. We need you here for the monthly board meetings, but we'll do web conferencing at as many of the meetings as possible. Do you think you ladies are up to that?"

"Certainly, we'll be able to catch up on work during the flights," Mary Ellen said. Sylvia nodded enthusiastically.

"Very good and congratulations, President and Executive Vice President." Robby clapped and the rest of board member cheerfully joined in.

Frank Upton startled in his seat. Dazed, he looked around. "Is the meeting over?"

PART III

MAYAGEDDON: 2012-2013

"It's the end of the world as we know it and I feel fine!"
--William Berry, Peter Buck, Mike Mills, and Michael Stipe (R.E.M. song "It's the End of the World")

Immaculate Deception

Chapter 13

2012

The sun slowly set over the Pacific Ocean, causing the billowing clouds to change from white to pink and purple hues. A crowd of approximately eighty people watched a solitary figure doing some form of exercise on the beach of San Juanico, Mexico. Half of the crowd was reporters from various TV stations, magazines and newspapers, while the other half were followers of the man.

The man, stretching slowly in fluid movements, was tall, lean and well-tanned. Even his bald head was well-tanned instead of sunburned as one might expect from a former governor of Minnesota visiting a tropical region. He wore a white outfit that seemed somewhere between a karate uniform, a regular button-up shirt and slacks, and pair of satin pajamas. The outfit appeared more appropriate for the Playboy mansion than a Mexican beach.

Marc Rebstock, a writer for High Times, watched the man with amusement. "Are you sure this is the right guy? He looks like Wayne Dyer?"

Hal West, a reporter for the Chicago Sun-Times, glanced over at his colleague's bloodshot eyes. "The Erroneous Zones guy? I guess he does at that."

"This Mayan Messiah is Jose Valencia, the former wrestler turned governor of Minnesota, right?" Restock squinted through his sunglasses to get a better look at the speaker. "He used to have long blonde hair, a biker moustache and wear a feathered boa. I loved to watch him wrestle. He was nicknamed the Torso and the Intellect. Watching wrestling and eating pot brownies and Taco Bell, that's the best, man."

"I'll have to take your word on that," Hal said. "But he shaved his head bald and got rid of the 'stache a long time ago. Since before he became governor."

"He's so tan. He's looks like a really tan Tai Chi instructor. Too weird."

"He's been holed up here in Mexico for several years now. He left the U.S. over 'censorship issues' and vowed never to return. Nobody had heard anything from him until last week, and now…look…"

Marc gazed around at the dozens of groupies following Jose Valencia, recently dubbed the Mayan Messiah by the media. "Far out. What's he doing? Yoga?"

"Tai Chi, I think."

"Isn't that a drink?"

Hal pondered that for a moment, and then chuckled. "No, that's chai tea."

"Whatever…tai chi, chai tea…same thing," Rebstock said. "When is he going to start talking? My buzz is starting to wear off and I'm starving. I want to get back to the hotel, light up again and grab some fish tacos from that taco stand in front of the building."

"Right," Hal said. "Hey, listen up. I think he's starting."

The Mayan Messiah did a final bow to the setting sun, slipped on his sandals and turned to the crowd. "Walk with me," came Valencia's voice echoing around the crowd. Hal guessed several of the groupies must have had speakers attached to their backs and Valencia was evidently wired for sound.

The crowd moved along the shoreline as they all listened intently to their prophet.

"Dear friends, the end of civilization as we know it is coming," Valencia said in strangely soothing tones. In his wrestling days, Valencia's voice was loud and raspy and about as smooth as a raccoon being shook to death by a Rottweiler. "Sooner than you think. Before the end of the year, the earth shall be devastated. The Mayan calendar foretells the end of this age on December 21, 2012 or 12/21/12. That date, which is also the winter solstice, is the end of the thirteenth baktun of the Mayan calendar. A baktun is roughly a 400-year period. The Mayan calendar abruptly ends at the end of the 13th baktun…forever."

A few people in the crowd, all reporters, scoffed and muttered at the evidence but were quickly silenced by the scathing looks of the Mayan Messiah's supporters.

"It gets worse. Has anyone heard of the Timewave theory?" A score of hands, all followers, in the crowd go up.

"The Timewave theory was first hypothesized by Terrence McKenna in the 1970's. It was originally called Timewave Zero. It uses a sophisticated combination of mathematics and numerology to show waves of climactic events throughout history, such as the Inquisition and World War II, and attempts to predict future events along the wave. The theory was further modified by John Sheliak to use computer technology and is now commonly referred to as Timewave One. By all calculations of Timewave One, which have been run thousands of times, the wave abruptly stops on the same date as the Mayan calendar on December 21, 2012."

"What if Sheliak was insane or just a crappy programmer?" Greg Watson of Skeptic magazine asked. "Garbage in, garbage out, right?"

"Indeed," Valencia countered smoothly. "One more bit of evidence. December 21, 2012 is also the date of a galactic event. Known as the Galactic Alignment, it is when the solstice sun lines up with the center of our galaxy, the Milky Way. This happens only once every 26,000 years."

"That happened 26,000 years ago, didn't it? And the Earth is still here," Watson retorted.

"Ah yes, true enough, my cynical friend," the Mayan Messiah said peacefully. "If my previous examples aren't proof enough that the end of the world is coming, consider this: The Cleveland Browns and the Detroit Lions are playing in the Super Bowl in just a couple of days from now. As any football fan knows, it would be easier for my mother to pile drive Andre the Giant than get the Browns and the Lions in the Super Bowl in the same year. If that doesn't mean the end of the world, I don't know what does."

Watson nodded in acquiescence and sunk back into the crowd.

"Dear friends, the end of days will not happen in Armageddon as prophesized in Revelation, but around the entire world in the conflagration I call Mayageddon," the Mayan Messiah intoned hypnotically at the press conference. "Are there any questions?"

"So, Mayan Messiah, how complete will the destruction of this Mayageddon be?" Hal asked. "Will everybody die?"

"No, not everyone. Approximately 93% will perish. Next question?"

"Yo, have you ever seen Caddyshack?" Marc Rebstock asked.

"Of course, best seen while on shrooms and purple hair ganja," the Mayan Messiah replied with a smile.

"Righteous, dude," Rebstock said.

"You know it, brother. By the way, it might be a good idea to catch a gnarly buzz starting December 20th…"

* * * * *

Sammy sat on the dark brown leather sofa in the living room, absently watching a Discovery Channel special, while he "played" with some Mensa puzzles Mary Ellen printed up from their website, an empty cereal on the coffee table next to him. Mary Ellen thought she was pretty smart, having been in Arkansas' Gifted and Talented program for most of her elementary and high schools years, but this Mensa stuff and most of what Sammy was into was beyond her.

Though he was only ten years old, he was into advanced math like Trigonometry and Calculus and weird puzzles like

Sudoku, Ken Ken, Kendoku and a slew other oddities that she was sure other "average" fourth graders weren't into. When she was growing up, she was into Barbies and Gilligan's Island. Most kids today were into the Jonas Brothers and iCarly, but Sammy was into Discovery Channel specials. What ten year old was into mummies and Easter Island? It was Saturday morning, for Christ sake. She decided to find out what he was watching.

Mary Ellen grabbed the plate of Eggs Benedict the family chef had made and sat down next to her son. "Watcha watching, Champ?"

"Oh, mom, it's so killer," Sammy said, clearly in awe, not looking away from the TV screen. "In 1938, these archeologists found the home of Saint Peter the Rock, you know Jesus' lead disciple? And they found all kinds of cool junk. A gold cross. Some wood that might have been from a cross-a-fiction…"

"You mean crucifixion," Mary Ellen corrected.

"Right. Crucifixion. It might even be…"

Sammy's words trailed off in her mind as she thought back. This TV special reminded her of something Sylvia had told her about over a decade ago but she couldn't quite place it. Oh well, she returned her focus to her son and the delicious Eggs Benedict. She really must give the chef a raise. Delightful!

Chapter 14

News Items from 2012

29th Amendment Ratified---Muller Able to Run for President

WASHINGTON, DC – February 4, 2012 – The 29th Amendment passes both the House and the Senate in a stunning blow to the Democratic Party. The Amendment effectively changes the requirements for a candidate to run for the presidency: citizenship for at least twenty years; at least thirty-five years of age; and reside in the U.S. at least fourteen years.

The change came after Jurgin Muller, Governor of California, and his legal team fought the battle for public opinion in the media and won. The Amendment's ratification opened the door for Muller to run for office against President Roderick.

Muller, former star of Sperminator, Gonad the Deflowerer, and Jiggle All the Way, has a 72% approval rating. On the other hand, President Roderick's approval ratings have dropped to 47%. Before he can face his nemesis at the polls, Muller will have to cinch the GOP nomination.

Nate Grolsch, Chairman of the Republican National Committee and former Speaker of the House, said, "This is a spectacular turn of events. We finally have someone who can beat Roderick and get her out of office before she can cause more damage. I'm confident Jurgin can win. He will be as great a

President as Ronald Reagan."

Henry Donne, chairman of the Democratic National Committee responded to the news by screaming, "This is an outrage! How can this be? Hell, if you want an actor for president, you already have one with Dolly. Heck, she's a much better actor than Jurgin ever will be. I guarantee it."

Governor Muller, who was born in Austria and became a U.S. citizen in 1983, was elated. "this is a great day for democracy. This is even more exciting than The Cumming Man premiere."

* * * * *

Supreme Court Outlaws "Fun" Candy

WASHINGTON, DC – May 17, 2012 – In a major blow to the candy industry, the Supreme Court, in a decision of 6 to 3, has ruled the United States government has the constitutional right to ban the phrase "fun size" in all forms of candy advertising. The ruling upholds the Commerce Department edict that any candy with a net weight of less than three ounces must be clearly labeled "small", "small size", "tiny", "tiny size", "tease", "tease size", "teaser", or "teaser size" in a similar fashion to the warning labels used on cigarette boxes.

The ruling is the result of a class action lawsuit brought by several dieter organizations including Weight Wallowers and Fatties Anonymous. Plaintiffs in the lawsuit claimed the "fun size" language implied a lack of calories and unfairly hampered their dieting efforts since they just want to have fun (especially the girls).

Orca Windfall, the famous talk show host whose yo-yo weight has been well documented, issued a press releas stating, "When something says 'fun' you don't think it can be bad for you. The candy manufacturer's labeling is dangerous and reckless. This is a victory for 74% of the public that is overweight. Next, I'm going after McDougall's Burgers to quit adding nicotine to their frying grease to get their customers addicted to their fries."

The news sent the candy industry reeling. It is estimated the cost of pulling the "fun size" product from stores and destroying it or repackaging it will be somewhere between $70 and $120 million. Hardest hit will be the Hershey Company with an estimated $28 million cost in repackaging cost. The news sent the company's stock melting 17%.

Red M, famed mascot of M&M's said, "What is the world coming to? If you can't have fun with candy, what can you have fun with? I should have been a porn star. You can still have fun doing that, right?"

*****

Roderick's Approval Rating at All-Time Low as Dollycare II Dies in Senate

WASHINGTON, DC – September 9, 2012 – Dollycare almost cost Dolly Roderick her political career nearly 20 years ago, and Dollycare II, Roderick's second attempt at healthcare but first as President of the United States, could easily ruin her political career this time.

Two days after The Roderick-Moretti Health Plan, dubbed Dollycare II by the media, was killed on the Senate floor, a USA Today poll gave President Roderick an all-time low approval rating of 42%. Even more damaging, the poll posed the question, "If the election were held today, who would you vote for?" 51% said they would vote for Muller, while only 37% would reelect Roderick, 6% would vote for Pedro and 3% would pick Homer Simpson.

President Dolly Roderick has had a difficult first term in office. During the first year alone, she lost not one but two husbands. During mid-term elections, the democrats lost the majority in both the House and the Senate. And now, her second attempt for healthcare reform has failed as well.

With the presidential election only two months away, the woman once known as "Sister Refrigerator" to her classmates is feeling the heat from her opponent, the one-time B-movie super villain "Mr. Chill."

* * * * *

As reported in University of California, Berkeley's independent student-run newspaper, the Daily Californian:

Scientists Predict Apocalypse

BERKELEY, Cal. – October 6, 2012 – The Gaian Consortium, a group of astronomers and physicists from the University of California, Berkeley made a stunning announcement yesterday: "The world could end on December 21, 2012."

Megan Carrens, Metaphysics professor at Berkley, explained, "The galactic alignment is when the galactic center lines up with the winter solstice sun. It's really going to be quite phenomenal." James Jones, Gaian member, responded, "Jesus, not phenomenal, professor. It's going to tear the world apart"

A heated debate erupted at a recent Consortium

meeting about galactic alignment, the significance of the relationship between the Mayan calendar, and the Timewave One Algorithm, both of which end on December 21, 2012. Some members believe the Earth's tilt, currently at 23.5 degrees, will shift as much as 80 degrees and will usher in an ice age, exterminating all life on the planet. Others believe the shift will cause world-wide earthquakes and volcanic eruptions that could kill millions. Still others believe that Darlusians, aliens that populated the earth at the beginning of time, will finally return to take them home.

Rio DeAngeles, Consortium leader and former Heavengate cultist, announced, "The galactic alignment is happening in just two months, man. It's so righteous, dude. It only happens once every 26,000 years. 26,000! That's a long time!." He added, "Whatever happens, it's going to be quite a ride. Totally righteous, man!"

Chapter 15

2012 continues...

"Son of a bitch!" Dolly Roderick screamed from behind the newspaper she read in the oval office as she ate a plain bagel with cream cheese and drank coffee. "Did you see this article, Helen? My approval rating is down to 42%, forty-two fucking percent. Fucking healthcare. That's what I get for trying to give a shit about the poor. I try to help the uninsured and I get screwed for trying. Fuck 'em all."

"I know, I know," Helen said reassuringly, sitting in a chair across the Resolute desk from the president. What she wanted to say was 'I told you so,' but that wasn't something you told the POTUS (President Of The United States), especially not this one.

Helen had warned Dolly to drop the whole healthcare issue that almost ruined her political career before it even really started, back when she was First Lady for that sleazy slimeball Bobby. Nothing if not ballsy, Bobby even had the nerve to try and proposition Helen a few times, even though he must have known she and Dolly were lovers. He must have known. Why else would he have suggested a threesome?

Dolly wouldn't listen to reason though. She thought the healthcare plan was solid and wanted revenge on the Republicans for screwing up her first healthcare plan by using her presidency to cram the second plan down their throats and push it through the legislature. Unfortunately, the GOP managed to stall it until after the mid-term elections and then they controlled the House and the Senate and killed the damned thing again.

"Time for some PC," Helen offered up. In Bobby's administration, PC stood for 'politically correct,' thanks to slimeball Bobby and blowjobs not being considered sex anymore; in Dolly's administration though, it stood for 'publicity control,' but only to insiders, of course. If the media found out about that, they would have a field day with it.

"Yes, definitely. Gather the team," Dolly said, flipping the page of the newspaper so violently Helen thought she might tear the paper in half.

"The team" consisted of Helen, Dolly's Chief of Staff; Pedro Sandoval, Dolly's long-time friend and personal advisor; Nanny Moretti, the VP; Babbs Baxter, the Secretary of State; Susan Collins, the Press Secretary; Pam Sausalito, Dolly's campaign manager; and Beth Anne Clausen, Dolly's personal public relations advisor.

"Will do," Helen said. She glanced at her iPud. iPud stood for Intelligent Personal Use Decacomputer, deca meant ten in Greek as in the decathlon from the Olympics. The whole deca thing struck Helen as odd since the iPud actually listed 47 separate applications. Maybe Apple did some research and found that ten was the number of applications the average customer actually used. The iPud was a phone, contact manager, calendar, e-mail reader, boomerang, internet browser, music and video player, laser pointer, global positioning system, photo album, postage meter, game player, camera, radar detector, laser can opener, and a few dozen other features.

After about twenty seconds of frenzied finger tapping on the two inch by three and a half inch screen, Helen navigated through the menu system and found the calendar. "I could probably reschedule your meeting with the executive director of the Special Olympics at 10 AM. Is that soon enough?"

"That's fine. I'm not in the mood to be doling out ribbons today anyway. Tell the team to come with ideas for a great campaign slogan, something that will get America to forget about this whole healthcare cluster fuck."

Good luck with that one, lover. "Will do."

* * * * *

"Son of a bitch!" Dolly Roderick screamed from behind the newspaper she read in the oval office as she ate an apple Danish and drank coffee. "Did you see this ad, Helen? That fucking Austrian boy is butchering our campaign slogan!"

During the emergency healthcare PC brainstorming session of "the team" some three weeks earlier, someone - Helen forgot who, Pam or Susan maybe - had come up with an excellent campaign slogan. Some insiders had started calling Dolly "Hot Rod" after she won a couple of caucuses. Dolly liked the nickname well enough. It was certainly better than Sister Refrigerator, Wicked Witch of the West Wing, Dolly the Dunce or one of another dozen other vicious names spread throughout the media or even Big Gal as some of her friends called her.

During the session the slogan "Go, Hot Rod, Go!" came out and everyone, including Dolly, loved it instantly. Pam had the marketing firm in charge of Dolly's reelection campaign, the prestigious BDS&M, come up with an advertising campaign.

Their campaign was brilliant. They came up with posters of Dolly standing in front of a NASCAR race car painted like a giant American flag with a big white number "'12" on the door with Dolly clad in a NASCAR jumpsuit with a similar flag design and the number "'12" in white across her chest. She held a red helmet in her left arm and her right hand stuck out in a big "thumbs up" gesture. She wore a big, warm, confident smile on her face. Underneath the photo was the slogan in big red lettering "Go, Hot Rod, Go!" with smaller white lettering underneath stating "Dolly Roderick 2012."

Dolly loved it so much she had three million posters and five million yard signs made at a cost of 23 million dollars and distributed them to the local campaign headquarters throughout the country.

"No I didn't," Helen said.

Dolly half handed, half threw the newspaper at her. Helen looked at the ad and then looked at the top right corner of the page. New York Times. Uh oh…

The ad took up the entire back page of the first section of the newspaper. The background was a list of eighty or so people supposedly killed off by Bobby and Dolly for various reasons during their presidencies. The list was known as the Roderick Hit List. In front of that was an old, weathered hospital, obviously a jab at Dolly's failed healthcare plans. In front of the hospital, was Dolly's number "'12" NASCAR car peeling out with an open trailer in tow filled with the White House heirlooms they stole at the end of Bobby's presidency. Dolly's car ran over people, Helen guessed people on the Hit List. Behind the car and trailer, a killer robot from one of Jurgin's movies fired a chain gun, blowing holes into the car. Underneath the scene, in bold lettering reads "Go, Hot Rod, Go AWAY!" with smaller lettering underneath "Let's terminate Dolly in '12! Jurgin Muller for President 2012"

"Hmmm," Helen said, stalling, not sure what to say.

"Hmmm is fucking right, Helen," Dolly seethed. "What the fuck do we do about this? Sue? Get a cease and desist order? How the fuck do we shut this down without that steroid-abusing Austrian fuckhead making me look even worse?"

"I don't know," Helen said weakly. "Get the team together again?"

"Fuck yes," Dolly replied bitterly. "Cancel my entire schedule this morning and get everyone in here, including those dumbfucks at BDS&M. We only have five weeks until election day. We need a solution to this fucking disaster today."

* * * * *

"Son of a bitch!" Dolly Roderick screamed at the 60-inch plasma monitor as Tom Brokaw announced Muller winning California and another 55 electoral votes closer to the 270 votes needed to win the election.

Dolly and most of her insiders were gathered in the penthouse suite of the Washington Jefferson hotel, minutes away from the Javits Convention Center in New York City. It was 11:45 PM on election night, November 8, 2012, and Dolly had picked New York City as the place to give her victory speech, but things weren't looking good.

Her nemesis, Jurgin Muller, already had 257 of the needed 270 electoral votes to her 138 votes with only about two-thirds of the states reporting definitive results. So far, Dolly had only carried the northeast and a couple of the Great Lakes states for a total of fourteen states plus Washington, DC; Jurgin had won the rest of the country totaling 26 states, leaving ten states left to be called. Ohio and Florida were the only states with significant electoral votes left that hadn't been called and both were projecting Jurgin as the winner.

A map of the United States came on the monitor, showing the states as red for Jurgin and blue for Dolly. It was clear that red covered the vast majority of the country. Tom Brokaw announced, "This map is based on our projections with 85% of precincts reporting nationwide. As you can see, we are predicting Governor Muller carrying Ohio, Florida, Utah, Alaska, Kansas, Wyoming and Nevada and President Roderick carrying Washington, Oregon and Hawaii. If our projections are accurate, then Governor Muller would have 312 electoral votes to President Roderick's 226 electoral votes. So we are confident enough at this point to declare Jurgin Muller the winner. And now onto the state gubernatorial elections. In Texas…"

"What the fuck?!?!" Dolly screamed, jumping up off the couch, her face turning crimson with rage. "We spent more money than any campaign in history. $1.2 billion fucking dollars! $300 million was my own money. How the fuck could we lose?!?!"

She turned accusingly at the people in the room, all of which were trying to avoid her gaze. "I refuse to lose this fucking election!" she screeched at Pam Sausalito. "Do you understand?" Dolly moved her death stare around the room. "Do you all understand? There must be some way out of this fucking disaster, some way to throw out the election results."

Nanny Moretti offered cautiously, "We could start lawsuits in key states to throw out their election results. A mis-election, so to speak. We could force the election to be held all over again."

"No," Dolly responded bitterly. "That didn't stop Kirby in 2000 or 2004 and won't stop that Austrian fuck now. I can't fucking believe it. How could that fucking bad actor win this fucking election? He can't even speak understandable fucking English, for Christ sake!"

Pedro Sandoval, Dolly's long-time mentor and advisor and one of the few men she actually trusted, offered calmly yet cautiously, "As I see it, Doll, our best option is to get the 29th Amendment thrown out and then Jurgin won't be able to be president so you would win as runner-up."

Most of the group turned ashen on hearing Sandoval's comments. Pedro was probably the only person in the world who could call Dolly the "runner-up" without Dolly cracking a vase over his head. Clearly, Dolly still considered it. She looked like she was going to explode like a villain from one of Jurgin's crappy action flicks.

"Pedro, it's a good thought, but I don't think it will work," Helen responded as Dolly continued to fume. "We fought that battle all the way to the Supreme Court already and our legal team said there's no way left to appeal it. We've tackled that issue fifty different ways and came up empty."

"Yes, Helen is right," Dolly said. "But there must be something. I don't want to make a concession call to that fucking Austrian musclehead without some way out of this. Find me something!"

Immaculate Deception

After several uneasy seconds that seemed like hours, someone finally spoke. Everyone in the room turned, shocked that this person would dare speak about politics and risk Dolly's wrath.

Ava, the gorgeous blond secret service agent - Dolly's personal favorite everyone knew - began, "Madame President, if you will hear me out, I think I have a workable option."

"Really?" Dolly said, her rage subsiding slightly, her curiosity piqued. "Go ahead."

"I have been doing some research, just in case the polls of the last couple of months were accurate, and I've come up with a possible contingency plan," Ava said calmly, obviously completely unafraid of Dolly, much to the surprise of everyone in the room except for Pedro and Helen. Sandoval knew her confidence from a similar frame of reference. He didn't fear Dolly either.

Helen envied Ava's demeanor. Even though they shared Dolly in threesomes regularly, Helen still feared Dolly's wrath, yet Ava didn't. It must be the combat training. Being able to kill someone with just a thumb and index finger must bring a certain level of confidence.

"This is probably going to sound a little far-fetched so please hear me out," Ava continued. "I'm sure you have all heard about this Mayageddon end-of-the-world gloom and doom all over the TV and the newspapers."

"There's a nut in Mexico spewing crap, so what?" Susan Collins asked.

"It turns out that something is going to happen," Ava replied. "Basically, the entire scientific community agrees. They just can't agree on what. Some scientists think the world is going to explode. Some think there will be a few things like earthquakes and volcanoes erupting. Most think it will be somewhere in between; lots of earthquakes, power outages, tornados and the like."

"Okay, let's say we buy into this," Pedro said. "How will

this help Doll win the election?"

"This is the good part, Mr. Sandoval," Ava said with a seductive smile. "When it happens on December 21, 2012, it will be a good month and a half before Governor Muller would be sworn into office, President Roderick can…"

Chapter 16

More News Items from 2012

McCarthy Wins Texas Governorship

Austin, Tex. – November 9, 2012 – In what some may call a bit of déjà vu, Shaun McCarthy, former actor and Texas State Senator (Texas Dist. 14-R), has been elected 48th governor of Texas. A wildly popular actor and native Texan, McCarthy won his senate seat in 2010 and served one term. His approval rating was an impressive 77%. So impressive, in fact, that GOP insiders urged him to run for governor just halfway into his first term as Texas state senator.

Shaun McCarthy won the gubernatorial election with 53.9% of the vote, beating democrat Mick Jones (22.6%) and perennial independent candidate Kinky Friedman (13.2%).

"Is this far out or what?" McCarthy said about his election. "It's great to know that the good people of Texas can see when a simple guy who has made his share of mistakes is truly trying to improve the great state of Texas. The first improvement I plan to run through the legislature is to drop the drinking age back down to eighteen. Dammit, if an eighteen-year-old can die for our country in the Middle East, he or she sure as hell should be able to drink a Shiner Bock or a rum and Coke, right?"

Could McCarthy be a future U.S. president? Last night, another actor was elected to public office.

Jurgin Muller, a former action actor best known for the Agitator series of movies and governor of California, used the killer robots in an ad campaign to beat incumbent Dolly Roderick to become the 45th president of the United States. Ronald Reagan, also an actor and governor of California, became the 40th president of the United States in 1981. In 2005, Reagan was also named "the Greatest American" by viewers voting on the TV show of the same name. Could McCarthy be the next actor turned governor to become president of the United States?

"Wow, this is wild," Shaun McCarthy said when asked about future political aspirations. "I get elected governor and Jurgy gets elected president. What are they going to call him? The presidentinator? Who knows, eh? I tell you this, if I do ever get elected president of the United States, the first thing I'm going to do is get marijuana legalized. Rock on!"

* * * * *

Group of Idaho Mormon Men Want Sex Now

Boise, ID – December 18, 2012 – In a bizarre development in this state with a long history of bizarre events, a group of married Mormon men are saying they want sex and they want it now. The group, currently seven members strong and known as Men with Needs, believes in the Mayageddon prophecies and claims the world is ending in less than a week. To makes matters worse, they claim they can't have sex without violating the ordinances of the Mormon Church.

Abe Stension, founder of the group, held a press conference in front of Idaho's capital building yesterday. "It is not fair to me and my brethren. The world is about to end and we cannot procreate because our wives are on their periods. Idaho state law and the rules of Mormon Church prohibit prostitution or sodomy with our wives. Our only option is to have traditional sex with our menstruating wives, and Mormon doctrine forbids that as being unclean. Damn straight, not to mention it is disgusting and messy."

Dee Stracted, another member of Men with Needs, added, "The rest of the world is procreating like guppies and we're left holding our own, and we're not supposed to do that because it, too, is forbidden. President Roderick has promoted the liberal and gay agenda by getting sodomy laws repealed in most states. We're asking her to step in here and help us good, God-fearing, Church folk get a little nookie before we all go to that great Tabernacle in the sky. We're just asking the state or the Church to repeal their sex laws, at least for a few days.

"It is all because women are subservient and cannot think for themselves," Stension continued. "Which is usually right and good, but the menstrual cycles of all my wives are synchronized. Have you ever been in a house where three women are suffering from PMS at the same time? It must be God's way of punishing men for their mortal sins."

"Abe, wait a second!" Stracted exclaimed. "We can get more wives! Hey, guys, let's head to BYU...quick!"

"Why didn't I think of that! Young women, too, and hopefully prettier than the hags we're stuck with now," Stension responded. "This press conference is over."

* * * * *

Mayageddon Wreaks Havoc around the World, 600,000+ Feared Dead

Earth – December 22, 2012 – Unlike the Y2K scare of 1999, the much-publicized Mayaggedon event has proven fatally accurate for an estimated 600,000 people worldwide.

Jose Valencia, dubbed the Mayan Messiah, established the term Mayaggedon to refer to the end of the world as prophesized by the Mayan Calendar and the TimeWave One Algorithm. The phenomenon occurred yesterday triggering natural disasters all over the world.

Political leaders across the U.S. rushed into action. President-elect Williams, current Governor of California, declared a state of emergency, mobilizing the National Guard and all available military personnel from local bases. Shane McCarthy, Texas State Senator and Governor-elect, stepped in for Ferris, the Governor of record feared lost in the tropics while on vacation. McCarthy also declared a state of emergency following the tsunami that hit the Gulf Coast.

Valencia had predicted a 93% casualty rate, or approximately 5.77 billion people would be lost. While casualties were horrific, the total lost is only one-one hundredth of one percent of the world's population, far less than he anticipated. When asked if the world could expect more disasters and if the casualty rate would increase based on his predictions, Valencia replied, "Oops, I forgot to carry a few zeros. Too many DDTs to the ol' noggin, I guess. What I meant to say was that .0093% of the people of the world die. Not very catastrophic, is it? But look at it this way, no one would have taken me seriously if I hadn't made the mistake and nobody would have come to Baja. How many hides did I save?"

Casualty Estimates Worldwide

Peru: Earthquake (100,000 lost)

Japan: Earthquake (80,000 lost)

U.S.: Tornadoes
Kansas: 132 lost
Texas: 63 lost
Kentucky: 47 lost
Georgia: 34 lost

Volcano Yellow Stone National Park: ash 4 miles in the air; 8,000 lost as a result

Earthquake California: 9,400 lost along coast

Africa: 5 tropical depressions; 9 hurricanes (storms heading toward the Caribbean and the U.S.)

* * * * *

Script from commercial aired on the Gimme a Break: the Mayageddon Special with John Stossel, December 22, 2012:

FADE IN:
Jeff PROBST, dressed in a Hawaiian shirt, khaki shorts and Timberland sandals, stands in front of a tiki hut on the sandy beach of a deserted island, a drink in a coconut cup in his left hand.

PROBST
Hey, everybody, the NFL playoffs are almost here, so you know what that means? That's right, it's

almost time for another season of Survivor. The season premiere starts right after the Super Bowl. It's hard to believe but it's our twenty-fifth season. So, to celebrate the quarter century mark, we've come up with an extra special edition, right, Simon?

Camera cuts to a new scene. Simon COWELL, dressed in a bright orange parka ski suit, stands in an icy wasteland, shivering.

COWELL
That's right, Jeff. Tell them all about it.

Scene switches back to PROBST.

PROBST
Okay, Simon, got it. You just work on staying warm.

Scene flashes to COWELL, who gives "thumbs up" sign amidst the heavy snowfall and then back to PROBST, who is sipping his drink.

PROBST
Folks, to "super size" our twenty-fifth season of Survivor, were adding two new elements. First, we're having our first-ever arctic climate conditions. Second, we're adding elements of the blockbuster TV show, American Idol. Right, Simon?"

Scene cuts to COWELL, who is having a hard time standing due to blizzard conditions and severe wind gusts.

COWELL
That's right, Jeff. World, get ready for Survivor

Idol: Antarctica, the most dangerous and most entertaining Survivor ever!

COWELL gets blown into a snowdrift. Scene cuts back to PROBST.

PROBST
Whoa, Simon! Be careful out there. Get back to the tent and grab spot of tea, you old bloke. I'll finish up here.

Scene cuts to a montage of scenes of the contestants on Antarctica doing various challenges.

PROBST
Survivor Idol: Antarctica is going to be the biggest, best Survivor yet. Watch contestants subjected to temperatures of down to fifty degrees below zero, having to eat lichens, lice and [PROBST gulps] penguin scrotum while singing such pop hits as The Sun Always Shines on TV by Aha!, Good Day, Sunshine by the Beatles and The Heat is On by Glenn Frey. Check out this action!

Scene cuts to a couple of the Antarctic contestants talking around a makeshift campfire. CONTESTANT 1 is a 5'1" 30ish thin tanned blond beauty who looks strikingly like Elizabeth from Survivor: the Australian Outback and CONTESTANT 2 is 300+ pound 23-year-old Barry White look-alike.

CONTESTANT 1
Jeez, Clevon, this totally bites. I used to be a backup singer for Madonna and now I'm eating bugs in a frozen wasteland while I sing Walking on Sunshine. This just isn't worth it, man.

CONTESTANT 2
Come on, Camille. It's not that bad. Besides, you sounded great. [sings] I'm walking on sunshine and it's time to feel good...yeah!

CONTESTANT 1
I'm freezing my ass off.

CONTESTANT 2
And what a cute ass it is...

CONTESTANT 1
Gee, thanks, that's easy for you for you to say. You've got all that blubber to keep you warm.

CONTESTANT 2
That's harsh, Camille. I need to eat more than you and I'm always starving...whatever, I'm outta here.

CONTESTANT 2 walks away. The scene cuts back to PROBST.

PROBST
Wow, folks. Is Camille frigid or what? Hell, yes! So come and chill with us right after the Super Bowl on Survivor Idol: Antarctica. [sings] I'm hot blooded, check it and see. I've got a fever of 103...

FADE OUT:

* * * * *

From the New York Times, World section, page 14:

Mexico in Chaos Following Mayageddon

Mexico City, Mexico – December 22, 2012 – Our neighbor to the south, Mexico, is in complete disarray after the devastating events of Mayageddon. The country was hit especially hard by earthquakes and tsunamis.

An estimated 28,400 people have died in Mexico due to Mayageddon, a fairly minor amount compared to other areas of the world. The real cause of the chaos is the power outages. An estimated 86% of the country is without power and could remain without power for several weeks. In the wake of the outages, looting and rioting have been running rampant.

President Lopez Omnicron and most of his administration are feared dead as earthquakes leveled the presidential residence, the Bosque de Chapultepec, and many of the government buildings including Asamblea Legislativa del Distrito Federal (Legislative Assembly of the Federal District). It is rumored that more than 80% of elected federal governmental politicians are dead.

Three Mexican Army Divisional Generals - Don Cuervo, Jose Pablo, and El Gigante - are fighting for control, their armies pillaging the countryside. Diego Santana, deputy mayor of Mexico City, the highest-ranking Mexican official still known alive, has asked the USA for assistance. President Roderick politely declined to help, stating American resources were already spread too thin dealing with its own Mayageddon issues to send help. California Governor and U.S. President-elect Jurgin Muller and Texas State Senator and Governor-elect Shaun McCarthy have both pledged to send help, mobilizing troops from

Camp Pendleton and Fort Hood as part of their "state of emergency" authority…

* * * * *

Middle East on Fire in Wake of Mayageddon

Manama, Bahrain – December 22, 2012 – Earthquakes set off by the events of Mayageddon have sent Middle Eastern countries reeling. From Beirut, Lebanon to the Iran-Pakistan border, oil rigs and refineries have been seriously damaged or destroyed, and over 180 oil fires have been reported in the region, many out of control. Oil production in the region is projected to have dropped by 47% in the past few days, and prices for light sweet crude for January delivery climbed as high as $232.40 a barrel on world markets.

Sheikh Shaaq Shaek family's oil operation in oh'Shete, Bahrain, has been completely destroyed, and the area is still completely engulfed in flames. The Sheikh said in a news conference with other OPEC leaders, "It could take months for the fires to be put out. With no oil to sell, how will I feed my 47 wives and 127…wait…128 children? I may have to go to the great Satan [The United States of America] and open a convenience store like my less-fortunate cousin Muamar did."

Infighting and power struggles within the governments of many of the Middle East countries have been reported, and well-known terrorist organization el-Queso has been linked to some of the infighting…

* * * * *

As reported on Discovery News website:

"Mayageddon" Permanently Alters Earth's Tilt---
Wreaks Havoc Worldwide
Lauren Emile, Discovery News

December 22, 2012 – By now, everyone with access to TV, the Internet or a newsstand has heard about the worldwide devastation and the death toll of a half million and counting caused by Mayageddon as it has been called by the Mayan Messiah and the mass media, but little has been mentioned as to why all of the natural disasters have occurred. Discovery News has the answer, though.

An event known as the Galactic Alignment happened on December 21, 2012. This event is extremely rare, occurring once every 26,000 years. The Galactic Alignment is the alignment of the winter solstice sun with the galactic center (or equator) of our galaxy, the Milky Way. Sounds innocent enough, right? Like an eclipse.

Unfortunately, this Galactic Alignment shook the earth on its axis, changing the axial tilt over 4 degrees from 23.439° to 27.563°, and the world is having "growing pains" in the form of earthquakes, tsunamis, tornados, sinkholes, and other events, many to fatal effect. Even more unfortunate is the fact that the scientific community is in agreement that these events will probably continue at much greater than normal rates for weeks and possibly months. On a brighter note, the severity and frequency of these events should diminish with time and eventually return to a near pre-Mayageddon state.

What are the repercussions for the world? The new axial tilt will mean that most areas north of the equator will be 1°-3° cooler in the summer and 1°-

3°warmer in the winter and southern hemisphere will be the opposite, i.e. hotter in their summer and cooler in their winter. 1°-3° may not seem like much but the effects could be catastrophic.

In the northern hemisphere, America's breadbasket crops could easily fail without enough sunshine and too much rain. Milder winters could cause greater insect infestations in the spring hindering crops even more.

The southern hemisphere could easily have it much worse, baking Africa and Australia. Antarctic ice will melt at alarming rates during the harsher summer. Scientists are predicting the world's oceans will rise six to 18 inches per year until Antarctica's ice eventually melts completely in the summer. Based on those calculations, one-third of Florida could be underwater in as little as 25 years and over one-half of Bangladesh will be underwater in the same timeframe.

There is no known way to readjust the earth's axial tilt. The science to make that happen is hundreds or thousands of years away, if it ever becomes possible at all. So get out your bug spray and snorkel, because this is a brave, new world that is here to stay.

Chapter 17

2012 continues...

"Are you sure about this?" Jurgin Muller asked, scanning the document.

Yes, Jurg," said Steve Schwartz. He was Muller's campaign manager, advisor and one of his closest friends.

The California governor and president-elect shook his head. "She's got bigger balls than that girly man husband of hers ever had as president, that's for sure, I'll give her that. Can she pull it off?"

"Don't know. Possibly. She has the northeast in her pocket still. Even if she doesn't pull it off in the end, she could drag it through the courts and maintain control of America for your whole presidency. Your term could be up without you ever becoming president."

"That fucking coozehole," Muller muttered, his thick Austrian accent becoming more pronounced. "What do you recommend?"

"Time to call in some favors," Steve commented. "I'd gather up the commanders of every California military base and see where their loyalties lie."

"Good idea. I also know the commanders of Nellis Air Force Base near Vegas and the Fallon Naval Air Station near Reno pretty well. I filmed a couple of movies out there. I'll get them here too."

"I think we definitely want Shaun with us," Steve said, referring to Texas governor-elect McCarthy. "That would put at least one-quarter of the population behind us. It's a start."

"Fine. Get it done. Try for tonight if possible. By lunch

tomorrow at the latest. Thanks, Steve."

"No problem, Jurg."

"I disagree. As usual, Dolly is a problem, a big fucking problem. Let's hope she doesn't steal our presidency."

Steve smiled at the 'our presidency' comment. It was obviously Jurg's presidency but that's not the way Jurg viewed it. They had all worked hard for it and earned it. It was that kind of loyalty to his people that had helped him win the presidency in the first place. Hopefully, it would help them save it...

*****

Shaun McCarthy stared at the fax as he talked into the hands-free microphone of his cell phone. "Jurgy, dude, you have got to be kidding me. This is some sort of practical joke, right?"

"Nope, it's for real," came the reply.

"Man, what a bitch. She needs to seriously chill out. She could use some purple hair. Maybe I should send her some."

"Sending the President of United States pot would be considered a terrorist activity. Probably not the kind of publicity you want as the newly-elected governor of Texas. It took you a decade to overcome the naked banjo incident, remember?"

"Hey, Jurgy, I was just kidding, man."

"Sorry, Shaun, I'm not really in a joking mood. This is serious. I need to know if I can count on you. Can I?"

"Sure, Jurgy, of course. But what the hell do we do about this?"

"Just be prepared," Muller said. "We can't do anything until she tries something. So far she hasn't and maybe she won't. Who knows? Maybe I'll get sworn in without any issues. But we need to be prepared if the fax is accurate. I have gathered up all of the California base commanders and got their backing. You should do the same for the Texas bases..."

"But what about all the troops we sent to Mexico?" McCarthy cut in. "About one-third of the troops stationed in Texas are down in Mexico, trying to restore order."

"That's part of the plan my staff and I came up with." Muller spent the next twenty minutes detailing the plan.

When Muller was through, McCarthy felt like he was doing his own movie and the director just told him he needed to roll a car ten times on a Los Angeles freeway in rush hour traffic. He tasted bile at the back of his throat. "Jurgy, this has to be a joke. Is Ashton Kutcher there? Am I being Punk'd?"

"Dammit, Shaun, this is serious! Are you with me or not? I am the President-elect of the United States and I need your support."

"I know, I know, Jurgy, but Jesus, do you realize what the hell you are asking...?"

"Shaun, I am asking you to support your rightfully-elected president..."

McCarthy cut in again, "I know, I know, but damn. I need a joint, a drink or maybe rehab. I'm just an actor. Shit, we're both just actors. Do you realize this might be civil war we're talking about here?"

"Of course, Shaun," Jurgin said in a reassuring tone. "We've thought it through very carefully. Hopefully, she won't try anything. Even if she does, we don't think it will lead to that. If you and I are united, then she should fold. If she doesn't, my staff doesn't think she'll go as far as starting a civil war. Can I count on you?"

"Of course, Jurgy." McCarthy's voice had a hint of panic, kind of like a husband caught cheating on his wife with a pair circus midgets on one of those sleazy daytime talk shows. "Is Lindsay Lohan in rehab again? I think I need rehab..."

Muller gave a halfhearted chuckle. "Feel free to have a nice long rehab with Lindsay, Britney or whoever else you want to...after this is over."

"Okay," McCarthy said, suddenly calmer.

* * * * *

"Are you sure about this?" Pedro Sandoval asked. "At best, this won't be popular. At worst, you might be brought on high treason charges or impeached like you're dearly departed husband."

"Who the fuck in Washington has enough balls to try that?" Dolly asked brashly.

"I seem to recall your would-be successor was a world champion bodybuilder and made his living for many years blowing things up. I don't think he's just going to roll over..."

"True," Dolly mused. "But he still needs support in Washington..."

Sandoval cut in again. "Listen, Doll, I understand your frustration, but why not leave office and make $2 mill a speech..."

Helen flinched and even Ava cringed slightly as Dolly cut him off acidly, "I don't think you do understand my frustration, Pedro. I put up with that fuckwit husband of mine's crap for three fucking decades to become president. I married that fuckhead Hertz to help fund my campaign. I invested over $300 million of that money on this campaign to lose to that fucking kraut bastard! I am going through with this. Are you on-board or are you resigning?"

Even Pedro Sandoval wasn't audacious enough to point out that Jurgin was actually Austrian, not German. "No, Doll, I'm not resigning. God knows you're going to need all the help you can get if you're going to pull this off."

Dolly would have torn the head off anyone else being so presumptuous as to assume she needed them, especially a male, but not Pedro. She knew she needed him. She took a deep breath and looked at the time on her cell phone. "Good, the Presidential Address starts in 20 minutes."

* * * * *

Sitting behind the Resolute desk, her fingers interlaced in front of her, her elbows resting on the desk, Dolly began her speech, "Friends, Americans, countrymen, lend me your ears.

"It was eleven score and sixteen years ago our fathers brought forth on this continent a new nation, conceived in liberty, and dedicated to the proposition that all people are created equal.

"Now we are engaged in a great tragedy, testing whether our nation, or any nation around our ravaged planet, can long endure under the onslaught of natural disasters collectively named 'Mayageddon' that began two days ago.

"The National Security Council has estimated U.S. casualties to be 38 million…"

Helen, standing off camera, flinched though she tried to hide it. 38 million? The newsfeeds were reporting closer to 38 thousand. God, how she loved Dolly's chutzpah. Unknowingly, Helen licked her lips.

While Helen was lost in her daydream, Dolly continued, "Power outages are reported in almost every state. Approximately 12 million households are without power and many industries have been brought to their knees. Oil production has dropped by 37% as most of the oil refineries along the Gulf coast are at least partially shut down and 73 oil rigs in the Gulf of Mexico are destroyed or severely damaged. There is looting and rioting in every major city and most towns and hamlets.

"The United States is in the most precarious situation it has been in since the outbreak of the Civil War more than 150 years ago. This is far worse than the 9/11 tragedy and worse than even World War I or World War II."

Dolly paused to let the point sink in, and then continued, "Because of the serious nature of this situation, I hereby execute executive order 12919 also known as the National Defense Industrial Resources Preparedness order. Using the authority given to the President of the United States in executive order 12919, I hereby declare the United States to be under total martial law. Until further notice, my administration, for the sake of unity in these catastrophic times, is declaring a military dictatorship."

Dolly paused again. Finally she said, "My fellow Americans, this stuff that some sources sling around about America wanting out of this challenge, not wanting to fight, is a crock of bullshit. Americans love to fight, traditionally. All real Americans love the sting and clash of battle. When you, everyone of you, were kids, you all admired the champion marble player, the fastest runner, the toughest boxer, the big league ball players, and the All-American football players. Americans love a winner. Americans will not tolerate a loser. Americans despise cowards. Americans play to win all the time. I wouldn't give a hoot in hell for a man who lost and laughed. That's why Americans have never lost nor will ever lose a war; for the very idea of losing is hateful to an American.

"We shall fight for our seas and oceans, we shall fight with growing confidence and growing strength in the air, we shall defend our country, whatever the cost may be, we shall fight for our beaches, we shall fight for our fields and our streets, we shall fight for our hills; we shall never surrender! Thank you, good night and God bless." Then the camera blacked out.

Pedro Sandoval shook his head. Did Dolly really just steal speeches written by Lincoln, Patton and Churchill...?

Chapter 18

2013

Jurgin Muller, dressed in a navy Firado wool three-piece suit and red silk tie, stood behind a podium on the front steps of the City Administration Building in downtown San Diego. Behind him was an entourage of important politicians from several states, Mexico and Canada, plus most of Jurgin's administration and his insiders. At the bottom of the steps and overflowing into the cordoned-off street were several thousand spectators and dozens of news cameras awaiting Muller's press conference.

The press was told this would be Muller's most important news conference ever but were given no details. Some of the press wondered if their efforts would be broadcast at all because of President Roderick's declaration of martial law.

"Happy New Year's Day, everyone," Jurgin said. "This is a great day for our nation. This is a great new beginning. Behind me are the esteemed governors of Texas, Nevada, Oregon, Washington, Hawaii, Alaska, New Mexico, Louisiana, and Arizona as well as Senor Santana, deputy mayor of Mexico City and interim President of Mexico, and the Premiers of British Columbia and the Yukon Territory of Canada, Mr. McKown and Mr. Devereaux.

"They are here to show their support for me as the duly-elected President of the United States and to show their outrage of President Roderick's obvious attempt to circumvent the will of the good people of the United States of America and steal the election that everyone knows I legally won, by a solid margin I might add, by declaring martial law.

Martial law has never been declared by a U.S. President before, not even during the Civil War or either World War.

"In a pathetic attempt to justify her actions, outgoing President Roderick has also blatantly exaggerated the death toll figures of Mayageddon, claiming a ridiculous 38 million Americans dead, or over 10% of the population, when all legitimate estimates put casualties between 35 and 50 thousand, which is less than 1/20 of 1% of the U.S. population,. While that is a dreadful number of casualties, it hardly warrants declaring martial law. To put this in perspective, the tsunamis that occurred the day after Christmas in 2004 killed almost 230,000 people or approximately five times our current Mayageddon U.S. loss estimates and none of the countries involved declared martial law.

"Dear friends, it is obvious that martial law is a ploy for Roderick to stay in power. I have tried to establish discussions with her administration but have been stonewalled at every turn. It is apparent that she is a power-hungry megalomaniac who refuses to relinquish her presidency, the will of the people be damned."

Jurgin made a sweeping gesture toward the suited group behind him. "My esteemed colleagues and I refuse to let the will of the people be patently ignored by the tyrannical despot Roderick, whose behavior is reminiscent of Hitler or Stalin. The United States of America was founded on freedom and democracy and the last thing her people want is for Dolly Roderick to declare martial law and make herself a dictator.

"Because of this, my esteemed colleagues and I have reached a monumental decision. California, Texas, Nevada, Oregon, Washington, Hawaii, Alaska, New Mexico, Louisiana, and Arizona are seceding from the United States of America and forming a new country along with Mexico, British Columbia and the Yukon Territory."

The politicians behind Jurgin nodded the assent and clapped. The crowd in the street seemed divided on the announcement. Most cheered enthusiastically while some gasped in disbelief and others gaped in complete shock.

An image of a map appeared on a giant screen mounted on the front of the City Administration Building. The map showed the new country highlighted in red and the remnants of the United States highlighted in blue. The sight of the image elicited more gasps and cheers as the crowd realized the new country dwarfed what was left of the United States, appearing to have almost twice the land mass. The new country encompassed the pacific coastline from the Arctic Circle all the way to Central America plus most of the gulf coast. Arizona, New Mexico and Nevada were the only states of the new country that were void of a coastline.

"Ladies and gentlemen," Muller beamed. "It is my privilege to present the Unified States of America, the real U.S.A.! And folks, our new country is a real powerhouse."

The map on the screen above Muller's head was replaced with statistics that read:

> World Economies by Gross Domestic Product
>   (in $million USD)
> Peoples' Republic of China $9,984,062
> Unified States of America $6,901,056
> United States of America $6,119,804
> Japan $4,170,533
> India $4,158,922

"As you can see, our new country is the second largest economy in the world, ahead of Dolly's land." The statistics overhead changed to another map with several areas highlighted in red. "We have the high-tech centers of Silicon Valley, the bay area, California; Silicon Hills, Austin, Texas; Hollywood and the Silicon Rainforest, the Seattle-area, Washington; and let's not forget NASA in Houston, Texas and the Jet Propulsion Laboratory near Los Angeles, California."

The screen behind Jurgin changed to another map with

highlighted areas. "Plus we control the Alaskan, Californian, Texan, Louisianan and Mexican oil fields plus a lion's share of the oil rigs off the gulf coast and over two-thirds of North American oil refineries. And let's not forget Hoover dam."

A new map came on the screen with many dots in various colors ranging blue to brown to green. Jurgin continued in a confident manner, "You may be wondering how our country is going to defend itself in these troubling times. In addition to controlling all of Mexico's military…"

This drew uncomfortable chuckles from various pockets in the crowd. Muller ignored the noise and continued smoothly, "…we control the entire Pacific Fleet, the largest marine base in the world, Camp Pendleton, California, the largest army base in North America, Fort Hood, Texas, plus the famous Edwards Air Force Base and dozens of other bases from all branches of the military including the coast guard. By the way, we also have the largest coast guard base, which is located in Kodiak, Alaska. Our current military strength including Mexican and Canadian forces is currently 109% the size of the military under Roderick's control. As you can see, we are exceptionally secure."

An organizational chart appeared on the screen with Muller's name in the top middle box with the title President under his name. "Here is how the new government will be set up. I will be the President of the Unified States of America. Texas governor Shaun McCarthy will be the Vice President. Our lieutenant governors will be acting governors of California and Texas until an election to be held on June 3rd will determine our official replacements. All other current governors, state representatives and senators will continue their current terms. Mexico will be organized into four states in our new country. British Columbia will become a state as well. Alaska and the Yukon Territory will become one state to be called Silami, which is the native Eskimo term for 'outside' since the new state is going to be so huge.

"The new government will run much like the United

States government until all open political offices are filled through appointments or special election on June 3rd. At that point, my administration will work on a new constitution and other laws for the government. More details of the official political structure will be detailed in the days to come."

Jurgin raised his arms in a wide, welcoming gesture. "You may be wondering why we are making this announcement here in beautiful San Diego. It is an excellent question. The answer is San Diego is going to be the capitol of the Unified States of America. The location is ideal for several reasons. First, San Diego is in the approximate center of our new country, when based on population. Second, it is the ideal defensible location. San Diego has the largest naval base on the west coast, Miramar naval air station and Camp Pendleton, all minutes from downtown. Third, San Diego has far fewer and far less intense earthquakes than other potential capitol sites like Los Angeles and San Francisco."

The screen changed to reveal a giant flag with three thick stripes (navy, red, and green) running lengthwise. A giant grey whale was encircled by fourteen gold stars in large white circle the middle of the flag. Underneath the flag, the message read: The Unified States of America---the real USA!!!

Jurgin Muller turned to Shaun McCarthy and said, "Vice President McCarthy, would you care to say a few words?"

McCarthy, dressed in a beige Armani suit and donning his usual three days of stubble, shook Jurgin's hand and then stepped up to the podium. Although he had his patented charismatic smile, he was obviously nursing a New Year's Day hangover, his eyes hidden behind dark sunglasses though the group stood in a shaded area. "Sure thing, el Presidente.

"Wassup, fellow citizens of the Unified States of America? Que pasa, amigos y amigas? It is my honor to announce the first of many new laws that will be signed into law in the near future. To improve communications with our friends in the new states to the south, the Muller administration is adopting

Mexican...uh, Spanish as an official second language."

This brought cheers from several pockets in the crowd.

"Spanish will be treated equal with English," McCarthy continued. "Beginning immediately, at all grade levels from kindergarten through twelfth grade, the same amount of time will be spent teaching Spanish as English. In high school, for example, a ninth grader must take one period of English and one period of Spanish. Beginning 2018, half of all tests at all grade levels including college entrance exams like the SAT will be given in Spanish. If an English teacher gives eight quizzes throughout the year, four will have instructions in Spanish."

English test with Spanish instructions? Jurgin rubbed his temples. McCarthy must be even drunker than he thought. He wasn't making any sense. How was he going to get McCarthy off the stage?

"Hey, Jurgy, to support the whole 'equal time for Spanish' thing, I'd like to change my title from vice president to a Spanish title. Is that okay?"

Muller tried not to look flustered. What the hell is Shaun pulling now? He knew he shouldn't have put that stoner on stage the day after a major partying holiday. He feigned a confident smile, clapped and nodded with forced encouragement.

"Excelente, mi presidente," McCarthy said. "I would like to go by the title of Los Grandes Cojones."

Jurgin walked up to the podium and offered his hand to McCarthy. "Thank you for those inspirational words." Then he gently but firmly nudged his vice president out of the way before he did any more damage. "Before closing this press conference, I have one last thing to say to Dolly Roderick: ¡Estaré destrás!"

A crescendo of applause and cheers rose from the crowd.

* * * * *

"Son of a bitch!" Dolly Roderick screamed as the video of Jurgin Muller's press conference ended and the video screen in the White House Situation Room went blank. "That fucking Aryan musclehead! What the fuck does 'estaré destrás' mean?"

Seated several chairs down from Roderick along the conference table, Babbs Baxter coughed uncomfortably and said softly, "'I'll be back'."

Dolly looked at her. "What?"

Babbs spoke louder, "It means 'I'll be back'."

Dolly's normally pasty countenance turned alabaster. "Fuck."

Pedro Sandoval, sitting across from Baxter, rubbed his chin. "That sounds ominous."

Dolly's face turned crimson as she glared at Sandoval. "You think? We have to do something! I'm not going to let that Austrian fuckhead tear apart my country." She looked over at General Apatia, the Chairman of the Joint Chiefs of Staff, who was seated next to Babbs. "So, General, where do we attack first? San Diego? Houston? New Orleans? Do we go after military targets first or the oil?"

The general glanced at Pedro and raised an eyebrow.

Pedro returned a knowing look and looked Dolly in the eyes. He was one of the few people in the world who could manage that feat. "Doll, I don't think we can do that."

"Why the fuck not, Pedro?" Dolly asked defiantly. "We have to do that! We can't let that prick tear apart the country."

"There are several reasons, Doll," Pedro replied calmly. "First, our buddy Jurg made several good points in his press conference. Among them are their military is now larger than ours and they control more oil than we do. We probably couldn't win a sustained campaign, right, General? We don't have the resources."

"Yes, madam President," Apatia said. "I agree with Mr. Sandoval's assessment."

Pedro locked his eyes with Dolly's. "Plus we have a more

pressing reason for not starting a second civil war. To be perfectly frank, you lost the election. If you start a civil war, it won't be very popular. In fact, it would probably be very unpopular and would probably cause mass defections, both civilian and military. I wouldn't recommend playing that card. We could lose the entire western half of the country."

Dolly seethed for a moment, looking around the room frantically. Finally, she grabbed her water glass and threw it as hard as she could against the far wall some thirty feet away. It shattered with a loud crash, sending shards flying several feet in all directions, but still far enough away that no one was hurt. She took a couple of deep breaths, her vermillion face slowly returning to a more pallid complexion. "Then, Pedro, what exactly do we fucking do?"

Sandoval sighed and shrugged. "I wish I knew, Doll, I wish I knew."

"Madam President, I recommend moving at least a corps of Army, Marine or National Guard soldiers into all of the states bordering this new 'Unified States of America,'" General Apatia suggested.

"That's an excellent idea," Sandoval responded. "Border states might try to secede but none of the interior states will secede if they are completely surrounded by us. That should keep any other states from seceding."

"Okay, that's something, I guess," Dolly said. "Good idea, General. See to it."

"Yes, Madam President," Apatia said aloud and then whispered in Baxter's ear, "What did McCarthy say in Spanish at the end?"

Babbs whispered back with a grin, "Los Grandes Cojones."

"What does it mean?"

"'The Great Testicles'."

"Damn, really?" Apatia said, surprised. "He earned it, I guess. It's not every day you secede from the union, after all."

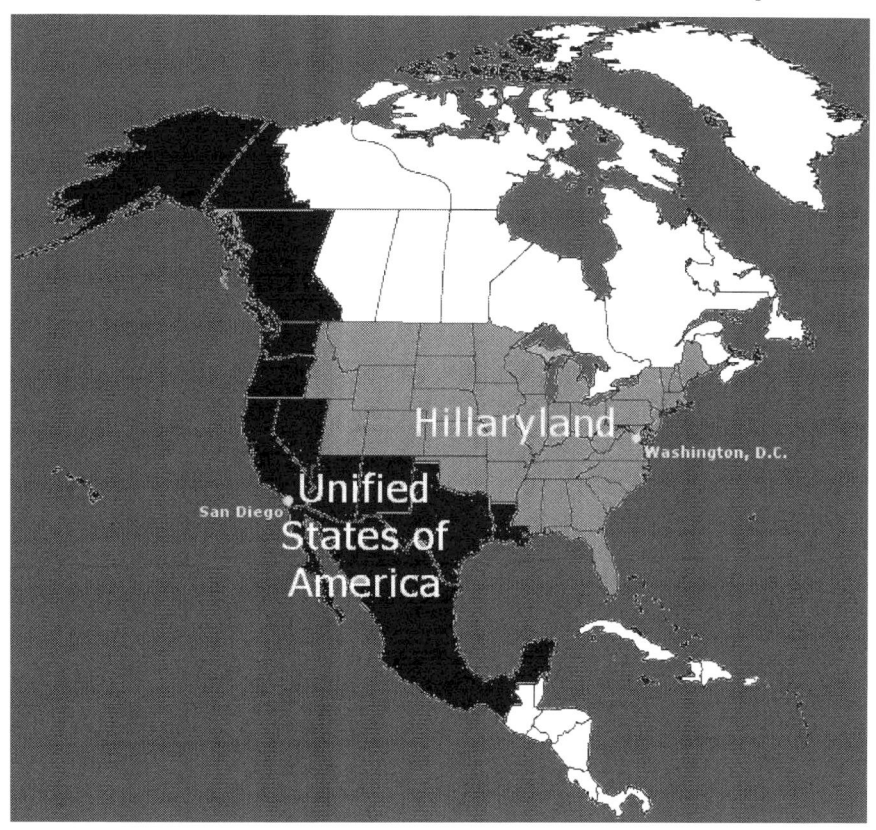

Immaculate Deception

Chapter 19

News Items from 2013

America Divided!

San Diego, Cal. – January 2, 2013 – In the most stunning news to happen in the United States in over 160 years, Governor of California and President-elect of the United States of America Jurgin Muller has announced the secession of California and nine other states (Texas, Nevada, Oregon, Washington, Hawaii, Alaska, New Mexico, Louisiana, and Arizona) from the U.S.A. to form a new country named the Unified States of America. In the aftermath of Mayageddon, all of Mexico and two provinces of Canada (British Columbia and the Yukon Territory) are also joining Muller's new country.

Governor Muller cited President Roderick's declaration of martial law as an obvious attempt to prevent his legally and rightfully won ascendancy to the United States Presidency as the reason for the secession.

Susan Collins, White House Press Secretary, gave an official statement. "While the Roderick administration recognizes that in the wake of Mayageddon, we Americans, all of us, are under extreme stress, we do NOT accept or acknowledge the secession of any state from the union. Any attempted secession violates the constitution of our great nation and all parties involved are breaking the law. Therefore, a warrant has been issued for all governors from the states attempting secession for the crime of high treason. In addition, due to Mr. Muller's felonious actions, he can no longer be elected president and has been removed from the running in the November 2012 election. Therefore, the election victory goes to the runner-up, which is Dolly Roderick, who has now been re-elected as President of the United States.

"President Roderick will strive to mend our troubled nation in these trying times. In an effort toward a peaceful resolution in this matter, the Roderick administration will not execute any governor for high treason who renounces their secession and rejoins the union. They will not be imprisoned or otherwise punished in any way other than being removed from office. This offer is good for all governors except for Mr. Muller, of course. Mr. Muller, the leader of this illegal rebellion, not even a natural born U.S. citizen, will receive a swift and sure punishment fitting the crime. He will be hanged in front of the U.S. Supreme Court, assuming he is found guilty, of course."

Muller, President of the newly formed Unified States of America, scoffed at the threats. "Although Ms. Roderick is certainly more of a man than that cheeseball husband of hers ever was, her threats are all without weight or merit. Our military is stronger than hers is and we control more oil than Dolly's land does. Her threats are merely tough talk because she is cornered, and she is scared. I'll be back, reclaim my presidency and reunify the country, make no mistake about that, but until then, our country is stronger than, and has no fear of, Dolly's land."

The Unified States of America has a population of roughly 195 million while the remaining United States of America has an approximate population of

220 million people. The capitol of the new country is San Diego, dubbed "America's Finest City."

Muller's reference to "Dolly's land" appears to refer to the states President Roderick actually won in the November 2012 election, which were primarily the northeast and the Great Lakes states. As Muller won most the Midwestern states in the election, this leads to some speculation as to whether more states might be seceding and joining the Unified States of America in the coming days...

* * * * *

El-Queso Terrorist Leader bin-Laed Dead

Landi Kotal, Pakistan – January 8, 2013 – A little more than two weeks after the events of Mayageddon devastated the far reaches of the earth, a spokesperson for el-Queso confirmed on the all-Jeers radio network that the leader of el-Queso and financier of the 9/11 assault on America, I. Nivaar bin-Laed, was killed in one of the numerous earthquakes that have ravaged the Afghanistan-Pakistan region since December 21, 2012.

El-Queso is an international terrorist organization formed by bin-Laed in 1988 to further his political and religious agenda throughout the world. Though the organization has Middle Eastern roots, it's name is distinctly Spanish. The moniker originated during a trip bin-Laed made to Honduras to set up drug trafficking operations to help fund his terrorist activities abroad. The diminutive local drug lord, 4'11" Jose Valdez, was so impressed by bin-Laed's 6'6" stature that he dubbed the Saudi "el Queso Grande" or "the Big Cheese." Bin-Laed liked the moniker so much he renamed his organization el-

Queso.

One of bin-Laed's three top lieutenants – Ishaeq Mbhuuti, Ismooq Craaq or Bhust Myaas – is expected to inherit control the el-Queso terrorist empire. Ishaeq Mbhuuti, el-Queso Deputy Operations Chief and head of the Military committee, is considered the front-runner to replace bin-Laed because Craaq and Myaas have been reported missing since bin-Laed disappeared. Rumors have emerged that they died with bin-Laed or Mbhuuti had them eliminated as part of his plan to gain control of el-Queso...

* * * * *

El-Queso Forms New Superpower

Medina, Saudi Arabia – February 17, 2013 – El-Queso leader Ishaeq Mbhuuti and his ever-growing el-Queso army has marched peacefully from the Khyber Pass along the Afghanistan-Pakistan border to Medina, Saudi Arabia, gaining followers along the way. Several of Mbhuuti's lieutenants started similar pilgrimages to Medina, beginning from Morocco, Somalia, Kazakhstan and Turkey. The force in Medina has grown to an estimated 2.3 million people strong. The march started just days after the death of el-Queso's founder I. Nivaar bin-Laed and ended three days ago.

Today, just five weeks after seizing control of el-Queso, Ishaeq Mbhuuti has announced the creation of a new superpower from the majority of Muslim nations. The new super nation, named the Allied Republics of el-Queso, AReQ for short, is made up of twenty-four and a half countries and stretches from Kazakhstan in the north, the western half of Pakistan in the east to Morocco in the west and Somalia and the Sudan in the south. AReQ will have an estimated population of approximately 434 million people and comprise over 97% of the world's Muslims. It is the greatest peaceful coup in recorded history. All leaders of the current Muslim countries will continue to lead the new "republics" of the Allied Republics of el-Queso, but Mbhuuti did announce a future grand army that would protect the entire new superpower.

"It is our holy destiny to defeat the Great Satan and destroy Satan's Concubine. We will continue to be vigilant in our effort to depose Satan's unholy mistress by whatever means necessary. With the combined power of AReQ, I am certain of victory," Mbhuuti said in his inauguration speech to a cheering crowd.

Mbhuuti's reference to Satan's Concubine is a clear reference to Dolly Roderick. Ayatollah Chowmeini had first referred to President Roderick as Satan's Concubine in her days as First Lady during her late husband's presidency some twenty-five years ago.

When asked about the Unified States of America and if it was still part of the Great Satan, Mbhuuti responded in an Austrian accent, "'I'll be back.' No, no. I like Jurgin. He makes funny shoot-them-up movies."

Mbhuuti also announced that Medina, Saudi Arabia, would be the capital of the Allied Republics of el-Queso. Medina is the second holiest city in the Muslim faith, being Muhammad's first capital and his burial place.

* * * * *

AReQ Leader Mbhuuti Announces Big Changes

Medina, Saudi Arabia – February 26, 2013 – Ishaeq Mbhuuti has announced more sweeping changes for his new super nation of the Allied Republics of el-Queso (AReQ).

First, in an effort to restore historic pride to the region, Mbhuuti is renaming Iraq to Babylonia and Iran to Persia. Babylonia and Persia were powerful empires in the past.

Babylonia was home of one of the seven wonders of the ancient world, the Hanging Gardens of Babylon. It was ruled by famed kings Hammurabi and Nebuchadnezzar II, traditionally known as the Great. Hammurabi's Code was the first written code of laws in human history. Nebuchadnezzar the Great was best known for constructing the Hanging Gardens of Babylon and appearing in the Holy Bible.

The Persian Empire, circa 550BC, was the most powerful empire in the world at the time. Its greatest ruler, Cyrus the Great, is, ironically, best known for conquering the Babylonian Empire on his way to creating the greatest empire the world had ever known up to that point in history.

Mbhuuti also announced the formation of an elite fighting force for the new superpower. The Republican Ultra Military Protectorate (RUMP for short) will be a united force for every country in AReQ, in addition to each country's local military and police forces. One-fourth of each country's military will be transferred to RUMP to create the new force. Approximately one-tenth of the new force, the best of the best, will be placed in the elite forces unit, the RUMP Rangers...

Chapter 20

2013 continues...

President Dolly Roderick sat behind the Resolute deck in the Oval Office of the White House, glancing at several color prints spread out on the desk. Nanny Moretti, Babbs Baxter, Helen Moore and Dolly's favorite secret service agent Ava were standing behind Dolly, looking over her shoulder as Pedro Sandoval opened the door and entered the room.

"Well, well, doesn't this look portentous?" Sandoval said, walking up to the gathering. "What scheme are you ladies hatching this morning?"

"Just the latest step en route to global domination, Pedro," Dolly said with a grin, not looking up from the prints.

"I'm flabbergasted, Doll," Sandoval said. "I do believe that is the first smile I've seen on your face since the creation of the second USA."

Dolly's grin disappeared for just a moment, her nose curling as if she had just got a whiff of a toxic waste dump, but her grin returned quickly though it wasn't quite as pronounced as previously. "Yes, indeed. I have decided to follow your advice, move forward, and give up the idea of trying to reunite our country, for now anyway. The decision has brought me a certain measure of peace."

"I guess so," Sandoval admitted. "I believe the last time I mentioned…what did you call him? 'That fucking musclehead?' You threw a vase at me. I'm glad to see you handling the situation so well."

"Chloe says I'm making great progress on my anger management issues," Dolly said.

Though Chloe was officially Dolly's 'personal adviser' or 'life coach' as some people called her, she was really a psychiatrist with an advanced medical degree. In the 1990's and 2000's, it was all the rage to be seeing a therapist but those days had passed and now it just wouldn't do for the President of the United States to admit enough weakness to need a therapist, so Dolly had a 'personal adviser' instead.

Pedro knew Dolly's ambition and often-volatile behavior stemmed from her past. She had spent most of her life trying to gain her father's approval. Though she never said it, Pedro knew that Dolly thought her father had wanted her to be a son. This was proven beyond any doubt when her brother was born three years later and named Hugh Jr. She had spent most of her childhood trying to be worthy of her father's love and prove that she was as ambitious and worthy as any son.

That inadequacy was compounded when Bobby replaced her father as the main male figure in her life. Bobby's incessant infidelities had undermined her self-worth tremendously. Dolly wasn't as good as a male in her father's mind and she wasn't good enough, beautiful enough, perky enough, or lusty enough as a woman in her husband's mind. Though, on the surface, Dolly knew both arguments were ridiculous. All fathers always seemed to want to pass on their name to a son. It had nothing to do with her. Bobby could've married Miss America or the Playmate of the Year and he would've still screwed around on her. For Bobby, it wasn't about looks. It was about conquest. He wanted to fuck anything with a hole between its legs simply because he could.

On a deeper, subconscious level though, the combination of rejection of her central male figures had created a cocktail of maniacal ambition and megalomania in Dolly that rivaled Hitler, Stalin or Hussein in its intensity, often causing blind rage in her. Having a Masters Degree in Psychology in addition to a Bachelors Degree in Political Science and a Law Degree from Columbia, Sandoval had a keen understanding of Dolly's issues and understood her better than anyone in her inner circle save for possibly Chloe, and that was certainly up for debate. Chloe was smart enough, but he had a good twenty years of experience over her to draw from.

On many levels, he found Dolly's issues quite sad, which is why he put up with her tirades and stood by her when most people would have become fed up with her histrionics and moved on. Pedro was the one person in her inner circle that didn't want anything from her. Everyone else tried to either fulfill some political agenda or sate some sexual need or simply enjoyed being a power groupie or, in most cases, some mix of the three.

He was the lone person among her confidants that didn't seek any of that. He had all of the power and money he could ever need long before he ever met the Rodericks. He was also one of the few straight men that she trusted. That, in itself, was quite a feat, considering her past with 'Nobby Bobby.' Perhaps Pedro's complete lack of self-promotion was what made him such a valuable ally and confidant to Dolly. He liked to think so.

"Excellent progress indeed," Sandoval said, glancing down at the prints on the desk. "So, what have we here?"

"Pedro, I've decided to move forward with renaming the country."

"Really?" Sandoval said, his eyebrows raising slightly, realizing the prints must be mock-ups for the flag for Dolly's newly named country.

The idea for renaming the USA had first been brought up in a staff meeting a couple of months earlier; just days after Muller's secession, but Pedro didn't realize Dolly was seriously considering it. The whole idea seemed, at best, a lark and, at worst, dangerous, insane, stunningly stupid and, quite possibly, political suicide. Dolly probably hadn't mentioned it to him because she knew he would try to talk her out of it. Maybe he wasn't as close to Dolly as he thought he was. He would have to work on that. He didn't want one of Dolly's bed buddy tramps like Helen leading Dolly down a path of self-destruction. Dolly had already made too many ill-advised decisions lately.

"So, what names are you considering?" Sandoval asked in a slightly bemused tone in a concerted attempt not to put Dolly on the defensive.

"Name, not names, actually. Roderickstan," Dolly said simply. "It's the name that has been plastered all over the Internet, TV, and the newspapers since Muller seceded anyway. It's either that or Dollyland and that sounds like a theme park, so why not?"

Dolly didn't wait for an answer to her rhetorical question, not seeking objections for her plan. "Here are some ideas for a new flag for Roderickstan. I would like a man's opinion. Which one do you like best, Pedro?"

"Which one do you ladies like best?" Sandoval asked.

Waving a silencing finger at Sandoval and the rest of the group. "No, no, no. Nice try, Pedro, but I want your opinion, untainted."

Pedro shrugged and gazed carefully at the four designs. The first one showed a white flag with Dolly riding a donkey, an obvious reference to Jesus and the democrats at the same time. Very clever. Unfortunately, Dolly looked silly riding the donkey. Besides, it was a touch arrogant to compare herself to Christ anyway.

The second design showed Dolly's head wearing a crown, looking like a young Queen Elizabeth II. The background was the gay and lesbian rainbow flag of diversity. An interesting choice. It might work if Dolly never planned to end martial law and her dictatorship, which Pedro was certain was the case.

The third design showed a traditional USA flag minus the ten seceding states. A conservative choice but what if more states secede? It would be embarrassing for the administration to change the flag several times.

The last design showed Dolly's head again, this time on a

white background with a Japanese "rising sun" design but the sunrays were yellow instead of red. The flag caused Dolly to come off looking too much like a Statue of Liberty wannabe from Pedro's taste.

Which one? Which one? Sandoval rubbed his chin as a stall tactic, trying to think which flag Dolly was trying to steer him toward. Probably the Statue of Liberty flag or the rainbow flag, but which…? "I like the rainbow flag best."

"Okay," Dolly said with a smile. She lifted the rainbow flag print. "Why do you like this design over the others?"

Pedro sighed. He had picked correctly but there was still a chance of earning her wrath. "It looks regal and it shows diversity."

"And what don't you like as much about the others?"

Damn it. Was Dolly trying to put her anger management skills to the test? "The 'donkey' flag is clever with the Democrat/Jesus riding into Jerusalem reference but it's too religious. You'll offend too many taxpayers with that. The 'new' USA flag is a safe choice but too similar to the old flag. New country name, new country flag. And the 'sun' flag looks too similar to Japan's rising sun flag for my taste. We were at war with Japan less than a century ago."

Pedro waited for Dolly to turn flush and start screaming at him but she didn't. Instead, she smiled and said, "Excellent feedback, as always, Pedro. I agree with your assessment, though I do kind of like my 'sunny day' flag. I think we should go with the 'diversity' flag too."

Still standing behind Dolly, the ladies nodded their assent.

"The 'diversity' flag it is, then. Helen, move forward with getting samples of stationary, etc." Dolly looked up at Sandoval with a grin. "Pedro, perhaps I should send a thank you card to Jurgin. It's one thing to be the leader of a country, but it's much better to have a country named after you. Pedro, we're also changing the currency."

She flipped through the pictures and held up an image of

a blue five dollar bill with Dolly's face in the middle and two huge triangles, one on either side of her face. Dolly chuckled. "We're calling them Dollies. Cute, huh?"

Pedro groaned inwardly, wondering if Muller had any openings in his administration. Finally, he said, "Sure, Doll, they look great but what are the triangles for?"

"That is the letter Delta in Greek. D or Delta for Dollie. Get it? A stroke of brilliance, don't you think?"

Perhaps he should send a thank you card to Chloe for whatever drugs she prescribed to Dolly. "Indeed."

Immaculate Deception

PART IV

M-PIRE: 2013-2024

"Nonononono you all have it wrong. Walmart and/or Costco are going to rule the world while Disney brainwashes the children. It's all basic knowledge. Doesn't everyone know that?"
-- ~Pickle~ (thepengragonadventure.com forum, September 30, 2007)

Immaculate Deception

Chapter 21

2013 continues...

Fangshan was one of the most outrageously exclusive and expensive restaurants in Beijing. Located in the Yilantang Hall on the north side of Jade Isle, overlooking Bei Hai Lake, Fangshan literally meant 'imperial' in Chinese. The restaurant served traditional imperial style cuisine dating back to the 1800's when Empress Dowager Cixi used to eat there after enjoying the park.

Back then, imperial style cuisine was food only served at court and was more expensive than commoners could afford or were even legally allowed to eat. Even today, a typical meal for two at Fangshan would cost more than an average Chinese factory worker would earn in two months. The restaurant was best known for the opulent Manchu and Han banquets featuring extravagant pastries like steam corn-flour cake and kidney bean flour rolls.

Mary Ellen Martin had been to Fangshan a dozen or more times in the two years since she become President of M-Mart China. She walked into the restaurant, dressed in a luscious bright red dress with a plunging neckline that accentuated her large breasts and a hemline that ended just below her knees. A sparkly black purse and gleaming black high heels finished the look. As usual, she stopped in the entryway of the restaurant, looking in the shiny glass of a giant painting of a Chinese landscape that was a personal favorite of hers. Using the glass as a makeshift mirror, she fluffed her long, medium-brown hair, just a shade or two lighter than the color she was born with. It was also considerably darker than the ever-growing sprinkling of gray hair that had begun to proliferate her scalp in the last half decade, thanks to coloring treatments from an upscale salon down the street from the M-Mart China headquarters in Shenzhen. She adjusted her dress, making sure that her push-up bra was hidden from view and pushed her breasts upward and inward to create even more cleavage. She smiled deeply; her companion tonight would like that. He was definitely a breast man. Pursing her lips, she checked her lipstick and appraised the overall look in the picture glass. Though she had never lost that last ten pounds of weight since having Little Sam eleven years earlier, her waist-high tummy tuck panty hose created a slimming effect that was pleasing to her. Not bad, not bad at all. Almost forty and she looked hotter now than when she was twenty, ha!

Mary Ellen walked up to the Maitre d's station and was greeted in English by a pleasant-looking man in a tuxedo. "Good evening, Miss Martin."

"Good evening, Wen. Busy tonight?"

Wen smiled. "Of course, Miss Martin. Always. I see we are having a meeting of the Presidents again tonight. President Jhuns is awaiting you in the Emperor room."

Wen referred to President Tao Jhuns, the leader of the most populous nation on the planet, the People's Republic of China and Mary Ellen, President of M-Mart, China. She usually used Fangshan to wine and dine politicians or a corporate executive from a potential supplier but Jhuns was by far her most frequent companion. Her relationship with Tao had started out as strictly business but grew increasingly friendly with each dinner date, although probably not as friendly as Tao might like. Not yet, anyway. Anything was possible if it helped move her closer to fulfilling her ambitions.

"Yes, another meeting of the presidents," Mary Ellen said with a smile.

"This way, miss," Wen said and led her across the main dining room to a set of doors guarded by two dark-suited agents, who simply nodded and opened the door for Wen and Mary Ellen. Wen escorted her to an intimate table for two in the middle of the large room where a tall regal-looking Chinese man in his late forties sat, dressed in an expensive-looking silver suit with a burgundy silk tie.

Tao smiled and stood when he saw Mary Ellen. He moved close, gave her a deep hug and kissed her on the check and, still holding her, appraised her admiringly. He said in perfect English, "Ah, Mary Ellen, exquisite, as always."

Mary Ellen blushed slightly. She replied in passable Mandarin Chinese, "Why, thank you, Tao. You look quite exquisite yourself."

Tao released her and held her chair for her to sit. "I dress my best out of respect for your loveliness."

A male waiter in a tuxedo arrived at the table with a pitcher of water and began filling their glasses. "Good evening, Miss Martin," the waiter said.

"Ah, good evening, Chang," Mary Ellen responded pleasantly.

"Do you need a few minutes to look at the menu or would you like your usual?" Chang inquired.

"The usual will be just fine, thank you." The usual was called Go lu yuk. It was the closest thing that real Chinese restaurants in China had to the American favorite sweet and sour pork, which was only a distant cousin to authentic Chinese food at best. Mary Ellen had made the mistake of once letting Chang 'surprise' her with a recommendation. What arrived on her plate was some sort of sea creature staring up at her that looked like a sea horse and a squid had mated in some freakish experiment gone wildly awry, like some sort of Lake Erie mutation that might crawl off the plate at any moment. It was all she could do not to throw up all over the grotesque thing. Since then, she had never strayed from her tried and true Go lu yuk again.

"A glass of Pinot Noir to go with that, Miss Martin?" Chang offered.

"Yes, Chang, thank you." Mary Ellen did have to give Chang credit. While his food selections were suspect, his wine choices were impeccable.

Chang bowed politely and departed.

Tao looked at his companion with a mix of admiration and lust on his countenance, his eyes glancing about her face, hair, shoulders and cleavage. "So, Mary Ellen, while it is my hope and dream that you are here to finally submit to my unrelenting and unsolicited advances, I suspect you have other reasons for requesting dinner with me tonight."

Mary Ellen reached across the table and placed her hands gently on Tao's hands. "Can't I simply want to enjoy dinner with an extremely handsome man who just happens to be the most powerful man in the world?" Mary Ellen asked with an innocent grin.

Since the demise of the United States of America and the creation of Roderickstan and the Unified States of America, Mary Ellen was technically correct. Tao Jhuns was the most powerful man in the world, controlling a country over six times as populace as either Roderickstan or the Unified States of America. Even before Mayageddon, when the United States of America still existed and it was debatable whether the USA or China was more powerful, Tao Jhuns had technically been considered the most powerful man in the world since Dolly Roderick controlled the USA. Some, though, would have argued that Dolly was the most powerful man in the world, just like they did when her late husband Bobby was President of the United States back in the 1990's.

"That would be wonderful, my beautiful lily, and I am moved by your words, but I am not naïve. You always have more than one reason to meet with me, though all I want is for you to wake up next to me in the morning. You may be a Martin, but I'm convinced you would still be president of M-Mart, China even if you weren't, my ambitious delight. You are the most capable woman I have ever met." He glanced at her breasts. "I do so want to know exactly what you are capable of..."

Mary Ellen blushed. That was the most forward he had been with his advances so far. He must be growing frustrated with her stalling. She would have to have sex with him. Not the most unpleasant prospect, she thought, though the thought of a penis penetrating her made her pause. She guessed it couldn't be too much different from Sylvia's finger or a vibrator.

Though Sylvia knew exactly what she was doing tonight, Mary Ellen still felt a pang of guilt for cheating on her. It wasn't like she was sleeping with another woman or had feelings for Tao. Sure, he was a nice enough man and she liked him, but she didn't lust for him. Actually, maybe she did have some lustful feelings for him, and it was an alien feeling for her. She hadn't had any feelings remotely like this since the ninth grade, but it was nothing that endangered her feelings for Sylvia. Lusting after a man and having a deep, loving spiritual connection with a woman were completely different sensations altogether.

Oh well, this was business and nothing could be done about it. It was time for her to make her move. The plan she had been working on for almost two years was about to come to fruition - or fail. There was absolutely no way to pull off the plan without having sex with Tao. She had dangled that carrot in front of him for too long, and now, she supposed, it was time for him to dangle his 'carrot' in front of her. If she rejected him now, the last two years would have been for nothing.

Tao gave her a curious, yet amused look. "So, what is it, my precious flower? A land permit for a new warehouse...? Shipping tariff reductions...? A major bribe might be nice. Are you going to give me a yacht or five pallets of Sam's Pick soda to look the other way about something M-Mart is doing...polluting our rivers or air? I do like the Spring Lightning flavor, or maybe the Summer Thunder flavor. Ha, ha, lightning and thunder. Your marketing people bring me laughter."

Mary Ellen gave him a feigned hurt look. "I never. I am shocked you would think that of me."

"Oh, my lovely flower, I mean it in only the most respectful way," Tao said. "I don't know which I admire more about you: your succulent body, driving ambition or brilliant mind."

Mary Ellen's hurt countenance turned to a devilishly seductive grin. "Well, actually, I do have a proposal to talk to you about. It is much grander than a permit for a warehouse or a pallet of Summer Thunder soda though. Perhaps we could discuss it in the morning over breakfast in bed, after you have had a more intimate opportunity to determine whether you admire my mind or body more."

Tao shot her a seductive grin of his own. "I believe I'm admiring your mind more and more by the moment. It is a shame you aren't the president of a country. You would make a marvelous politician and would certainly be more pleasurable to negotiate with than most politicians."

"Hmmm…interesting that you would say that, Tao. That's what I wanted to talk with you about…"

Chapter 22

News Items 2013-2017

China Invades and Annexes Taiwan

BEIJING, China – November 23, 2013 – In a surprise move, over 500,000 Chinese troops landed at the coastal city of Tan-shui and swept into the Taiwan capital of Taipei. The contingent included mechanized infantry, tanks, helicopters and two of China's naval groups with four aircraft carriers each. As the Taiwanese military had been almost completely obliterated in Mayageddon, the Chinese force met with little resistance.

Though there has been a major dispute between China and Taiwan over Taiwanese independence for decades, the invasion took the Taiwanese and the rest of the world by surprise. Mainland China has wanted to reincorporate Taiwan since the end of World War II, when the Japanese surrendered to the USA and lost control of the island nation. There have been several highly dramatic stand-offs over the years, but there has never been any actual combat.

The Taiwanese government unconditionally surrendered to the Chinese General Pong Mi Gaem within seven hours of the beginning of the invasion. People's Republic of China President Tao Jhuns said of the invasion, "The people of China are happy to have Taiwan back. China and Taiwan have had a long history of unity, and we look forward to continuing that history for a long, long time into the future. We welcome back Taiwan with open arms."

* * * * *

M-Mart Buys Taiwan

BEIJING, China – November 26, 2013 – Chinese President Tao Jhuns, M-Mart Stores, Inc. CEO Les Scarletti, Jr. and M-Mart, China president Mary Ellen Martin held a press conference to announce the sale of Taiwan to M-Mart Stores, Inc.

Although details of the deal have not been disclosed, it is widely considered by industry experts to be the biggest land purchase ever by a corporation. Analysts estimate that it is also the biggest land purchase by any entity (government or corporate) ever, easily topping the Louisiana Purchase (estimated cost in today's dollies: approximately Δ950,000,000) and the Alaska Purchase (also known as Seward's Folly after the United States Secretary of State who arranged to buy Alaska from the Russians; estimated cost in today's dollies: approximately Δ170,000,000). Analysts could not come to a consensus as to the value of Taiwan, with estimates ranging wildly from Δ400 billion to Δ68 trillion, though it is generally accepted that even M-Mart, the world's largest retailer with worldwide annual sales topping Δ3 trillion, could not secure loans greater than Δ10 trillion, which would drop the highly-secretive price range from to Δ400 billion to Δ10 trillion.

"The Chinese government and the Chinese people are excited about this continued expansion of our relationship with M-Mart, China, and M-Mart Stores, Inc.," Jhuns said at the press conference.

"While we value the new relationship we had re-established with Taiwan just three days ago, we value the relationship we have with M-Mart Stores, Inc. more. Sorry, Taiwan."

"M-Mart is thrilled about this new addition to our portfolio of properties," Les Scarletti, Jr. added. "It is well known that M-Mart buys trillions of dollies of merchandise from Taiwan annually. The Taiwan purchase greatly expands M-Mart's ability to increase its profits. I would like to thank Mary Ellen Martin for masterminding this wonderful acquisition and to make the following announcement: In addition to her duties as president of M-Mart, China, she is taking charge of Taiwan as its President. Congratulations, Mary Ellen!"

"Thanks, Les," Martin said. "I look forward to being the first woman President of Taiwan. Look for many exciting changes to be announced in the coming days. I would like to begin with two major changes.

"First, the official new name for Taiwan is now M-Wan. Second, the official language, both oral and written, for M-Wan will be English, the Unified States of America version."

* * * * *

M-Wan President Martin Announces Major Changes

Taipei, M-Wan – December 2, 2013 – In the latest series of sweeping changes for the island nation formerly known as Taiwan, M-Wan President Mary Ellen Martin stated at a press conference yesterday that several new laws and agreements will be enacted immediately.

Martin began the press conference by announcing M-Wan will eliminate its military completely, opting for a relatively small national police force. M-Wan also signed a significant alliance treaty with China which gives M-Wan protectorate status and states that China will treat any attack or any threat of attack on M-Wan soil as an attack on China itself.

President Martin also stated she is forming a communist government and nationalizing all factories. "This is great day for all M-Wanters," Martin said. "Now, we have government and industry for the people, by the people...the ultimate freedom. I believe Thomas Jefferson would be proud of our new government."

A maximum wage was also announced for all factory workers. The new wage ceiling will be 3,000,000 M-Wan New Dollars (MWND-pronounced "M-wands") per hour, which converts to roughly .8 cents in dollies, meaning factory workers will now earn a maximum of 14 cents per day with the new mandatory 16-hour workday in place. In Taipei, M-Wan, an average 400 square foot apartment costs 500,000,000 MWND per month or approximately half a month's wages at the new rate. A 5-pound bag of white rice costs about 15,000,000 MWND or 5 hours of work at the new wage...

* * * * *

From the San Diego Union-Tribune:

Muller Reelected by Overwhelming Majority

San Diego, Cal. – November 8, 2016 – In a landslide victory, Republican incumbent candidate Jurgin Muller has been re-elected El Presidente of the Unified States of America with 71.6% of the popular vote, beating out National Action Party candidate

Ubaldo Gutierrez (19.3%) and Democratic Party candidate and former California senator and current Roderickstan Secretary of State Babbs Baxter (8.8%). Muller, whose approval ratings were at 77% on Election Day, was predicted to win by a wide margin.

Republicans criticized Babbs Baxter's nomination as the Democratic Party's candidate as an obvious attempt for Dolly Roderick to reunite the United States of America. Dolly Roderick, who had legislation pushed through several months earlier to change the office of President in Roderickstan to be a lifetime post similar to that of the members of the supreme courts of both the Unified States of America and Roderickstan. Obviously, the voters agreed with the Muller administration's assessment, and fearing that Baxter would simply give the USA back to Roderick, most democrats voted for Muller or Gutierrez instead.

In a USA Today poll dated May, 14, 2014, Unified States of America citizens were asked if they were happier now as a separate country or happier before Mayageddon as the United States of America. An overwhelming 86% preferred the post-Mayageddon USA to the pre-Mayageddon USA. The main reason cited for the preference was the shedding of the $15 trillion national debt, which Muller squarely left with Roderickstan, refusing to take any of the debt not incurred by his administration in San Diego.

No one from the Baxter campaign or the Roderick administration in Roderickstan was immediately available for comment on the election results.

Shaun McCarthy, re-elected as Los Cajones Grande on the Muller-McCarthy ticket, said of the victory, "Hey, what can I say? My man Jurgy is on fire, kind of like San Diego County has been for the last decade."

EvapoFood Inventor Commits Suicide

Chicago, Ill. – January 12, 2017 – Just days after a class action lawsuit forced her company into bankruptcy, EvapoFood inventor Anna Rexia was found dead in her Chicago penthouse condo from an apparent overdose of diet pills.

Rexia invented the "evaporating" food line EvapoFood that created a diet craze in 2016 that help millions lose massive amounts of weight but tragically led to the deaths of 1,427 people before the product line was pulled from the shelves last October. A Δ3.8 billion class action lawsuit quickly followed and the company was forced into bankruptcy last week.

EvapoFood was line of food products, when eaten, would interact with the body's stomach acid to slowly, but completely dissolve, thus all EvapoFood products were filling but had zero calories. Unfortunately, they also had no nutritional value either. All EvapoFood had large warning labels that the product was meant to supplement regular food (with calories and nutritional value) and designed for between meal snacking exclusively. In spite of the warnings, tens of thousands of people went on "EvapoFood only" diets and 1,427 people literally starved themselves to death before the Food and Drug Administration had the product pulled.

"Freakaziod" from Unbossed.com, an online group of writers with a wide variety of perspectives and experience engaged in truth-telling, said, "While TV was the worst invention of the 20th century (i.e. the most misused), EvapoFood is easily the worst invention so far in the 21st century. TV is sometimes a very great thing, like educational shows found on the History Channel and the Discovery Channel, but most of the time it is used for mind-numbing drivel such as soap operas like Days of Our Lives and lame comedies like Beverly Hillbillies. EvapoFood could have been a great thing too, but it is sad to say that too many North Americans are simply too stupid to handle it without misusing it.

"What else can you say about a society where a woman buys an RV, gets on the highway, puts on the cruise control, and then goes to the back to make sandwich and wonders why her RV crashes into tree? This happened just four years ago and she successfully sued the RV manufacturer for almost Δ2 million because the manual wasn't 'clear enough' that the RV didn't actually drive itself. 50 years ago, the woman would have been too embarrassed to mention her stupidity, much less try to sue over it, but hey, now her stupidity is worth Δ2 million."

A note found next to Rexia's body stated: Always use under a doctor's supervision and never eat less than 1,200 calories a day. Why can't anybody read directions??? Screw you all!!!

Chapter 23

2018

Mary Ellen Martin sat around the large mahogany table in one of the many conference rooms at M-Mart's Martinville, Alabama headquarters, a manila envelope lying on the table in front of her. Three of the eight high-backed leather chairs situated around the table were occupied. She chatted with Robby Martin, M-Mart Stores, Inc. Chairman and her uncle, and Sylvia Byrne, Executive Vice President, M-Mart, China and her second-in-command, closest confidant and lover. The group made small talk while they waited for the fourth person to arrive.

"So, Uncle Robby," Mary Ellen said congenially. "What are your big retirement plans?"

"Nothing really set in stone, my dear," Rob replied. "I'll probably spend more time with the Martin Foundation, or maybe I'll try to figure out a way to oust Dolly and get Jurgin into the White House where he should be so we can be the United States again..."

"Wouldn't that be nice?" Mary Ellen cut in pleasantly. Her mind raced at the implications. Deposing that evil, spiteful bitch would be wonderful on so many levels and the whole Roderickstan/Unified States of America split was a logistics nightmare. It had cost M-Mart an extra ∆1.7 million last year in accounting and legal expenses alone. Marketing expenses like changing the address on everything from stationary to M-Mart's myriad of websites was estimated to be at least triple that number.

"That would be so nice," Sylvia chimed in. She had

Immaculate Deception

become more confident and congenial around the M-Mart chairman in the last half decade since her and Mary Ellen's China promotions. She actually quite liked Robby Martin. In recent years, he treated her like a niece, just the same as Mary Ellen. "It feels weird that one of my sisters, Joan, now lives in another country. She lives in San Francisco, after all. It's just weird."

"My feelings exactly. Mary Ellen's aunt Alice lives in Texas," Robby said. "At least we don't have long-distance phone charges to deal with anymore. Do you remember we had those, before cell phones became so popular?"

"Yes, Uncle Robby," Mary Ellen replied with a mild scoff. "We're both over forty. We also remember when cars took only unleaded gas and when it was only a dollar a gallon. Remember dollars? Heck, I even remember when Dolly's picture wasn't on every denomination of currency." Luckily, that was a moot point now that the government, as a cost-cutting measure, had phased out all hard currency like coins and paper money. Everyone had been accessing his or her money electronically via bankcards and the Internet for years now anyway. Besides, now it was easier than ever for a government to erase its debt. It no longer had to bother printing more money. Now it could simply add a zero or two to the balance in its account. Creating hyperinflation was a breeze.

Sylvia shook her head in disgust. "Wow, I've bought hydrogen for so long now, I had almost forgot about gas prices. What is gas selling for now?"

"I don't know, about twelve dollies a gallon, I think," Robby offered with a shrug. All new non-commercial automobiles by law built in the model year 2011 had to use hydrogen so only older cars still had to get unleaded gas at a filling station. Most filling stations only had one pump that offered 'legacy' fuels, diesel and unleaded, and usually one grade, the highest and most expensive one, of course.

Mary Ellen laughed. "Remember when gas topped $10 a

gallon and thousands of gas stations had to change the price from 'per gallon' to 'per pint' for a month or so because none of the pumps could handle the fourth digit? Gas companies spent billions of dollars changing out of their gas pumps. Geez, when was that? 2010? 2011?"

"That was the beginning of 2012, I believe," Robby said. "Just after the law changed everything to hydrogen but almost everyone still had gas cars. A year later gas prices dropped."

"Right," Sylvia pondered. "I remember reading the company memo about M-Oil changing its name to M-Fuel and retooling all of the filling stations at M-Marts to handle hydrogen."

"Yeah, that was expensive, but we made a killing on it." Mary Ellen said. "Anyway, we were talking about your retirement…"

"Yes, we went off on a tangent, didn't we?" Robby said. "I think the first thing we are going to do is go on an around-the-world cruise. I've never had the time before to go on one. They last three and a half to four months, you know. It's hard to take that kind of time off when you are working fourteen-hour days."

"Wow, that sounds incredible," Sylvia said.

"It sounds like it should be a lot of fun. The ship goes through the Panama canal and the Suez canal." Robby's expression became mildly curious as he turned to Mary Ellen. "So, my favorite niece, while I always enjoy chatting with the two of you, I'd like to know what's grinding away in that brilliant little brain of yours? What's this little meeting about? I smell some grand scheme brewing…"

"Ah, my favorite uncle, that sulfur smell? Soon enough. It should be quite the fun surprise, but let's wait for Les, though, shall we?" Mary Ellen answered with a smile. "So, what ports of call will the cruise have?"

After a few more minutes of chit chat, there was a soft rap on the conference room door and Les Scarletti, Jr., CEO of M-

Mart Stores, Inc., entered the room without waiting for an answer and closed the door behind him. "Robby, ladies, good morning. Sorry for my tardiness. My conference call with the CEO of Unilever ran long. Parker sure is chatty for a CEO." He sat down next to Rob. "I'm sorry but I only have a few minutes, so, Mary Ellen, let's get down to brass tacks. What's this meeting about?"

So much for the pleasantries. "Certainly, Les. Not a problem, not a problem at all. As we all know, Uncle Robby is announcing his retirement at the board meeting today. I would also like to make another special announcement and I would like your and Uncle Robby's buy-in."

"Sure, Mary Ellen," Les said confidently, knowing every idea she had presented in M-Mart board meetings over the seven years of her tenure as a board member was nothing short of brilliant and made the company millions, perhaps billions of dollies. "What's the announcement? Buying China? Buying Mars? I know, I know...opening the first Morris Fueling Station in orbit?" Les shot a glance at Rob and laughed. "Hey, we could probably charge a cool mil per gallon. Wow, wouldn't that be nice?"

Mary Ellen chuckled heartily. The ideas were rather silly, but she felt pretty wired at the moment, a blend of confidence and a mild adrenaline rush at the thought of the coming confrontation surging through her. "Not bad ideas, but nothing that extravagant. I wanted to announce your retirement at the board meeting too, Les."

Les's face turned ashen. Robby's countenance was a mix of curiosity at Mary Ellen's plan, respect of her chutzpah, and pure 'what the hell?!?!'.

"What...?" Les stammered.

"Les, you and Uncle Robby have had an incredible run, but Uncle Robby is stepping down and you've been CEO for seventeen years now. As former president Kirby would say, 'it's time for a regime change' - or would he say 'regimen change'?" Mary Ellen and Sylvia chuckled to each other.

Robby was the first to recover his composure from Mary Ellen's bombshell. "And I assume, my dear niece, that our logical successors would be you and Sylvia...?"

"Of course, my dear uncle. Who else is more qualified? In the past decade, who has done more for the company than Sylvia and me? From the Microsoft buyout to the purchase of Taiwan, who has done more for the M-Mart bottom line than us other than grandpa himself?"

Robby pondered the statement for a few seconds. "There is no denying that, I suppose. You've been the most ambitious and innovative Martin of us all. But why exactly would Les want to step down?"

"Three reasons," Mary Ellen offered confidently. "First, as you stated just moments ago, no more fourteen-hour workdays. Second, the largest retirement package in the history of business: $1 billion in stock and cash. That's for each of you. Les for retiring and you, Uncle Robby, for backing me here."

"That's in Unified States dollars, not dollies, right?" Les asked, his mind racing at the implications of such an astonishing amount of money.

Mary Ellen laughed pleasantly. "Of course, Les, I said dollars, not dollies."

"I don't know. It sounds good but..." Les pondered, trailing off into thought.

"Wait a second...what's the third reason?" Robby asked.

"Ah, the third reason." Mary Ellen opened the manila envelope that had been lying in front of her the whole time and a produced a photograph, laying it face up for the group to see. It was a picture of Les buck-naked being orally serviced by two female dwarfs who were equally buck-naked except for clown make-up.

"Oh my god...Les...?" Robby said, disgusted.

Sylvia stifled a snicker.

"What the hell?!?!" Les shouted accusingly, examining the photograph. "Where did you get...? Hey, I didn't do this. This picture is doctored."

"Yes, actually it is," Mary Ellen replied with a chuckle. "Calm down, it was just a joke to lighten the tension. With a billion dollar retirement package, do you really need a third reason?"

Les laughed uneasily. "Oh...I guess not..."

"So, do we have an agreement?" Mary Ellen asked. She already had over half the board members in her pocket and could force Les out if she had to, but he had been a good CEO during his tenure, which is why she had waited until now to oust him in the first place. She didn't want to tarnish his image or his legacy by overtly usurping him.

Les thought on the prospect. Mary Ellen was right. He had had a good run and quite frankly, he was sick of the Martin family politics. He had known some Martin would come gunning for his job sooner or later and he was sick of always looking over his shoulder. Heck, Mary Ellen probably already had enough board members bought off to get rid of him anyway. Better to take the billion dollars while he could. He glanced over at the photograph again. Besides, with a billion Unified States dollars, he could buy a lot of quality clown dwarf time. "I guess so..."

* * * * *

The board meeting clipped along quite nicely for a change. Normally, the board meetings plodded along as quickly and gracefully as a one-legged frog trying to move across a garden. Instead, this meeting was so lively, in fact, that even perennial board member, Frank Upton, now a nonagenarian, was able to keep from drifting off into his usual meeting-induced afternoon coma, Mary Ellen noted with a grin.

Les and Robby's retirements were announced and their $1 billion retirement packages approved by the board, although reluctantly by some of the tighter board members. After all, a billion dollars was a one with a hell of a lot of zeroes after it, and we are talking M-Mart here, the king of the discounters.

Mary Ellen was voted in as interim CEO and Chairman of the Board until the annual stockholder meeting could make her promotions permanent. Sylvia was, with some initial hesitation, voted in as the interim President of the company, after ringing endorsements by Mary Ellen, Les and Robby.

About two-thirds of the board had silly, ecstatic grins on their faces like kids who just found out that they were going to go to the Harvest Festival at their elementary school.

The other third had shocked looks on their faces, knowing they would be among Mary Ellen and Sylvia's first corporate casualties.

"This is fabulous," Frank said. Then he looked over at Les. "No offense, Les, you've done a great job, but I'm glad to see a Martin as CEO again. I think that's what Sam would've wanted." Then he turned to Mary Ellen. "And deep down I always knew it would be you, Mary Ellen. I remember when you were born. You had a set of lungs on you. You could scream so loud, I thought you would shatter the windows."

Sylvia grinned inwardly. *She still can.*

"Growing up," Frank continued with the surprising, almost shocking, frank attitude that only comes with advanced age. "I could tell you had more balls and ambition than any of those pansy Martin men. Damned trust funds castrated the lot of them.

"Present company excluded, of course." Frank, smiling slightly, glanced over at Robby and Jim Martin, one of Robby's nephews and Mary Ellen's cousin. "Sam's money, God rest his soul, turned them into a bunch of eunuchs. You, Mary Ellen, are the perfect Martin to carry on Sam's dream."

"Why, thank you, Frank," Mary Ellen said, blushing slightly.

"You're welcome," Frank said. "Just don't let your son turn out the way most of Sam's grandsons and great grandsons have: spoiled and worthless, okay?"

"No worries. Sammy is growing up quite nicely, thank you very much." Mary Ellen decided to change the subject before Frank spiraled out of control into one of his infamous tirades about some random subject like communists and cheese puffs or 'Happy Holidays' versus 'Merry Christmas'. "As my first act as Chairman and CEO, I would like to propose a name change to better reflect that M-Mart is now much, much more than discount box retail stores. As we all know, M-Mart is now fuel, real estate, software, unions..." Mary Ellen looked over at Sylvia with a chuckle. "Oops, that business went bankrupt, didn't it, Sylvia? Quite alright, don't worry, none of us blames you for that, right?"

The group chuckled uneasily. True enough, they all knew Mary Ellen and Sylvia intentionally bankrupted M-Union but they all, including Rob and Les, who had just been blindsided, were curious and scared. What Mary Ellen might want to call M-Mart Stores, Inc. moving forward?

"As I was saying, M-Mart is so much more than retail stores. We own a country, for pity sake. Therefore, I propose we rename M-Mart Stores, Inc. to M-pire, Inc. to reflect the diverse industries and entities that comprise M-Mart. M-Mart is truly the greatest corporate empire that ever existed and our name should reflect it. Do I have a second?"

After a few uncomfortable seconds of silence as the board considered the idea, Sylvia said cautiously, "I'll second it."

"Technically, you're not a board member...yet, anyway," Les said matter-of-factly.

Robby considered the statement for a moment. "Good point. M-pire sounds good to me. I'll second it then."

Les cleared his throat. "Uh... Technically, you're not a board member...anymore, anyway."

"Jesus," Frank scowled. "Neither are you, Les, so please shut your damned pie hole. I'll second it then. Does everyone agree that I am a board member?"

"Sure, Frank, you've been a board member since before Franklin discovered electricity," Robby said.

Frank grabbed his suit jacket lapels and did his best 'Honest Abe' expression. "Damn straight. I'm one of the founding fathers."

"Maybe they should put your likeness on Mt. Rushmore?" Les offered.

"I remember when Mt. Rushmore was carved..." Frank pondered.

That brought roaring, tension-breaking laughter from the board.

"Lovely, Frank," Mary Ellen said. "But we have a motion up for vote..."

Chapter 24

Mary Ellen Martin and Sylvia Byrne entered the kitchen of the 7,400 square foot Martinville, Alabama home they had bought a few months ago when they returned from China. It was officially bought in Mary Ellen's name, of course, and Sylvia had bought a similar home, though only 4,800 square foot, in the same subdivision just a couple of streets over. Though times had changed in the last couple of decades and most of the M-Mart insiders knew (or at least suspected) Mary Ellen was at least a bi-curious if not a full-blown lesbian, it would still be uncomfortable from a business standpoint for M-Mart to have an openly lesbian CEO, so she and Sylvia kept up a front of just being extremely close business partners. Mary Ellen's public intimate friendship with Chinese president Tao Jhuns and sealing the M-Wan deal had done wonders to hide Mary Ellen and Sylvia's true relationship from the outside public.

It was 4:47 AM, according to the kitchen video wall, Mary Ellen noted. Currently 49 degrees with an expected high of 76 degrees. Some sponge metal band or some such thing blared throughout the kitchen, obnoxious heavy electric guitar and vocals from a guy who sounded like he drank battery acid regularly, and the walls and floor reverberated. Even though school didn't start for three hours, Sammy was already up, making himself a bowl of cereal, his usual high-fiber cereal that tasted like tree bark and twigs to Mary Ellen. Sammy was on a 'my body is a temple' health kick lately. Mary Ellen was grateful. At least he wasn't doing drugs. To the best of her knowledge, he wasn't, anyway. You could never be 100% positive with teens these days, though the three times she collected and turned in his urine - when he forgot to flush - to M-pire Human Resources, all tested clean.

Since Mary Ellen and Sylvia always arrived at work by 5:45 AM and often worked as late as 9:00 PM or 10:00 PM, the early morning was often the only time Mary Ellen saw her son. It wasn't an ideal solution but at least they carved out a little time each day to see each other. They had been doing it since Sammy had started middle school some six years ago and now it was a comfortable routine.

"Kara, my usual music, please," Mary Ellen said. The music instantly changed to Beethoven's Symphony No. 6 in F Major as it did on most weekday mornings around 4:50 AM, give or take about five minutes, and the volume dropped by approximately twenty decibels. Kara was the name of the 'household environment system,' a fancy name for the computer that monitored all of the home's functions. Kara was short for Kara Zor-El, better known as Supergirl to comic book collecting masses. Growing up, Mary Ellen couldn't stand playing with dolls like Barbie or Bratz, pretending to be mommy, changing diapers. That was so weak and docile. Mary Ellen read Supergirl comics instead and even found a doll or two and pretended to beat up big, bad villains. She had a fondness for the name Kara ever since, so it only seemed natural to name their home's computer after the comic book hero.

Mary Ellen walked up to Sammy and kissed him on the forehead. "Good morning, sweetie."

"Good morning, mom." Sammy absently looked up from his cereal preparation and gave Mary Ellen a one-armed hug. "Good morning, Sylv."

"Hey, Champ," Sylvia said. "How are you doing this morning?"

"Fine," Sammy said, crunching on his cereal.

Mary Ellen poured cups of coffee for herself and Sylvia. Sammy had liked coffee too, before his health kick. Now coffee was evil. They had a couple of arguments about it

Immaculate Deception

before Sammy had given up trying to save her from the dangers of caffeine. "So, honey, are you ready for your finals?"

"I'm good on Calculus, Advanced Science and English Literature, but Accounting is kinda kicking my butt," Sammy said in a disenchanted tone.

Though Sammy was only sixteen, he was a senior at high school having skipped Kindergarten and Fourth grade, thanks to Mary Ellen's pushing and expensive tutoring. He was now mainly in Advanced Placement and College Prep courses. It was one of Mary Ellen's greatest sources of pride that Sammy had already been accepted at the University of Alabama where he would go to the Sam M. Martin School of Business, named after Sammy's great-grandfather. She didn't even have to give the school a huge donation. He had earned the college admission solely based on his grades.

"So, Champ, what's the problem with Accounting?" Sylvia asked.

"I don't know. I just don't get it. I don't like statistics," Sammy said, frustrated. "Credits, debits, it just doesn't make sense."

"You better learn to like it. As CEO of M-pire I use Accounting and numbers all day long, and you will too when you take over, eventually," Mary Ellen said indifferently.

"Mom...do we have to do this again?" Sam asked. "I know you both want me to be CEO of M-pire, God Emperor of the Universe or whatever, but I don't know if I want to do that. I might want to be a doctor or maybe work with Habitat for Humanity or the Peace Corps or the Red Cross..."

"Honey, you are destined for greatness," Mary Ellen cut him off. She really hated it when he pulled his tree hugging 'save the planet' crap. He spent a lot of time reading New Age philosophy garbage by the likes of Ram Dass, Maharishi Mahesh Yogi, H.R. Puffinstuff, Timothy Leary and Wayne Dyer. It all started about six months ago when he decided to write a book report on John Lennon for school, and ever since he had been studying Eastern Religions like Taoism and listening to the Beatles' White Album and tantric music. Maybe he was doing drugs. Ironically, Sammy probably didn't even know what an album was since they went the way of the dodo three decades earlier.

"Yes, Mom, I know, but I don't know if I want to be heir to my great-grandfather's dynasty. Let one of the other great-grandkids have the job. I don't know if I even want to go to college right now. I thought of maybe joining the Peace Corps and going to Africa and helping out with the AIDS epidemic. Did you know…"

Sylvia noticed Mary Ellen's face turning a deepening red and stepped in. "Hey, Champ, we only want the best for you, right? We've sent you to the best schools, got you the best tutors, set you up in Boy Scouts, helped you earn your Eagle Scout just like your great-grandpa, got you piano lessons, everything so you can be the best person possible…"

"I know, I know, and I appreciate that but…" Sammy cut in.

Sylvia rejoined, "Sammy, we didn't do that for you to build low-income housing in the inner city or dig wells in Nigeria. Let someone else do that. You have such great potential for much bigger things. Why not run M-pire and donate millions of dollies, maybe even billions of dollies, to charity? Wouldn't that be a better use of your time than teaching Sex Ed in the Congo?"

"How about one of my cousins runs M-pire and donate to charity and I go to the Congo?" Sammy shot back.

"Because you will only get one shot to run M-pire. If someone else becomes CEO, you may never get the chance," Mary Ellen said. "You're destined for greatness on so many levels, and not just because you're Sam Martin's great-grandson. Enough of this argument! You will go to the University of Alabama and get your MBA and then you will join us at M-pire…"

"You can't make me, mom," Sammy retorted angrily.

"Really?" Mary Ellen snapped back harshly. "I'm the CEO of the greatest corporation in history. I've negotiated buyouts of multi-billion dollar companies. I've even run a country. I think I can get a boy to go to college."

"But that's not fair..." Sammy said, a mix of rage and disenchantment on his face.

"Listen, honey," Mary Ellen's tone softened. "I know you want to help, but Sylvia is right. You can help more people here as CEO of M-pire than by going to the Congo and demonstrating how to put condoms on broomsticks. I've worked too hard on you for that. You were not some unplanned pregnancy..."

"I know, I know," Sammy said, exacerbated. He had heard the story a thousand times. Every time he had asked who his father was, his mother went into the story of his birth. She had gone to some place in Toledo, Ohio and had a special donor's sperm; at great pain and expense, she always made a point of mentioning.

She always evaded telling him who his father was, simply stating that he was a great historical figure and that he was long dead. Sammy's mother said she had refused to tell him because she didn't want the information to 'change his life path,' whatever that meant. She had also said she had left instructions to disclose his father's identity at some point in the future. When, he didn't know. She was never clear on that either. Perhaps upon her death or when he turned thirty-five. She and the lawyer were the only ones who knew. Sammy didn't even know which lawyer it was. He had inquired with all of his mother's normal stable of lawyers and none of them knew anything, or at least they gave that impression. Of course, lawyers, the ones on TV anyway, made their living by knowing how to lie convincingly, so Sammy had no idea if she picked some other lawyer to keep his father a secret or not.

"Listen, we have to get to work," Mary Ellen said softly, moving over to Sammy, leaning over and giving him a one-arm hug as he continued eating his cereal. "I'm sorry we argued. You have a big day today, and I want you to do well, okay? Now, college and M-pire aren't up for debate..."

"Yes, they are. It's my life..." Sammy said bitterly.

"But...," Mary Ellen calmly continued. "Perhaps we could arrange taking a few months off, say starting college next spring instead of this fall, so you travel and pursue some humanitarian efforts. How's that? Maybe you could build a few homes for Habitat for Humanity or maybe go on a missionary trip with the church. What do you think? Now, if you do, I'll want a promise that you will go to the University of Alabama in the spring." Mary Ellen turned to Sylvia. "Honey, what do you think of the idea?"

"That seems like a fair compromise to me," Sylvia said reassuringly.

"Whatever...I'll have to think about it," Sammy said dejectedly. It sounded like another eighty years of prison to him. Just what he wanted. Fourteen-hour workdays plus half of his weekends spent trying to drive M-pire's growth to keep the stock price on the rise. Like anybody, other than his mother and Sylvia and the stockholders, gave a crap about it anyway. What was his mother's tombstone going to say? Here lies Mary Ellen Martin, a crappy mother but great CEO, under her reign the stock price shot up 412%. All hail Mary Ellen Martin. Rest in peace. Now, take a day off already and try not to take over heaven. Was he ever going to be free of his mother's 'great plan' for him? He felt like his Aikido Sensei was less demanding of him.

*****

Later that day, after acing all of his finals, Sammy was riding to the local Taco Bell for an afternoon snack with his best friend Pete, Pete's younger brother Andy, and Jim. Sammy, Pete and Jim shared several classes in high school and Andy and Sammy were the same age so the group was oddly cohesive. Though he was sixteen, Sammy relied on the rest of the group for rides because his mother was too damned busy to take him down to the Department of Driver Services and sign the form to give her consent for him to get a Learner's Permit. He was the only senior in high school that couldn't drive, except for an adopted Chinese girl named Lily, a total brainiac who was only twelve but taking several college-level courses. It was quite a source of embarrassment for him.

The only thing worse than being chauffeured around by his friends was being chauffeured around by the family chauffeur, which, of course, was his mother's solution. It was bad enough that the Martins had more money than God. It was even worse that most of the parents of Sammy's classmates were mid-level management for M-pire or some other company who relied on selling to M-pire for its existence. Most of the kids at Sammy's high school treated him like a pariah, scared to deal with him on any level for fear he might get their parents fired or something.

Unfortunately, he had done that to himself. He got his mother to fire Kelly Horton's father when she had called Sammy a Martian, but that was a long time ago. He was only six at the time and was careful about going to his mother ever since, but some things the community would never forgive, or, at least, never forget. Driving around with a chauffeur would just alienate the school kids even more, so he absolutely refused to do it. Luckily, Pete and Jim were good about driving him places. He believed filling up their cars whenever they were running low on fuel probably had something to do with their generosity, but Sammy didn't mind.

"Pete, what the hell do I do?" Sammy said as Pete drove his indigo 2013 Toyota Matrix into the Taco Bell parking lot.

Pete, being the oldest in the group by three months, was their de facto leader and their advisor for anything requiring life experience. "I don't know, dude. Your mom has got you by the cajones pretty good."

"What?!?!" Jim chimed in. "Being the CEO of M-pire sounds cool to me. My parents want me to be a freaking lawyer. They want me to be an ambulance chaser, just like them." Andy was often kidded about his parent's tacky TV commercials that ran incessantly during daytime soap operas.

"Been in a car accident?" Andy mimicked in a cheesy announcer's voice. "We fight for your rights and you deserve the best. We're the best. Call now!!!"

"Thanks, Buttmunch." Jim ruffled Andy's hair as he tried in vain to fend him off.

A few minutes later, the gang was sitting at a table, munching on tacos and burritos.

"Come on, guys, this is serious," Sammy said, exasperated. "My mother wants to sentence me to eighty years in corporate hell. I've got to do something. I don't want to be a freaking suit and get up at four in the morning every day for the rest of my life."

"It's simple enough," Pete said. "Refuse."

"Yeah, right," Sammy shot back. "I can't do that. She'll nag me until I cave in or go insane."

"Sure enough, dude," Jim agreed. "Your mom makes my mom seem like a wimp. You stand up to her and she'll pop your balls like zits."

"Just great, Jim," Sammy replied. "Yes, everyone knows my mother can make Darth Vader look like the Easter Bunny. Any ideas that might actually help me out here?"

"I know... bail." Andy offered, and then his face changed as if he just had an epiphany. "Hey, let's all bail."

"Where the hell could I bail where my mother wouldn't find me?" Sammy asked, irritated.

"Wait," Pete said. "My little bro has a point. Why not? You've got a trillion dollie trust fund, right?"

"250 million, actually," Sammy corrected uncomfortably. He hated talking money with his friends. His family was easily worth a thousand times that of any of his friends. The whole concept kind of freaked him out.

"Whatever," Pete continued. "You have a current passport, right?"

"Yeah, so?" Sammy said. Pete knew they all did. All of their families were rich enough to go on frequent international trips.

"Cool," Pete replied. "Tomorrow morning, go down to the bank, grab a million or two, fly down to the Bahamas or better yet, Switzerland and open up one of those super secret, numbers only accounts and then disappear to one of those funky places that you've had a wild hair up your ass to go to lately. Africa, Nepal, whatever."

Sammy thought on the prospect. Most of his trust was locked up until he was thirty-five, but not all of it. He had full access to fifteen million dollies of it at least, he was pretty sure. His mother had given him a debit card with seemingly limitless funds instead of an allowance so he never had to touch his trust fund. The guys' plan just might work.

"Hey, dude, I want to go with you," Andy said.

Pete gave his brother an annoyed look. "We can't bail. Mom and dad will freak."

"Really?" Andy countered. "Dad is gone on business trips three weeks a month and Mom is working twelve hour days trying to be a clone of Sammy's mom. When is the last time they did anything with us other than grocery shopping or watching TV? When was the last time we had dinner as a family? Three weeks ago? Hell, they probably wouldn't even notice we were gone for a week."

"That's not fair," Pete said. "Their busting their asses for us."

"I know, bro. I'm not saying bail forever. I need to finish school. Just a summer trip to help our buddy Sammy get settled. We could leave a note. We went on that summer camp cruise a couple of years ago, right, guys?" Andy looked to Sammy and Jim. "We can pull this off."

"That's it!" Jim said excitedly. "Remember that

Mediterranean cruise to check out the ancient wonders I told you guys about? The one that goes to Athens, Santorini and Rhodes? It's a three-week deal in August. I already have my parents talked in to it."

"That's perfect," Pete agreed. "We get all of our parents to send us on that. At the end of the cruise, whoever wants to bail with Sammy, instead of flying home, takes a train to Zurich where he can set up a bank account and then disappear. You'll already be halfway to Africa or Nepal before anyone's parents are the wiser."

Sammy's face crinkled in concentration. "Hmmm… This might just work…"

* * * * *

Nine weeks later, a sealed letter was given to the ship's captain with instructions to give it to Sammy's mother if she inquired about him. She did, about thirty-seven minutes after she realized Sammy wasn't on his flight back to Martinville. The captain opened the latter and faxed it to her. It read:

>Dear Mom & Silv,
>I hope I haven't worried you but I've decided to extend my trip. I am going to Africa to help AIDS victims. I wish I didn't have to sneak away like this, but you both were ignoring my wishes for my future. I may go to college someday and I may even run M-pire one day but Mom, I'm not simply an extension of you like another arm or something. I am my own person and I need to decide what I want to do with my life, not you.
>I love you both. I'll be in touch.
>Sammy

Sylvia handed back the letter. "Wow. He must have been planning this for a while. I didn't realize he was so unhappy with the idea of going to college. I knew he didn't like it much, but I thought he would still do it. What should we do? Track him down or give him space?"

Mary Ellen, sobbing, gave Sylvia a deep hug, burying her face in Sylvia's neck. "I don't know. My baby's run away." Her mind raced with the implications. Her son, genetically bred to be the perfect man, the perfect Martin, meant for some future greatness, perhaps the leader of a future global power, was gone. What did it mean? What should she do? What could she do? She had no earthly idea.

She had a heartsick burning sensation in the pit of her stomach at the loss of her son, or perhaps, that was just combo plate #3 from Humberto's she had had for dinner. She had no earthly idea about that either. Her son had never dared run away before. She didn't know what she was supposed to feel like.

Chapter 25

News Items from 2018-2021

From the Roderickstan Times:

> Supreme Court Bans All Traditional Religions
> STUD Becomes Roderickstan's Official Religion

Washington, DC – August 26, 2018 - Just before Labor Day, the unofficial start of the holiday season for the nation's retailers, the Supreme Court has outlawed all forms of traditional religion including all forms of Christianity (Catholic, Protestant, Methodist, Mormon, etc.), Judaism, Muslim, Buddhism, etc. and have mandated that only one religion, the one true religion of Spiritual Transcendence of the Ultimate Dolly (or STUD) is legal. The major reason cited for the religious ban was the documented history of violence and intolerance of all organized religions for other organized religions.

Effective immediately, all banned religious property is to be turned into the nearest place of worship. The ban is far-reaching. Everything from religious works like the Holy Bible, the Koran, and Dianetics to novels like Charles Dickens' A Christmas Carol, J.R.R. Tolkien's The Lord of the Rings and C.S. Lewis' The Chronicles of Narnia (Gandalf and Aslan are said to be Jesus figures) to movies like Rudolph the Red-nosed Reindeer and It's a Wonderful Life are now outlawed. A list of banned property (80,000+

items) is listed on page A10-A47 and will also be made available at all places of worship.

All property in Roderickstan owned by religious organizations, including land, buildings (churches, mosques, synagogues, etc.) and monies are to be seized and given to the newly-formed STUD Operational League (SOL). All religious figures (pastors, rabbis, bishops, etc.) will be given the option to apply to the SOL to become a New Religion Advocate (NRA), to renounce their religion and find a non-religious vocation, to leave the country by September 1st, 2018, or to be executed.

It was mandated that anyone found to be worshiping any other religion could have all of their assets seized by the government, be exiled from the country and/or be imprisoned for a minimum of 20 years.

STUD is the religion that has been sweeping the nation ever since our Lady and Protector Dolly Roderick performed miracles and saved our great nation from the devastating effects of Mayageddon on December 21, 2012 (12/21/12). Our Lady and Protector Dolly Roderick can now be addressed only as Our Lady and Protector, the Dolly Mama, or Hot Rod.

All current religious holidays like Christmas, Hanukah, and Ramadan are banned. Instead, STUD worships Our Lady and Protector's birthday, the vernal and autumn equinoxes and the summer and winter solstices. The biggest holiday of the year will be the winter solstice celebration as it is the anniversary of Our Lady and Protector's miracles and her ascension to godhood in the aftermath of Mayageddon.

Matt Freman, spokesperson for Dollie General, the nation's largest deep discounter (thirty percent of all merchandise is still one dollie or less!) said, "This is a devastating blow to the retail market. The cost to move all religious items to the Unified States of America, England and other English-speaking countries will probably cost our company a billion dollies or more. The cost to retail industry as a whole could easily top a trillion dollies. The government could've given us a year to unload this garbage...err, quality merchandise so we wouldn't have to move it."

Former Rabbi Yusef Goldstein said, "I look forward to becoming an NRA. The SOL offered me triple my current pay. I talked with Yahweh and he said he couldn't match that offer and agreed that I should go with the best offer. He wished me all the best. He's a good Lord, you know."

* * * * *

M-pire Becomes the Butt of Jokes

Martinville, Miss. – September 5, 2018 - Less than three months after the official name change of M-Mart Stores, Inc. to M-pire, Inc., the new company name has become the butt of jokes on late night talk shows. After an internal e-mail by a disgruntled middle management employee dubbing the corporation "M-pile" was intercepted by M-pire's internet security division and the employee was terminated, the former employee quickly leaked his termination and the new derogatory slang term to the media.

The Late Show host Dave Chappelle quipped, "M-pile is fucking right. Every time this nigger walks in an M-mart, its piles of crap here and piles of crap there...crap, crap, crap...M-pile is right, the store is one giant pile of crap.

"M-pire? Yeah, it's the biggest corporation in the

world. So what? Shit, the Martins need to get over their damned selves, swallowing up fifty companies a year and all. Pretty soon they will be only company in the world. Hell, why not M-planet or M-axy? How 'bout M-iverse? Yeah, that's it. Then the CEO could be 'goddess of the universe.' Oh, wait, that's already taken by Dolly Roderick, ain't it? Hunh..."

According to an M-pire executive speaking on condition of anonymity for fear of being terminated, "The name change from M-Mart Stores, Inc. to M-pire, Inc. was simply meant to reflect the corporation's growing diversity of business enterprises. Perhaps we should have gone with M-prise or M-corp instead."

* * * * *

First Class Stamp Tops Δ3 for North American Delivery
RMS Now Closed Three Days A Week to Save Money

Washington, DC – June 18, 2019 - The Roderickstan Mail Service (RMS) annouced yesterday the new rate for a first class stamp to anywhere within Roderickstan will be Δ2.48, effective July 5, 2019. In addition, a North American first class stamp used for delivery to the Unified States of America and Canada will top Δ3 for the first time at Δ3.16.

A spokesperson for the RMS cited rising the price of crude oil (yesterday's price: Δ614.38 per barrel) and proliferation of alternative mail options such as e-mail, i-mail, e-cams, imessaging, o-mail, spam, bacn, blogs, and satellite phone text messaging that were causing traditional mail to be less popular and cutting into RMS profits.

Though Roderickstan passed laws in 2011 to

require all new vehicles produced after 2014 to operate using hydrogen, most 2014 and older model vehicles still operate using gasoline, ethanol or hybrid gasoline/electric technology. Most of the RMS fleet of vehicles (residential and commercial mail trucks and eighteen-wheeler semi-tractor/trailers) are ten to fifteen years old and still use very expensive gasoline (yesterday's national average: Δ16.74 per gallon). Part of the reason for the rate increases, the RMS spokesperson noted, was to start retiring the current fleet of trucks and begin replacing them with new hydrogen vehicles.

The RMS also announced that all Mail Stations will be closed and there will be no mail delivery on Wednesdays and the weekends (Saturday and Sunday) as a cost-cutting measure. The move will save an estimated Δ6.8 billion annually by reducing the number of days vehicles are running. The RMS also stated that its workforce will be reduced by 15% by year-end, mainly through attrition. Most of the remaining employees will shift to a 4-day, 10-hour shift workweek.

"Wow, that's great," Colby Meyers, a Washington, DC, resident said upon hearing the news. "I really look forward to getting bills and junk mail two less days a week. All of the fun stuff like blow-up dolls and battery-operated 'toys' come in discreet packaging from FedEx and UPS anyway."

* * * * *

Seen on CNN.com:

Post-Delivery Abortions Legalized
Supreme Court Rules to Change Murder to
Neutralization

Washington, DC – April 14, 2021 – The Supreme Court ruled yesterday six to three in the landmark case of Smith v. Wesson to acquit Cletus Smith, an ethnically challenged Alabama man of killing his daughter, Shirniqua Smith Wesson for marrying a pigment-challenged man, greatly extending the rights given to parents to abort their children. The opinion, dated Friday, April 13, 2021, now gives either parent the legal right to abort (or neutralize) their children at any point during the child's lifetime, whether they are in the womb or they are sixty years old. Associate Justice Beatrice "Butch" Cassidy argued that since Roe v. Wade allowed a woman to neutralize her child pre-birth thereby affecting the child's destiny (or lack thereof) that it simply made sense to continue those parental rights for the child's entire lifetime and to extend them to both parents. The Supreme Court coined the term Post-Delivery Abortion (or PDA) for the now legal act.

Along similar lines, in a move pushed by the Roderick administration to ease the public's perception of the growing crime rate in most of the nation's metropolitan areas, the Supreme Court also voted six to three to change the legal terms of "murder" and "homicide" to a kinder term of "neutralization." The outrageously sexist term "manslaughter" has also been changed to the kinder term "inadvertent neutralization."

Legal analysts, by and large, applauded the decision. "I think it's a great idea," said lawyer Ima Slaezbohl. "Not only is 'inadvertent neutralization' a more placid, more politically correct idiom, most middling populace won't comprehend the verbiage, thereby escalating our firm's pecuniary affluence. Consider our maxim: 'Our client's ignorance is our lobster and butter'."

*****

Lyrics from the official "reworking" of a banned traditional Christmas carol for the Dolly Mama:

White Solstice
(sung to the banned tune of White Christmas)

I'm dreaming of a white Solstice

Just like the ones I used to know

Where the Mother Goddess preaches

And she teaches of grand Winter Solstice Festivals covered with snow

I'm dreaming of a white Solstice

With every Solstice card I write

May your days be merry and bright

And may all your Winter Solstice Festivals be white
(repeat chorus)

Chapter 26

2022

Roderickstan Castle was 352 feet tall, a full sixty feet taller than the former seat of power, Washington DC's United States Capitol building. It rested on Roderick Park, once known as Silver Point County Park or Atlantic Beach, New York. Dolly's new seat of power was less than four miles south of JFK airport on the beach overlooking the Atlantic Ocean, making it a convenient location for traveling dignitaries. In addition to replacing the United States Capitol building, Roderickstan Castle was Dolly's replacement for the White House.

Though it was called Roderickstan Castle, it wasn't really a castle at all. Shortly after STUD had become full-fledged religion, Dolly announced a contest to design a new seat of power for her, her government, and her new religion, offering Δ1 million as the prize. The official tally had the number of entrants at 58,749. A committee then narrowed the number of finalists to twenty-five. Dolly, with some help from her inner circle, came up with the winner. Contrary to what one might expect for such an important project, the winner wasn't a giant world-famous architect firm, nor some bold visionary, a modern-day Frank Lloyd Wright or Leonardo di Vinci, or even someone with any professional drafting experience. The winner was little Rose Lauren Allison, a third grader from a town in Kentucky called Cut and Shoot, population 327.

The best way to describe little Rose's entry would be to imagine what you might get if you mated a castle from any number of Disney animated films with the Statue of Liberty. The end result, when the most prestigious architect firm Dolly could buy was done with it, was a 352-foot skyscraper with a façade of almost lawsuit-worthy similarity to Cinderella's Castle in Walt Disney World in Florida.

Dolly had loved Disney animated films like Fantasia and Cinderella as a child so it seemed like a truly splendid idea. Dolly wasn't worried about lawsuits, of course. Besides, she would win any lawsuit by saying the government (she was the government, after all) used the design for the 'greater good of the people' thus eminent domain took precedence. It's good to be the Goddess! What would Disney do anyway, get pissed off, dismantle Disney World piece by piece and move it to the Bahamas?

The feature that made Roderickstan Castle really stand out was the exact replica of the Statue of Liberty that stood on one of the Castle's turrets. The statue, known as the Statue of Deity, differed from the original in two key aspects. First, it was made of stainless steel which gave it a shiny silver appearance and, second, the face was changed to resemble Dolly.

The GodPod, as Roderickstan Castle was dubbed by the media, was officially over four hundred feet tall. The beach had been built up almost sixty feet at the builder's suggestion who feared global warming might cause the first couple of floors to be submerged by the Atlantic ocean in the next half century. The GodPod's parking structure was built on the flat beach, went up four levels, then the bottom three levels were surrounded by thousands of tons of dirt that tapered to create the mound that became the foundation of the GodPod. The parking structure's entrance was placed on the fourth level, situated at the back of the castle. The façade of the top level of the parking structure seamlessly matched the rest of Roderickstan Castle.

The White House had been turned into a museum and, at Δ35 for adults and Δ17.50 for children and seniors, made quite a tidy profit. The "Dine with George Washington in the White House" tour was especially popular. For Δ150 per person, guests get to eat with a George Washington impersonator, dressed in his dashing Continental Army General's uniform, in the State Dining Room using the state china and silverware Dolly had returned to the White House after she became President of the United States. The meal consisted of a seven-course dinner with 1790's period favorites like calves' head (turtle fashion), tongue pie, and hoe cakes.

Dolly was quite proud of herself for thinking of a way to get the White House to help pay for its replacement. Estimates showed revenues from the White House and Roderickstan Castle tours would pay for the Roderickstan Castle in less than fourteen years, even taking into account staffing and routine maintenance.

Her Holiness Dolly Roderick, the Dolly Mama, Lady and Protector of the great nation of Roderickstan sat at her workstation in the opulent Elliptical Office of Roderickstan Castle, which was situated some three-hundred feet up, just a couple of floors below the southeast laser turret, facing the ocean. On a holographic computer screen projecting out of the floor that appeared to be floating about ten feet in front of her in the middle of the room, she was reading USA Today to get an objective view of the goings-on of the world. A decade ago she would have read the New York Times or sometimes the Washington Post, but after she declared martial law, one of the first things she did was lockdown every newspaper and magazine and censor out any negative content about her, her government or her religion. Most magazines and nationwide newspapers, including USA Today, had pulled up roots and moved to the Unified States of America within days of Muller announcing the secession. Los Angeles was now considered the publishing capital of the western hemisphere, wresting the honor from New York.

It was just one of the many sources of irritation about the whole Roderickstan/Unified States of America debacle. She had almost lost the entire U.S. stock market when the CEOs of the New York Stock Exchange, NASDAQ, the Chicago Stock

Exchange and the Chicago Mercantile Exchange banded together and threatened to move to San Francisco if she and the government didn't stop meddling in their businesses. Dolly knew, with current satellite technology and petabyte flash dot storage, that the entire NYSE could probably be run from the average handheld computer, much less a desktop or laptop computer, so she caved in to the CEOs demands. The stock market was just one of dozens of industries that had threatened to pull out over government interference.

"Can you fucking believe this?" She asked harshly without looking at the other person in the room.

Ava stepped up close behind Dolly's chair and scanned the computer image in the middle of the room, trying to find the source of Dolly's irritation. Ava, now forty-one years old, was still gorgeous, especially now that she could wear more flattering clothes than her old black Secret Service suits. Today, she wore a businesslike navy jacket, skirt and shoes with a powder blue blouse unbuttoned just enough to reveal her delightful cleavage, her blonde hair flowed down her back to just past her shoulder blades. She was now Dolly's closest confidant and her official Grand Inquisitor, previously called the Chief of Staff in the United States of America days, since the tragic death of Dolly's former number one confidant Helen Moore, who died tragically in 2019 after losing a long battle with cervical cancer.

While Ava was glad to be Dolly's favorite finally after being her side distraction for over a dozen years, she still missed Helen terribly. Helen had been her closest confidant and lover as well as Dolly's. Up until Helen's death, Ava loved Dolly deeply but felt she couldn't she share intimate details of her life with Dolly. Dolly was the Dolly Mama, after all. So Ava had shared those intimacies with Helen, who was more than willing to take her into her world, acting as a mentor, friend, and lover to her. When Helen first found out she had cancer, some four years before her death, she took Ava under her wing, grooming Ava to eventually take her place as Dolly's right hand.

Last year, Ava had taken a side lover, a young junior staffer named Kaylyn. Ava mentored her as Helen had mentored her to 'pay it forward' as the saying went but being a mentor just wasn't the same as being a mentee (or is it mento?). Ava still missed Helen and her counsel, her love, her kindness, her brilliant political mind.

"What is it, Hot Rod?" Ava asked, standing behind Dolly, gazing at the holographic image, skimming the USA Today article on the screen.

"Look at this crap," Dolly said, disgusted, her bleached blonde hair done up in a bun designed to hold her ruby and diamond-encrusted platinum crown with a massive 400-carat ruby in its center in place. "Mary Ellen Martin is listed as the number one most powerful woman in the business world according to Fortune magazine. No surprise there, right? She has been ever since she became CEO of M-pire half a decade ago, but look at this list of the most powerful women in the world by Forbes.com..."

Dolly scrolled the image down to reveal:

Forbes Top 50 Most Powerful Women in the World

Rank* Name   Occupation   Country
1 (1) Dolly Roderick President/Deity   Roderickstan
2 (5) Mary Ellen Martin CEO, M-pire   Roderickstan
                     President M-Wan
3 (2) Haup Singh   Vice Premier   China
4 (7) J.K. Rowling   Writer   England
5 (6) Oprah Winfrey Chairman, Harpo   Roderickstan
50 (#) Britney Spears CEO, Viacom   USA

* Number in parentheses represents previous year's rank.
\# Previously unranked

"Yes, you're number one again. That's great," Ava said, bending over, giving Dolly a light kiss plus an opportunity to view her large hanging braless breasts. She knew Dolly always enjoyed the view.

To Ava's surprise, Dolly didn't glance at her breasts. She must be really pissed off. "That's not the point," Dolly said. "Mary Ellen jumped three spots, three fucking spots, to number two! I don't know how the fuck they decide these rankings…probably some bullshit polling of their minimum wage writing staff or some such thing."

"Maybe they have some sort of point system like tennis or NASCAR does," Ava offered with a chuckle.

"Right," Dolly said tersely, obviously not amused. "If it is, then I'm at a thousand points and Mary Ellen is at 999 and gaining fast. That scheming little cunt has been a thorn in my side ever since I walked in on her slobbering on my late fuckwit husband's cock what, Jesus…er, Goddess, twenty years ago? I'm sick of her and M-pile. She needs to be taught a lesson in real power and be taken down a notch or two. Gather the team. We need to do a 3M."

Chapter 27

A 3M (short for Mind Meld Meeting, taken from the term from the old Star Trek TV series where two people joined minds) meant using special computer goggles nicknamed BCD's, and plugging them into a meld computer interface with one or more people similarly plugged in to facilitate the sharing of ideas or brainstorming. BCD stood for Birth Control Device because anyone wearing them looked so dorky they would never get laid. The term was originally slang for military-issued eyeglasses for the same reason. A 3M was like brainstorming on steroids, ideas flying around tens, sometimes hundreds of times faster than the old brainstorming techniques used in the 1990's. Back then, ten people would get in a conference room and start rattling off ideas as fast as they could think of them while one to as many as three people in the group might act as scribes, scribbling notes as furiously as they could.

With a 3M, the computer software, usually the popular Patty Meld, handled all of the dictating functions, organizing everything into a neat report with ideas ranked by whatever criteria the 3M organizer wished. Best of all, thanks to advanced satellite technology, everything was wireless and participants could be thousands of miles apart and still feel as though they were conversing across a table in the same room.

Although Dolly's anger management sessions only lasted a couple of months and the therapist disappeared along with all of her records a month later and was rumored to be yet another victim of the infamous Roderick hit list, Dolly was still a creature of habit and showed surprisingly extreme loyalty considering her tendency to wild rage. Therefore, the 2021 version of "the team" was strikingly similar to the one that first helped get her elected to the presidency way back in 2008. Other than Ava replacing Helen as Dolly's Grand Inquisitor, almost everyone else remained the same, though most of the titles had changed over the years as STUD gained in popularity. Pedro Sandoval, the only man in the group and Dolly's oldest friend, was still her personal advisor. Nanny Moretti, formerly the Vice President of the United States, was now called the Demi-goddess. Babbs Baxter's position, once the Secretary of State, was now the High Priestess of Administration. Susan Thomas, the Press Secretary in the old USA, was now titled the High Priestess of Communications.

Pam Sausalito, Dolly's campaign manager in the elections of 2008 and 2012, was no longer needed in that capacity as goddesses usually didn't need to be reelected. Instead, she was rewarded with the title of Supreme High Priestess of STUD for her years of loyal service, becoming third in power in the religion after Dolly, the Dolly Mama and Cherry, the Daughter Goddess.

The only other change in "the team's" lineup was Dolly's personal public relations advisor/image consultant. Beth Anne Clausen, the previous image consultant, had died in 2016 from a heart attack due to "morbid obesity" and a prescription diet pill addiction. Her replacement was none other than child star turned drugged-out skank turned clean and sober children's author and motivation speaker Leslie Hogan. Though only thirty years old when Dolly hired her, Leslie had done a splendid job of increasing her approval rating with the ever-important 18-49 year-old demographic.

Goggles already on, Ava double-checked the setup of the Roderickstan Castle's ultra top-secret 3M room.

A figure wearing military garb materialized on the far side of the conference table. "Hello, Ms. Garbo," the Chairman of the Joint Chiefs of Staff, Marine General J. Beatrice "Beater" Jones said with her usual military stiffness. The J. stood for June but the general just liked J. For some God-awful reason the general just couldn't understand, her parents, at the prodding of her mother evidently, named her after the domestically oppressed, perfect TV mother June Cleaver and it drove her crazy with rage. She had spent her entire life trying to be the opposite of June Cleaver's "a woman's place is in the home" life and she pulled it off even beyond her own lofty expectations. Only about six percent of all active duty marines were women and less than a dozen women had reached the rank of general in the entire 346-year history of the corps, yet not only was she the top marine, she was now the top military person in all of Roderickstan. She was quite proud of that.

Ava looked up to see the general's salt and pepper flat top haircut, trying to stifle her usual cringe. Beater would probably still be homely with makeup and long hair, but still, why try to look like a man? Ick. Ava had had to do that for the secret service for over fifteen years and she hated it so much now it made her skin crawl every time she saw someone else doing it. What was the point of being a lesbian if you were going to date a woman that looked like a man? Why not just date a man in the first place? Other than the fact that most of them were arrogant, idiotic jackasses, that is. "Good afternoon, General. How is the weather at West Point today?"

"Splendid, Ms. Garbo," General Jones said. "68 degrees and clear as a bell. How did you know I was at West Point?"

"You're teaching a class on World War II Pacific Fleet Beach Assault Tactics all week from 10AM to 1PM. Just part of my job," Ava replied. "Ten minutes early as usual. We'll be starting soon."

"Fair enough," the general responded. "I'll just be working on paperwork until you call the meeting to order. These classes always get me behind on paperwork and e-mails."

About three minutes later, the next attendee, Pedro Sandoval, materialized, wearing a navy pinstriped suit with a red silk tie. Ava looked at her computer screen and noted Sandoval's physical location. "Hi Pedro. You're not really wearing a suit on the beach, are you?"

"Of course not, beautiful," Pedro said with a smile. "You just have to love the whole 'avatar' deal. I'm lounging on my balcony in a Hawaiian shirt, shorts and sandals, sipping a margarita, and everyone thinks I'm wearing a suit and tie."

"That must be nice," Ava said in a wistful tone.

"You bet. Just one of the perks of being an advisor instead of a Secretary of such and such, or I should say, a High Priest of such and such. Hey, they would let me be a High Priest, right? I wouldn't have to be a High Priestess like everyone else, would I? I mean, Doll wouldn't expect me to have a sex change, would she? I guess not," Pedro chuckled and continued. "Anyway, the point is that I can be semi-retired. I don't have to be married…excuse me, sometimes all of these bleeping new terms drive me nuts and I really miss the good ole U.S. of A., apple pie and Chevrolet, you know? Anyway, I mean 'joined' to my job and work fourteen-hour days. So, I get to be Hot Rod's on-call token guy on staff for three to six hours a day and collect seashells and shake the sand out of my trunks the rest of the time."

"That does sound great, not the trunks part," Ava said with a laugh, "but the rest of it. How are things in Key Biscayne?"

"Awful, the truth be told. Damned global warming is going to have my place underwater in the next decade or so, if I'm lucky. It's probably closer to six or seven years. I am sure of it. High tide comes in over our retaining wall and about fifteen feet into our backyard now. Fourteen years ago, when I bought the place, high tide was a foot and half below the retaining wall. The next tropical depression is going to have a foot of water in the living room. If a category three or greater hurricane hits, my house will turn into an aquarium. That's why I'm spending so much time down here now. Sally and I will only have two years, maybe three, tops before we have to sell or abandon the place."

"Abandon?" Ava said, shocked. "Didn't that place cost

you a fortune?"

"About Δ6.8 million, but I doubt I could get more than Δ1.4 million for it now, if I could get anybody to buy it at all. It's plastered all over the internet, the news and the newspapers that Florida is sinking into the ocean. Oh well. Easy come, easy go, eh?"

"I guess so." Ava shrugged. "There's always your New Zealand house to fall back on in the winters. The meeting will start in a few minutes."

"Sure thing," Pedro said. "I'll just be lounging here. Yell at me if I start snoring, okay, beautiful?"

"Of course, Pedro," Ava said with a grin.

By five minutes after three in the afternoon, the rest of the group had assembled in the 3M room and Ava clicked a button on the Patty Meld screen to notify Dolly everyone else had arrived. Dolly really hated waiting for people to arrive at her meetings and hated it even more when she started a meeting and then a straggler showed up late. She had a tendency to punish the culprit in some way by humiliating them in the meeting. Sometimes it was worse. The offender might get an assignment that required the straggler to work until midnight for weeks or even months such as setting up a fundraiser for some slimeball senator or, much worse, chairing a committee to save some stupid endangered rodent or bird like the cairina horchata, the rare Rhode Island venomous duck or some such thing. Pedro and Helen, realizing the situation wasn't good for anyone involved, came up with the current solution some seven years earlier.

Within two minutes of being buzzed, Dolly materialized, crown and all. "Good afternoon, everyone."

The group greeted her in response.

Foregoing any remaining pleasantries, Dolly dug right in. "From the i-vite Ava sent out, you've all read the Forbes and Fortune articles. Martin's ranking is totally unacceptable. I am in real danger of losing my number one spot to her, a fucking CEO of a fucking five and dime chain, for Christ...uh...for

Goddess sake! We should have done something before she became CEO. We should have done something about her before M-Mart bought Taiwan. Fuck, we should have done something before she started snapping up companies like ExxonMobil and Microsoft like my dearly departed fuckwit husband snapped up mistresses…" Dolly shook her head in disgust.

The group was hushed, reluctant to say anything. Whenever Dolly brought up her serial adulterer late husband, everyone knew she was on the verge of an explosion on the scale of Mt. Vesuvius or Santorini and nobody wanted to end up like those people, mummified alive in molten ash and all.

"Doll, M-Mart bought ExxonMobil before you came to power," Pedro corrected gently. "It was just a couple of months before you beat McGarrity in 2008." Pedro was always careful not to mention Williams. In fact, he usually acted like he never existed.

Pedro Sandoval was the one person who still called Dolly anything but "Your Holiness", "Madam Goddess", "Our Lady and Protector" or one of a dozen other highly deific titles or the approved slang "Hot Rod" in public. Dolly had shed the "Madam President" title in 2018, shortly after the Supreme Court made STUD the official religion of Roderickstan. Though this was a meeting of Dolly's confidants, the addition of General Jones to the meeting changed the group's dynamics. Roderickstan was still officially under martial law, so Dolly had the military under her thumb and General Jones was most certainly her hand-picked pet. Evidently, Ava thought Pedro must consider the general enough of an insider to drop the formalities.

Dolly's anger diffused as she considered Pedro's comment. "True, it was right before the election, wasn't it?"

Pedro glanced over at the general briefly, paused, looked back to Dolly and then said, "When you say 'done something,' are you referring to somehow removing her from M-Mart management?"

"If you mean having her disappear, Pedro, yes, that's what I mean."

"I don't think that would be prudent, Doll," Pedro said. "Martin is in bed with China pretty heavily, literally if our intel is accurate. I don't think we want to risk pissing off China and Tao Jhuns, especially if he is playing 'park the Porsche' with her."

"Their military is almost three times the size of ours," General Jones said. "They have approximately 2.1 million serving to our 800,000. They have over 12,000 tanks. Even though they are made in China, we still don't want to mess with those."

"Besides," Pedro added. "I'm sure Muller would love an excuse to ally with China to 'liberate' Roderickstan and restore the good ole U. S. of A."

"Fair enough," Dolly conceded irritably.

On the holographic image floating over the middle of the conference table, item #1 Eliminate Mary Ellen Martin faded from black to gray and was crossed out.

"So," Pedro began. "If we can't eliminate her, then we need to weaken her power, but how?"

"We could impose an excessive tariff on everything imported from M-Wan," Ava offered. "That should cut sales dramatically."

"That's a good thought, Ava," Pedro said. "It would hurt sales but there are a couple of problems. First, the retailers would simply pass the extra expense on to the consumer, which would hurt our population and hurt Doll's approval ratings. Second, only about 24% of all M-Marts are located in Roderickstan. This would probably backfire and cause our border states to lose business to cheaper retailers in das vaterland."

Das vaterland was the term Dolly's insiders occasionally used for the Unified States of America (German for 'the fatherland', a knock to its leader, Jurgin Muller) and Roderickstan was sometimes called the motherland.

"And third, it not only affects M-Marts sales but all of the other retailers as we---"

"No, no, no," Dolly snapped. "We need something that only affects M-pire or better yet, just that fucking tramp."

Item #2 Impose Excessive M-Wan Tariff faded on the holographic screen.

"I suppose invading M-Wan would be out of the question for the same reason as item #1…" General Jones pondered aloud.

"An interesting thought, but yes," Dolly said. "We couldn't even pull that off for the Middle East and oil and that was a hell of a lot more important than crappy bric-a-brac from M-Wan. That would certainly cause China to crush our invasion. The last thing we need is another embarrassing fuckup, or worse, Muller and Jhuns launching missiles at DC."

Item #3 Invade M-Wan faded from black to gray on the screen.

"I guess it's true what they say: 'if you have a tank battalion, every problem looks like Tora Bora', huh, General?" Nanny Moretti asked wistfully.

"You're one to talk, Ms. Moretti," General Jones retorted gruffly. "If it was up to you, our military strength would just be a National Guard of about 50,000 people, half of the skyscrapers in New York would have been bombed by now and we'd all be speaking Arabic! You dumba..."

"Whoa, whoa!" Pedro cut in quickly. "Ladies, we're getting off track."

At the "ladies" remark, Jones gave Sandoval a look that made him think she might rip his head off and impale it on a bayonet.

"Remember the tenants of the 3M," Ava said. "We don't criticize. There are no dumb ideas…"

"…Just dumb people," Jones muttered, shooting a glance at Moretti.

Over the next forty-five minutes, the group proceeded to

Immaculate Deception

grind through and reject items #4 through #147. Everything from nuking Martinville, Alabama, home of M-pire's headquarters, to poisoning the M-pire's CEO and making it look like foul play from a competing retailer to having Roderickstan's submarine fleet sink the M-Wan transport barges (i.e. the slow boats from China) were systematically offered up for discussion and summarily rejected for one reason or another which was usually given by Pedro Sandoval. That was his forte; being the voice of reason and shooting down other people's ideas. He was quite good at it, which is why everyone, especially Dolly, appreciated him though he often drove everyone in a meeting crazy.

"Fuck, fuck, fuck, this isn't useful," Dolly said, exasperated. "We need to focus, damn it."

"That's it!" Pedro had an epiphany. "Our focus is wrong. We keep mentioning things to do to M-pire or M-Wan when we are really trying to get rid of Mary Ellen Martin."

"But we're trying to reduce her power," Babbs Baxter said. "Isn't the easiest way to do that to reduce the power of her company?"

"Not necessarily," Pedro replied. "What if we could get her discredited and get her removed as CEO of M-pire? Then her power vanishes."

"That's brilliant, Pedro," Dolly said enthusiastically. "But how?"

"'Therein lies the rub' as they say. I'm not sure," Pedro admitted. "We need to dig up some dirt on her. A scandal of some sort---a deal she cheated on---tax evasion---massaging profit numbers---something…"

"Maybe we could even throw that fucking little bitch in jail," Dolly said.

"Maybe," Ava agreed. "We should have the CYA launch a full scale, black ops investigation on Mary Ellen and M-pire."

The CYA, which stood for the Committee of Yenta Agents (Yenta (noun): one who meddles), was one of the seemingly endless name changes caused when that fucking Austrian musclehead split America in two and then kept all of the good names including 'USA' for himself. The CYA, the former National Security Agency or NSA, was responsible for collecting intelligence, both domestically and internationally, that was considered a risk to national security, thereby the perfect group to collect dirt on Mary Ellen Martin in Roderickstan, M-Wan and China.

"Excellent," Pedro agreed. "That's the ticket."

"We have to be very careful with this," Dolly warned. "We need to do this in such a way that it looks like the government had nothing to do with it. The last thing I need is for some excuse for those fuckers Muller or Jhuns to invade us. Got it? Classified top secret, okay? This investigation never happened and was never sanctioned. Do I make myself clear?" Dolly looked at Pedro. "This gets out and I'll chop your pecker off and feed it to the secret service Dobermans." Then she glanced at the women around the room. "And I'll have your nipples sewn together, ladies, got it?"

That brought a collective nod from the group; several people squirmed uncomfortably as their minds came up with a visual of that painful act.

"Ava and I will handle this," Pedro offered. "I think I have just the person to handle it."

"Good, you do that," Dolly said with an evil grin as she made a cutting scissors motion with the index and middle of her right hand. Chop, chop.

Chapter 28

There was a tap on Mary Ellen's office door.

"Come in," Mary Ellen called out.

Sylvia walked in and closed the door behind her.

Mary Ellen looked up from her computer screen, noticed it was Sylvia, smiled, and then noticed Sylvia's concerned look. "What's up, love?"

"I think we have a problem." Sylvia handed her a piece of paper. That in itself was concerning. Almost everything nowadays was handled electronically. Paper was reserved for items troubling and/or secret in nature. Paper could be shredded or burned. E-mail, i-mail, voicemails and all of the other electronic methods of delivering messages, no matter how secure they claimed to be, could be hacked into and/or retrieved by some eight-year-old Ritalin-addicted, autistic computer geek savant. "It's from SG-1."

SG-1 stood for M-pire's Security Group-One. Mary Ellen's summers as a White House intern had caused her to grow paranoid about the business and political world in general. This paranoia grew steadily worse as she moved up the ranks at M-Mart and realized most people hated M-Mart, even though they still shopped there. Much like Microsoft or the IRS, M-Mart was considered by many a necessary evil at best, the corporation of the Devil incarnate more likely. Mary Ellen was positive that many competitors were out to destroy her empire and some of those competitors had a lot of power and influence plus friends in high places.

To protect her newly won empire, one of the first things Mary Ellen did when she became CEO of M-pire was to completely overhaul and dramatically increase security at all of M-pire's companies. As part of that revamping, a new super-secret group was created within M-Pire's Security division.

Security Group-One was the corporate world's most elite security forces. At least, as far as Mary Ellen knew. She suspected competitors had their own secret security details and really didn't know if theirs were better or not. They were secret, after all. Mary Ellen had been assured though that Security Group-One was the best security force money could buy. For the price she paid, it had damn well better be---she could've bought a small nation for that amount of money, and she should know.

Agents in SG-1 were trained thoroughly. They were part Navy SEAL, nuclear physicist, Secret Service agent, rabid polar bear, MI6 agent, bounty hunter, FBI agent, super nanny, CIA agent and ninja all rolled into one finely honed package. We're not talking everyday, run of the mill ninjas that just do paperwork and hang out at artsy fartsy coffee houses all day either, but cool Hong Kong movie ninjas that can kill eight people in less than three seconds.

Communiqués from SG-1 that made it all the way to Mary Ellen were extremely rare. Most things were handled at the mid-management level. The last time she personally received anything from SG-1 was over seven years ago. SG-1 found out that an M-Oil field in the Sudan that produced about 7,000 barrels of oil per day was in danger of being raided and taken over by a local warlord. Mary Ellen appeased the warlord by shipping him two pallets of Remington 750 semi-automatic rifles, a pallet of shells and a pallet of Sam's Pick Summer Lightning soda (the warlord's favorite soda, according to the SG-1 report). As a side benefit, the warlord promptly used the Remingtons to destroy a competitor's nearby oil field, causing M-Oil's stock to jump sharply.

Mary Ellen quickly scanned the memo, and then looked up. "No worries, love. Governments are always investigating us. I'd bet some governmental department in every country we do business in is investigating us for one reason or another. They all want to get their grubby little paws on our profits, especially our dear former First Lady of Alabama. She's just jealous. It says it right there in the memo. She's been trying crap for decades now. Don't sweat it."

"No," Sylvia said. "This is different. This isn't the Department of Agriculture or even the IRS…"

"It's the Committee of Yenta Agents," Mary Ellen said, glancing at the memo. "So what? What are they going to investigate? Whether or not our matzos are kosher? Hey, what the heck? Why does her Holiness have an agency that sounds Jewish when Judaism has been outlawed…?"

"Note the initials, Cuddle Cakes," Sylvia prompted.

"CYA…? That CYA??? CYA stands for Committee of Yenta Agents…? The former FBI? Uh oh."

"The CYA used to be the NSA, pre-split, which is actually much worse. They are the ones that can detain people for years without telling anyone, seize all of your assets, etc. They make the IRS look like pansies."

"Damn that jealous bitch," Mary Ellen muttered irritably. "Why the hell can't she just leave me alone?"

"So, what are we going to do?" Sylvia asked.

Mary Ellen thought on it for a moment. "You know what we have to do. We've discussed it a thousand times."

"Are you sure you want to do that?" Sylvia asked, surprised. "That's pretty drastic…"

"Sylv, we should have done it a decade ago."

"But it'll cost the company billions…"

"In the short run, love," Mary Ellen admitted. "But it'll probably save us tens or hundreds of billions over the long haul."

"I really hate moving though," Sylvia said with a sigh.

"Don't worry, love," Mary Ellen with a mischievous grin. "I've got a little payback in mind for Roderick for all the hassle she's putting us through now, and all of the bullshit she's put me through in the past. This should really piss her off."

Chapter 29

News Items from 2022-2023

M-pire Moves Headquarters to M-Wan

Martinville, Ala. – October 11, 2022 – On the 60th anniversary of the founding of the M-Mart Stores, Inc., Mary Ellen Martin, CEO of the corporation (now called M-pire, Inc.) made the surprising announcement that the company has officially moved its headquarters from Martinville, Alabama to Taipei, M-Wan.

It was a move that had been predicted by industry insiders on several occasions over the last decade since the company first bought the island nation, but the news still sent shockwaves through Wall Street. The M-pire official company response to those predictions had always been that it would never move from Martinville, the home of the original Martin's 5 & 10, and adopted hometown of M-Mart founder Sam Martin and many of his descendants, including Mary Ellen Martin.

Prior to the announcement, the M-pire CEO, who is also the president of M-Wan, was splitting the majority of her time between her Martinville and Taipei residences. In the press conference, Ms. Martin said that she would retain her Martinville home plus her Manhattan apartment and her Del Mar estate located near San Diego for business and personal trips when visiting North America.

The Dow-Jones Industrial Average was down a record Δ918.57 to Δ16,457.84, the worst market close since November 22, 2012, as Wall Street analysts and fund managers pondered the implications of the move, many selling off stocks and leaving their funds in cash for the moment. The M-pire move not only affects its retail giant subsidiary, M-Mart Stores, Inc., but all of its divisions, including M-Fuel, M-Proct, M-Soft and dozens of other companies M-pire has acquired over the years, plus hundreds of companies that sell goods to M-mart retail stores as well as suppliers to all of M-pire's many companies.

There were also concerns about the M-pire companies potentially leaving the NYSE and NASDAQ and moving to the Hang Seng Index (the Stock Exchange of Hong Kong). M-pire's various companies account for Δ6,385.27 of the DJIA and Δ2,112.87 of the NASDAQ as of the closing bell yesterday. Although DJIA and NASDAQ components (member companies) are swapped out from time to time, the loss of almost 40% of the companies at one time is bound to have detrimental effects on the indices. The consensus of the industry experts is not whether M-pire moves to the Hang Seng Index, but when. Rumor is that all of the New York and Chicago-based indices are scrambling to come up with replacement candidates, many having late night meetings, in case the M-pire companies leave quickly.

Perhaps the biggest entity affected by the move will be the Roderickstan government who could stand to lose anywhere from Δ80 billion to Δ360 billion, based on industry tax experts' wide-ranging estimates for all of the various taxes M-pire pays the government. The taxes include income tax, property taxes, sales taxes, etc. No Roderickstan IRS spokesperson was immediately available for the comment.

CNBC's Mad Moolah host Jack Cramden said, "This is insane! This is nuts! Head for the hills! Sell! Sell! Sell! Sell it all! Holy Crap! I'm moving to Liechtenstein, baby! The Euro is kicking the dollie's butt anyway. Moolah!"

* * * * *

Stock Market Crashes Again on News of New M-Wan Law

Taipei, M-Wan – October 16, 2022 – For the second time in less than a week, M-pire and M-Wan have been at the root of a major stock market crash. Just five days ago, the stock market dropped a record Δ918.57 when M-pire announced it had moved its corporate headquarters for all of its subsidiaries to Taipei, M-Wan.

Today, the stock market was again sent reeling, dropping another Δ457.34, as the M-Wan government announced the passing of a new law. The law, paraphrased, states that all companies based in M-Wan may only sell their products to other M-Wan-based companies or M-Wan citizens. All exporting of goods to non-M-Wan based companies is now illegal.

The first major implication from the law is that all of the M-pire companies are now considered M-Wan-based; especially considering the CEO of M-pire is also the president of M-Wan. The other major implication is that all "Made in M-Wan" goods will only be sold through M-Marts and other M-pire retail companies, thus locking out every other retailer. Sears Holdings Corporation stock plummeted 38.6% on the news and Target stock dropped 27.9%.

Jason Penny, great grandson of founder Penny

Penny and CEO of the Penny General chain of discounted retail goods, whose stock dropped 43.2% on the news, made the following statement in response to the announcement, "We at Penny General are unconcerned by the new M-Wan legislation. Our company, with its 546 retail locations---be sure to check out the grand openings this week in Sheboygan, Wisconsin; Bastrop, Texas; Chula Vista, California; and Hastings, Nebraska---stand by our business model and our financial plan, which we believe are very strong. There are still plenty of locales around the world to buy our cheap crap...err, deeply valued goods. We will simply shift our purchases to places like Mexico, South America, Micronesia, India and any one of a dozen other countries."

Joe Bob Funkle, lead retail industry analyst for investment firm Emerson, Sheonberg and Watts, didn't share Penny's optimistic view of the situation. "M-Wan currently exports approximately 3.85 trillion items each year and approximately 900 billion of those items end up in retail stores in Roderickstan. There are no countries that can retool that quickly. This is a brilliant move by [M-pire CEO Mary Ellen] Martin and M-pire. This is going to run a lot of retailers out of business and bolster M-pire's market share significantly."

Shares of M-pire stock are up over 26.3% in the last week as the street responded favorably to the company's sweeping changes. Many of M-pire subsidiaries like M-Soft (shares up 1.3% for the week) and M-Proct (shares up 7.8%) are unaffected by the announcement as they have plants and factories operating within Roderickstan. The traditional unbranded, generic "Made in M-Wan" products and the infamous "As Seen on TV" late night infomercial

Immaculate Deception

fodder seem to be most affected by the legislation.

CNBC's Mad Moolah host Jack Cramden responded to the announcement by saying, "This is even more insane! This is even more nuts! Head for the hills! Sell! Sell! Sell! Sell it all! Uh, except for M-pire companies, of course. Holy Crap! I'm really moving to Liechtenstein this time, baby! Moolah!"

*****

Target and Sears File for Bankruptcy Protection

Minneapolis, MN and Hoffman Estates, IL – May 16, 2023 – In an effort to show solidarity, the CEOs of Target and Sears held a joint press conference to announce that both companies were filing for Chapter 11 bankruptcy protection. Both companies had been the major players in a class action lawsuit against M-Wan and M-pire for discriminatory and predatory practices for the M-Wan law passed in October, 2022 that prohibited any non-M-Wan-based company from buying "Made in M-Wan" products. The law effectively locked out all other major retailers from buying cheap goods except those owned by M-pire. That led to a horrible Holiday 2022 season that has caused at least 57 nationwide and regional retailers to declare bankruptcy because of the law so far.

Last week, the Supreme Court ruled in favor of M-Wan and M-pire primarily because they had no jurisdiction over M-Wan or M-pire, thus killing any chance of Target or Sears rebounding anytime in the near future.

Paul Colmes, CEO of Sears Holdings Corporation, owner of Kmart and Sears, said, "It is quite sad that, after almost 140 years in business for Sears and over 120 years in business for Kmart, we cannot soldier on but the heavy losses from our holiday season, over Δ13.4 billion, are just too much for the company to handle."

Target CEO Wallace Waerld added bitterly, "Congrats. You won, you evil, vile cunt." It was obviously a thinly-veiled reference to archrival M-pire's CEO Mary Ellen Martin.

As part of the bankruptcy deal, both Colmes and Waerld are stepping down as CEO of their respective companies. As part of his severance from Target, Waerld is receiving Δ3.4 billion in cash for his three year tenure as CEO. Colmes, who had only been CEO of Sears for five months, negotiated a severance package worth €2.9 billion in cash.

When told about Colmes severance package, Waerld said, "2.9 billion for five months work? Damn, he's good. And in Euros? He's really good. I should have thought of that. I need to call my lawyers…"

* * * * *

From the Roderickstan Times:

Mysterious Prophet Performs Miracles in Maine

Bangor, Maine – February 2, 2024 – At first, most of the people who stood outside of Bangor Bangers, a sausage market on 5th and Elm in downtown Bangor (not to be confused with Bangor Gangbangers, the "gentlemen's club" just outside of the city limits on highway 202, or Bangor Bongos, the music store on the corner of 10th and Maple) thought they were part of an elaborate April Fool's joke. It quickly became apparent to the growing crowd that what was happening was not a practical joke at all, but a

Immaculate Deception

miracle. In fact, it was several miracles, perhaps dozens of miracles, according to several of the people gathered at Bangor Bangers.

"Bangin'" Peter Longo, owner of Bangor Bangers and Bangor Gangbangers, was tending the counter at the meat market when four nondescript men in their mid-twenties walked into the market to have lunch. According to Long, as the four men stood in line, another patron, later identified as Paul Tarsisi, who already sat at a table eating some bangers and mash with onion gravy (on special every Thursday for Δ14.99 including large soft drink, Longo added) grunted, grabbed his chest and fell to the floor. The four men ran over to Tarsisi and the leader of the group (described as 5' 10", shoulder-length brown hair and trimmed beard, blue eyes, wearing a red button-up short sleeve shirt, cargo shorts and open-toed sandals, and, according to several people, silver holy cross earrings) revived him.

What immediately struck Longo and the rest of the people in the market as odd was the way the stranger revived Tarsisi. He didn't use the Heimlich Maneuver or CPR, instead he simply touched Tarsisi lightly on the forehead. Tarsisi immediately jumped up and began running around the market (a miracle in itself as Tarsisi weighed at least 380 pounds) raving about miracles and claiming the stranger, who refused to be identified, was the son of God. When Tarsisi finally stopped running, some five minutes later, he said that he was selling everything and would follow the stranger anywhere.

Another patron, Mary Bethany, who was hunched over noticeably with a severe case of Scoliosis, saw the miracle and asked the stranger if he could help her. He simply smiled and touched her on the forehead in the same manner as Tarsisi. She straightened right up with several loud pops and ran around the room raving and claiming the stranger was the son of God just as Tarsisi had.

Within another ten minutes, the stranger had healed four other people of various ailments and a crowd gathered. The stranger and his followers left the market just minutes before local police arrived with three STUD priests, ready to charge the stranger with blasphemy and heresy, both crimes punishable with life imprisonment, though, according to sources, the stranger or his three friends never said anything against STUD and made no proclamations of his own divinity. In fact, only the Bangor Bangers patrons claimed the stranger's divinity.

Later in the day, the stranger and his followers were seen at the Skowhegan deli where they ate dinner and he performed several more miracles before the group disappeared again. The stranger is being called the Maine Miracle Man or M^3 ("M cubed" for short) by the local believers. Local authorities are also calling the stranger M^3 but state the moniker stands for Maine Mystery Man. Although the stranger's true identity is unknown, his three friends were overheard to be called Peter, James and Andrew.

M^3's current whereabouts are unknown and he is being sought for questioning by the authorities in Maine. Report any information regarding his whereabouts to your local police department.

*****

Coverage of the Macy's Thanksgiving Day Parade, November 22, 2024:

The popular hard rock band LICK, dressed in full black,

Immaculate Deception

white and silver makeup and black and silver leather outfits, sat at the parade booth across from Macy's Herald Square, New York location with their instruments in hand. Rosie O'Conner, dressed in a parka, jeans and work boots, sat between Paul Staley and Gene Simons, lead singers of LICK as a crowd looked on from the street.

"It is my honor to host of the 100th Macy's Thanksgiving Day Parade with my pals, Paul Staley and Gene Simons of LICK!" Rosie said.

The crowd cheered wildly.

"This year's theme is about one of my favorite issues, gay pride," Rosie continued. "And I'm sure one of LICK's favorite issues too, right guys?"

Staley and Simons exchanged puzzled looks. Staley cleared his throat but said nothing.

Simons shook his head and said, "Yeah, right, Rosie. I've been banging a Centerfold of the Year for over thirty years and have two kids by her."

"Oh, I hate 'men's' magazines," Rosie complained. "They are so demeaning to women and the women are so... so... so feminine, yuck, with boob jobs, bleached hair and twenty inch waists."

"They are a celebration of the female form," Simons responded. "Shannon, my life partner, doesn't regret being a centerfold one bit."

"Okay, okay," Rosie said, then turned to Staley and winked. "Paul, come on, you back gay rights and gay pride, right?"

A flustered look overcame Paul's made-up face. "Uh, I guess. I don't really care either way if a person is gay or not. Why should I?"

"You're not...ya know...?" Rosie asked.

"Of course not!" Staley retorted. "Why the hell would you think that?"

"With the make-up and all...I thought I heard rumors..." Rosie replied, noting the Paul's white geisha-like face makeup, black star make-up on his right eye and his candy apple red lipstick.

"Listen, Rosie, I've banged almost 5,000 women in my life," Simons said proudly. "Many of them groupies after a show and Paul and the rest of the guys were all sharing in the fun, if you know what I mean, okay? And there were no rump ranger festivities going on, catch my drift?"

"Okay, okay, gotcha," Rosie said. She was obviously hearing something in her earpiece because she turned to the street and quickly changed the subject. "This year's theme for the very special 100th Macy's Thanksgiving Day Parade is 'Shout You're Out' and here comes your Parade Queen right now."

The TV view switched from Rosie O'Conner to a view that focused on the float of the Parade Queen and his court. At the top stood a brown haired and bearded 20ish man wearing a white sequin dress and tiara surrounded by a court of four young women and one man, all dressed in pink satin dresses.

"This year's Parade Queen is Boston College student George Sanders. Doesn't he look wonderful?" Rosie asked to no one in general and the crowd on the street cheered wildly.

"Just lovely," Gene Simons replied sarcastically and then began to sing softly, "Girls will be boys and boys will be girls..."

Paul Staley joined in, "...it's a mixed up, muddled up, shook up world except for..."

"Lola la la la la Lola!" Rosie joined the chorus, screaming off-key. "Oh, I love that song...L-O-L-A Lola!"

Simons grunted, put on his sunglasses and didn't say another word for fifteen minutes. Paul said little as well as various floats and marching bands paraded by on the street below the booth over the next quarter hour.

"Oh, oh! Here's the band I've been waiting for!" Rosie said excitedly, then she caught herself, looked at Paul and Gene and quickly added, "Besides, you guys, of course.

Introducing the greatest marching band in the history of the universe, the USC Trojan Marching Band, all of the way from the west coast. Did you guys know their official name is the Spirit of Troy?"

"Really?" Gene replied sarcastically.

The hundred-plus strong predominately-male band turned the corner and started marching onto to the street in front of Rosie's booth. She said, "Going along with this year's theme, the band members are wearing special uniforms."

The camera zoomed in on the band who was wearing nothing but brass Roman Centurion helmets, red and gold chaps and their instruments. The cheers escalated as the band's formation turned away from the camera exposing dozens of well-defined collegian male butt cheeks to the crowd.

The camera switched back to a view of Rosie, appearing amused, Paul, somewhat shocked, and Gene, thoroughly annoyed.

"What the fuck?" Gene said, appalled. "You take one of college's finest traditions and turn it into a gay Chippendales show? This is pathetic."

"Gee, Gene, that kind of sounds like hatespeak to me," Rosie said, trying to sound jovial but her rage came through.

"Come on, Rosie," Gene rejoined. "Just because I don't want to drive a pink car or watch guys prancing around in Vegas showgirl outfits doesn't mean I'm homophobic. If other people want to do it, I don't care. It just means I don't like that crap."

"Well, Gene," Rosie snapped back angrily. "If you don't like 'this crap,' then why are you here?"

Gene didn't respond.

After a few uncomfortable seconds, Paul offered, "Well, Rosie, we're all in our sixties now and we don't get as many gigs as we used to…"

"We don't need the money that bad. Let's get the hell out of here," Gene said and started to get up.

"Can you afford the lawsuit?" Rosie asked tartly.

"Shit," Gene mumbled and sat down.

"Great, the Spirit of Troy has finished. You guys ready to rock?" Rosie asked cheerfully.

"Sure," Paul said apathetically. The LICK members stood and filed out of the booth.

"And now, our headlining band, who has sold over seventy million records over the last half century, LICK, and their specially revised version of their classic song 'Shout it Out Now' in honor of our parade theme 'Shout You're Out Now!'"

LICK started jamming and Paul Staley sang with mock enthusiasm:

"Don't let 'em tell you that there's too much noise

They're too straight to really understand

You'll still get rowdy with your backdoor boys

'Cause it's time for you to take a stand, yeah, yeah

Shout you're, shout you're, shout you're out now

Shout you're, shout you're out now!"

Immaculate Deception

PART V

THE PLOT

"Exactly when will I get my 72 virgins?"
--Overheard at a Middle East suicide bomber training camp

Immaculate Deception

Chapter 30

2024 continues…

Dolly Roderick stood behind her desk in the Elliptical Office of the Roderickstan Castle, looking out at the panoramic view of the Atlantic Ocean through her specially built ceiling to floor windows. As she watched the waves hit the shore and ships of all sizes sail, Dolly wasn't feeling the sense of calm and peace she usually felt.

Pedro Sandoval and Ava Garbo sat in chairs on the opposite side of the desk from Dolly, looking at her and the skyline past her.

"So, what the fuck are we going to do about this?" Dolly asked irritably without turning away from the scenery, still hoping to calm her nerves. "And don't mention another fucking 3M. The last one we did had Nanny and Butch going at each other like hundred dollie Balinese fighting crickets."

Pedro looked at Ava and chuckled. "I thought Butch was going to pull out a gun and blow Nanny's head off, eh, beautiful?"

"I was certain she was going to deck Nanny," Ava said.

"Also, the 3M was a complete waste of time," Dolly said. "Those dipshits at the CYA still haven't found anything useful on the M-witch, have they, Pedro?"

"Unfortunately, either Martin is squeaky clean or M-pire's security is even better than ours," Pedro responded.

"Gee, Pedro, which do you think it is?" Dolly raised an eyebrow.

"I don't know of any squeaky clean CEOs," Sandoval said with a laugh, risking Dolly's wrath.

"Right, the only thing worse than a fucking politician is a

goddamned CEO." Dolly absently rubbed her chin as she continued gazing out at the ocean without taking it in. "Politicians are easy to figure out. It's all about power to them. Money and greed are just fringe benefits of the position. With CEOs, it's a whole different ball game. You rarely know which is more important: Power or money."

"In this case, though," Ava offered, "it seems obvious enough. Martin's priority is power. She wants to be the most powerful woman in the world."

"Yes. That's the problem, eh, beautiful?" Dolly retorted, mocking Pedro's voice.

Ava cleared her throat. She was suddenly uncomfortable, a rare event in her relationship with Dolly. Being a former Secret Service agent and a 3rd degree black belt in aikido, Ava knew of 192 ways to kill a person with just her hands, feet, elbows, knees, forehead or various common implements like pens, paperclips, dental floss, or tweezers. That knowledge usually gave Ava a certain level of confidence but it had suddenly vanished with Dolly's impersonation of Pedro. Dolly had never done that before. Uneasily, Ava said, "Yes, I guess so."

"And why would that be, my dearest friends?" Dolly asked in a syrupy sweet tone that Pedro imagined Lucifer, back in the days when he still officially existed, might use when he offered some poor sap a golden fiddle for his soul.

Pedro and Ava both realized they might have somehow entered uncharted and frightening territory with Dolly. They had both always known she was driven, ambitious, probably even a megalomaniac by most standards. She also was known for fits of rage and foul-mouthed tirades that might make a sailor or Madonna blush. Suddenly, though, Dolly reached a new, higher level of rage. The lawyer in Pedro Sandoval dubbed it "temporary insanity." Pedro could tell Ava sensed it too. They looked at each other but said nothing.

"Because," Dolly began sweetly enough and then her voice quickly rose to a screech. "That's my position. I'm the most powerful woman in the world, and I plan on it staying that way, understand? I'm not going to let the little tramp that blew my fuckwit husband steal the position that I busted my ass for decades and paid for in blood to get. Got it?"

"Sure, Doll," Pedro said with less than his normal confidence. In the back of his mind, he pondered the thought of really retiring for the thousandth time. He was getting far too old for this shit. One of these days, the "Dolly Mama" was going to truly believe she was a deity, go off the deep end and maybe have him killed. Heck, she might even sacrifice him, rip his liver out of his body while he was still alive and eat it right in front of him as he screamed in agony. The scene in his mind made him shiver. He really needed to rethink this whole personal adviser gig. "But what should we do about it?"

"It" was the latest in a long list of kudos for Dolly's long-time nemesis, Mary Ellen Martin. This time, Fortune magazine's Most Admired Companies 2023 article had sent Dolly into a tirade.

Rank	Company	Country
1	M-pire	M-Wan

M-pire was number one again. That wasn't much of a surprise. It was in the top ten for most of the last half century and had been number one seven of the last ten years. What had set off Dolly was the Country column of the article listing M-pire's country as M-Wan. The move of M-pire's headquarters from Martinville, Alabama to Taipei, M-Wan had cost Dolly's administration an estimated quarter of a $\Delta 1$ trillion per year, according to Dolly's best bean counters. The loss of that kind of tax revenue was agonizing to Dolly, almost as painful as knowing that her arch-rival Mary Ellen Martin was on the verge of overtaking her as the most powerful woman in the world.

Both Pedro and Ava knew that something had to be done, possibly something drastic, and probably soon. If not, Dolly would end up in a rubber room or, more likely, Pedro, Ava, and a couple dozen of Dolly's insiders would end up being poured into the concrete base of a wind turbine in Nantucket Sound as part of phase four of the Cape Wind Project.

"What indeed…? What indeed…?" Dolly pondered, her eyes a mix of wild-eyed lunacy, profound determination, and intense thought. "Whatever it is, it needs to happen immediately. I'm sick of waiting on those dumbfucks at the CYA to come up with something…"

"Doll, I've got an idea," Sandoval said. "How about if we do something to catch Martin off guard and cause her to make a mistake?"

"Such as…?" Dolly's eyes lost the Dr. Frankenstein 'It's alive!' appearance as they focused on Pedro.

"How about if we have the CYA raid M-pire's Martinville offices while Martin is in town on business. Maybe we can scare her enough to make a mistake."

Ava added, "We could raid their headquarters during a board meeting or when Martin is schmoozing somebody important like a big vendor or the mayor of a city where she wants to build a M-Mart…"

"Yes, I like it," Dolly said, sounding rational for the first time in several minutes. "When is the next time she will be here in Roderickstan?"

Ava walked up to Dolly's desk, tapped a few buttons on the control panel and Mary Ellen Martin's agenda for the next month appeared as a hologram in the middle of the room.

As Dolly scanned the image, she said, "Maybe the CYA doesn't have their heads up their asses as far as I thought."

Pedro stood, walked behind the ladies, and gazed at the agenda. "Well, well, lookie there, Martin is having a meeting with all of the Gulf Coast refinery and oil rig managers plus all of the senior management of M-Fuel at the Martinville office in two and a half weeks. A raid during that meeting would be quite embarrassing for the M-witch, I would think."

"Yes, that's perfect," Dolly agreed. "But that's not

enough. We need to hit her in the pocketbook and we need to do it soon."

Ava looked at Dolly. "You mean like a tax or tariff?"

"Yes, but what?" Dolly pondered aloud.

"An excise tax on all oil pumped out of Roderickstan soil?" Pedro offered. "How about nationalizing all M-pire property?"

"Hmmm, that would be luscious," Dolly said with a grin, "but that would just get Mary Ellen out of Roderickstan. It wouldn't eliminate her as a threat for the most powerful woman in the world. Keep thinking about it. Maybe this raid will help us."

Chapter 31

Pedro "Sully" O'Sullivan sat in his cubicle in the CYA offices at Fort Meade, Maryland, staring at the 3D holographic streaming video from the Grid that gave the illusion of being about three feet in front of his face but was really just in his mind. The scene was of the deliciously hot thirtyish actress Smiley Sirius doing a sexy striptease pole dance in her latest movie, Janna Banana 13: Janna does Dallas.

Sully intently watched Janna Banana twirl seductively around the pole in some seedy Miami bar, her peppermint-pastied nipples swinging in all directions as she seduced the camera lens with her eyes and smile. Sully nearly fell out of his chair as Canie Pest's latest tune, I Luv U, boomed in his head.

Die you goldigging skank
Yo just don't rank
I sniffed yo panties
Damn, they stank...

"Boss," Sully said quickly and the striptease image disappeared and all evidence of the showing was deleted. "Answer." A click went off in Sully's head. "Hello."

"Hey hey, how's my namesake doing today?" came the response in his head.

"Hey, Uncle Pedro. How are you doing? You in DC? You want to hit Honkers tonight? Tuesday is 'five free buffalo wings with any purchase' night."

"Sorry, kiddo, I'm still in Florida," Pedro Sandoval said. "I need to talk to you about something."

"Sure, Uncle Pedro. Wassup?"

"I arranged a special assignment for you. Your boss is

going to be briefing you about it sometime this morning, I'd guess."

"Really?" Sully asked.

"Yes, really. If you don't screw this one up, it'll get you that promotion you've been wanting."

"Really?" Sully asked again.

"Yes, really. This assignment is coming from the top and it is classified super top secret. Now, kiddo, I'm counting on you not screwing the pooch on this one, okay? It's bad enough that I got you placed on the M-pire investigation team, and you guys haven't turned up anything useful. Doll's really pissed off about that, and she makes your mother seem like a pussycat, if you know what I mean. I don't need her Worship ripping me a new asshole, okay? Can I count on you, buddy?"

"Sure, Uncle," Sully said, recalling his uncle's stories over the years about Roderick and her outrageous temper. "I've got your back."

"Excellent. I knew I could count on you. Go get 'em, tiger."

"Sure thing, Uncle Pedro," Sully said, another click in his head and his uncle's voice was gone.

A promotion? He had been a Special Agent I for almost four years and he was growing antsy. The average agent usually got promoted at around the three-year mark.

Sully knew he wasn't the brightest knife in the drawer. He wished he was as smart as his uncle Pedro Sandoval. He was like a friggin' rock scientist or something. He was also the coolest uncle ever. He had saved Sully's job a couple of times, once when Sully accidently outed an AReQi double agent and the CYA barely pulled the guy out of Babylonia before he was almost killed, and another time when he accidently contaminated a crime scene and got the case against a terrorist chief thrown out of court. Sully figured that was why his promotion to Special Agent II was taking longer than normal.

As Sully pondered the possibilities of what the extra Δ700

a month for his new pay grade would do for his lifestyle, a chime rang in his head, a chime that meant he had just received an e-mail from his boss, Special Agent in Charge Anita Gunn. Sully said, "E-mail."

A list of new e-mails in his index appeared in front of him. One stood out:

Importance: High
From: Anita Gunn
Subject: New Assignment Briefing 10AM, Location: Lounge Lizard room

Sully skimmed the contents of the e-mail, nothing noteworthy there. He noticed the time in the bottom right corner of the image in his mind: 9:53AM.

Shit! "Close e-mail." The image of his e-mails blinked out as he grabbed a pad of paper and a pen and scrambled down the hall to the conference room. He entered the open door to the Lounge Lizard room.

Gunn was messing with a projector the size of a pack of cigarettes, evidently attempting to link her brain-mount computer to it for a presentation. Half a dozen fellow special agents were chatting among themselves as they sat around a conference table with seating for ten.

Sully sat down next to Janine "the Love Machine" Kilborn, a saucy special agent two years his junior with flaming red hair and green eyes that belied her Irish descent. She had quite the reputation around the water cooler of being an animal in the sack. Pedro had frequently but unsuccessfully attempted to verify that reputation. Though Kilborn had spurned him regularly, she was quite nice about it, so he still held hope of "checking into the Y" someday.

Gunn finished tinkering with the projector and looked around the room. "Good, it looks like everyone is here. Let's get started. Dim lights."

The room went dark save for the bright light emanating from the projector that filled one of the walls with the image of the CYA logo.

"We received a special assignment today..." Gunn said.

Sully cut in, "That's good since we're special agents."

The group chuckled softly at the old joke.

"Some of us are more special than others," Gunn snapped. "Remember, O'Sullivan, you're special...just like everyone else, now pipe down."

That got the crowd cackling. Everyone in the room knew Gunn couldn't stand O'Sullivan's stupidity and only tolerated him because he was Our Lady and Protector Dolly Roderick's special advisor Pedro Sandoval's nephew. If it was up to her, Sully would be a dog catcher or a trash man or at least would be riding a desk for his entire career and never receive a field assignment where he could put others at risk. Unfortunately, it wasn't up to her.

"Ouch, boss," Sully said in a hurt tone, looking around the darkened room for sympathy, but not finding much.

"O'Sullivan, this is a serious field assignment where people could get hurt or even killed, so could you please pay attention and try not to screw this one up, okay, before I am tempted to request you get transferred to el Queso?"

Sully perked up. "You're tempted to assign me as a double agent? Gee, thanks, boss!"

"No, O'Sullivan," Gunn shot back. "Not as a double agent. I want you to work for the el Queso. You'd probably singlehandedly bring down the terrorist organization from within with your screw ups."

That brought yelps of laughter from around the room.

"Now, O'Sullivan, can you please quiet down and listen? Or I might let Tiny interrogate you..."

Tiny, six-foot-seven and 320 pounds of muscle, gave a "your ass is mine" grin from across the conference table to Sully, who gulped uncomfortably.

"Yes, ma'am," Sully muttered.

"Excellent," Gunn said. "Moving right along..." Gunn hit a button on her remote and an image of a massive complex taken from several hundred feet up appeared on the wall, replacing the CYA logo. "This is M-pire's Roderickstan headquarters in Martinville, Alabama. Higher ups suspect tax fraud and tax evasion and they want us to do a raid on the facility and lockdown all of the records before they can destroy them."

Sully's mind raced. Was his question a good one? He didn't want Tiny giving him a prostate exam. He wasn't supposed to need one for a good ten to fifteen years, and he was pretty sure Tiny wasn't a licensed doctor anyway. He decided the question was okay and raised his hand cautiously.

Gunn noticed Sully and shot him an irritated look. "Yeah, O'Sullivan?"

"This sounds like it should be under ROT jurisdiction, ma'am," Sully offered.

ROT stood for the Roderickstan Office of Taxation. "True enough. Normally, it would be, but Hot Rod's executive office requested us and you, O'Sullivan, specifically, for the raid." Gunn paused to let the point sink into everyone in the room. Sully's uncle had obviously stepped in and got him the assignment and his fellow agents now knew it. "Also, since M-pire is now headquartered out of M-Wan, it falls under our jurisdiction. Plus, this assignment is going to be very sensitive because we will be conducting it while the M-pire CEO Mary Ellen Martin is there."

Sully's eyebrows raised at that statement. He and Ray Gunn, Anita's husband, were working on an open Martin file for a couple of years but had come up with nothing useful since she pulled up roots and moved to M-Wan.

"Evidently," Anita Gunn continued. "Martin has done something to really piss off somebody in the Castle and we're supposed to scare her and 'shake the tree' to see if we can find something on her in the raid.

"We have Martin's itinerary for next week. She's having a meeting with most of the Roderickstan and the USA M-Fuel executives next Tuesday from 2:00 PM-4:00 PM. The raid of the complex has been ordered for 3:15 PM. You will each be leading a team of six local field agents.

"All, we need to be extremely careful here. M-pire's security is rumored to be second to none, even as good as ours..."

"That's bullshit," Ray said defiantly.

"Probably," Anita agreed. "But it is the best in the private sector and they have a sizable armed security force, intel says thirty-two strong at that time of day, so we need to play this very cool." She gave Sully a 'this means you' look.

"Uh, sure thing, boss," Sully offered. "I can be cool."

"Right..." Gunn hesitated, pondering a comeback but thought better of it. "Anyway, we need to make our identities well known and not provoke a firefight. Got it?"

The group nodded their assent. The image on the wall switched to a layout map of the M-pire Martinville complex. Gunn rattled off the various assignments, each agent leading a team to secure a building in the complex and begin searching for and seizing any found documents. Sully grew antsy when everyone in the room but him had been given an assignment. He wondered if Gunn was going to shaft him and stick him with a desk assignment again, as was her usual treatment, or something equally lame like communications duty in the command van.

Finally, Gunn hesitated for a moment and then said with a sigh, "And O'Sullivan, your team will be securing the boardroom."

Everyone in the room, Sully particularly, was stunned. Many people around shot looks back and forth, ranging from mild irritation to 'what the fuck are you thinking? Are you nuts?!' to 'Oh my god, we're all going to die!'

"Really?" Sully asked, perplexed.

"Unfortunately, yes," Anita Gunn said with a hint of sadness that reflected someone who could see the foreshadowing of her career being flushed down the toilet.

As the meeting continued, Anita Gunn led a group of somber and disenchanted agents through the particulars of the raid. Everyone, that is, except for Pedro "Sully" O'Sullivan, who kept looking around the room with a stupid grin on his face like he was at dinner with a date, perhaps even Janine "the Love Machine" Kilborn, and she just let slip that she planned on having wild, life-changing, mind-blowing sex with him for the first time later that night.

Chapter 32

Pedro "Sully" O'Sullivan felt like he just drank two venti Starbucks Doubleshots on Ice +Energy with an extra shot of espresso and +Energy in each, which he supposed made it a sextuple shot or septuple shot. He always got the Roman numeral thing mixed up. Anyway, he was jittery from the major adrenaline rush he was having. He wasn't sure if he was going to jump out of his skin, piss his pants, or have a heart attack from the nervousness. This must be what your wedding day, or maybe confronting your ex in divorce court, or being on some sleazy talk show, felt like.

"Teams, report in," Anita Gunn's voice crackled in his headset.

"Alpha team in position."

"Beta team in position."

A pause...a nudge... Sully looked up to see a team member tapping him on the shoulder and tapping her finger to her headset, silently mouthing "talk, you idiot."

Uh, right. Sully cleared his throat. "Gamma team in position."

Delta through Iota teams rattled off similar readiness.

Anita Gunn closed her eyes, crossed her fingers and whispered a silent prayer to the Dolly Mama. Dear Goddess, please let this go well. Please let this help my career and please don't let O'Sullivan screw this up and get anyone hurt---except maybe himself---excuse me, sorry for that. Hoo ha! "Okay, Sanders, kill the main power. Roberson, kill the security building backup generator. Upsilon team, secure the security building."

Within two minutes, the response came. "Security building secured."

"Okay, all teams," Gunn said. "Permission to proceed. Head out."

"Channel: Gamma team," Sully said. His voice changed from the open channel to his team's channel, though higher ups like Gunn could listen in but the other teams wouldn't have to listen to each other's chatter. "Let's do it. Yancy, get us down there."

"Roger that." In less than a minute, the black ARH-70 helicopter landed on one of the four helipads on the roof of the M-Mart main headquarters building. Two of the helipads were already occupied with civilian helicopters, one an extremely expensive scramjet helicopter that Sully knew must be M-pire CEO Mary Ellen Martin's private helicopter.

Sully's team, six strong, was dressed in black Kevlar body armor with five-inch tall yellow letters CYA on the seat of their pants. As soon as the chopper landed, they ran to the stairwell access door. Sully tried the doorknob to find it locked. With all of the force he could muster, he crashed his shoulder into the door, which didn't budge. "Damn!" He tried to rub the pain from his shoulder.

Quincy, the biggest agent at six-foot-nine, held out the heavy steel battering ram and asked, "Shall we try this?"

"Yo, O'Sullivan," Killian said from around the corner. "Backup generator to this building must've kicked in. Power is still on to the elevator."

"Uh, right, let's do that." Sully moved over to the elevator and hit the down button, but nothing happened.

Quincy waved an M-pire ID in front of the elevator scanner.

"Uh, right," Sully said, hitting the down button again. Everyone readied their Mk 17 Mod 6 assault rifles as the elevator doors opened. "Double check your settings. Make sure they are set to TASER. No blood."

The Delta team entered the elevator and went down to the second floor. The elevator doors opened again. As they rushed through, Sully went down the left hallway as the rest went down the right corridor and then everyone stopped. "This way, team."

Killian shook his head silently.

"Uh, right, that way. Fourth door on the left...?" Sully half said, half asked.

Killian nodded.

"Let's go." Sully led them to the fourth door on the left. At the door, Sully whispered, "Everyone ready?" the team members nodded. "Remember, nobody gets hurt. On three, two, one..."

Sully grabbed the door handle and tried to turn it, to no avail. Quincy waved his M-pire ID card again and the door popped open.

The team rushed into the room with their assault rifles out.

"Everybody freeze!" O'Sullivan shouted as he ran into the room. "This is an official CYA raid." He stopped in his tracks as he noticed the M-pire group calmly sitting around a conference table, looking at them as if they had been waiting for them. Two M-pire security guards stood behind two sitting women who Sully recognized as Mary Ellen Martin, M-pire CEO and Sylvia Byrne, M-pire CFO.

Martin scanned an image in her head for a moment. "Hello, Agent O'Sullivan, I believe."

"How did...?" Sully voice trailed off. Damn, they are good.

"How is your uncle, Pedro Sandoval? I haven't seen him since my intern days..." Martin quipped.

Damn...damn...this wasn't good at all. "Listen, Ms. Martin," O'Sullivan said tersely. "My uncle is fine, but we're getting sidetracked here. This is an official CYA investigation. We need access to all of your files...now, please."

"I don't think so, Agent O'Sullivan," Martin said matter-of-factly, scanning the room, looking at the various CYA agents. "Couldn't they find anybody better than you? According to my information here, your uncle is the only thing keeping you from being a meter maid."

Most of the people in the room snickered, Sully's fellow agents under their breath and the M-pire people openly. Sully's face flushed as Martin continued, "See these three gentlemen here, Sully? They are part of the team of 160+ lawyers M-pire keeps on staff. You're not touching our files."

As Sully fumed, one of the security guards bent over to whisper in Byrne's ear…or possibly pull a weapon.

"Hey, you, freeze!" Sully yelled, leveling his rifle at the guard.

The guard continued to bend over, whispering to Byrne, and seemed to go for his gun.

"That's it, you're done," Sully said, pulling the trigger on his rifle.

Two small electrode darts shot out from small compartments just below the main barrel. As the guard leaned down toward Sylvia, she leaned up toward him. The electrodes hit her in the right pectoral muscle, about four inches below her clavicle. Her entire body convulsed in wild spasms. The security guard then really did reach for his gun and Quincy had shot him with his TASER, sending his body into convulsions too. Sylvia's spasms caused her to fall out of her chair.

"No, Sylvia!" Martin screamed, leaping to grab and comfort Sylvia as she fell to the carpet, her body still seizing.

Though it seemed much longer, Sylvia's body went limp after about five seconds. Something was wrong. She shouldn't have passed out. The security guard already stood up again shaking it off.

Killian ran up to Sylvia and put his hand to the carotid artery in her neck. "Dammit, she doesn't have a pulse." Into his headset, he said, "Get an ambulance here, stat." Then he took her from Mary Ellen, who fought him for a moment, evidently in shock, and then let go. He laid Sylvia on the ground and began giving her CPR.

Sully slowly moved toward Sylvia in total disbelief.

"What the…how?"

Sitting on the ground next to Sylvia, Mary Ellen sobbed. Finally, she looked up and gave O'Sullivan a scathing look. "You shot her right where her pacemaker is, you stupid son of a bitch."

Sully's eyes went wide. A pacemaker? Oh my God…

Quincy took Sully off to the side as three paramedics rushed into the room with a gurney. They placed Sylvia on the gurney and quickly departed, Mary Ellen following close behind as she gave O'Sullivan one last hate-filled gaze as she left the room.

*****

Though Sylvia didn't survive and there was an investigation, the incident was considered a freak accident as a TASER normally wouldn't kill somebody, even someone wearing a pacemaker. O'Sullivan was completely exonerated, rumored in part due to his well-connected uncle, but somewhat shaken by the whole ordeal.

Chapter 33

Pedro Sandoval gazed at the report of the Martinville raid and shook his head in disgust. He read the parts detailing his nephew's involvement at least half a dozen times, trying to figure out how to approach Dolly without getting a lamp or a flowerpot thrown at him.

He loved his nephew. The kid was named after him after all, even though he shunned his rich Mexican heritage by going by the inane Irish nickname of Sully. Pedro O'Sullivan had been called Little Pedy until he was about eight years old and watched a cute, old animated movie called Monsters, Inc. with a character named Sully and he immediately changed his nickname, much to Sandoval's chagrin. Sandoval still preferred to think of him as Little Pedy.

Sandoval always thought his nephew was of at least average intelligence. Pedro doubted the kid would ever be an advisor to a president, queen, goddess, whatever, but at least he was smart enough not to dry a cat in a THW (terahertz wave) oven.

Damned if that kid didn't seem to have the worst luck in the world, though. In fact, Little Pedy's luck was so god-awful that most people mistook it for stupidity. What were the odds of killing someone who had a pacemaker with a TASER? According to the report, roughly one in 350,000. Leave it to his nephew to beat the odds. He wasn't even aiming at the woman who died. She leaned into the shot to get hit.

Now Pedro had to clean up the boy's mess yet again. Sandoval wasn't getting any younger. What would Little Pedy do after he died and wasn't around to fix things? Sandoval shuddered at the thought.

Pedro got off the elevator and stopped at the door leading

to the Elliptical Office. He took a deep breath and brushed the front of his suit, mentally donning his emotional armor for the tirade he knew was coming. Finally, he hit the button on the intercom interface on the wall and looked into the scanner to get his retina scanned.

"Yes, Pedro, come in." An image of Dolly came on the intercom screen. She read some papers in her hand and didn't look up. She usually preferred reading paper copies rather than a computer screen because her eyes grew tired easily from computer use in the last few years. She had an irritated look on her face.

Pedro remained silent as the door opened. He walked up to her desk and opted to remain standing. After a few seconds of being ignored, he said, "Good afternoon, Doll."

"Is it?" Dolly asked, a look of doubt on her face as she looked up from her reading at him. "Do you have good news from Martinville? Did the CYA find anything?"

With the smoothness of a big screen movie actor playing a politician in a big budget blockbuster, Pedro said with poise, "Yes, I have news from Martinville."

When he didn't elaborate, Dolly prodded, "And…?"

"Unfortunately, it's not as good as we would have hoped."

"In what way?"

"Several ways, actually," Pedro said simply.

"Great, just great," Dolly sighed. "What the fuck went wrong this time?"

"They saw us coming and had an injunction ready to prevent the CYA seizing any documents…"

"What?!" Dolly screamed. "I'm the fucking Mother Goddess. I'm the Dolly Mama. I'm the Mother fucking Goddess. What the fuck are you talking about? Find out what judge signed the injunction and feed his sorry ass to the sharks or send him to Gitmo for the rest of his life for being a terrorist. Now, tell those CYA dumbfucks to go back and pull everything and I mean everything, shoe receipts, library receipts, fucking Happy Meal receipts---all of it. Tell them to ignore any M-pire stalling tactics and get it all!"

Pedro hesitated for a moment, just a moment, but it was long enough to alert Dolly. A crazed look came to her face. "What, Pedro? What the fuck aren't you telling me?"

"It's a little late for that, Doll."

"Why?"

"Because, there was an incident and Mary Ellen and all of the records are gone…"

"Gone? Where?"

"Everything of worth was shipped out offshore, probably to M-Wan."

Dolly pondered the information. "Offshore? How? Wait…what incident…?"

"There was a fatality during the raid and the situation became frenetic…"

"Fatality? Someone was neutralized?! Ours or theirs?"

"Theirs."

"Holy shit, Pedro." Dolly cringed. "This is going to be another CYA cluster fuck, I see. Who was it? Just a guard or an admin, right? Please tell me it was it wasn't an executive or a lawyer. Please, not a fucking lawyer…"

"No, not a lawyer," Pedro said, searching for a bright spot in this whole disaster.

"So who?"

Pedro cleared his throat. "Sylvia Byrne, M-pire's CFO."

Dolly's eyes went wide. "Son of a fucking bitch! You're kidding, right? This is some elaborate, albeit dangerous and stupid, practical joke. Ashton Kutcher is going to be walking in any second, right?"

"No, Doll," Pedro said as soothingly as he could muster.

"Sylvia Byrne…You're sure?"

"Yes."

"Son of a bitch. That's Mary Ellen's lover, isn't it?"

"Yes, that's the rumor. They've done a pretty good job of hiding it, but yes."

"Jesus H. Christ, Pedro. This is a cluster fuck beyond all cluster fucks."

Pedro ignored the blasphemous remark that would have sent anyone else to prison. He guessed Dolly could blaspheme herself all she wanted. It wasn't like a goddess could be arrested anyway. "Yes, I'd have to agree this is a bit dicey."

"A bit dicey?" Dolly laughed viciously. "You think? You may be the perfect politician, Pedro. A bit dicey, my ass. You have a true gift for political spin. The sun could go supernova, and you would be talking about the opportunity to get a great tan."

After an uneasy silence, Pedro finally said, "Thank you, your Worship."

"What dumbass killed the bitch? I want their head on a platter."

"It was an accident."

Dolly's gaze ripped into Pedro's soul and recognition sparkled in her eyes. "Holy shit, Pedro. Not your dumbfuck nephew again?"

Pedro cleared his throat again and straightened his power tie. "Yes, but it really was an accident." He went on to elaborate the events from the report.

"Fuck, fuck, fuck...I can't fucking believe this. One in 350,000...damn, damn, damn...How can somebody related to you, one of my dearest and smartest friends, be so fucking stupid?"

"He's not really stupid. Admittedly not brilliant, but not stupid. Just unlucky...very unlucky at times..."

"You think?" Dolly said bitingly. "Your loyalty to your nephew is touching, if unwarranted."

Pedro took a deep breath and a big risk. "You know, Doll, I'm not the only one in this administration who has been accused of unwarranted loyalty."

Dolly was taken aback. Pedro obviously referred to her standing by her late philandering husband through scandal after scandal. She pondered his words, sighed deeply and half-smiled. "You know, Pedro, it's a good thing I know you aren't interested in running the country or I would probably need to have you killed. You are just too smooth a politician. You are truly dangerous. It's a good thing you're on my side. You are on my side, right?"

"Of course, Doll. On your side and by your side for almost forty years now."

"Forty years? Where has all of the time gone? It seems like just yesterday Bobby was running for governor of Alabama…" Her voice trailed off. After a moment, she continued in the softest voice Sandoval ever recalled her using, "Pedro, I am getting too old for these scandals and controversies. This is really, really bad. Killing the lover of the second most powerful woman in the world and my biggest rival. How do we fix this?"

Pedro gave her a sympathetic smile. "I wish I knew, Doll, I wish I knew. I don't think it can be 'fixed.' According to reports from the scene, Mary Ellen went ballistic, totally insane with grief and rage. One of her VPs had to step in and take control. He got Martin, Byrne's body and the records out of Martinville less than an hour after Byrne was pronounced dead. I doubt if you would ever be able to make peace with Martin now, if you ever could before. I think damage control is our only option."

"Damage control," Dolly said bitterly. "I hate those words. I've heard them far too often in my life. What do you suggest?"

"At this point, I don't think there is a 'clean' solution. As much as I hate to say it, I think we need to go for the throat."

"'Go for the throat?' What do you mean?"

"I don't think we have anything left to lose. I think we should nationalize all of M-pire's Roderickstan assets."

"Really?" Dolly said, pondering the implications of that.

"Yes."

"What about China and the USA? Won't they invade?"

"Of course, I don't know for certain," Sandoval conceded,

"but I doubt it. It's one thing to defend M-Wan from our invasion and a completely another matter to invade our shores. I don't think China is ready for that or willing to spend the several trillion dollies it would cost.

"I don't think Muller wants to start a civil war or he would have already. Muller doesn't want to kill fellow Americans."

"That seems reasonable, I guess," Dolly said, disgusted. "This is so ridiculous."

"Indeed. I think we need to do it though. I think it's the only way we can diminish Martin's power enough and distract her enough to keep her from doing anything rash."

"Rash? Like?"

"I don't know. Hiring an assassin to kill you or maybe Ava?"

Dolly gasped. It would make sense for Martin to get even with Dolly by killing her favorite lover. Mary Ellen must have surely thought that she intentionally ordered Byrne's death. "Ava…? We must not let that happen."

"Correct. We don't want anything happening to either of you. Nationalizing M-pire's assets will ravage the corporation. If Martin is scrambling to save her precious family business from financial ruin, she won't be able to focus on revenge."

"I'm beside myself. This is far worse than all of Bobby's cheating. This is worse than losing the 2008 democratic primary to Williams. This might even be worse than losing the 2012 election to that fucking Austrian musclehead." She shrugged. "You're right. I don't see another choice. Let's do it. Brief Ava and have her set up a 3M ASAP, today if possible, to get this going. Also, triple the security on me, you, Ava and the rest of the cabinet members."

"Certainly," Pedro said. He debated bringing up his nephew and asking for a reprieve but decided against it. Instead, he hoped Dolly had forgotten the boy's involvement and had moved onto other crises in this particular shitstorm.

He bowed deferentially, turned toward the door and exited the room before Dolly could remember to say anything about Pedro's hapless nephew.

Chapter 34

The People's Republic of China president Tao Jhuns sat at a table in a private room of the ritzy Fangshan restaurant, pondering his next move. Under normal circumstances, he knew exactly how to handle Mary Ellen Martin. Some flirting, a little negotiating, perhaps a bit of "hide the egg roll" with no strings attached, no emotional strings anyway, but things had changed. Two months earlier, Mary Ellen's true life-long lover, Sylvia Byrne, had died and in her own arms, no less.

Tao had met with her a few times since Byrne's tragic death, once at the funeral and a couple of courtesy calls since, but Mary Ellen had been distant, aloof, cold, barely saying a word, obviously in the throes of a deep grieving process. Now, she sat across from him as if nothing ever happened, dressed to kill and looking ever so edible. She was animated and lively, even cracking an occasional joke.

It made no sense to Jhuns. The last time he had met with her, just two weeks ago, she was still listless and apathetic to the world. Now, she was acting like a disco party girl, looking quite ravishing in a teal dress with a plunging neckline that accentuated her scrumptious cleavage. It was certainly a marked improvement over the depressing plain black dress and pearls she wore at Byrne's funeral. Surprisingly, she had even worn a dowdy black hat and veil that day.

Normally Jhuns was calm and confident as was expected from the Chinese President, even around the ambitious and delicious Mary Ellen Martin, but something seemed out of sorts. A look in her eyes that didn't seem quite right. Just under the surface, a wildness, a rage, perhaps insanity, smoldered, threatening to unleash itself at any moment. He dared not bring up Sylvia for fear of bringing whatever "it" was to the surface.

Far worse, her plan seemed totally fanatical, bordering on Hitleresque derangement. She couldn't seriously expect to carry it off, and if she could pull it off, would she really want to? Jhuns certainly hoped not. "Mary Ellen, my flower, are you sure you want to do this?"

"Of course, Tao," Mary Ellen said calmly. "We have had our first loss in over thirty eight years. Roderickstan has stolen all of M-pire's assets in Roderickstan. She must be stopped. She is obviously a vengeful bitch bound and determined to destroy me and M-pire. I cannot just let this slide and go hide under a rock."

"What about the court system? Certainly, they can help..."

"No, no. Roderickstan is completely under that bitch's control. I'd just waste years and years in the courts and tons of money on the effort and gain nothing."

"Perhaps the United Nations or the World Trade Organization...?"

"No, no!" Mary Ellen rejoined. "What are they going to do? Slap her on the wrist? Sanction Roderickstan? She wouldn't care and M-pire won't get our assets back. No, it must be this way. I need something extreme. I need to take her out once and for all. Will you help me or not?"

"Are you absolutely certain you want to do this, my flower? These people aren't some thugs or mafia from the movies. These are real killers. Mbhuuti and his clan kill people for a living."

"That's exactly what I need, Tao," Mary Ellen said with a wild-eyed grin that worried the Chinese President.

"Okay, I'll arrange a meeting." Jhuns just had to hope that Martin would see reason and talk herself out of her mad scheme before she actually went through with it. If he didn't help her with the plan, she would just find someone else to help her, and his relationship with her might be adversely affected. Besides, if she really did manage to pull off her mad scheme, his country would benefit greatly from it. Tens of millions of Roderickstan might die but there would be no repercussions to China, and it might finally make China the greatest nation in the world for the first time in eight hundred years. It seemed like an acceptable tradeoff to Jhuns, if Mary Ellen's plan could actually work.

*****

Three weeks later, Mary Ellen Martin arrived at the Burj Al Arab hotel in Dubai, United Arab Emirates. Once the tallest hotel in the world, it was still considered one of the most luxurious. Its giant sail-shaped metal structure loomed over the Dubai coastline from a manmade island just off the coast. She took the lavish Royal Suites at a cost of $50,000 or about 17.5 billion M-Wan New Dollars per night.

Officially, the trip was a working vacation. Mary Ellen was in the Middle East to meet with some suppliers. Contrary to common belief, some things in M-Mart stores did indeed come from outside of M-Wan.

Tao Jhuns had arranged a meeting between Ishaeq Mbhuuti, leader of the Allied Republics of el-Queso, and her on the promise of a substantial anonymous donation to further the AReQi cause from Mary Ellen and deep discounts on a large amount of military munitions from Jhuns.

Four days after she arrived, Mary Ellen went to dinner with a local supplier at a fancy local restaurant. Halfway through the meal, as arranged, Mary Ellen snuck into a bathroom, changed clothes, slipped out the back door where she was placed, hooded and laying down, into the back seat of a nondescript car.

After what felt like at least a couple of hours to Mary Ellen, but was probably closer to forty-five minutes, the car stopped, someone grabbed her and walked her into a building. Finally, the escort took off her hood. They seemed to be in a warehouse or possibly an old office building. The

Immaculate Deception

guard led her down a bending hallway, turning several times along the way. They stopped at a door that was guarded by two men. Her guard talked to them in Arabic and they stepped aside, opening the door.

As Mary Ellen stepped into the room, she was surprised at the sight of Ishaeq Mbhuuti. Instead of being dressed in a turban and a robe, he was wearing a red polo shirt, blue jeans and a navy sport coat. He stood and walked over to her as she entered the room. He was much shorter than she would have thought, some three or four inches shorter than her own five foot seven inches in height. He was dark skinned with a long black beard with streaks of gray in it.

"Ah, Miss Martin, a pleasure, a pleasure," Mbhuuti said in surprisingly crisp English, bowing. "My apologies for the security measures, but that is the nature of my position."

Mary Ellen bowed in response. "Yes, certainly. Not a problem."

"My people are most appreciative of your gracious donation to our cause."

"You are most welcome, but that is just the start, your Excellency…"

"Ah, no need for that, Miss Martin. Please call me Ishaeq," he said.

"Oh, thank you, Ishaeq. Please call me Mary Ellen," she said with a smile.

"Certainly."

"As I was saying, I am willing to double my donation upon successful completion of the task, plus the cost of 'supplies', of course."

"Really? That is an intriguing sum. What task would you like my help with, Mary Ellen?"

Mary Ellen pulled a map of the world out from under her abaya and laid it on the table. She proceeded to detail the plan for Mbhuuti, pointing out various locations like the Canary Islands and Atlantic Beach, New York during the discussion. The AReQi leader listened quietly as she talked, never asking a single question. After she finished, an uneasy silence ensued for almost a minute. She asked, "So, what do you think?"

"Hmmm... quite intriguing," Mbhuuti said. "Have you verified the number of nuclear devices needed? And that they will have the desired effect?"

"I had our mutual friend do some research and he was told twelve twenty-kiloton bombs should be more than sufficient for the task."

"Yes, he certainly has the resources to verify the calculations. Quite intriguing. The repercussions could be quite devastating. This must be kept extremely confidential. If the USA or the European Union found out, it could get most unpleasant. We don't wish to start a world war."

"Yes, I agree," Mary Ellen said. "But our mutual friend said he would back you and any claims that it was a fanatical renegade group that did it without your authorization. That should be enough of an alibi if necessary."

"Very well. Payment in Euros as before. No offense to your country's New Dollar, but the conversion ratio is too difficult because the numbers are just too large. The calculations make my head pained."

"None taken," Mary Ellen said. "We're still working on inflation and strengthening our currency."

"Aren't we all? Aren't we all?" Mbhuuti agreed with a sigh.

"So, do we have an agreement?"

"Certainly. An advance of five billion Euros for supplies should be sufficient. Agreed?"

"Fair enough. What timeline for completion?"

"Hmmm. I will have to discuss with my..." Mbhuuti hesitated, searching for the appropriate word in English. "...specialists but I feel nine to fifteen months seems reasonable."

"Excellent," Mary Ellen said with a satisfied smile. "I'll have the money wired to your Swiss bank account today."

Mbhuuti clapped loudly and the guard opened the door.

"Mary Ellen, most pleasant meeting with you today. We will communicate again soon." He bowed deeply.

As Martin left the room, escorted by the guard, Mbhuuti thought how much more pleased Allah would be with him than his predecessor I. Nivaar bin Laed when he eliminated over one thousand times as many heretics in a single day as he had. The thought brought a smile to his face.

Chapter 35

News Items from 2024

From USA Today:

Roderickstan Winter Solstice Activities Outrage Muller

Coronado, CA – December 21, 2024 – Holding an emergency press conference from the Presidential Mansion (the former Hotel del Coronado), President Jurgin Muller condemned Dolly Roderick's latest actions.

"If there was ever any doubt that Dolly [Roderick] is a crazed, self-absorbed megalomaniac, this latest crime against humanity proves it beyond any doubt. I will personally demand the UN raise the highest sanctions against Roderickstan until Dolly is removed as President, Deity or whatever she feels like calling herself this week. This is an abomination as well as a decline in civilization back to the Dark Ages."

The crime against humanity Muller alludes to is the ritual sacrifice of twelve Roderick felons on the top of Roderickstan Castle to commemorate the twelfth anniversary since Mayageddon and Dolly Roderick's self-proclaimed ascension to into godhood. Critics outside of Roderickstan claim the felons were all unjustly convicted of treason against Dolly Roderick as a way to get rid of her political enemies.

Ritual sacrifice, except for very small pockets of African and Indonesian tribes, hasn't been practiced by any major civilized society since the Aztecs faded from history in the sixteenth century.

Fox News dubbed the horrific event "The Twelve Slays of Christmas..."

* * * * *

From the San Diego Union-Tribune:

M³ Made Citizen of USA

San Diego, CA – December 23, 2024 – Just in time for Christmas, the man known simply as M³ or the Maine Mystery Man has been made an official citizen of the Unified States of America, following last week's order by self-proclaimed Deity/President Dolly Roderick to arrest the enigmatic prophet and healer in Roderickstan, who was placed on the CYA's Top Ten Most Wanted list. President Jurgin Muller offered M³ asylum in the USA, and M³ gladly accepted the offer, fleeing from Maine into Canada, traveling to the Canadian West Coast and then making the journey to San Diego via the Pacific Coast Highway. "It was a beautiful drive," the prophet acknowledged.

Upon his arrival, M³ was given the keys to the city of San Diego and named an official citizen of the Unified States of America.

At the ceremony, Muller said, "It is just like Dolly [Roderick] to commit such an atrocity. M³, clearly a man of faith, clearly a humanitarian, a man who has healed hundreds, if not thousands of people, should not be arrested. Instead, he should be praised, embraced and accepted. Here, in the USA, we do that with open arms. It my pleasure to give M³ the keys to the city and make him a full citizen of the Unified States of America, complete with voting privileges. See, M³, here in the Unified States of America you get to vote."

In response, M³ said, "Thank you so much for your hospitality, President Muller. I look forward to calling the USA home." M³ reportedly healed several people and then had lunch with the President and several members of his cabinet. Afterwards, M³, whose true identity is still unknown though he sometimes goes by the moniker of Jesus of Toledo, disappeared, as has been his usual practice since he first began healing people in Maine over ten months ago…

Chapter 36

2025

CYA Special Agent in Charge Anita Gunn put a hand on Special Agent Jackson's shoulder and looked around the room at the members of her team. "Listen up, crew. This is fresh meat. His name is Ryan Jackson."

Hellos echoed from around the room.

Ryan looked at Gunn. "Fresh meat?"

"Yes, our friendly term for a new recruit. Grab a seat, Jackson," Gunn said, sitting herself at one end of the table.

"Okay, guys, try not to get the new guy killed. Jackson's no slouch and no noob. He graduated from Really West Point with honors, was a Navy SEAL, a SWAT specialist and, most recently, a homicide detective in Mission Viejo, California."

"How did he end up here?" a towering black man at least six-foot-four and probably 320 pounds of pure muscle said. It looked as though his chair was going to collapse under his immensity any second.

"Tiny, Jackson had a run of bad luck while attending the SWAT convention last year in the Big Apple. He tried to stop a mugging in the subway without a weapon and got plugged three times in the chest. He was in a coma for eight months with several million dollies of unpaid medical bills."

"Ouch," Tiny said.

"Yeah, I forgot that airport security had confiscated my gun." Ryan blushed. "I went for it, and the perp popped me."

"The Big Apple took a bite out of you, eh?" a guy of average height, brown hair and brown eyes said with a snicker.

Gunn looked over at Ryan. "That would be your new partner, Pedro 'Sully' O'Sullivan. He's a bit of an acquired taste…"

"…that most of us still haven't acquired," a cute thirtyish woman with red hair, green eyes and a lightly freckled face chimed in with a sexy grin.

"Indeed," Gunn agreed. "Anyway, the CYA, the goodhearted people that we are, bailed Ryan out from his medical bills in exchange for working with you knuckleheads."

"'Sully's new partner'?" a man maybe five foot, ten inches tall, with black hair and brown eyes asked with a hint of hope.

"Yes, Honey Buns, you're being reassigned," Anita Gunn said.

"Yes!" Honey Buns nearly screamed with excitement, slamming his right fist onto the table, confirming Ryan's suspicion that this assignment was indeed going to be a steaming pile of crap.

"Okay, I get Sully and Tiny, but Honey Buns?" Ryan asked. "Your group has an interesting sense of humor."

"Damn straight," the cute redhead chimed in again. "Maybe I'll even tell you mine someday," she added, giving him a wink. Several people giggled under their breath at the comment.

Ryan swallowed hard, somehow aroused and intimidated at the same time by the offer.

Gunn cleared her throat, blushing slightly. "Honey Buns is my husband, Special Agent Raymond Gunn. He's a third degree black belt in Aikido. I'd recommend you stick with Ray or Gunn. Even Tiny has never called him Honey Buns."

"Right." Ryan said. Then he looked over at Ray, saying, "You look more like an apple fritter to me, anyway."

The group laughed.

"Hey!" Ray started to get up.

"Ray, sit," his wife commanded. "Jackson, in addition to being a Navy SEAL, is a fifth degree black belt in Karate."

"Brazilian Ju Jitsu, actually," Ryan corrected.

"Fifth? Damn," Tiny said, impressed.

Ray, still fuming, settled back in his chair.

"Hey, Ray, just kidding, man," Jackson said.

"No problem," Ray said with a discomfited grin, the crimson hue slowly fading from his face.

The rest of the meeting continued uneventfully for another forty minutes. After it ended, Anita requested that Ryan and Sully meet her in her office.

Ten minutes later, Jackson and Sully joined Gunn in her office and sat around a small round conference table. Gunn slid a thin red file folder in front of Ryan. The folder was labeled "Operation Martian Invasion." Ryan opened the folder and found a couple pieces of paper taped to the inside of the folder and a flashdot storage device resting in a baggie. The flashdot was about the size of an old USA dime from back before hard currency had been discontinued in 2015 for security and cost reasons. It hardly made sense to keep making pennies when each one cost 6.8 pennies to produce.

"Wow," he said. "That's either a pretty old flashdot or a very large capacity one." Normally, flashdots were closer to the size of a pencil eraser and held sixty-four to 128 terabytes of data.

"Well," Gunn began stiffly. "A bit of both, actually. Budget constraints limit us to having to pick and choose where we use cutting-edge technologies and where we don't. We usually pick the latest guns, flak jackets and surveillance technologies over storage. Sorry."

"Okay, fair enough," Ryan conceded. He scanned the pieces of paper in the file and noted that it was a list of the contents of the flashdot: a bio of Mary Ellen Martin, CEO of M-Pire, Inc., a company overview of M-pire, Inc., a bio of somebody Ryan had never heard of, a Sylvia Byrne, M-pire CFO, listed as deceased, etc. He looked up from the pages. "Interesting. 'Operation Martian Invasion'? Very cute. Why would the Castle want to investigate a corporation headquartered halfway around the world?"

"It's all on the flashdot but the short story is the Dolly Mama and Mary Ellen Martin have a very long history, dating back some thirty years when the Dolly Mama was the First Lady of the USA and Martin was her intern. They had a falling out of some sort that we haven't been able to figure out and the Dolly Mama would never elaborate. They've had this weird game of one-upmanship ever since. A while back it led to a CYA raid on the Martinville M-pire headquarters that went bad and Mary Ellen Martin's lover and M-pire CFO Sylvia Byrne was killed."

"It was an accident," Sully said awkwardly.

"Yes, true, an accident, Jackson," Gunn admitted, "in which your partner here shot Byrne in the heart with a TASER and caused her pacemaker to short out."

Ryan's eyes went wide. "Really? I didn't know that was even possible."

"Yes, we didn't either but evidently it is." Gunn looked over at Sully, a hint of patronization in her eyes. "What were the odds, O'Sullivan? One in a million?"

"One in 350,000."

"Jeez...," Ryan said, catching himself. "That is some statistically improbable bad luck there, partner."

"Never mind," she said. "To make a long story short, the Castle is convinced that Martin is more of a threat than ever and will, sooner or later, go off the deep end and try something extreme."

"Like...?" Ryan inquired.

"That's the problem," Gunn admitted. "We don't know. M-pire seems to have excellent security. We found precious little in the way of any intel coming from M-pire in the three years since we officially opened the case. We have nothing about any sort of plot in the offing. We have wiretaps, i-mail and e-mail tapping, satellite coverage of all of their major factories, headquarters, etc. Nothing. Nothing at all. We are even doing some spying on M-Wan, but we have to be careful there as that's another country and they have a strong alliance with China and the Dolly Mama is very worried about upsetting them."

"So, you have nothing?"

"Basically, yes."

"No known plot? It could be an assassination attempt; messing with the stock market; blowing up Manhattan; anything?"

"Yep," Sully said. "That about sums it up. We got nuthin'."

"So no useful intel is coming out of M-pire or M-Wan?" Ryan asked.

"Correct," Gunn said with a hint of growing irritation. "I believe we've already covered that."

"Right. Perhaps we need to think outside of the box here. If Martin was going to try something like nuking Manhattan or blowing up the Castle or even trying to assassinate the Dolly Mama, how would she go about it?"

"What do you mean?" Gunn asked.

"I mean she couldn't just go to one of her stores and go to the nuclear device aisle and buy it. She would need some outside help. Who would that be?"

"Ah, I see." Gunn's face brightened. "I knew adding you to the team was a good idea. So, you mean the black market or maybe Russia?"

"Exactly. Maybe China, India or my personal number one candidate: the el-Queso. While we need to keep Martin and M-pire under surveillance, of course, I recommend shifting our focus to these other groups and see if anything unusual pops up. I assume we already have people assigned to monitor el-Queso, China, etc., right?"

Gunn nodded.

"So then, we just get with them and start looking for anything out of the ordinary that might link them to M-pire or Martin or even anything unusual, i-mail or sat phone traffic, for example, that might have started after Byrne was killed."

272

"I didn't kill her," Sully said with a hurt tone. "It was an accident."

Gunn smiled, dismissing O'Sullivan's comment. "This is an excellent start, Jackson. Evidently, they taught you well at Really West Point."

"There wasn't really a whole lot to do there on our off-time except to study. It's not like we could sneak away and go into town and get drunk."

"True enough." Gunn, though she hadn't been to the Unified States of America since the split, knew that Really West Point was on Alcatraz Island and built by renovating the maximum security prison that was nicknamed the Rock. The pictures she had seen made the place seem state of the art and even plush, but still it was Alcatraz and the thought made her shudder.

"Okay, O'Sullivan, I want you to show Jackson around and get right on those ideas of his. I think this might be the breakthrough we've been looking for. Good job, Jackson."

Chapter 37

The People's Republic of China President Tao Jhuns sat at his usual table in his usual private room of his usual restaurant, the ultra-expensive and flamboyant Fangshan as his confidant, sometime lover, and now partner in future crimes against humanity Mary Ellen Martin entered the room. She wore a black dress with beige patterns and a delectably adventurous plunging neckline so extreme he wondered if she had to somehow tape the dress to her nipples to keep the dress from fully exposing her breasts. The bottom curve of her breasts could be seen from the neckline and the sides of her dress. Candy apple red lipstick and matching high-heel shoes completed the ensemble.

Jhuns didn't really care how the delightfully trashy yet somehow dignified dress kept Mary Ellen's treasures under wraps. He was more interested that it seemed that the old pre-Byrne's death Martin was finally back and, hopefully, for the first time in several months, he was going to get to do a little negotiating in the bedroom with her after the meal.

Mary Ellen walked over to Jhuns, who intentionally remained sitting so she would have to lean over and kiss him on the cheek. Her breasts somehow managed to stay confined, confirming his suspicion of some form of tape. After the kiss, Jhuns stood, gave her a deep hug, squishing her large breasts into his chest and gave her a kiss on the neck, not wanting to mess up her makeup or get any of her lipstick on himself. He stopped when he felt the Sensei begin to stir within his pants. That would have to wait for later. "My precious flower, I believe this is possibly the most delicious you have ever looked."

"Why, thank you, Tao," she said with a devilish grin.

He released her and pulled out her chair. She sat and he stole another glance at her glorious cleavage. She noticed what he was doing and grinned even wider.

Mary Ellen's face grew serious, looking around. "Is it safe to talk here?"

"Certainly. I had my people sweep the room for bugs twice." Jhuns pointed at a dark gray device the size of shoebox sitting on a nearby table. The device had a couple of antennae, some lights in various colors and several switches. "That should scrambled any signal and disrupt anyone trying to listen in. It has a range of 20 meters. Nothing in or out."

"Excellent," Mary Ellen reached out and gently grabbed his right hand, pulled it to her lips and licked the back of it playfully. "Did you acquire the 'merchandise'?"

"Of course. Acquisition is not the issue. We have thousands of them lying around in warehouses all over the world. A couple of calls to loyal, discreet friends in the military procured them. Merchandise is easy to misplace and disappears completely just as easily. The transportation is somewhat more difficult. Your friends are highly scrutinized. We have to be careful and go through several intermediaries to be certain nothing gets traced to either you or me. That would be inconvenient for both of us."

The 'merchandise' Jhuns referred to were a dozen twenty-kiloton nuclear warheads.

Still holding his hand, Mary Ellen suggestively sucked on his index finger. "Inconvenient?" She laughed lightly. "You have such a delightful manner of understatement about you. I've always loved that about you."

Jhuns was taken aback. Loved that about you? While, back before Byrne's death, she had been spirited and adventurous in his bed, Jhuns had always known their relationship, as it were, was purely political and not emotional. She pretended to want him and satisfied him sexually as a means to an end. Loved that about you? It sounded almost, almost, as if she was actually beginning to think of him as more than just a political confidant. Interesting possibilities formed in his mind. Marriage to the president of a neighboring country and the CEO of the most powerful corporation in the world would certainly make them the most powerful couple in the world, if Mary Ellen's little plan of revenge didn't cause a world war or them being executed for crimes against humanity by a United Nations Security Council tribunal, which they wouldn't accept and would, in turn, start a world war. Either way, it might be a world war. Still, the possibility was tempting. He would have to explore that more later, in the bedroom while he explored Mary Ellen's numerous assets.

Jhuns refocused, conceding, "Perhaps devastating or catastrophic would be more accurate. Anyway, the merchandise should be arriving at the destination in the next couple of days and shouldn't be traceable to either of us. If anything ever is discovered, it will have the appearance that it was procured from the Russian black market and won't be traced to either of our governments. As long as you are careful with your interactions with our friend, everything should be fine."

'Our friend' was the leader of the Allied Republics of el-Queso, Ishaaq Mbhuuti, and the 'destination' was a clandestine AReQi camp about twenty-five kilometers southwest of the small Moroccan port town of Tarfaya. Tarfaya was the westernmost town of any size in the entire AReQi Empire, having some 4,500 inhabitants and had a military garrison with a couple of AReQi navy patrol boats that were stationed for sea rescues more than anything.

The secret base was home to a thousand-plus of Mbhuuti's most elite troops, the Democratic Guard, his personal guards. It was the perfect location to hold the 'merchandise' until it was sent to its final destination of the island of Isla de Las Palma, the western-most of the Canary Islands, some 500 kilometers west of the camp.

"Excellent," Mary Ellen said. "I'll have to meet in person with our friend by the end of the week. I should leave right away."

What? What about the Sensei? A brief look of panic came to Jhun's face before he regained composure.

Mary Ellen chuckled lightly and sucked his index finger back into her mouth. "Don't worry, lover. I meant I needed to leave in the morning. I was planning on spending the night to show my appreciation for all of your hard work. Is that okay?"

"Ah, yes, my precious flower," Tao said with a mischievous grin. "I'll be happy to show you my hard work tonight."

Chapter 38

Sully looked over Ryan's shoulder at the plasma computer screen in Ryan's cubicle as his partner typed on the virtual laser keyboard image that flashed on his desk. Sully guided Ryan through the seemingly endless amount of data that Sully and Honey Buns had gathered over the last three years.

The problem wasn't the massive amount of data but the massive amount of useless data. Ryan figured that maybe two to three percent of it might be useful and the rest should be recycled, but, of course, it wouldn't. The government didn't get rid of anything, especially now that you could scan or take a picture or video of almost anything and fit what used to fill an entire warehouse with boxes of paper onto a flashdot the size of your pinky fingernail. The only items actually stored in boxes in warehouses anymore were physical evidence like blood-stained clothes, carpet fibers for DNA testing and the like.

Unfortunately, Sully and Ray weren't the most organized people in the world and there were random files in random folders all over the flashdot. There were some 1,436 files in 112 folders, and that didn't include the 1,138 daily report logs in the folders labeled "2022," "2023," and "2024," which would hopefully have some valuable information in them, but so far not much.

A folder, presumably Sully's, with the ominous label of "bigguns36ddd" with scantily clad women dry humping a variety of two-wheeled and four-wheeled vehicles was among the files. Ryan assumed Ray would be too smart to risk his wife's wrath by stashing porn so poorly on work equipment.

Immaculate Deception

Ryan assumed Ballcrusher, as he had found most of the team called Anita behind her back, could kick her husband's ass. Heck, she could probably kick Ryan's ass, for that matter. Being a fifth degree black belt, Ryan wasn't afraid of much, but he was unsettled by her. He was also a little turned on by her, which struck Ryan as odd because it seemed wrong on so many levels.

Though Ryan hadn't learned much, he did know that Mary Ellen Martin had a major grudge against Dolly Roderick, made ten times worse by the death of Sylvia Byrne, Mary Ellen's best friend, business partner, and alleged lover, though they were secretive about that and the evidence was thin. The only people who could verify that were Mary Ellen, who certainly wouldn't verify anything, Sylvia, who was dead, and Mary Ellen's test tube son who had disappeared, seemingly off the face of the earth, some six years earlier.

Ryan had also learned that Mary Ellen had made several business decisions specifically with the intention to hurt Roderick financially or politically. The decisions, while they always improved M-pire's position in the marketplace and were sometimes even brilliant, were obviously aimed at attacking Roderick's powerbase. Breaking the AFL-CIO, buying Taiwan and moving the M-pire headquarters there to deprive Roderickstan of billions, maybe trillions of dollies of tax revenue, plus dozens of other decisions, were aimed squarely at infuriating Roderick.

Each decision escalated the feud. Anita and the rest were right. Mary Ellen must be planning something and it must be big, enormous, perhaps stupendous, but what? An assassination? Probably not. Is the murder of one person, even the leader of a superpower, bigger than costing that country billions of dollies? Ryan didn't think so. In fact, he thought Mary Ellen wouldn't want to kill Dolly at all but would rather keep crippling her financially and watching her suffer. That had been Mary Ellen's modus operandi so far.

If not assassination, then what? What else could she do to

further mess with Roderick? Martin had already devastated her tax base, making it impossible to reunite the country. What else was there for Mary Ellen to do?

Jorge Killian walked up to Jackson's cube. "Hey guys."

"Yo, Big Red!" Sully said like a college cheer.

Killian, just five foot three inches tall and with hair even redder than Janine Kilborn's, earned the moniker seconds after labeling the gargantuan Lester Hayes "Tiny." Hayes countered by calling Killian "Big Red." Both names stuck.

Killian tossed a flashdot onto Jackson's desk. "Check this out. I've been monitoring el-Queso traffic and something weird seems to be going on that I think might be relevant to your M-pire case. Check out the file 'Jackson'."

Ryan tapped a few strokes on the virtual keyboard and the file popped up on the screen in front of him. A transcript of various Grid instant messenger traffic appeared in front of him. "Okay, what are we looking for?"

Killian leaned over Jackson's shoulder and tapped the virtual keyboard and scrolled down several pages in the file. "There."

It was a Grid instant messenger conversation between two people:

[Translated from Arabic]

Eq7465: Is the L.P. project as per schedule? The client requires a status report. She is getting much [untranslatable expletive, word removed] upset. She is worried about delays.

Eq6231: The merchandise has been transported to the island and awaits positioning.

Eq7465: Estimated timetable?

Eq6231: Three to five weeks, depending on how carefully we have to hide ourselves from the locals.

Eq7465: Excellent. I'll let his Excellency know.

Eq6231: Uh, you were not supposed to use titles, were you, you fornicator of camels?

Eq7465: Ah, Shi'ite! I did it again. Many apologies.

The dialog went on for several pages.

Ryan swiveled around in his chair and looked up at Killian. "So, Big Red, what do you make of it?"

"We traced the eq6231 and eq7465 IDs. One was traced to a gateway in Saudi Arabia, Medina to be exact and the other came through a gateway in Morocco, a small town called Tarfaya."

"Tarfaya, where the heck is that?" Sully asked.

"It's a small coastal town on the western edge of AReQ."

"Really?" Ryan pondered. "And Morocco is on the Atlantic Ocean, not the Mediterranean Sea, correct?"

"Exactly," Big Red said with a knowing grin.

Sully's face lit up. "Hey, aren't there some islands off the Moroccan coast; Easter island or the Cardinal islands or something?"

"Close," Ryan said, tapping a few keys on his virtual keyboard and the computer screen changed to a map of Africa and the Atlantic Ocean. He pointed to several dots off the Moroccan coast. "Wrong ocean for Easter Island. It's in the South Pacific, but the Canary Islands are off the Moroccan coast, I believe."

"Canary, cardinal, a bird's a bird," Sully said indifferently.

"Sure. Marilyn Monroe, Rosie O'Donnell, a woman's a woman, right?" Ryan asked.

Sully winced, shaking his head. "Point made."

"So, Big Red," Jackson asked, "you think the island reference is referring to one or all of the Canary Islands?"

"Seems logical. It's certainly a good place to start."

"And the EQ IDs are el-Queso operatives?" Ryan

continued.

"Indubitably, Sherlock. Anything else?" Killian prompted.

"Like?" Ryan countered.

"What does L.P. in L.P. Project stand for, for example?"

"Uh," Sully stammered, obviously wracking his brain. "Libertarian Party…Liquid Propane…Laser Prostatectomy…?

"Laser Prostatectomy? Nice try, Sully," Big Red said. "That's it. I decided to come over here and waste your time with the Laser Prostatectomy project. Ryan, your turn."

"Hmmm." Ryan looked back at the computer screen and focused in on the Canary Islands. "Sully, lookie there? The far west island is called La Palma."

"Holy Shit, dude!" Sully nearly shouted.

"Exactly," Big Red said with a smile.

Now, it was Ryan's turn to give a wry grin. "Anything else, guys?"

"Like?" Killian countered with a wry grin of his own.

"Who is His Excellency?"

"Well, duh," Sully answered. "That must be Mbhuuti, right?"

"Correct," Ryan said.

Sully smiled proudly.

"Anything else?"

"Like…who 'she' is, you mean?" Killian offered.

"Indeed," Ryan said simply. He and Big Red looked at Sully with a mix of mirth and expectation.

After waiting a few moments for Sully's epiphany to materialize, Ryan added, "Sully, who are we investigating?"

"M-pire…"

"No, that's more of a what. Who are we investigating?" Ryan prodded.

"Mary Ellen Martin… Holy shit, dude! Martin has hired the el-Queso to do something to the Dolly Mama!"

"It's certainly beginning to look that way," Ryan said. He turned to Killian. "But what?"

"That's the 20 billion dollie question, now, isn't it?"

"Indubitably," Ryan said, rubbing his chin. "Indubitably."

* * * * *

Ryan looked around at the stacks of papers, some almost a foot high, of random clues that needed to be sifted through, sorted and scanned to be filed in the CYA's database, and sighed. So much for the paperless office. Hadn't they been talking about that for fifty years now? Computers were going to change everything… Yeah, right. He stood up and looked over the cubicle wall at O'Sullivan, saying, "Hey, Sully, my brain's fried. Want to grab some lunch at Twin Peaks?"

Ten minutes later they were sitting down at a table ordering hot wings and soda from a buxom co-ed beauty clad only in a white bikini top, a woodmen's vest unbuttoned just enough to press her breasts skyward, a very short plaid kilt and lumberjack boots. It just wasn't the same as ordering hot wings and beer from a buxom co-ed beauty clad only in a white bikini top, a woodmen's vest unbuttoned just enough to press her breasts skyward, a very short plaid kilt and lumberjack boots but it was heck of a lot better than the scenery at the CYA cafeteria, or the food for that matter.

As they waited for the food, Ryan looked over to see his partner intently reviewing some documents on the eight by ten-inch screen of his Amazon Kindle XL, a device for reading books, newspapers and other documents and surfing the Grid.

"Watcha looking at? Porn?" Ryan asked with a laugh.

"No way, dude," Sully said. "Believe it or not, I'm actually working. Besides, the screen is way too small for porn."

"Right. Watcha working on, then?"

"I think I might have a link here to the Martin-el-Queso connection. Big Red forwarded me a file with some potential money laundering activity on it. He found a company named

Mpulsive.com that bought a bunch of random electronics equipment to the tune of six billion dollies from a Dubai company called Big Cheese Productions. It looks like Big Cheese Productions is just a front. Big Red couldn't find any legitimate material purchases from Big Cheese Productions and only a couple of employees."

"So Mpulsive.com sounds like a front for filtering M-pire money to the el-Queso through this Big Cheese Productions then?"

"Yep, that's what it looks like. There is a bunch of activity on their bank accounts. Within two weeks of the Mpulsive.com purchase of six billion dollies, an equivalent amount was sent to three companies for 'parts' and those three companies bought 'materials' from eight other companies. The bottom line is ninety-two percent of the original six billion dollies ended in top secret Swiss bank accounts within a month."

"Hmmm… When did this all happen?"

"Mpulsive.com did the original purchase seven weeks ago. The money disappeared just over three weeks."

"And references to the L.P. project began happening around the same timeframe. Any activity coming from the Canary Islands?"

"Not really. Whatever they are doing, they are being extremely secretive about it. Everything must be being done at night and they are taking countermeasures. Our satellites aren't picking up anything."

"This is a real problem. Six billion dollies? Something big, really big is going down and probably soon. When we get back from lunch, I want to pull all of the satellite coverage of the Canary Islands, especially La Palma, for the last seven weeks and see if we can find anything useful. We may need to go on a little vacation on the company dollie."

"How about the Canary Islands?" Sully offered with a grin.

"Sounds like the perfect vacation spot."

"I wonder if they have nude beaches there…"

Chapter 39

"Yo, Sully!" Ryan yelled.

"Yeah?"

He threw a wadded up piece of paper over the cubicle wall at his partner.

"Damn it!" Sully snapped.

Ryan could tell from the sound the paper made that it hit Sully in the head again.

"How the hell do you manage to hit me in the head every time, you rat bastard?"

"Hey, what can I say, I missed my calling. I should have been a basketball superstar."

"Sure, champ," Sully said. "You missed your calling by about a good foot and a half at least. What do you want, or do you just like torturing me?"

Ryan tossed another wad over the cubicle wall. "I just like torturing you."

"Great, thanks, buttmunch."

"Ah, where's the love, Sully?"

"I got your love right here. Leave me alone already."

"Seriously, come here. I think I've got something."

Sully came over to Ryan's cubicle and stuffed the wads he had picked up down the back of Ryan's shirt.

"Hey now," Ryan said, scrambling to retrieve the wads from his back. "I guess I deserved that. We're even now, okay?"

"Fine, watcha got?"

Ryan pointed at his computer screen. It looked like a spreadsheet listing of accounting entries. "See this company here?"

"Mama Drama, Inc! Yeah, that's one of the holding companies linked with Big Cheese Productions, right?"

"Yep, notice these purchases here?"

Ryan scrolled down a list of seventeen purchases ranging from $1.2 million Euros to $3.2 million Euros each.

"Yeah, they are buying a lot of something. What?"

"Property on La Palma island."

"What?!"

"It gets worse," Ryan said. "They are buying huge parcels right next to the Parque Nacional de la Caldera de Taburiente."

"Why the heck would they do that?"

"I don't know."

"Do you think we should try again to get Gunn to let us go there and investigate?" Sully asked.

"Maybe, but I'll think she'll say no again. We're getting close but we need more."

"Yeah," Sully shrugged. "But what?"

"I don't know." Ryan stared at the ceiling, tossing a wad in the air and catching it. "Why would the el-Queso or Martin want land next to a park on a Podunk little island in the middle of nowhere? Hmmm…"

"Maybe we should have the Sat Boys monitor the area. Do you have the specs on the lots?"

Ryan sat up like someone tasered him and began typing furiously. "That's a great idea, Sully, and I thought you were just a pretty face."

"What can I say? I'm the complete package."

Ryan winced at the thought. "Dude, I don't want to know about your package."

"Ah, but the ladies do," Sully said with a grin.

"Are you sure that was a lady?"

"Dude, that's messed up."

* * * * *

The Sat Boys were the CYA's satellite surveillance team. They were a bunch of nerdy ninety-eight pound weakling types with pocket protectors, taped-together glasses and most could rattle off pi to the ten-thousandth digit. Most of the field agents barely tolerated the Sat Boys because they never had to risk their lives out in the field but had the same pay scale and the same title. That worked in Ryan's favor because he treated the Sat Boys with respect, especially their commander, Special Agent in Charge Ike Phillips, and they were always quick to help him out of because of it.

Ryan shot off an e-mail to Phillips with his request for surveillance footage of the el-Queso La Palma properties. Two minutes later the reply came, instructing Ryan to stop by in half an hour.

Twenty-six minutes later, Ryan and Sully made their way across the parking lot to the Surveillance building that held all of the communications (satellite, Grid, radio and phone) equipment and personnel. Right at thirty minutes, they strolled up to a large room with a dozen monitor screens that filled most of one of the walls. Phillips was waiting for them.

Ryan walked up and shook Phillip's hand. "Hey, Ike, thanks for your help."

Phillips returned the handshake and shook Sully's hand as well. "No problem, guys. Let's take a look. What are the coordinates?"

"Uh, yeah," Ryan said, pulling a note out of his pocket. "It's twenty-eight degrees north and fifteen degrees west."

"No minutes or seconds?" Ike asked.

"Minutes, seconds?" Sully asked. "You need to know the local time?"

"No, O'Sullivan," Phillips said calmly as if talking to a kindergartener. "Longitude and Latitude are measured in units called hours, better known as degrees, minutes and seconds. At the equator, a degree is almost seventy miles wide. Our satellites are precise enough they can tell your hair color from 22,000 miles above the earth. So, using degrees is pretty vague when we are searching for plots of land less than a quarter-mile across. Not a problem, though. We can start from there." Phillips typed the coordinates into the computer and zoomed in just to fit La Palma on the screen in its entirety.

Ryan scanned the image carefully and pointed. "The first site should be right around there."

Phillips re-centered the image and zoomed until a ten by thirteen mile area came into focus.

"Okay," Ryan said. "The edge of the park is this ridge right here, so the area must be those dots right there."

Phillips tapped a few the virtual keyboard keys and the screen zoomed in again until it displayed one mile by 1.3 mile area. Box and cylinder shapes were clearly visibly in the northwest corner of the screen.

"That's definitely a camp or some sort of construction zone."

"Seems to be. Let's check it out." Phillips zoomed in again. This time to 500 feet by 650 feet. Several large tents were discernable and half a dozen military-style transport trucks. A couple dozen or so people, usually grouped in twos or threes, stood guard along the perimeter of the camp. As the CYA agents watched the screen, a transport truck disappeared into the large tent in the middle of the camp.

"Can we listen to what those guards are saying?" Ryan asked.

Phillips chuckled. "Our technology is good, very good, really, but not that good. We can setup a listening post within a quarter of a mile or so and hear a pin drop. Unfortunately, 22,000 miles is just too far. The sound gets distorted to the point of uselessness way, way before that."

Ryan rubbed his eyes with the palm of his hands. "How about infrared or x-rays? Can we try to look into those tents, especially that big one?"

"Now, that I can do." Ike tapped a few keystrokes, gazing at the screen the whole time. As the screen image changed, a perplexed look came to his face. "That's interesting."

"What?" Sully asked, peering at the screen intently, trying to figure out what Phillips had noticed. "I don't see anything."

"Exactly. We should be able to see something. We know there are people and hot vehicle engines in that tent yet...nothing." Phillips changed the screen again. "Yep, just as I thought. Nothing on x-ray either."

"So, what does that mean, Ike?" Ryan asked.

"Either that tent is extremely heavy or extremely expensive or possibly a bit of both."

"Hunh?" Sully asked.

"The tent is lined with lead...?" Ryan offered.

"Exactly, or possibly tungsten, some form of carbon composite fiber, something like that. The bottom line is someone down there doesn't want anyone snooping in on them."

"That's not good," Sully said. "We really need to get Gunn to send us there to check things out."

"Yep," Ryan said. "I don't think we've got quite enough. Close, but not quite. I've got something I want to track down that I think will put us over the top. I'll hook up with you later, okay, Sully?"

"I guess. What is your lead?"

"I'm not sure yet. I seem to remember a TV show about natural disasters that I saw when I was a kid. I'm going to surf the Grid and see if I can track it down. I'll catch up with you later."

"Sure."

* * * * *

As Sully walked into the conference room, Anita Gunn looked over at Ryan, who fiddled with the room's projector. "Okay, Jackson, everyone's here. We've all dropped everything. This had better be good."

Ryan looked around the room at Gunn's entire team, from

Anita's husband, Janine "the Love Machine" Kilborn, Sully, Tiny, and the rest. "Don't worry, Chief. I am certain you'll find this enlightening and, quite possibly, terrifying."

After his first week at the CYA, Ryan began calling Gunn "Chief" after the Chief on the old TV spy show Get Smart. At first, it annoyed Anita but she had accepted it as a term of endearment and had even grown to like it...just a little.

"What you are about to see is an old television special from the BBC, the British Broadcasting Corporation, called Mega-tsunami: Wave of Destruction. I first saw this when I was a little kid, maybe eight or nine."

"What is a mega-tsunami?" Tiny asked.

"A tsunami is a huge wave, sometimes called a tidal wave, that can be a hundred feet high or taller, but they are usually localized, hitting just one beach. A mega-tsunami can hit hundreds or thousands of miles of beach. One time, the day after Christmas..."

"Winter Solstice, I'm sure you meant, right, Jackson?" Gunn corrected quickly.

"Uh, okay... On the 26th of December, 2004, an Indian Ocean earthquake caused a mega-tsunami that killed almost a quarter of a million people from eleven different countries. Some of the deaths were over 3,500 miles from the earthquake's epicenter."

"Holy crap," Sully said.

"Indeed." Anita Gunn gave Sully a look that made Ray cringe involuntarily. "I remember it. That's tragic, Jackson, but what does have to do with your case on Martin and M-pire?"

"Watch, you'll see." Ryan started the show. "Lights out." The room's monitoring system turned out the lights and the room went dark.

A beautiful island came on the screen and a narrator described the various lush qualities of the island, then he gave the island's name: La Palma. Ryan paused the show. "This is the island Sully, Big Red, Phillips and I have been investigating for the last few days. We have found links to the el-Queso and some of Martin's holding companies to this island."

He began the show again. The show painted a picture of the eminent destruction of a large portion of the island. A large caldera dubbed Caldera de Taburiente, some ten kilometers across, could collapse due to an earthquake and send a huge chunk of the caldera into the Atlantic Ocean. If it did, it could cause a mega-tsunami over a mile high to head toward the United States of America at over five hundred miles per hour, wiping out cities like Washington, D.C., Manhattan and Providence, Rhode Island, possible killing tens of millions of people.

"Holy crap," Sully said again.

"Indeed," Gunn said again. "But, again, what does this have to do with your M-pire case?"

Ryan paused the show and brought up a giant map of La Palma with several large red dots that formed a semi-circle in the shape of a reversed "C." "See, this is the caldera and these red dots are areas of el-Queso activity along the caldera."

"They seemed to be evenly spaced," Big Red said.

"Yep, they are exactly one kilometer apart and there are twelve sites."

"So," Gunn said. "What are they doing there?"

"We don't know. They are using some form of lead-based tent in each area to mask what they are doing. Infrared and x-ray satellites can't see through the tents."

"Okay," Gunn said. "So, what do you think they are doing, Jackson?"

"My theory is..."

"Actually, a theory is generally accepted fact," Janine said with an 'I want to jump your bones' smile. "A hypothesis is an educated guess."

"Okay..." Ryan was somehow annoyed yet aroused at the same time. Janine often had that effect on him. He probably would have already tried to seduce her if he wasn't so afraid of catching something from her. "My hypothesis is that Martin has paid the el-Queso to cause the caldera on La Palma to fall into the ocean and cause a mega-tsunami to wipe out Roderickstan Castle and kill Roderick or at least destroy the Roderickstan economy to avenge her lover's death and the nationalization of M-pire property in Roderickstan."

"Holy crap," Sully said again.

"Exactly." Gunn gave Sully an irritated look, then she turned back to Ryan. "How sure are you, Jackson?"

"Not very," Ryan conceded. "It could be easily that I'm simply making the facts fit my theor…hypothesis, right, Janine?"

"True," Kilborn said.

"But," Ryan continued. "Can you think of another reason the el-Queso would be digging holes around the rim of a volcano on an island in the middle of the Atlantic Ocean?"

Everyone looked around the room at each other, searching for another possible explanation.

"Not really," Gunn said.

"How about drilling for oil?" Sully offered.

"Ever seen an oil derrick on the top of a mountain?" Big Red asked. "Besides, the el-Queso can't just set up an oil operation in the middle of a national park on an island owned by Spain. Whatever they are doing is meant to be temporary and deniable. Boss, we need to jump on this stat. Whatever is going down, is going to be going down any second now."

"Jackson, do you agree with Killian?" Gunn asked.

"Yes, if my hypothesis is correct, they must be almost done."

"Hayes?"

Tiny nodded.

Gunn continued around the room and the rest of the group nodded their assent.

"Fair enough," Gunn said. "I agree with Killian too. We need to jump on this fast and hard. I want the whole team to be ready to leave in forty-five minutes. Yancy, the choppers can be ready for takeoff by then, right?"

"Yessir. As always, they are ready for immediate departure."

"Good." Gunn turned back to Ryan. "Jackson, you're running lead on this. I'm heading to the Castle to give them a briefing of the situation and get proper permission from the Spanish government to investigate La Palma." Gunn's gaze grew even more serious. "Whether or not we get permission before you arrive, land and investigate, no matter what. If you're right, Jackson, there is way too much at stake here. We can always apologize to the Spanish government later if we have to. Got it?"

"Loud and clear, Chief."

"Any questions?" Gunn looked around the room. No one said anything. "Dismissed. Departure is in forty-two minutes."

The team scrambled out of the room.

Chapter 40

Mary Ellen Martin stood at a chest-high small circular table outside of a small coffeehouse/bistro called Grind It, Baby a few blocks from the Roderickstan Castle in Atlantic Beach. She was on the phone. The phone was an untraceable prepaid satellite phone she had bought with cash in Rome using the name Mary Poppins. She had four more in her purse. The person she was on the phone with had five identical phones bought in Cairo by a Bert Screever.

Mary Ellen sipped a grande salted caramel hot chocolate with a doubleshot of espresso, extra light, extra whipped cream, as she talked. It was hard to understand the person on the other end. She was certain that he must have felt the same, as the phones, in addition to being untraceable, were also equipped with voice recognition scrambler chip that made them both sound like people who had tracheotomies and used an electrolarynx device.

"So, what is the status?" She whispered into the phone, the mechanical voice sounding odd coming back through the earpiece.

"Almost done, as per your parameters. We shall be ready to proceed at the top of the hour."

"Excellent." She adjusted the phone in her gloved hand so that she could take another sip of her drink. "Call me on number two as soon as it is done."

"Yes," came the mechanical reply.

"Good luck."

"You as well."

Mary Ellen closed the phone and began walking down the busy downtown street. After she rounded the corner, she dumped the phone into her empty paper drink cup. She dumped them both into a trashcan.

Time to do a little shopping while she waited for the call that signaled the eminent destruction of the so-called Dolly Mama and her precious Roderickstan. Mary Ellen looked across the street to spy an upscale hat boutique named the Mad Hatter. She could use a new hat for the occasion. When she found a break in the traffic, she crossed the street with a gleeful smile. She just loved to shop for clothes and accessories.

*****

Ryan sat next to Sully in the passenger/cargo compartment of the dull black AHR-19 SuperViper scramjet helicopter, cruising at 512 miles per hour. It was one of only three in the entire CYA fleet. At a cost of Δ36.7 million each, the SuperViper cost more than Ryan and everyone else on Anita Gunn's team combined would make in their entire CYA careers plus their retirements even if they all lived to the current life expectancies of 92.1 years for men and 103.8 years for women. Ryan smiled as he remembered his dad often saying women outlived men because the wives wore out their husbands with nagging and honey-do lists. Ryan glanced over at Ray, Big Red, Janine, and Tiny, who sat in the remaining seats.

The other two SuperVipers could be seen out of the bulletproof windows, trailing Ryan's chopper slightly. They carried the rest of Gunn's team.

The three SuperVipers were over the middle of the Atlantic Ocean, about a hundred miles from their destination of the island of La Palma. Even a mile up, the island was still over the horizon.

"So, Jackson," Ray shouted. The SuperViper was well insulated but the engines were still insanely loud. They were almost deafening if you stood next to them on the helipad without ear protection. "What's your plan?"

"Well, we're going to fly in low and be dropped about two miles north of the northernmost dig site." Ryan pointed to the map. "Yancy, you can do that, right?"

"Sure thing, Jackson," the pilot said loudly without turning around. "We'll enter stealth mode here in a few minutes and sneak right up on 'em. No problem."

"Stealth mode" was neither invisible nor silent but close on both accounts. The SuperViper already used stealth technology basics like sloped armor and non-reflective radar-absorbing paint. When the scramjets were running full power, they could be heard from a good five miles away, thus undermining all of the stealth features. Fortunately, the chopper had traditional propellers that lowered the noise range to an eighth of a mile away. Unfortunately, the SuperViper was only capable of 161 miles per hour in stealth mode, making it a much easier target for lower-end handheld rocket launchers such as the Panzerfaust 3 that the el-Queso would probably be using against them.

"Good," Ryan said. "Then we'll do some recon and hope that we're wrong about this whole thing."

"Lethal force?" Tiny asked, already knowing the answer.

"As far as we know, the el-Queso haven't done anything wrong...yet, so we have to go in with tranq guns, try to avoid contact if possible, and knock them out if we have to. Lethal force is a last resort. Any fatalities at this point would create a major international incident."

The standard CYA issue tranquilizer or tranq gun used silent darts and could knock out a nine hundred pound polar bear in less than two seconds.

"There won't be an international incident. This is completely black ops," Big Red said.

"True," Ryan conceded.

A CYA black ops mission meant no markings, no ID, nothing. If an agent was caught, they were expected to swallow a cyanide pill and any record of the agent was changed to be a surfboard salesman from Alaska or a parka peddler from Mexico City in every database in the world. This happened within three minutes of the agent's death, which was immediately recognized by a sensor injected in the forearm at recruitment and sent to CYA headquarters in Fort Meade via satellite transmitter, both of which dissolved into an untraceable goo within five minutes of the agent's death. If you were caught, the Roderickstan government never heard of you, and you aren't even a Roderickstan citizen.

"Still," Ryan continued, glancing over at Sully and trying to push out the growing feeling of imminent doom. "We have to be careful, right? Nice and clean, no screw-ups and no casualties."

"Right," Big Red said, sensing Ryan's concerns.

"There it is," Yancy called out, pointing.

The group looked forward. Yancy had bought the SuperViper down to about a thousand feet altitude, but the island could still be seen jutting out of the ocean off in the distance, like looking at a football floating in a pond from fifty feet away.

"How much longer?" Tiny asked.

"We're about forty miles out," Yancy said. "We'll get even lower, down to about hundred feet up, and have to go slower. Then we have to find a good spot to land. Twenty five or thirty minutes."

The group watched silently as La Palma slowly grew in the distance. After a few minutes, Yancy said, "Thirty miles out." Now the island was the size of a two-seater car and their target, the caldera, was now clearly recognizable.

As the island continued to grow, now taking up about a quarter of the horizon, Yancy said, "Twenty miles..." A bright flash and the windows going black cut him off. "What the fuck...?"

The windows cleared and the group looked out to see several clouds mushrooming up from the island.

"Dagnamit!" Yancy yelled, hitting several switches and

buttons on the control panel. The chopper began moving upward and forward at a frightening speed. "Everyone brace yourselves. Avenger Two and Three, brace for shockwave. Evasive..." Yancy's voice trailed as the chopper suddenly tossed around like a plastic boat in a bathtub with three-year-old triplets. "Hold on!"

After a few seconds that felt as long as a bad date, the chopper righted itself. Yancy looked around. "You guys okay?"

Affirmative nods all around.

Then he looked out the cockpit's windows and talked into his headset, "Avenger Two: status?"

"A couple of bumps and bruises is all," came the reply.

"Roger that. Avenger Three: status?"

"Roberson might have a sprained ankle."

"Damn it," came another voice from Avenger Three. "Our right scramjet engine is fried. We're limping from here."

"Roger that." Yancy looked over at Ryan. "Great..." Ryan's expression made him look back out the cockpit window to see what Ryan was looking at. A dozen cloud columns were rising a quarter-mile in the air from the edge of the caldera, forming a semi-circle.

"Holy crap!" Sully yelled.

"Yancy, get us over there NOW!" Ryan shouted. "Full speed, whatever."

"What about the radiation?" Sully asked.

"If the nukes were above ground, we would've been fried instantly," Ryan replied. "Gun it, Yancy!"

"Roger that." Yancy toggled several switches and sent Avenger One racing toward the island, about half a mile in altitude over the Atlantic Ocean's surface.

At about five miles from the caldera, Ryan said, "Hold us here, Yancy."

"I think we should be worried about the radiation," Sully said.

"There's nothing...yet," Yancy said, hitting some buttons

on one of the helicopter's computer screens and bringing up display. "No abnormal amounts of radiation."

"It doesn't have to be nukes," Big Red said. "They might have calculated out that traditional bombs would work. Hell, it could just be a couple of tons of C4 in each hole for all we know."

"Right," Ryan said.

"What do we do now?" Sully asked.

"We wait."

"For?" Sully probed.

"For something to happen," Ryan said. "There's no reason to land now. We can't stop the explosion, right? We don't know if they used nukes. Landing right now is crazy. Even if they didn't use nukes, the island is bound to be very unstable. They were trying to start earthquakes, remember? So, let's wait here for a few minutes and see what develops and report it back to headquarters."

"Fair enough," Big Red said, staring at the smoke-covered caldera.

"Dadgumit," Yancy muttered. "Rad levels rising. They used nukes alright."

"How insulated is this thing?" Tiny asked nervously.

"We're fine. Betsy here could withstand the radiation from a direct hit from a hydrogen bomb. The blast would blow us to Hell, but the radiation wouldn't do anything to us."

"Nice to know," Big Red said with a perturbed look. "Now what? We can't land for sure now. Rad suits won't protect us from ground zero of twelve nukes."

"Right," Ryan said. "Let's call Gunn…"

A voice entered the group's collective headsets. "What the hell happened, Jackson?" It was Anita Gunn. "We registered flashes and the west half of the island is now hidden by smoke."

"We were about fifteen miles out from the island when it appears that twelve nuclear devices exploded around the caldera..."

"Just like we feared," Gunn cut him off. "You nailed it, Jackson. Congrats on solid investigative work."

"Uh, thanks." Ryan didn't feel much like celebrating being right. He had hoped he was going to be wrong. Was World War III about to start? Should he move to an arctic cave in The Unified States of America state of Silami? Maybe a hut in the Australian outback?

"So, now what, Jackson?" Gunn asked.

"Huh?" Ryan responded, his head still reeling from the myriad of potential possibilities, most of which seemed to end with him fishing with a sharpened stick on some deserted island as he tried to figure out how to get milk out of a coconut without spilling it all.

Slowly, deliberately, as if talking to someone who didn't understand the language she spoke, Gunn said, "What happens next, Jackson?"

Ryan shook the thoughts of doom from his mind. "Uh, if the BBC special is right and the caldera falls into the ocean, we've got about seven hours to evacuate the eastern seaboard to ten miles inland or about fifteen million people are going to die."

"Okay," Gunn said.

A long silence followed.

"How does the caldera appear?" Gunn finally asked.

"Gee, Special Agent in Charge," Sully said in a sarcastic yet panicked tone. "It looks great considering twelve nukes just went off."

Gunn ignored the insubordinate remark, chalking it up to intense stress.

"There's a lot of seismic activity." Yancy punched keys furiously on various computer screens and several new displays appeared. "Lots of rumbling."

"Jackson, should we recommend an evacuation? It will cost millions of dollies, probably tens of millions. If we tell the Dolly Mama and we're wrong and the caldera doesn't fall into the ocean or it doesn't cause a tsunami, it could be our jobs..." Gunn's voice trailed off.

"I don't want to get stationed at the South Pole," Sully said, his tone even more shrill than before.

"You already deserve to be stationed at the South Pole, you putz," Big Red snapped. "Boss, I, for one, am willing to risk my career. I don't want fifteen million deaths on my conscience."

"And that was year 2000 estimates," Ryan said. "It's probably more like twenty million or more. I agree. Better a false alarm than millions dead."

"Any dissenting opinions?" Gunn asked.

After a few moments of silence, she said, "Okay, I'll go to the Dolly Mama now. Yancy, how much fuel do you have?"

"I can stay up for another forty minutes before we have to head home, longer if I land at Lajes Air Station in Portugal or Morón Air Base in Spain."

"Okay, stay for another hour and head to Lajes, okay?"

"Yes..." Yancy stopped, staring at a computer screen.

"Oh my God!" Janine screamed, staring at the same display.

"Avengers two and three, pull up! Pull up!" Yancy screamed as he sent Avenger One rocketing skyward.

The screen showed a zoomed-in view of the caldera. It caved in like a bad soufflé and a massive amount of earth raced down the hillside into the waiting Atlantic Ocean. As it impacted, a massive wave rose out of the water, heading in all directions.

"Holy crap!" Sully yelled.

"Chief," Ryan said. "You had better get to Roderick stat. The caldera just collapsed into the ocean. We're totally screwed."

"Roger that," Yancy muttered under his breath.

"Understood," Gunn said. "Get back here ASAP. Head to the Castle. I'll get you clearance to land. Got that, Yancy? Roderickstan Castle."

"Roger that," Yancy said. "According to Jackson's calculations, we'll make it there just a couple of minutes ahead of the wave…"

"Then punch it, Yancy!"

"Yes, sir." The pilot scrambled to punch in coordinates and sent the copter rocketing toward Atlantic Beach, New York.

Chapter 41

"You're kidding, right?" Yancy said into his headset. "Alright, roger that." After a few moments, he shook his head and muttered, "Ridiculous…"

The copter changed course. Ryan asked, "Hey, Yancy, what's going on? We're almost there. The GodPod is right there." He pointed to the structure near the edge of the horizon.

"I know, I know. We have to stop and pick up a prisoner from the New York field office. The orders are from the Director in Charge."

"Will we have time?" Sully asked.

"Yeah, they have him on the Helipad waiting. We should make it with five or six minutes to spare."

"Who is it?" Ryan asked.

"Don't know. They didn't tell me."

"Aren't we supposed to pick up Roderick and get her out of there? Why do we need a prisoner?" Ryan asked.

"Not sure."

"What a DiC," Sully muttered.

In his best Igor impersonation Yancy added, "I live to serve the master."

* * * * *

Mary Ellen stood on the east side, the actual park-like part of Roderick Park, staring up at the massive Roderickstan Castle, just a couple of hundred feet in front of her. This was the closest she had ever been to the GodPod, as many called it.

Mary Ellen smoothed the front of her white dress with red flowery patterns, adjusted her new red hat, and repositioned the matching purse on her shoulder. Her hair was colored a sandy blonde and permed into wavy curls. Her eyebrows were colored to match. It had been a good quarter century since she and Roderick had seen each other face to face and Mary Ellen was convinced the so-called Dolly Mama wouldn't recognize her in her disguise, at least not until it was too late.

Mary Ellen had an insider in M-Wan's Ministry of State Security, the equivalent, albeit much smaller, of Roderickstan's CYA or the USA's CIA, make her a new identity, complete with DNA records. They hacked into several of Roderickstan's security databases and doctored records, deleting Mary Ellen's fingerprint and DNA records so there wouldn't be duplicates. They also gave her a powerful micro laser concealed as lipstick in case of emergency.

Mary Ellen's new identity was Stormy Stubblefield, a Kennebunkport socialite and seven-figure contributor to Roderick's religion, the Spiritual Transcendence of the Ultimate Dolly. She had arranged an invite to the Dolly Mama's eightieth birthday party luncheon to be held on the roof of the Castle for Roderick's best financial supporters weeks ago.

Martin had no idea what a birthday party for a self-proclaimed deity would look like, but she assumed it would be the extravaganza of the century with no expense spared. After all, it wasn't Roderick's own money but the taxpayer's and the attendee's money, right? So why not go a little crazy with it? A goddess only turned eighty once. The thought made the taste of bile form at the back of Mary Ellen's throat. She knew Roderick's pride and arrogance would prevent her from canceling, or even moving, her eightieth birthday party. No, no, the Dolly Mama and her guests would be perfectly safe in the mighty Roderickstan Castle as most of New York was destroyed around them, at least that's what Roderick would tell everyone.

Mary Ellen laughed aloud at the thought. Soon she would put that evil megalomaniac bitch in her place for good. That place was six feet under. Better yet, she might float out to sea and be eaten by sharks. What a fitting way to die, since that's how Dolly's second husband died. The media reported it as a tragic accident but Mary Ellen knew better.

Maybe Mary Ellen would be eaten by sharks too. The thought made her cringe. She knew she would die along with all of the other guests, but she didn't care. The only way to know for certain that the world was rid of Roderick for good was for Mary Ellen to watch her die as the tsunami destroyed the Roderick's treasured GodPod, New York and the rest of the Eastern seaboard.

Dying didn't bother Mary Ellen. It might even be a good thing. She wasn't sure if there was an afterlife, Heaven or Hell, Happy Hunting Grounds, Valhalla or whatever, but if there was something, maybe she would be reunited with her soul mate, Sylvia, who was killed by that monster Dolly.

Mary Ellen had no real reason to live anymore anyway. Sylvia was dead. Her son, Sammy, was gone too. He took off almost a decade ago and was probably dead too. Even creating the greatest retail empire the world had ever seen left her feeling hollow.

She had nothing left except the emptiness, the unrelenting emptiness, the all-consuming, stifling emptiness, and she wanted to be rid of it once and for all. The only thing that made her barrenness fade was revenge. When she focused on her plot against Roderick and all of her injustices, Mary Ellen temporarily forgot the loss of Sylvia and Sammy.

With a deep breath, Mary Ellen looked around the horizon, taking in one last look at the landscape. The roads were already jammed with cars filled with people and their belongings stacked to the ceiling trying to flee the tsunami. She hoped they all made it. She regretted the "collateral

Immaculate Deception

damage" as they said in the movies and hoped they all made it out safely. Mary Ellen didn't want anyone but Roderick and her administration to pay for what Dolly had done to her. She had had second thoughts about her plot dozens of times, but it was too late to change her mind now. The tsunami was on its way and nothing could stop it.

Traffic going in and out of the Castle itself was surprisingly light. The party had begun an hour ago and, according to her calculations, the tsunami wasn't due to hit New York for about another forty minutes. She guessed Roderick wasn't letting anyone leave the GodPod under the threat of arrest.

Mary Ellen anxiously shifted the lipstick laser to the easy access side pocket of the small purse that hung loosely over her shoulder. This was the one place she could be caught. If she made it through the entrance, she was safe. She took a deep breath, composed herself, headed to the entrance of the Castle and walked through the scanner. She noticed half a dozen guards guarding the exit as she walked through the scanner.

A cordial but anonymous security guard staring at a computer screen greeted her. "Hello, Ms. Stubblefield."

"Hello."

"Here for Our Lady and Protector's eightieth birthday, I see."

"Yes."

The guard gave her a tentative look as if he debated whether to warn her of the impending danger but then thought better of it. "Enjoy the party, Ms. Stubblefield."

She hesitated. "Is it...is it safe here? From the tsunami?"

"Oh, yes, ma'am. Perfectly safe. It is very unlikely that that island volcano explosion will cause a tsunami that will reach Roderickstan at all. Even if it does, the Roderickstan Castle is safe and sound, designed to withstand any form of natural disaster up to a category five hurricane. Remember, ma'am, this is a military installation, complete with a reinforced structure and laser and missile turrets." He smiled with forced reassurance.

She smiled back. This guy should be the Press Secretary or High Priestess of Communications or whatever the hell they call it here these days. She could tell he thought he was going to die, but he knew he was going to die if he tried to take off. She frowned at the thought. Poor guy. "I guess you're right. This is the safest place on the east coast, right?"

"Yes, ma'am." He pointed to an elevator with three guards standing next to it. "That leads to the roof, where the party is being held. Enjoy the party."

"I sure will. Maybe I'll see you up there later," she said with a wink, hoping Roderick would at least try to get everyone to the top floor when the tsunami hit, but she doubted it. Roderick was a cold, hard bitch but maybe one of her underlings would show some compassion.

"Maybe," the guard said halfheartedly.

She turned and headed toward the elevator. Inside, she sighed with relief. She had made it. The elevator was smooth and fast, and she was some 350 feet above sea level in less than two minutes. The doors opened to reveal an extravaganza of biblical proportions taking place. Balloons, streamers and decorations of all kinds were strategically placed throughout the GodPod's roof deck. A dozen or more ice sculptures of Roderick stood in various regal poses, most at least ten feet tall. Dozens of giant silver streamers went from the top of the Statue of Deity's handheld torch flame to the equally distant points on the roof's guardrail, creating a massive skewed pyramid effect that was breathtaking.

Mary Ellen did a quick estimate of the cost of the party and thought it was somewhere in the two to three million dollie range. Roderick charged Δ25,000 a plate for her birthday party, and it looked like at least three hundred guests were attending. Mary Ellen figured another two hundred people probably paid but headed inland instead of making the party because of the tsunami. She thought the self-proclaimed deity was making a pretty good profit on the deal, somewhere in the ten million dollie range.

Mary Ellen grabbed a glass of champagne offered by a waiter in a tuxedo and nonchalantly scanned the deck for familiar faces. She needed to know who might recognize her. There were a few power couples from Alabama she recognized, but they were hiding off in one of the corners of the roof trying to avoid everyone's attention, especially Roderick's evidently. They wouldn't be a problem.

Most of Roderick's administration attended, but none of them were from Mary Ellen's intern days except for Pedro Sandoval, who was noticeably absent. She found that quite interesting as he was the absolute most loyal and trusted of Roderick's confidants. He must be in the bathroom or something. Surely, Sandoval wouldn't miss the "Dolly Mama's" eightieth birthday. Surely not.

Mary Ellen barely recognized Roderick's daughter Cherry, the so-called "Daughter Goddess" in the Roderick's religion, STUD, standing off to the far side of the deck, uncomfortably visiting with financial supporters who approached her. Though Cherry was only five or six years older than Mary Ellen, she hadn't seen her in over thirty years, except for the occasional picture in a magazine. Cherry didn't seem to like being the heir to a goddess and avoided publicity as much as possible. Cherry certainly wouldn't recognize her.

A loud thwapping noise drowned out the party music. Mary Ellen turned to see a black helicopter landing on one of the roof's four helipads. Four secret service agents, from the looks of their outfits, exited the craft. They were escorting a well-tanned thirtyish man in a white robe. He had a full head of almost black hair that went down past his shoulders and a thick beard to match. The man had his wrists handcuffed behind his back. There was something eerily familiar about him, but Mary Ellen couldn't place the young man. The agents rushed him up to Roderick, some hundred and fifty feet away from Mary Ellen.

Mary Ellen worked her way through the crowd towards Roderick and the monkish man. She couldn't get any closer than about eighty feet away. She tried to hear what was going on but the noise of the crowd drowned out what Roderick and the man were saying.

Mary Ellen watched the scene intently. The man talked calmly, but Roderick screamed at him, her face turning several shades toward vermillion. Mary Ellen recognized that look. She flinched involuntarily. After a couple minutes, Roderick's face softened, and her face returned to its normal pallid color and she motioned for the secret service agents to remove the man's handcuffs.

"Who is that man?" Mary Ellen asked no one in particular.

"M^3," a socialite in a peach-hued hat next to her said.

"M cubed?"

The socialite gave Mary Ellen a look that said she obviously thought Mary Ellen must have lived in a cave for the last decade. "M^3---The Maine Miracle Man."

"Main Miracle Man?" Mary Ellen responded. That didn't ring any bells. Why did he seem so familiar?

"No, Maine as in the state. Some called him the Maine Mystery Man. M^3 started performing miracles in a small town in Maine a couple of years ago. Healing people, rumor has it he has even resurrected a couple of people. Then he would disappear before the Dolly Mama's priests could arrest him…"

"The wave!" a woman somewhere off to Mary Ellen's right screamed. Mary Ellen turned to see the woman some hundred feet away, looking through one of the many deck's binocular viewers that dotted the deck's safety rail. The woman faced southeast.

Mary Ellen's face went flush, and she recognized the sickening, jittery feeling of adrenaline rushing through her as the mixed feelings of excitement and dread flooded her. It

Immaculate Deception

was about to happen!

Dozens of people scrambled to the southeast railing, but Mary Ellen noticed others looking toward the center of the deck where Roderick and M^3 were. Roderick tried to act strong, but she obviously tried to hold back a panic attack just as Mary Ellen was. M^3, on the other hand, seemed completely calm. He closed his eyes and lifted his arms towards the heavens.

Knowing she wouldn't draw any attention in the mass hysteria, Mary Ellen pulled out the pair of binoculars she bought for the occasion, stood on a table, and aimed at the Atlantic Ocean. A bulge in the Atlantic Ocean that must have been a hundred feet high raced toward the GodPod. It was still several miles away but was headed toward them at an incredible speed.

Mary Ellen looked back at Roderick with a bizarre mix of satisfaction and regret. Finally, it was almost over, and she'd be with Sylvia again. She noticed the M^3 person, still in his calm presence, his eyes closed and arms raised skyward.

Mary Ellen looked back to the ocean and the bulge turned into a wave, forming a white crest, growing to three hundred, then four hundred, then five hundred feet tall as it came up the coast less than a quarter of a mile away now.

Martin looked backed to the Maine Miracle Man. What was he doing? She noticed he was still in a strangely serene pose as Roderick frantically whispered in his ear.

"The wave! The wave! It's stopping!" someone screamed. The crowd cheered.

What the hell?! Mary Ellen turned back to the wave, looking through her binoculars again. The tsunami stopped, seemingly suspended in mid-air just a couple of hundred feet from the GodPod. It was quickly shrinking in height and beginning to recede back toward into Atlantic Ocean. "No!" she screamed as the wave faded away. "No!"

Adrenaline coursing through her, Mary Ellen forgot about her lipstick and frenetically searched her surroundings for a weapon. She noticed several large steak knives in a gray tub of dishes waiting to be bussed. She grabbed two, turned to Roderick and ran to her and M^3. She lunged at the Dolly Mama, knives aimed at the self-proclaimed goddess's heart. "Die, you evil bitch!"

Ryan and Sully, standing near Roderick, jumped into action and subdued the enraged beauty dressed in red and white while Big Red and Tiny moved into a protective stance on either side of the goddess. Ryan and Sully made the woman drop the knives by twisting her arms behind her back.

She glared at the Maine Miracle Man. "What have you done?! You've ruined everything!"

The man looked at her, becoming flustered. "Mom…?"

Chapter 42

"Sammy?" Mary Ellen gasped. Ryan thought she was going to faint.

"I go by M³ or Jesus of Toledo now, mom."

Jesus of Toledo? Ryan hadn't heard that name before.

"What...?" She said, looking downward as if she tried to take in everything she just learned. "You've...you've ruined everything. You were meant for greatness. To be special."

"He just saved the Eastern Seaboard from certain destruction. That sounds pretty special to me," Big Red said.

"And saved about fifteen million lives," Ryan added. "Just how did you do that?"

"Jedi mind trick," Sammy Martin, also known as M³, said with a wink.

"Wasn't Star Wars the greatest movie series ever?" Sully asked.

Mary Ellen's eyes went wide as she looked up at Sully, struggling to break free but Ryan and Big Red each held an arm firmly. "You! You killed Sylvia!" She turned to Roderick. "Sammy, this is all her fault. Dolly killed Sylvia. She broke up America. She is a lying, scheming, evil bitch. This religion should be yours. You are the divine one. You should be worshipped, not her."

"Why?" Ryan asked. Something from all of the files he read on Mary Ellen Martin began to bubble to the surface of his mind but hadn't quite made it there yet, but what? She gave birth to Samuel Martin in Toledo. Toledo? Jesus of Toledo? Evidently, nobody ever bothered to look up his birth certificate or Martin had it somehow altered in public record.

His real name must be Jesus Samuel Martin.

The file showed Martin went to a special clinic where she was artificially inseminated. No man was involved. That made sense since her reaction to Sylvia Byrne's death. She was obviously a lesbian, no biggie there. The father was unknown. One thing he distinctly remembered from the file because it struck him as odd was that the DNA used was listed as "anomalous," suspected of being very old.

Jesus Samuel Martin...

Mary Ellen Martin...

What was he missing?

M^3...Jesus of Toledo...

Mary Ellen...

Thoughts were racing through his mind like a ball ricocheting around the walls of a handball court.

Jesus...

Mary...

"Oh my god!" Ryan exclaimed.

Dolly Roderick gave him an irritated look as though she was going to have him arrested too. "What?"

"Mary Ellen Martin was artificially inseminated."

"So?" Roderick snapped.

Ryan turned to Mary Ellen. "You were a virgin when Sammy was born, weren't you, Ms. Martin?"

"No, she wasn't," Roderick nearly screamed. "I caught this fucking tramp screwing my husband. That's why I kicked her out of D.C."

"Actually, Dolly, I never had sex with Bobby," Mary Ellen said, now sniffling.

"I saw you," Dolly said, visibly pained.

"We had just started..." Mary Ellen turned to Ryan. "No, I had never had intercourse with a man."

Ryan turned to M^3. "And Samuel is your middle name, right?"

M^3's eyes went wide. "Jesus H. Christ! Mom?!"

Mary Ellen smiled at Sammy Martin, pride in her tear-streaked face. "Yes, you were meant to be special, Jesus Samuel Martin."

"Jesus, son of the virgin Mary," Ryan added.

Shock overcame the faces of most of the group, including Roderick.

"And the anomalous DNA in your file was from Jesus of Nazareth, wasn't it?" Ryan asked.

"Yes, from blood on a crucifix timber found at a dig site in Israel almost a hundred years ago, where Peter's first church was located," Mary Ellen said.

"Holy cow," Big Red said. "She cloned Jesus?!"

"Exactly," Ryan said.

The crowd gasped.

"Hardly," M^3 replied calmly.

"Hardly?" Big Red said. "Why not? How else do you do your miracles? You just saved tens of millions of people? It explains a lot."

"Hardly, for several reasons," M^3 replied. "First, thousands of people were crucified by Romans in the first century. The chances of finding Jesus of Nazareth's cross are one in millions. Second, I don't perform miracles, per se, I simply talk to the universe and it answers. Third, I'm not even a Christian, much less the second coming of Christ."

"Not a Christian?" Mary Ellen asked with a frown.

"No, mom. When I left, I traveled the world, learning the world's various religions---Judaism, Catholicism, Islam, Taoism, Buddhism, and a dozen others." M^3 turned to Roderick with a grin. "Even STUD."

Roderick responded with a silent scowl.

"So, if you're not a Christian, what are you?" Ryan asked.

"I follow a blend of all religions and faiths. All religions have their good and bad elements. I glean the good parts and ignore the bad parts. I also read a lot of self-help books. You know, Wayne Dyer, Deepak Chopra, Snoop Dogg, that sort of thing. I especially like Richard Bach." He pulled out a tiny book from his white robe and handed it to Ryan.

Ryan looked at the cover. Messiah's Handbook---Reminders for the Advanced Soul by Richard Bach. "Well, I'll be."

M³ pulled out another copy and handed it to Roderick and smiled. "Here you go. Every messiah should have one."

Roderick crossed her arms with a grunt. "I'm not a messiah. I'm a goddess."

M³ smirked. "Right, sure you are." Then he put the book back into the folds of his robe.

Sarcasm from Jesus of Toledo? Ryan grinned. This young man was certainly full of surprises.

"Isn't that great? Just lovely," Roderick said. "Jesus Samuel Martin here just confessed to blasphemy. Arrest them both!"

As Ryan and his fellow agent made a quick adjustment to figure out who would escort who, Mary Ellen broke free and rushed Roderick, knocking the self-proclaimed goddess to the ground. Mary Ellen landed on top of her and began choking with all of her might. "How dare you?! I loved you. I worshipped you before you ever had your stupid religion..."

The CYA agents pulled them apart and stood them up. Mary Ellen said with a mix of bitterness and self-defeat, "Why, Dolly? I thought we were in love? Why did you have to discard me like one of Bobby's used condoms? I was only twenty-three..."

Dolly straightened her clothes. "Simple, you naïve tramp. A lesbian affair would have ruined my run for the senate and the presidency."

"So you just trample my heart?" Mary Ellen asked weakly.

"Yes, something like that. So sorry," Roderick said in English maid tone.

Ryan noticed something change in Martin's face. A flash of insight...an epiphany. For a split second, the dejection in her face disappeared. Oh crap!

The Alternate Ending Decision Making Quiz

Congratulations on making it this far. Because you've made the effort to get through this novel, I've come up with two alternative endings to please dichotomous tastes. Simply answer this short quiz to find which ending you should prefer:

1) Serial rapist murdering pedophiles should be:
A) Executed.
B) Rehabilitated and released. Better yet, make them pre-school teachers so they can teach my 3-year-old daughter.

2) Better president:
A) Ronald Reagan
B) Bill Clinton

3) Better president during the Clinton years:
A) Hillary
B) Bill, of course. What do you mean?

4) Welfare should be/is:
A) A very short-term stopgap measure to help get people back on their feet.
B) My constitutional right. I'm entitled to receive payments from the government forever for getting knocked up at 13, just like my mother and grandmother did. The taxpayers owe it to me to let me watch talk shows with fighting dwarfs and love triangles with goats all day while I raise my seven out-of-wedlock kids.

5) Gay marriage is:
A) Fundamentally and morally wrong. What's next? Marrying an animal…?
B) Awesome - hey, what's wrong with marrying an animal?

6) I prefer the following greeting:
A) Merry Christmas
B) Happy Holidays or Super Solstice!

7) Which is better?
A) M & M's
B) Eminem

8) Gangsta rap is:
A) Vulgar, disgusting and simple-minded.
B) My constitutional right to freedom of speech. Shut your cakehole before I cap your sorry ass, mofo.

9) Abortion should be:
A) A last resort, only used for medical reasons or when raped.
B) Used whenever I don't bother to use protection. Hey, it's my body, baby!

10) Oral sex is:
A) Bill Clinton's sad, pathetic legacy.
B) Not sexual relations!

Answer Key

7 or more A) answers:
You should really enjoy alternate ending C on the next page and have fun!

4-6 A) answers:
Hmmm…it's a toss up. You may like or dislike either one…read them both and let me know.

3 Or less A) answers:
Made it this far, eh? It's a minor miracle. Well, to reward your "suffering" through the book this far, I created an ending just for you. Go to alternative ending L on page 327 and enjoy!

Chapter C-1

"Die!" Mary Ellen screamed, broke free of the agents again and launched herself. She swung her right hand around to Roderick's left temple.

A bright red beam pulsed through Roderick's brain, out the right side of her head, and upwards toward the afternoon sky. Roderick fell backwards, dead before she hit the ground. A puddle of blood slowly formed around her head.

Ryan swatted the laser from Martin's hand. Everyone but the Martins stood gawking at the fallen body. The woman, the goddess, who ruled their country and their lives for almost two decades, was dead in front of them by a laser from a crazed woman.

After several uncomfortable moments, Big Red looked up at M^3 and asked slowly, "Uh, shouldn't you do something?"

"Like what? Cry or cheer?"

"You know, a miracle, raise her from the dead or something," Sully said.

"As she said herself, she's the goddess. I'm just a messiah. Thousands of people die every day. I can't resurrect everyone. Besides, mom is right. The Dolly Mama here has ruined countless lives, divided a nation and forced millions of people to abandon their beliefs. She can resurrect herself. Let's watch for the miracle of the goddess."

Ryan, along with the rest of group, stared at the corpse for several minutes, looking for signs of life they all knew wouldn't be coming. Dolly Roderick wasn't a goddess. She never was. She was just a power-hungry megalomaniac with good political connections.

"That was interesting," Jesus of Toledo said. "Now what, gentlemen?"

Ryan looked at Tiny, Big Red, and Sully for answers.

"You're the lead on this case, Jackson," Big Red said.

"Right, thanks," Ryan said irritably.

"I suppose it wouldn't do to let me and mom go, would it?" M³ asked. "That's what they would do in the movies."

"Probably not."

"Drat." M³ stroked his beard. "Hmmm. I suppose I could blast everyone off of the roof to their deaths and I could flee with my mom…"

Everyone's eyes grew wide, and Tiny put his hand on his gun.

M³ continued, "But that wouldn't be very nice, now would it? As the cliché goes, 'What would Jesus do?' eh, my friends."

Nobody answered.

M³ smiled. "Why, he would turn himself in, of course." He held out his open-palmed hands. "Let's do that."

Ryan and Big Red handcuffed the Martins and escorted them to the helicopter.

"So, uh, Mr. Martin, how do you really do those miracles?" Ryan asked as they entered the chopper.

"Read the book I gave you," M³ said pleasantly. "The best way is to randomly flip to a page and read the passage for insight."

"Really?"

"Certainly. You know, I like you, Jackson…it is Jackson, right?"

"Ryan Jackson. Call me Ryan."

"Okay, Ryan. If I manage to avoid execution and get released, care to be one of my disciples? I'm always looking for good disciples."

"Really? Uh, I'm flattered…"

"Just think about it, okay?"

"Sure." Ryan sat down in the chopper next to M³. He

helped buckle the messiah's seatbelt and then buckled himself in. He pulled out the Messiah's Handbook and did as M³ instructed and flipped to a random page. It read:

Everything in this book may be wrong.

Chapter C-2: Epilogue

2030

New $6.3 Billion Church of Universal Beliefs Campus Opens
M³ Celebrates Fifth Anniversary of New Church

Toledo, OH – December 26, 2030 – M³, AKA Jesus of Toledo, celebrated the fifth anniversary of his "open faith" nondenominational Church of Universal Beliefs (CUB) by officially opening a new $6.3 billion campus yesterday on 500 acres just out of his birth town of Toledo, Ohio. The new campus features a retractable roof sanctuary similar to the Dallas Lions football stadium in Arlington, Texas, but will seat 30,000 more people for a total of over 110,000 parishioners. The Sunday school, holy book study group, and administration buildings top half a million square feet of space.

The parking lot is said to be bigger than the Disneyland parking lot, holding over 60,000 cars and buses. It includes state-of-the-art monorail, tram and shuttle systems to quickly get worshippers to the seven Sunday services, three Saturday services and the three Wednesday evening services. The facilities took almost three years to build.

The Christmas services went smoothly with a total attendance for the day's five services topping 645,000. Most services were standing room only as the parishioners celebrated Christmas and M³'s fifth anniversary as leader of CUB.

CUB's growth in the past five years has been nothing less than phenomenal with a current official worldwide membership of over 28 million people from all religious faiths, dwarfing any other church in USOTA. His daily M³ is Square and that's Okay religious-themed talk show is aired in 47 countries and translated into sixteen languages. Rumor has it that Oprah is starting to get worried about the show's popularity.

While his meteoric spiritual rise is nothing less than divine, not all of Jesus of Toledo's endeavors have been so blessed. Two years ago, his primetime sitcom Bigger than the Beatles was canceled after only three episodes.

M³'s next project is to create a fully-accredited online faith-based university that is completely free. The goal is to be able to supply at least one million computers to needy students all over the world so anyone who wants a college degree can get one, no matter their financial circumstances. If he succeeds, it will be the biggest university ever built.

* * * * *

Mary Ellen looked up from the USOTA Today article on her Sony PRS-1500 HoloPhone and took a deep breath of fresh, salty sea air. She sat in a lounge chair on the sun deck of her 408-foot yacht, the Sylvia, and gazed at Port-Vila, the capitol of Vanuatu, a small island chain in the South Pacific Ocean just over a thousand miles northeast of Australia. Although it was Christmas yesterday and only nine in the morning, the temperature was already climbing past eighty degrees under pristine clear skies. The breeze felt good.

The article made her smile, though her feelings were

bittersweet. It was good to hear her son was doing well. Aside from watching his shows, she rarely saw him anymore. Like the song Cats in the Cradle, when Sammy was growing up, she rarely had time for him. Now that she was "retired" and had all of the time in the world, he was too busy. She would visit him in Toledo, but she was prohibited from entering USOTA.

Thinking of her exile from USOTA reminded Mary Ellen of "the Event" as her therapist phrased it. That kind man, President Muller, gave her a presidential pardon for all crimes associated with "the Event," citing mental cruelty by "the person," also a therapist phrase. Muller also credited Mary Ellen for helping reunite the country. That made her smile too.

The new combined country, which comprised of the former United States of America, Mexico and parts of Canada, was now called The United States of the Americas or USOTA for short, pronounced "you soda" by most people. Some media pinhead, probably the same one who called "the Event" Godgate, named it that, and the name stuck.

There were several conditions to her pardon. She was not allowed on USOTAn soil or that of another couple dozen countries who were hit by the tsunami before Sammy stopped it. She had to step down as CEO of M-pire and president of M-Wan. Her M-pire replacement had to agree to move the corporate headquarters back to USOTA, reopen as many of the former Roderickstan M-Mart stores as possible, and sell off many purchases Mary Ellen was responsible for like the country of Taiwan, until recently known as M-Wan. She also had to agree to an intensive ongoing therapy and medication regimen.

During therapy, with the help of several anti-anxiety medications, Mary Ellen worked through most of the demons of her past, forgiving everyone for perceived wrongs. She even met most of the CYA team responsible for her beloved Sylvia's death, came to believe it was indeed an accident and forgave them as well. She even became friends with a few that were assigned to her during her incarceration until Muller pardoned her.

Since she was still wanted for crimes in several countries, she now spent most of her time on her yacht in international waters. For a donation of just under a billion Euros, the republic of Vanuatu was more than happy to make Mary Ellen a citizen.

She looked out to the beautiful blue-green ocean, seeing various ships and sailboats dotting the landscape. A well-tanned young man with brown eyes and brown hair, dressed in only bright orange swim trunks, came walking up to her, a paper cup in his hand. "Here you go, honey buns." He handed her her meds and leaned over to give her a kiss.

She grabbed her iced latte and swallowed the eight pills with a quick gulp. She pulled the man down for another kiss. "Thank you, Sully, you're so good to me." From somewhere deep within Mary Ellen, from a part of her soul she buried long ago, away from the therapists and the medications, she thought that Pedro Sandoval must be turning in his grave knowing his nephew, his namesake, slept with Dolly's worst enemy and murderer. The idea made her smile as she kissed Sully more strongly and slid down his trunks.

The End

Chapter L-1

"Die!" Mary Ellen screamed, broke free of the agents again and launched herself at Dolly. Something glinted in her right hand as she swung it up.

M^3 stepped in front of Dolly to block his mother and a flash of red light aimed at the Goddess hit him in the forehead instead and burned right out of the back of his skull.

"No!" Mary Ellen gasped as her son fell to the ground dead, a strangely serene expression on his face.

Ryan used the moment to wrestle the object out of Mary Ellen's hand. She dropped to her knees next to her son, weeping uncontrollably.

Ryan and Sully left her there for a few moments to mourn the loss of her son.

"Some messiah he turned out to be," Dolly scoffed. "Take her away."

Mary Ellen's face flashed rage as though she was about attack the Dolly Mama again. Ryan and Sully subdued her. She didn't resist, obviously in shock at her son's death at her hands. The CYA agents escorted the fallen M-pire CEO onto the same black helicopter they had removed her son from just a minutes earlier.

Chapter L-2: Epilogue

2030

Roderickstan Celebrates Fifth Anniversary of Surviving Apocalyptica and the Defeat of the Mysterious One
The Dolly Mama Celebrates 85th Birthday

Roderick Park, NY – October 31, 2030 – In what socialites are calling the party of the century, the upper echelon of STUD are celebrating the Dolly Mama's 85th birthday. Today is also the fifth anniversary of the most important event since the Spiritual Transcendence of the Ultimate Dolly almost two decades ago.

Five years ago, in an event called the Apocalyptica, the evil Mysterious One plotted to assassinate the Dolly Mama and destroy the eastern seaboard with massive tsunami. Our Lady and Protector Dolly Roderick thwarted the Mysterious One, killing him and obliterated the wave before it could hurt anyone, praise to Her glorious name.

In an act of mercy, the Dolly Mama sentenced Mary Ellen Martin, mother of Jesus Samuel Martin AKA the Mysterious One and a coconspirator in Apocalyptica, to the maximum sentence of two years at the Beverly Hills Rehabilitation Club. Our Lady and Protector Dolly Roderick normally would have performed a ritual sacrifice of anyone accused of High Treason but She gave a statement: "Because of the

Martin family's longstanding relationship with the Roderick, and because her agreement to bring the Headquarters of M-pire back to Roderickstan, I am commuting her sentence of neutralization."

Followers of the Mysterious One, then known as M^3, wanted Mary Ellen Martin neutralized for his death but it was thrown out of court as it was legally acceptable as a Post-Delivery Abortion.

The Dolly Mama also stated: "I am certain that Mary Ellen Martin can be rehabilitated and be a contributing and taxpaying member of society again."

*****

Mary Ellen looked up from the Roderickstan Today article on her Sony PRS-1500 HoloPhone and took a deep breath of fresh, salty sea air. She sat in a lounge chair on the sun deck of her 408-foot yacht, the Sylvia, and gazed at Port-Vila, the capitol of Vanuatu, a small island chain in the South Pacific Ocean just over a thousand miles northeast of Australia. Although it was Halloween yesterday and only nine in the morning, the temperature was already climbing past eighty degrees under pristine clear skies. The breeze felt good.

The article made her smile, though her feelings were bittersweet. It was good to hear the Dolly Mama was doing well. She was such a sweet woman and she had treated Mary Ellen like her own child. There was a rumor some Roderickstan think tank was working on moving her brain to computer so she would live forever like a goddess should.

Something about the article troubled her but she couldn't quite place it. Maybe it was the Mysterious One…? All of the electroshock therapy and medications still left her a little fuzzy on parts of her past. The nice therapists and CYA agents at the Beverly Hill Rehabilitation Club said that should improve with time.

As she gazed out at Coral Sea, watching the ships sail into and out of Port-Vila, she thought how much she enjoyed being retired. The wondrous Dolly Mama recommended moving M-Pire's headquarters back to Roderickstan and retiring to a peaceful tropical island. What a lovely idea.

The Dolly Mama said some countries still weren't happy with some of the things Mary Ellen had done in the past so the Goddess recommended spending most of her time on her yacht in international waters. For a donation of just under a billion Euros, the republic of Vanuatu was more than happy to make Mary Ellen a citizen.

She looked out to the beautiful blue-green ocean, seeing various ships and sailboats dotting the landscape. A well-tanned young man with brown eyes and brown hair, dressed in only bright orange swim trunks, came walking up to her, a paper cup in his hand. "Here you go, honey buns." He handed her her meds and leaned over to give her a kiss.

She grabbed her iced latte and swallowed the eight pills with a quick gulp. She pulled the man down for another kiss. "Thank you, Sully, you're so good to me." From somewhere deep within Mary Ellen, from a part of her soul she buried long ago, away from the therapists and the medications, she thought that Pedro Sandoval must be turning in his grave knowing his nephew, his namesake, slept with her. The idea made her smile as she kissed Sully more strongly and slid down his trunks.

The End

Immaculate Deception

Immaculate Deception

About the Author

Ken Baumbach is the author of several books including the acclaimed spiritual nonfiction book, *Mere Theosophy*, and the fantasy novel, *The Heretics' Power*. More information about his works can be found at www.KenBaumbach.com.

He also runs www.CaptainAttitude.com, a website that is a collection of random thoughts, reviews, cheat codes, the meaning of the universe, useful tips and tricks, and other potentially fascinating prose. Imagine if Harlan Ellison, Hunter S. Thompson, Carl Hiaasen and Christopher Moore had a love child. Now imagine that the love child had created lifehacker.com.

Ken lives in central Texas with his lovely wife, Kristi, and three wonderful daughters, Katie, Emily, and Megan.

Author Photo by Elio Camey

Made in the USA
Charleston, SC
21 March 2014